About the Author

Martin JP Devaney has a degree in drama from Trinity College Dublin. He is the author of the book *The RTE Writer's Guide* for RTE Commercial Enterprises/Blackwater Press. He has written one-off plays, comedies, dramas and series for RTE Radio One as well as short stories for RTE Radio One and BBC. He has written for RTE television; has produced a comedy quiz show for Radio One; produced/written several short films; has had plays produced in Ireland, America, Canada, Australia, and Poland. He worked on Sky 191 where he produced over ninety-nine weekly television shows, winning a national media award.

For more author news please visit Martin's website:
www.martinjpdevaney.com

How to Murder Your Dear Wife
(and Get Away With It)

Martin JP Devaney

How to Murder Your Dear Wife
(and Get Away With It)

Pegasus

PEGASUS PAPERBACK

© Copyright 2024
Martin JP Devaney

The right of Martin JP Devaney to be identified as the
author of this work has been asserted by him in accordance
with the Copyright, Designs and Patents Act 1988

A CIP catalogue record for this title is
available from the British Library

ISBN-978 1 91090 383 4

Pegasus is an imprint of
Pegasus Elliot MacKenzie Publishers Ltd.
www.pegasuspublishers.com

First Published in 2024

Pegasus
Sheraton House Castle Park
Cambridge CB3 0AX England

Printed & Bound in Great Britain

To my darling wife, who has put up with me in good times and bad. I wish she was here to share the publication of this work of FICTION.

Prologue

Everyone dies. Most don't know when. My wife, Laura, for example, does not realise that her time is up during the Lough Ree International Pike Festival.

I know because I'm going to kill her.

Despite evidence to the contrary (see above) I don't think that I'm a bad person. I pay my taxes, walk our dog and I simply cannot empathise with those who lay an unkind hand on others. As a teacher (vice principal to be pedantic), I've reported abuses of all kinds when I've seen them.

I could add that I was woke before it was a thing.

I've supported those who champion progressive causes.

When I registered to vote in Ireland, I gave my Number One to presidential candidate Mary McAleese – and it wasn't just because I fancied the girl who canvassed for her, a girl who soon became the reason why I remained in Ireland after graduating from Trinity. She, however, decided that saving whales was more important than saving our marriage.

That's gratitude for you.

Laura, whom I married years later, once found my ex's social media page. It depicted Michelle in a powerful twin-engine Zodiac, harassing a Japanese whaler off the Falkland Islands. She somehow had managed, in high seas, both to take a selfie and piss off Japan.

Laura noted that my ex was having a bad hair day. I remarked that even a top-of-the-range GHD might struggle in a South Atlantic gale.

I slept in the spare room that night.

The mistake in speaking aloud was mine and plays no role in my wife's imminent demise. Unlike the minke whales who writhe at the end of an explosives-tipped harpoon, her passing is going to be both swift and bloodless. She would be furious if I ruined her Egyptian cotton bedsheets. We couldn't really afford them, but they do set off the room.

Murderers can be nice.

Although you probably shouldn't turn your back on one.

I'll not rejoice when it is done (I'm not a monster) but I anticipate learning to live with being a widower. My neighbours will gift buns. I'll find tinfoil wrapped meals left in the porch. There will be talk of my stiff upper lip. I expect that I can overcome feeling guilty— I just don't want a jury declaring it.

I plan to get away with it, BTW.

I'm therefore writing these notes for an audience of one.

Me.

Notes that will both document the evolution of this perfect crime and remind me why I set out on this homicidal pathway in case my resolve weakens. As someone from my home county once wrote:

"Conscience makes cowards of us all."

Shakespeare himself would surely sympathise as these notes sink with the memory card below the surface of the lake (remember when I mentioned about getting away with it?). My tragedy is that this story will never grace the pages of *The Times Literary Supplement*. It's fated to remain forever lost in time, like Homer's *Margites* or Roy Batty's memories of the Tannhäuser gate, at the end of *Blade Runner*.

No one can ever know how I reduced the world's population (7.8 billion) by just one.

Part I

The Medieval Age

"What is better than wisdom? Woman. And what is better than a good woman? Nothing."
Geoffrey Chaucer

Laura

80

Laura does not deserve to die, TBH. If we were to rank individuals who should be pushed under a bus, with wild-eyed despots at the top of the list, then Laura could be found way down – well behind cold callers and those who never replace biscuits in the staff room (you know who you are).

On the one hand, she has some tremendous qualities. She's an excellent mother to her son (more on him later) and the Health Service Executive would say that she carries out her nursing duties diligently and effectively.

She once represented the county in the Rose of Tralee pageant. One time I persuaded her to show me the videotape of the final where – as part of the hidden talent spot – she bravely tackled an antique hurdy-gurdy. She asked me what I thought, and I told her that she looked good in a sash.

I again spent the night in the spare room.

She did look good in a sash. I remember thinking how gorgeous she was when I saw her for the first time. She was pretty and blonde and drunk. She was out on a pub crawl with her emergency room colleagues while I'd just come in after a fruitless day's fishing and had asked the barman for tea. We'd met when we shared a table at the Lough Ree Inn. She'd heard my English accent and in her drunken state, kept asking me if I knew the queen.

I later told her, that I had no luck on the lake that day, but I was lucky to land her.

She told me never, ever repeat that.

She refused my invitation to take her out fishing. She laughed and said if she wanted to be cold and wet, she'd buy a convertible. She admitted that she'd lived her whole life in the Midlands and had never been out on the lakes. She said she'd seen *Titanic* and look how that turned out. She did however say that she liked good food.

Also dessert.

I said I liked good food as well.

Her eyebrows furrowed.

She laughed for some reason and then picked out a restaurant flier from the countertop and slowly fanned herself with it.

I asked her out for dinner.

My best friend Suzanne told me I was punching above my weight when I married Laura. More on Suzanne later (she gets her own chapter).

We married quickly. I suspect that one reason was that Laura thought a brother or sister would be good for Liam.

I didn't want to allow her time to change her mind.

I also thought being a dad would be glorious, and like a dog reacting to a whistle, I'd drop Liam off at the childminder before running in through the front door, summoned by a phone call after a temperature check. I'd risk life and limb as I'd stumble up the stairs, stripping as I went.

However, Liam remained an only child.

And despite me bringing him to every adventure centre and petting zoo in the Midlands, he still only ever referred to me by my first name.

The unexpected gap in our world allowed me time to discover how little I knew my wife. She pleasantly surprised me about how adept she was at changing a plug, but I'd fret at the way she'd leave a room like a tornado had passed through it. I'd follow behind, picking clothes off floors and slipping them onto hangers.

Could she never learn to put away the half-empty milk carton?

However, we did have much in common.

We both liked films but it's maddening how she'd tell me to play a New Release on Netflix but then promptly nip out for a wee. Wouldn't anyone get frosty after spending five minutes watching a blockbuster on pause, while exhausting the crisps?

That said, Laura is also genuinely nice.

I never knew her father as he had passed away before I met her, but I was on the scene to observe how she never failed to spend an evening with her mother in the care home, even though the poor woman hadn't a clue who Laura was.

However, being nice doesn't pay the bills.

The reality is that the treadmill we find ourselves on is not living.

We are held hostage by a mortgage that sucks up my teaching salary while her nursing income does little more than keep the lights on. Any spare cent we earn is swallowed up by her now adult son who still lives with us— despite the helpful publications I'd leave casually around the house like a U.S. Green Card application or *The Lonely Planet* guide to Australia.

Liam (I said I'd get to him, didn't I?) attends the local technological university and is in his fourth year. Unfortunately, three of those years comprised a first-year repeat and a sabbatical where he needed to find himself.

More often than not, he finds himself in his room banging either his drums or the local talent with equal gusto.

Liam – via the Bank of Mum – manages to spend an inordinate amount of time on the road pursuing "gigs". Once, my phone tracker revealed that he was in Morocco.

I thought he'd just gone to the shops.

He is the product of Laura's first marriage. His dad walked out on them when Liam was barely weaned (not that he's showing much sign of that yet, regardless) and was last seen boarding a Ryanair flight to Stansted.

It almost goes without saying that Laura and I don't go out much, for financial reasons. When the country went into lockdown due to a viral pandemic, Laura remarked that it didn't make a blind bit of difference to us. We were already on lockdown. Just not a governmental mandated one.

She was in the kitchen leafing through the mortgage statements at the time, a mortgage we took out late in life and whose final payment is due at retirement – or at the death of one of the parties referenced in the life assurance policy.

She mused, 'I'm worth more dead than alive,' and we laughed.

It appeared that our policies would cover the mortgage if one of us did not make it to sixty-five. So that allowed us twenty years of avoiding war zones, lightning strikes and enormous round bales of hay (It happened in Westport. Very sad, an American tourist died while zooming in on the statue of Saint Patrick with his camera phone. He was oblivious to the runaway bale that fell off a trailer before accelerating downhill and over him. On the plus side, the video he was making went viral).

Laura and I sipped tea as she pored over the statements at the kitchen table. I watched her file them one by one into a shoebox and I couldn't help but recall how her health service post comes with a healthy pay-out should she check out early.

It would be of some comfort for those of us who are left behind.

I could not help thinking as she sighed and slid the shoebox under the kitchen dresser. *Must I wait until I'm presented with a gold watch before I have a proper holiday?*

What's the point in retiring if I'm going to be too old and infirm to enjoy it?

An unbidden thought crossed my mind. *Do we struggle together, onward to a distant finish line, or does one of us take a shortcut?*

I wondered if I should suggest that she should get out more, however, she's already been to Westport.

It seemed likely that she'd make it to retirement. Her downtime hobbies revolved around the local chapter of the Society for Creative Anachronism— a medieval re-enactment group. There is nothing inherently dangerous in mastering the brush and pen strokes of calligraphy or weaving a rope from hemp, although her attempts in recreating cooking from the Middle Ages did have me spend three days within sprinting distance of a toilet. Oftentimes, it was just an excuse to sample types of mead.

On the positive side – I watched as she dunked a digestive into her mug – she struggled with a few extra kilos but nothing that could place her in imminent danger, as I discovered, of cardiac arrest. I burst a blown up paper bag behind her once.

My mistake was to do it while she was cooking. I was scraping lentils off the ceiling for a week.

The thought of ending my wife remained just a vague notion, a little like the fleeting daydream we all experience after we hear of a lotto winner grasping an oversized cheque. We imagine it is ourselves on the cusp of receiving begging letters, instead of generating them.

Murder.

Surely it flits briefly through all our minds at some point. Who does not nurse dark fantasies of pushing a dictatorial boss out a window or taking a cricket bat to a childhood bully?

Come on. It's not just me.

Some couch potato assassins may not follow through for moral reasons or because murder is still considered a crime in most jurisdictions. Then again, how likely are they to carry out murder most foul if their only experience of crime is via a DVD box set?

I suspect, however, that the main reason most people don't cross to the dark side is simply that they fear they may be caught. Killing might not be easy but getting away with it is surely the harder part.

This notion, therefore, entertained me only briefly before being parked in that part of the mind reserved for passing fantasies, like the one where I wake up with Brenda (from four doors down) and, yes, of course, she also gets her own chapter.

However, *Murder Most Foul* – the idea, not the 1964 film staring Margaret Rutherford – dusted itself off and burst through the barrier of its parking garage one particular morning when my mobile phone rang.

Dervla and Dennis

79

Laura was very sorry, but she had run out of petrol. I had to leave the examination study hall and jump into my car. The AA no longer responded to our calls, and I suspected that a klaxon would sound in the rescue centre whenever either of our phone numbers appeared on their switchboard.

My hands whitened on the steering wheel as I whipped around slow drivers. Did I not remind her that she was running low? Did she not say that she would take care of it "first thing"?

I mused, as I overtook a tractor, that life might be less chaotic without her.

Dervla Kennedy, our Home Ec teacher, appeared in the passenger seat (in reality this probably didn't happen, but morphine-linked memory fragments form imperfect jigsaws. More on this later).

'Hello,' I would have said to her as I accelerated towards the town centre, keeping the car a shade under the speed limit.

'Mister Devaney,' she might have replied before burying her head in her smartphone, scrolling for city breaks.

A thermometer appeared in her mouth.

Again, this is likely to be pure imagination as I'm almost certain it never happened.

She carefully checked her temperature and entered data onto her phone.

'Edinburgh has some great deals going,' she may or may not have said.

'Does it?' I replied (this exchange probably happened in the staff room when she popped by during her last maternity leave).

'We're thinking of mid-January.'

I sighed. Next year, I would be booking September substitutes as Dervla added another sprog to the world. The woman had barely set foot into a classroom in eight years as she cleverly timed her maternity leave to coincide with the first week of term.

The streets narrowed as I approached the town centre, skipping around other vehicles with millimetres to spare. Annoyance had leadened the foot on the accelerator. It was imperative that I return quickly. I'd left Miles Murphy in sole charge of the exam hall. A man so unsuited to the pressures of teaching that he spent much of his workday hiding in the WC, claiming diarrhoea. If the students, quietly sitting their final state exams, sensed weakness then smartphones would be retrieved, and Google would become their new BFF.

Chris, the school principal, had promised to step in but Chris was Chris. More on him later.

The console in the dashboard dissolved from a display of local radio channels (stay with me) and words formed.

"Fail to prepare and prepare to fail."

It made sense and I nodded. Twenty years of laying out rosters, exam schedules and coordinating parent/teacher meetings meant that I've also learned a thing or two about planning. I could give Dervla a run for her money. Pick a topic and I'll run up a PowerPoint presentation on it within thirty minutes (with handouts). I am aware of the complexities and the nuances of scheduling. If Dervla can pop out eight kids on demand, then I can certainly deal with the permanent removal of one individual from our housing estate.

How hard could it be?

'I can't do this anymore,' I snarled, as I swerved into oncoming traffic, overtaking one car, and ducking in behind another.

Horns blared.

There was a cough from the back seat. Dervla's husband, Dennis, grinned amicably back at me in the rear-view mirror.

'However, plans fail, feck it,' he said.

'Who's talking to you?' Dervla snapped back at him and returned to her scrolling.

'I said I was sorry,' Dennis replied sullenly.

Whatever did she see in him?

Perhaps it was that he had a master's in something or other, and he'd never been sick a day in his life. He'd run for his county as a younger man. Maybe it was just the DNA she craved, for he had the personality of a paper bag.

'I'll give you sorry,' Dervla shot back. 'When I was ovulating that time, where was I? A clue. There wasn't an Eiffel Tower out the window.'

'I know I forgot to renew my passport,' Dennis murmured. 'How many times must I apologise?'

'I should have gone anyway,' Dervla said, 'brought your sperm in a tube.'

'You know I am here, right?' I said.

I overtook a bread van, one eye on my newly acquired passengers while the other scoped out the bridge, peering ahead of me for Laura's car.

The town of Athlone began as a Bronze Age settlement along the banks of the River Shannon— the longest river in the country. A nineteenth-century stone bridge spans the river. On one side, the narrow main street meanders haphazardly among winding side streets, a product of a time when town planning involved little more than ensuring streets had sufficient space to channel cattle, carts, and British cavalry. A squat castle dominates one side of the bridge, its cannon emplacements built and primed to prevent a French fleet from sailing upriver, an invasion fleet which would not arrive until the twentieth century, when foreign language students descended on the town. Custume Bridge had probably been open to two-way traffic for more than one hundred and eighty years. It took my wife just a moment to convert it to a single, lumbering lane.

I could not have been more mortified. It's not even like this was the first time. How often would we perform this dance? Her car breaks down more regularly than a millennial on *Love Island*. And yet, this is the same woman who can quickly ramp up an emergency room, from dealing with a few Patrick's Day dancers, nursing twisted knees to absorbing the victims of a major road traffic accident.

I have told her; the fuel warning light is not a decorative feature.

Dark thoughts continued to push forward. Would I not be better off without her? Life would surely be easier. Could I make it happen?

A fresh message appeared on the console.

"Don't do the crime if you can't do the time."

Was I the only one seeing this? I glanced about. Dervla continued to scroll while Dennis watched the streets pass rapidly outside his window. I guessed he'd said all he had to say.

My mood changed abruptly as I ground down through the gears. The LCD warning made sense. Even Dervla's plans can fail. After Dennis forgot to renew his passport, a weekend away in Paris became a two-day trip to a damp, Kerry bedsit.

Clearly, he did not rise to the occasion as she was due back at work in September.

The word around the staff room is that Dennis is required to keep it in his pants until Christmas.

I noticed Laura's car parked forlornly on the road, halfway across the bridge.

I flicked the indicator lever and bumped awkwardly up onto the footpath (I noticed she had forgotten – again – to turn on her hazard warning lights).

I thought, if the master of planning, the legend that is Mrs Kennedy, can fail, what chance do I have? I do not want to appear, haggard and drawn, in an Amazon Prime documentary, a shot of me being led away in handcuffs, the voice-over commenting: "He almost got away with it, too. One mistake meant the difference between freedom and a life behind bars."

I sighed deeply and glanced around. Alone at last. My companions had finally vanished.

Who was I kidding? I was not trained for this. The only thing I'd ever killed was a child's enthusiasm. In an unguarded moment, I'd once told a student that the world needs more fitters than dancers.

Then the irony of the situation hit me: possessing the requisite skills could even be counterproductive. How could I convince a jury that I had nothing to do with the discovery of the late Mrs Devaney down a well if I, for example, trained with the SAS in the school holidays? Maybe the optimum dispatch method should be so outlandish that no one would ever believe it to be intentional?

My reverie was interrupted by the click-clack of my own hazard warning lights.

I took a deep breath, ratcheted the handbrake up an extra notch, swung the door open and in the same, swift motion stepped out of the car.

That's when I got creamed by the bread van.

The incident demonstrated how a life-changing decision can be pinpointed to a single moment. A newscast about a terrorist act could inspire someone to join the army. A visit to the beach could trigger an impulse to sail the world or start a sun-lounger rental business.

My road to Damascus moment occurred neither in Damascus nor technically on a road. I was literally above one, though – the R446 that passes over the bridge. I flew high through the air, and it seemed that time slowed as I reached the apex of my trajectory.

I spied a fisherman, wearing a hat to protect himself from the summer sun, casting a line downstream at the weir; a couple in matching tee-shirts cycled along the far bank; cars, backed up along the bridge, honked impatiently. I felt like shouting, 'Sorry for the bloody inconvenience!'

At that moment, I understood that no memorial would be erected to me. The best I could hope for was a mention in some drivers' texts explaining why they were late home for lunch. Anger washed over me. It was not right that my next appearance in print should be in the obituary column of *The Westmeath Independent*. There were crossword puzzles that would remain uncompleted, jigsaws unassembled, books I'd neither read nor write, lovers that I would not take – it could happen. My neighbour, Brenda the brunette, sprang to mind.

I suspected that she had a soft spot for me. Must I always regret not following the trail of smoke into her back garden? I could have offered to help her burn her errant husband's possessions in the bonfire. He was a plumber whose aftersales services did not feature in any registered fitter's manual, so she kicked him out, but not before he had replaced the gas boiler with an improved condensing furnace. I respected her for that.

Meanwhile…

Death seemed imminent. It was so unfair, somebody deserved this more than I.

Laura!

Why couldn't she have filled the petrol tank?

The laws of gravity and physics kicked in and I became transfixed by the bridge parapet, that grew larger.

This is going to hurt was almost the last ignoble thought to pass through my head as I anticipated what the impact of nineteenth-century ashlar limestone might do to my twenty-first-century anatomy. I braced in anticipation of agony with the added soupçon of death.

However, my degree is in drama (you'll have noticed) and not physics. If it had been the latter, then I probably would have computed factors such as momentum, mass, and trajectory in my calculations. I was therefore somewhat surprised to find myself sailing, unharmed, over the cast-iron balustrade.

I could see a future opening up after all. A future that involves me asking if Brenda needs her garden trimmed. What are neighbours for after all? I'd need to be rid of the person who almost sent me into orbit first. Brenda wasn't the type of person who did affairs. I would have to be a person of the utmost respectability and integrity to turn her head. If I had to end Laura to achieve that, so be it.

My momentum continued and I plunged into the river. I sank deep but soon popped back up again, treading water to stay afloat. It was bone-numbingly cold, despite the early summer sun, but the Arctic it was not.

I was astonished. There wasn't a bruise on me. Thankfully, bull bars had long since been banned in Ireland and the bread van possessed a five-star NCAP safety rating for vulnerable road users. Its bonnet's energy-absorbing construction ensured that it was like being hit by a hotel mattress.

Heads popped over the bridge parapet. Onlookers snapped away on camera phones. I guessed that someone might get around to throwing me a lifebuoy once they updated their Instagram pages.

I waved.

'I'm okay,' I yelled.

That's when skipper Viking Mike, taking sightseers out for the tour of Lough Ree in his motorised, longboat replica, ran over me.

Laura

78

My eyes fluttered open and discovered Laura standing over me in uniform.

'Welcome back, stranger,' she said.

In reflex, I half rose, grasped a plastic knife from a tray and weakly poked her in the breast. The plastic utensil folded under the pressure.

Laura placed her hand over mine, removing the knife, and I fell back on the hospital bed.

'It's all right,' she said, 'you're in a safe place.'

I moaned.

I was in agony but registered that I was in a ward and that there were several other occupied beds. I'd be emailing VHI later. After all, I'd selected the option for a private room as part of my health insurance, then again, did I recall a direct debit bouncing back as unpaid?

My left arm was lost in a big plaster cast. My right leg, sheathed in a plastic brace, was raised, dangling from a metal support. My other leg was wrapped in bandages and propped up with a support under the heel. It looked like I was being prepped either to deliver a baby or be rogered mercilessly. Tubes snaked into my arms.

Another tube appeared out of my pyjama bottoms.

Someone farted noisily. I wasn't entirely convinced that it wasn't me.

I moaned again in pain and watched her adjust settings on an infusion pump that regulated the fluids going into my arm from a bag hanging over me.

'Should you be doing that?' I groaned.

'You do know I work here?' she said. 'This is what I do.'

'I thought you weren't supposed to mind family?'

'You're right but circumstances change when you've got three staff nurses calling in sick, locums struggling to stay on their feet after consecutive twelve-hour shifts and an on-call doctor who could not be more clueless. Half of us wonder if he downloaded his registration. The other half feel he's incapable of even doing that.'

I attempted to force face muscles into sympathetic mode but instead, it looked like I'd sucked on a lemon.

'If there's a petition you want signed, I'm your man.'

I grimaced. My whole body ached.

I watched a drainage bag fill with urine.

My urine.

'I swear, some of these young nurses think they can ride all night and still rock into work.'

'Laura,' I interrupted and nodded towards the potential audience watching TV or reading magazines around us. Ears started to perk up.

'What?' she asked.

'This isn't a private ward,' I mumbled. 'And why isn't this a private ward? I pay premiums, premia, premia's? A lot.'

'Oh don't be such a prude,' she said. 'I don't mind who or what they get on top of as long as they show up fit for their shift.'

I don't actually have an issue talking about sex. Laura however can talk about the subject in a way that would make a longshoreman blush.

'You know one of them vanished into the supply cupboard with the physiotherapist, where she screwed him sideways and every which way.'

I coughed but she didn't take the hint.

'I'd say her gee was red raw at the end of it.'

I'm not sure what Florence Nightingale would have made of it.

I've asked her to dial the rhetoric back when we've decided that there was nothing on Amazon Prime worth watching and as soon as the dishwasher had been filled. If this confluence of events coincided with her son being out of the house, then my luck was in and I'd seize the moment, placing clothing neatly aside on the chest of drawers. I would plead with her as I drew the bedroom curtains to keep it down but just when I'm generating a head of steam, she shouts out, 'Hang on, I've still got the remote—' before rummaging underneath the duvet and placing the television control on the locker. 'Now, where were we?'

It's hard enough to concentrate on matters at hand while trying to filter out what she is saying, at the same time keeping an ear cocked for Liam stumbling back home from the off licence.

In truth, such encounters had grown rarer and rarer lately. I'd begun to prefer walking the dog around the estate. It's not that sex is overrated, it's just not worth messing up the Egyptian bedsheets, sometimes.

'At any time stop and ask how I am,' I said.

'How are you feeling?' she asked after a beat. I caught the roll of her eyes.

'There's not a bit of me that doesn't ache. Can bruises have bruises?' I rubbed my stomach and instantly regretted it as pain lanced through me.

'Those are haematomas, technically.'

'As if being in agony wasn't enough. Now you have my mind racing. Am I going to be all right?'

'Martin, you'll be out of here in no time, we need the beds.'

She pressed a plastic object into my hand. It was like a ballpoint pen attached by a cable to a pump.

'Press the switch on top if you want to boost your pain meds,' she said.

I thumbed the switch, but everything still felt the same.

'Nothing's happening,' I whimpered. 'If I'm badly injured, you can tell me, I can take it.'

'Like the time you were bitten by a spider and called the emergency services.'

'It was a black widow.'

'False black widow,' she said.

'I didn't know that at the time,' I snapped back. 'You do know that arachnophobia is a real thing? You being the medical expert and all.'

Laura took a breath. 'You're not dying. Everything is intact and will heal. You broke your arm,' she said, 'and damaged some joints. The leg brace is there until the ligaments heal.'

'So my future as an Irish dancer is not in jeopardy.'

She smiled. 'I thought the English were famous for their stiff upper lip.'

'I was run over by a boat,' I replied. 'No school in the world prepares someone for that.'

I was feeling sorry for myself. No teacher alive regrets anything more than being out sick during the summer holidays.

'Your mother rang,' Laura said. 'She's going to pop over for a flying visit. Your dad has to stay and mind the van.'

My parents were both retired. My father (the Irish connection) left County Mayo when he was fourteen for England. He'd found work as a navvy before meeting my mother in Birmingham. They were married at sixteen. Long story short, they'd bought a campervan after retirement, and now permanently resided on the 18th fairway of The Royal Cedar Golf Club and Spa to the chagrin of the owner who had bilked them out of their pension fund.

Laura smiled.

I'll say that for her, she always had a lovely smile.

'We're all glad that you're going to be okay.'

'Who are you again?' I asked.

A panicked expression crossed her face before she smiled again. 'Bastard.'

'I am not sure if I'll be as good as new, though. I may never fill a dishwasher again.'

Her brow furrowed. 'I'm glad that you are taking it so well. It was a close call. I felt sure that my last vision of you alive would be you sailing over the bonnet of my car.'

'Well, even if I hit it, you've got step-back insurance,' I replied. 'You'd only have to pay the first hundred euros.'

She continued regardless. 'It's a pity I didn't have the phone out recording. That entry into the water would have earned you an eight-point average if the judges from Red Bull were present.'

'I'll just have to give it another go.'

'Still,' she leaned over and gently touched my uninjured arm, 'you were lucky.'

'Not that lucky so that I avoided the afternoon sailing of the Viking boat.'

She nodded, wistfully. 'I'm just glad to have been there for you.'

It seemed churlish to point out that I wouldn't have been in the situation in the first place if she had filled her bloody car with bloody unleaded like she'd bloody well promised.

'I can only tell you,' I said instead, 'that I truly appreciate you being here. I'd shake your hand, only I'm not letting go of the pain relief and I'm more tied up than an S and M customer who wants their money's worth.'

I felt a dart of pain in my arm. I moaned and thumbed the switch. 'You sure this thing is working?'

She glanced about her before adjusting a setting on the pump. 'Here you go. I'd hate that your last words to me involved swearing.' She smirked at the irony. She was alluding to a Sunday afternoon tryst, several months previously, where I'd tried to censor her.

I wanted to remind her that I wasn't against swearing per se, but I was losing the power of speech. We English have great swear words. We just don't tend to use them during sex. In fact, we speak very little during the main event. It's not really the time for a chat.

'How's that?' she asked, watching my eyelids flicker.

I felt pain recede. 'Better,' I said, fighting the urge to drift away. 'What do you mean by my last words?'

'As you sailed through the air. Right before you vanished over the side of the bridge. I could clearly hear you giving out about the van driver.'

'What did I say?' I mumbled.

I could feel my eyes closing as the pain eased and happiness filled my veins.

'You bloody bitch.'

Maggie

77

Never have I had such dreams. It was like the visual cortex of my brain switched from viewing the world via a cathode ray tube to an ultra 5k screen.

I found myself revisiting a memory of being dragged out our front door by Barney, our half-cross Pomeranian. Street lights flickered on. We were only four houses along when Barney hit the brakes and took a keen interest in a wheelie bin. The deserted street stretched out before me. I glanced up at the house nearest us. The upper storey had all the lights on. A woman, Brenda, appeared in one of the windows. Her dark hair was tied back in a ponytail. She draped fabric over a mannequin and peered intently at it as she adjusted the cloth, applying pins held between her lips. She wore a thin bathrobe that suggested nothing underneath and stared at the mannequin in a way that would make it blush if it had a pulse. I guess she felt that the fall of the drape was just perfect.

The intimacy of the moment washed over me and even then, I knew that I was straying into dangerous, uncharted territory. I was steps away from participating in an innocent ramble and appearing in a line-up.

I tugged on the lead to move on and glanced down, but Barney was hunched over, his hindquarters in the midst of a massive evacuation.

My heart pounded as Brenda placed one hand very lightly on the shoulder of the mannequin; lowering her touch, she slowly smoothed the fabric into place.

Barney circled his excrement and suddenly barked happily.

Brenda swivelled her head to face the window, but I was already gone, scurrying homewards with Barney heavy in my arms.

I heard a hospital monitor beeping loudly and I noticed a hospital bed on the street, a nurse hovering nearby, staring down at a patient under a blanket. *Now that is something you don't see every day*, I thought and edged in close, still holding the dog.

I could not be more surprised to discover that the pyjama-clad patient was me.

And then I was back in the hospital.

The nurse and several doctors quickly formed a scrum about me as my eyes opened. Their anxious glances made me wonder if my credit card had been declined. I felt my heart rate increase. *Stay calm*, I thought. *Try to reassure them.*

'Try the Visa,' the bedbound me mumbled. 'I beg you. I can't go public.'

I struggled to form more words to let them know the three-digit security code on the back.

'Seven-oh-seven,' I gasped, but no one was taking notes.

Hopefully one of them had a good memory and a card reader amongst the equipment they were wheeling in.

I opened my eyes again and found myself staring at a television set slung from the ceiling. I registered that the movie *The Hunger Games* was playing. Could someone fetch caramel popcorn?

A blurred figure edged in, half-blocking the screen. My brain struggled to pull focus until it revealed, in full HD, Dennis and Dervla Kennedy standing at the bottom of my bed. Dervla kept one eye on her phone. Her thumb scrolled ceaselessly. Dennis stared awkwardly at his feet, like he'd been dragged into the lingerie section of a department store.

'I've seen this,' I murmured.

Jennifer Lawrence fired an arrow through an apple stuffed in the mouth of a roasted boar.

'It's the first one,' I declared. They must have believed me because neither of them looked up at the screen. A thunderous fart shook the bedclothes. At least this time I knew its provenance.

'Oopsy,' I said. 'I'd say they heard that in France.'

Some sentient part of me recognised that I was under the influence of chemical compounds. I did not know what they were, but they were awesome. I twisted my neck and noticed a middle-aged man in the next bed licking at an ice cream.

My tongue poked out and wriggled as I tried to taste it.

He yanked the ice cream back in case I possessed the tongue-snagging powers of an American Bullfrog.

I squinted at Dervla.

'Are you really here?' I asked her.

'Doing our turn, Martin,' she said. 'We're all on a rota.'

'That's wild,' I giggled. 'Will you let me know if you two are doing the bold thing in January?'

'I'll get a nurse,' Dennis announced and ran out the door.

'Is it true you sent a DNA sample of his to the lab before you agreed to marry him?'

A nurse appeared. 'All right?'

'I mean you can tell a lot from a swab.'

Dervla stiffened. 'We were just going,' she said and hurried out the door without looking back.

I registered that I was alive unless the afterlife involved hospital wards and cable television.

'You know where you are?' the nurse asked, checking my pulse.

'The semi-private ward,' I replied. 'And thank you for at least that. The Visa card was good then?'

She peered into my eyes and appeared satisfied. 'You're some man for the visitors,' she said.

Someone laughed to my side. A little bit of quiet please, Jennifer Lawrence was speaking to me from the television.

'Your sister is here to see you,' she added, 'but she's just going to have to wait. I'm just going to get the doctor to look at you first.'

'My sister?' I asked the nurse's back, as she walked out the door.

A delicious warmth coursed through me. I grew up believing that I was an only child. Who knew?

Maggie Geraghty-Philbin, chair of the Parent's Association, strode in and plonked down in the visitor's chair beside my bed. She was a thin, stern-looking woman. I wondered if I should offer her a sandwich.

'Hiya,' I slurred. 'Maggie. Are you my sister?'

Maggie glowered. 'Sometimes you need to cut through the red tape.'

'I've always wanted a sister,' I confessed. 'Someone to look out for. Someone to introduce me to her friends. Will you introduce me to your friends?'

'I certainly will not.'

She reached over, grabbed a remote and the television blinked off.

An urge to kill rose within me, undiminished by tranquillisers. If I'd had two working hands, they'd have been wrapped around Maggie's throat. Jennifer Lawrence and I had a connection.

'Hey,' someone protested three beds over. 'I was watching that.'

'It's about Ruairi,' Maggie said, ignoring the filthy looks being thrown her way. 'He remains suspended.'

'Ah, Ruairi. The little shit.'

'Excuse me?'

'Sorry,' I said. 'Your son is not so little. Big brute of a shit, in fact.'

I'd never spoken to her like this before. I'd always been hamstrung by the protocols of office. There were expectations on how to speak to members of the public whose children were in our care. The drugs, though, permitted thoughts to flow unfiltered through my lips. I had better be careful what I might say. I could admit to anything.

'Anything like what?' Maggie asked.

'Did I say that out loud?'

'Yes, you did.'

My mind, despite being foggy with medication, knew enough to change the topic but my voice box never got the memo.

'I've made up my mind I'm going to murder—'

I interrupted myself. That was surely out loud.

'To murder who?' Maggie asked.

I winked with all the subtlety of a panto villain. 'A pint,' I said. 'I'm going to murder a pint.'

She raised her eyebrows in disbelief, how dare she not believe me.

'And kill,' I improvised, 'an urge… to kiss. Tell me you feel the same way.'

It wasn't the best save in the world, but I wasn't exactly firing on all cylinders.

Maggie was unamused. She leaned in. 'As if you haven't enough broken bones already. Now I'm warning you, Martin, but Ruairi needs to be allowed back. As soon as the holidays are over, I expect that his backside will be warming a desk, or you'll know all about it.'

I grinned happily as Maggie rattled on. She didn't know about my secret weapon. I felt for the fob under the pillow.

She pressed down on my leg, and I yelped.

'Don't doubt me, Martin. I'll do whatever it takes.'

I felt plastic under my fingertips, seized it and pressed the button frantically but nothing happened apart from a bemused look from Maggie.

I noticed that the drip of magic and sweetness had disappeared and that I'd been thumbing the top of a ballpoint pen.

I guessed that no one had noted my security code after all.

Chris

76

I wore a dark eye mask to blank out the light. I slid it upwards onto my forehead as a nurse greeted me with 'Good morning. How are you feeling?'

Like I'd been sleeping.

I'd spent the morning feeling sorry for myself, but no one noticed.

She took my temperature with a handheld scanner attached by a cord to a trolley. I did not know what she'd been told but it was safe with me.

I was experiencing the worst headache of my life. I moaned. It was like I had just got back from auditioning to be MMA champion, Conor McGregor's punch bag.

'Can you give me something?' I begged. 'I'm in the horrors here.' I managed to catch her rolling her eyes. I guessed that she was thinking of the new mothers upstairs, who would ask for a mug of tea while having a team of seamstresses repairing their fun palaces.

'Sorry. But I'll try and get you an Aspirin.'

'Aspirin?'

I wanted the good stuff. Before I could protest, she moved to the next patient and continued taking vital signs. She smiled in my direction as she worked, and I sucked in my stomach. It's a challenge to appear debonair when there's a half-filled urinary bag slung to the side of your bed.

I threw her an impish grin anyway but then realised that she was not maintaining an eyeline.

I turned my head and saw a newspaper being held out beside me.

I groaned and pulled the eye mask back down.

'Look who's back in the land of the living,' the man said and folded the paper.

I rolled the eye mask back up.

Chris, the school principal, remained sitting. He helped himself to a sweet from my locker.

'I don't think visiting is for another hour,' I said.

Chris ignored me. His eyes followed the nurse around the ward.

'So they tell me that you are out of the woods?' he said.

He adjusted his tie. It was an unconscious gesture made to draw attention to the quality of the silk, setting off a hand-made suit. The suit probably cost more than the car I drove. He then peered at his watch—an expensive Swiss timepiece, until it was noticed by the nurse. Chris was perpetually on the make. As one of the teachers succinctly once put it, 'If he could, he'd mount the crack of dawn.'

Chris didn't need to work. Word around the staff room was that he remained in the job solely to permit a run at Ms Clancy the Maths teacher. She was a former Ms Ireland finalist who later married the runner-up. She was also an outspoken advocate for LGBTQ+ rights but Chris just interpreted that as playing hard to get.

'So am I out of the woods?' I asked.

'Are you?'

'That's literally what you just said.'

'Oh, right.'

The nurse moved out of the room and Chris remembered why he was there.

'You were lucky,' he said. 'More than lucky.'

'Hard to tell from here.' I held up the encased arm. 'I'm keeping a plasterer in a job so that's a positive.'

'Could have been worse. You putting in a claim then? I would. The incompetent morons.'

'A claim?'

He hesitated as he'd said too much. He reached into a pocket and dangled a set of car keys. 'You'll be wanting these back soon. Laura said I could borrow your car while you were resting.'

He made it sound like I was having a spa day.

'Did she?'

'My Seven Series is in the garage,' he said louder for the benefit of the nurse who had just walked back into the room. He leaned in close and whispered to me, 'getting graffiti removed.'

Chris popped the last sweet from my bedside locker into his mouth. He was not just here to wish me well. The reference to the vandalism could mean several things but I picked the likely option.

'Suzanne?'

He nodded and lowered his voice again. 'She tagged the car. The thing is she mightn't stop at that, she was spotted buying a five iron. Would you have a word?'

I nodded painfully. 'It's on my to-do list.'

'You're a trooper. You can see why I picked you as my best man.'

I did not realise at the time that the role would involve a lifetime commitment. It was true that he'd asked me to be his best man – perhaps because every other man he knew loathed him. That's what you get when your life ambition is to sleep your way through the female population of Westmeath, marital status notwithstanding. It's not even that I actually carried out all of my best man duties. Suzanne, his former fiancée, also happened to be my best friend and therefore not likely to react with lethal force if I showed up at her office. She had never forgiven him for the humiliation of being texted on the way to the church, that he was "having second thoughts".

This was right after he had rung McGinley's boat yard to buy a Shannon cruiser.

He'd been idly opening some of the wedding cards that morning when a lotto scratch card tumbled out. Turned out to be a big money winner and while he was now unsure about wanting a bride, he knew that he definitely wanted a boat.

He coughed again. 'Take as much time as you need,' he said.

As if I had a choice.

'It may not be a good time but we've to let Kyle go.'

'Do we?'

Kyle was a new addition to the staff. He was a former Marine who had come to Ireland to meet the love of his life, whom he had discovered in an internet chat room.

'What's he done now?' I asked.

'It's more like our sports hall is on hold again. The planner said there might be rare newts on the site.'

'The planner that Kyle pushed through a window?'

'Now you get it.'

'You'll have to do the honours,' I said. 'I'm out of action.'

'Hello,' Chris said. 'He's killed people.'

'I heard it was either him or the Taliban.'

'What if he takes it the wrong way?'

'Maybe we should let the Department take care of it.'

'That probably will be for the best.'

He surveyed me again. 'I'm sorry,' he said, loudly. 'If only I had been out on my cruiser, I could have saved you.'

He was to be admired, he'd turned the topic expertly around to himself and somehow slipped in his boat reference.

'Is that the time?' Chris said. He held up his watch again. 'I'd better go, have to help out at the homeless shelter.'

Athlone has a homeless shelter?

Chris was all smiles as he swiped some toffees from the locker of a sleeping patient, while his gaze remained fixed on the nurse as she moved between patients. It was like watching a heat-seeking missile locking onto a fighter jet.

'I mean, if we don't mind the orphans, who else will?' he said.

The nurse checking the pulse of a patient, nodded sympathetically.

If there is one thing worse than being an orphan, it's being a homeless one.

Parents

75

My mind raced as my limbs healed and they weaned me off tranquillisers. I found it almost impossible to sleep in the hospital bed as I dangled like a deer caught in a fence. I would remain awake as patients about me snored. One morning, as I waited for the sunrise, I heard the sound of a smartphone ringing. I glared around me. Who could be disturbing the ward at this hour? I realised that it was my phone. I grabbed it from under my pillow to kill the call but accidentally accepted a video call from my mother.

'Hello, son,' she called out brightly. 'Bad time?'

'It's fine,' I whispered back, watching her adjust the phone camera to fill the screen. She was sitting in the front of the campervan, behind her, a golf course stretched out, down to the sea.

'We're so sorry, I could not come over in the end,' she said. 'They were threatening the bailiffs on us but I made them tea and told them we were old. One said that I reminded him of his gran. I sent them off with jam tartlets.'

The owner of the golf course had tried everything to have them removed but each time he had been outmanoeuvred. 'He may be rich,' my mother had said, 'but we are armed with a lifetime of experience.' The owner's dream of hosting a Master's was being dashed by the ongoing presence of my parents squatting on his course. I had told them that they should just give up. He was untouchable. Why not just settle down? There were plenty of places that they could retire to.

My mother had dismissed the notion outright. 'We did look into a care home,' my mother had said, 'however it smelled of wee. Your father also said it was too full of old people.'

They decided that they could not rest until justice was done. 'He took us for our savings,' she'd said. 'Not just us.' They had discovered that he was a director of the vulture fund that had collapsed but not before financing a private golf course and spa retreat. They'd sold their flat, quietly purchased club membership, bought a deluxe campervan and drove it onto the course. They had carefully examined the club rules – it included parking, but nowhere did it prohibit someone from setting up residence. They'd remained there ever since. 'We're much happier here,' my mother had said. 'I've lovely views of the sea and your father has plenty of room to plant his potatoes.' I imagined an apoplectic owner discovering root vegetables growing in the fairways.

'So to what do I owe the honour?' I said. 'And do you know what time it is?'

'We just wanted to see how you were. We are up early as there's an ITV crew setting up. I think this one is *Good Morning Britain.*'

'Good lord,' I said. My parents had become somewhat of a cause célébre. Celebrities were lining up to support them in their campaign against corporate business. It was the publicity that was probably keeping them alive. The owner knew that the local constabulary couldn't overlook him accidentally running over his two squatters with the greens' lawnmower, despite the massive Christmas hamper that he'd leave annually into the station. In addition, my mother played bridge with the superintendent, and my father installed power showers for anyone in uniform for the cost of a pint.

'Your father says, "hi,"' she said. 'Have to go and handcuff myself to a golf cart. The producer says she likes the optics of it,' and cut the connection.

I was welcome home anytime. However, my room had long since gone and the best that I could now hope for was a pull-out cot in their camper.

I cast an eye around the ward. No one seemed to notice my morning call.

Ireland was supposed to be a place with a quiet pace of life. A respite from the rat race. Instead, I'd been run over by a boat and had more debt than a small African country. My future likely involved delivering pizza in the evenings after school.

I experienced a flashback to the boat rolling over me.

Laura caused this.

Something needed to change.

In my mind's eye, I conjured up a whiteboard. I sketched words with my free hand and words appeared in my presentation.

"Martin Devaney."

I added text underneath using a dramatic font.

"Assassin."

That felt good. I was channelling my inner ninja. I surveyed the room. None appeared impressed. The ungrateful sods. They were present at a crucial moment, a lot like those who attended U2's first gig in Whelan's, but this audience slept on.

I wrote "Skills" as a headline. Underlined it. Underlined the underline.

I should not rush into this, I had so many skills. Hard to choose from them all really. Should I list them in alphabetical order or lethality rating?

Time passed. The sun rose as I wrote but as quickly erased the words. In frustration, I wrote, "English grammar".

My audience remained as unimpressed as I was. George Bernard Shaw cruelly once said that some men do, but that others teach. I had not any experience with unarmed combat. I'd not been in any special forces and my knowledge of IEDs was strictly limited to what I'd observed in Desert Storm films. Even if I knew how to make one, where was I going to find an unused artillery shell? eBay?

I glanced about me. Questions anyone? Anyone? I was met by faint snores.

I erased the words from the presentation and wrote in "Fishing".

Fishing?

I settled back in the bed as the words faded away like smoke.

There was something in that. I had skills as an amateur fisherman. I had a fully equipped workshop full of lures that I fabricated myself. Perhaps I should toy with the expression to make swords into ploughshares by doing the exact opposite.

I nodded, albeit painfully. I had skills, I just had to apply them. Somehow.

It was this minor detail that eluded me.

I closed my eyes to imagine the scenarios that I could create, using nothing more, than superglue, twine and welded metal scrappage. In my mind's eye, I saw Laura turning on the microwave before ducking down for a dish, oblivious to a butcher's cleaver swooping down from the ceiling. I saw her walk towards the stairs, snag a tripwire but pause to look in the hall mirror, as a huge concrete ball rolls past. I imagined her placing a hand on the handle of the downstairs toilet door but changing her mind, without ever hearing the growling from the wild animal that I'd forced inside.

I grimaced. Who was I kidding? Each idea was more unfeasible than the one before. Laura was a smart woman. She'd notice anything that was unusual and would be unlikely for example, to step onto a camouflaged tarp-covered pit in the garden.

I felt exasperated. Perhaps I'd feel inspired after I ate something. I pulled the wheeled table beside the bed around and positioned it over my lap. An untouched meal from the previous evening occupied centre stage underneath a plastic cover. I removed it, revealing a congealed plate of mash, chicken, and peas.

I stared before stifling a fit of laughter. A patient stirred and peered over.

A solution had literally been served to me on a plate.

'This could work,' I said aloud. It was not a plan that might grace any CIA in-house bulletins, but all options should be explored.

I adjusted the plate in front of me, picked up the knife and separated each food item into uneven triangular segments.

'You must really like hospital food,' the patient said, watching me.

I smiled. I certainly did.

I felt like shouting "eureka," but Archimedes had beaten me to it. He may have discovered how to measure the volume of an irregular object while bathing, but I had discovered something a lot more useful.

And it didn't involve me running into the street in the nip either.

Laura

74

The perfect murder involves using available resources. If I commanded a retinue of henchmen, then I could take one aside to whisper into his ear. After exchanging knowing nods, my marital status could be reset before lunchtime.

However, I didn't have any henchmen, I didn't even have online followers. I thought more would have appreciated the mention of my prizewinning pike when a picture of it was posted on the social media page of my angler's club. It measured a whopping hundred and five centimetres from its mouth to the tip of its tail. It only garnered a few *Likes,* most of which were mine using various school PCs.

I stepped up to the cork noticeboard in my kitchen. It was a mass of sticky notes, bills, and leaflets. I peeled back the electricity bill stamped Final Demand with my unplastered arm, to reveal a healthy food guide. It featured a drawing of a plate of food that was divided into uneven sections. Meats occupied a small segment, while vegetables occupied a larger portion. It looked just like the meal that I'd toyed with in the hospital. I must have remembered the image and parked it somewhere in my brain. I would plaster the school with such leaflets, targeting teenagers who think that they will live forever but who were more focused on *Likes* than living. It was ironic but a strategy for killing had been printed by the Health Service Authority. I pointed out the leaflet to the dog. 'This tells you what you should eat,' I said.

Barney, flat on the floor, opened an eye.

'If you think about it,' I continued, 'what if I just did the exact opposite?'

Barney yawned but passed no comment. Perhaps he was considering the implications of what I was saying.

I turned and grasped the frying pan handle and rolled sausages, sizzling in lard. I had only been home a few days after being discharged from the hospital and I still had an arm encased in plaster, but one arm remained free. It was all I needed to treat Laura to an all-you-can-eat full-on Irish breakfast.

With all the trimmings.

Laura woke up in surprise as I elbowed the bedroom door open, a tray held precariously over my plastered arm. I moved stiffly as one leg remained encased in its plastic brace.

'You shouldn't be doing this,' she said, sitting up. She took the tray from me. I was pleased as I'd hardly spilt a drop of the full-fat cocoa on the way up the stairs, and most of the breakfast remained on the plate, despite the presence of enough grease to launch a ferry.

Her eyes widened at the plates. 'Oh, two eggs?'

'Some sausages, rashers and pudding. No trouble at all.'

'Okay,' she said dubiously. 'I appreciate the effort.'

'Nonsense,' I said. 'I'll be at home for the summer. It can be our new thing.'

'This is too much,' she said, spearing a sausage with a fork.

'Nothing is too much for you.'

I backed out of the room and returned to the kitchen.

Herein lies the perfect crime.

You can kill your lover with kindness.

Pile on the saturated fats until the heart gives in and no jury in the world would convict you. I imagined them rolling their eyes as the barrister representing the director of Public Prosecutions, addressed the court.

'I now call on Martin's accomplice, Mrs Dolan of *Dolan's Pastries and Cream Buns* to take the stand.'

Death by calories would be an easy method of murder. All I had to do was feed Laura like she was training for the Olympic swim team.

I dipped the frying pan into the sink.

The words "Calorie Killer" in congealing fat, formed on the frying pan.

I rinsed the pan, revealing new words.

"Fool proof."

I rinsed the pan again. "Cons" appeared and underneath, "Might take a while."

This could be a problem as I had already decided on a date to attain Mission Accomplished. There are few things more motivating than a deadline, and another publicity leaflet on the notice board provided it. The Lough Ree Pike Fishing Festival took place later in the year. The large influx of strangers to the town would in turn create a source of potential fall guys as I continued to explore other lethal options. It would be foolish after all to keep all my fried eggs in one basket.

I was also mindful that Brenda wouldn't wait forever.

I dropped the pan into the sink before stretching my good arm to the back of a cupboard underneath, reaching for the deep fat fryer.

I placed it on the countertop.

In the meantime, while alternatives were being explored, I'd learn to coat Mars Bars in batter.

Mrs Keena

73

The key to a good Leaving Certificate – or where I grew up, A levels – is just like the committal of a perfect crime. It's all about the homework. Time spent learning the soliloquies of Hamlet could mean the difference between a Trinity offer and a place in an institute of technology that can only be located on a sat nav. In the case of murder – a fail grade may mean fifteen to twenty in Mountjoy Prison. So, research is crucial but therein lies the rub (as fellow Warwickshire man, Shakespeare himself would say). It's all very well Googling, "How to commit the perfect murder", but such things stand out in any subsequent investigation. It's hard to explain away your reasons for downloading a DIY Ricin recipe to a Garda while your wife lies cooling in the living room.

Research, therefore, has to go hand in hand with security. The Normandy landings would not have been the success they were if Churchill had been cavalier with the forties version of a Twitter feed – carrier pigeons that coo in a German accent. Don't mock, birds have dialects too. It was on the BBC.

I concluded that I needed to purchase a "burner." An internet-enabled smartphone that can't be traced back to the purchaser. I could blissfully explore tips on ligatures, for example, from the high stool on our kitchen island. An island incidentally comprising of a black granite top that I fought against. An island that cost me a month's salary that sits beside a perfectly good table and six chairs that no longer serve any purpose except as a repository for the shopping.

The justifications for murder just keep mounting.

Liam had left for college and Laura had offered him a lift. I rolled out of bed when I heard the door slam and sidled into the ensuite. I rinsed my hair using a red dye that I'd picked up in the chemist (with cash).

This was not easy considering the limited movement of my plaster-encased arm and that I was warned not to get it wet.

I slid on tracksuit bottoms over my leg brace, put on an old sweater and topped it off with a baseball cap. This did completely obscure my hair, meaning that the dyeing was somewhat pointless, but such trials and errors should help avoid other trials (see what I did there).

I even placed on a pair of glasses that I'd picked up in the St Vincent de Paul charity shop (again with cash). I baulked when I looked in the hall mirror; I almost didn't recognise myself.

Confident in my new altered appearance, I walked into the sitting room and slowly peeled back the curtains.

Today I was to purchase my new device but first I needed to slip past our next-door neighbour Mrs Keena and make it undetected out of the housing estate. This was easier said than done. To return to the World War Two analogy: The Great Escapers only had to cope with eight hundred armed members of the Luftwaffe on the wire. I had Mrs Keena to circumnavigate. In addition, I had an arm in a cast. There would be no tunnels dug this morning.

Mrs Keena was a retiree who had taken it upon herself to keep the estate a crime-free zone. She had come downstairs one morning and found a burglar rooting through her kitchen cabinets. She'd been terrified but it was he who had called the emergency services, to remove the knitting needle from between his shoulder blades. She'd applied for a shotgun licence after that but was refused when a representative of An Post – the Irish postal service – objected. She'd already opened the door to a postal worker while fielding a replica AK47. The postman had to be sent home with 'his nerves.' The local Gardaí agreed and no weapons, live or otherwise would be permitted.

Undefeated, she took to patrolling the estate with a notepad on the lookout for anyone acting suspiciously. If the housing association budget could have stretched to it, then she'd have had searchlights installed at the entrance to the estate. Residents would joke about it but to be fair, we'd not had a burglary in years. Alarm companies would send novices into our estate for a laugh.

I watched as Mrs Keena pulled up her jacket and stepped through her front gate onto the path. She peered up at the bird box she had installed on a tree opposite her house. The bird box remained uninhabited, just like the others she'd commissioned around the estate intending to make the estate more nature friendly. It shouldn't have been a surprise as her cats had decimated the local wildlife.

Her cats were the reason why Mrs Keena barely spoke to me. She had never forgiven me for backing over one of them.

Accidentally.

She'd then caught me placing the flattened pet in my wheelie bin.

I ask you, would it have been better to leave a cat corpse on my driveway?

She meandered onwards on her inspection tour. It would take her a good twenty minutes to circumnavigate the estate. I would just have to wait until she rounded a corner before I limped at speed towards the sole entrance/exit to the estate. I did not want to have to explain where I was off to and nor did I want her to wonder about my sudden change of appearance.

It might be even worse if I was unrecognisable because then Mrs Keena might go nuclear on me.

Residents still whisper across the timber fences that divide our back gardens. Ostensibly, they're pruning back deadwood but inevitably they're adding legs to the story of the foreigner who inadvertently wandered into the estate at four a.m., thumbs under the straps of his backpack.

The way that he was described to emergency services by an adrenaline-fuelled Mrs Keena ensured the dispatch of both an armed response unit and the Garda helicopter. Mohammad Aswan was caught in the beam of the helicopter searchlight, in mid-urination at a tree. He'd been abruptly tackled to the ground by a burly Garda who was under the impression that he was dealing with a suicide bomber. The arresting Garda was awarded a Scott Medal for bravery (he didn't know that the man was merely lost and looking for a house party).

The matter was eventually settled on the steps of the High Court after a formal apology by the state for breaking a refugee's legs.

Mrs Mina Olsen in 24 mused aloud on the neighbourhood social media group, asking why didn't anyone stop to wonder why a suicide bomber might be targeting an Irish housing estate in the Midlands? Joseph O'Brien in 32 *liked* the comment.

Mrs Keena faded gently from the scene for a time, nursing her humiliation, but re-emerged stronger than ever.

Somehow, she worked out that Mina was secretly carrying on with Joseph. They had been ultra-careful, only meeting in bed and breakfasts, at least two counties away. However, Mrs Keena managed to put it together, revealing the scoop at the resident's association AGM. None were more surprised than committee members Mr Olsen (chair) and Mrs O'Brien (treasurer) at the unexpected inclusion in the AOB portion of the meeting about their respective partners. Within days, "For Sale" signs were erected as households imploded. More than one household had their house swept for surveillance bugs.

I cracked the door open and watched Mrs Keena approaching the corner of the estate. I would step out the moment when she rounded the corner.

The lads in Stalag Luft III didn't realise how fortunate they were that they did not have Mrs Keena in the watch towers. They could have avoided the fate of captured escapees that were put up against a wall. The Gestapo weren't known for their hugs and muffins.

On the other hand, the prisoners were memorialised in a feature film starring Steve McQueen. So, there is that.

Hector

72

I made it out of the estate undetected and hopped onto a bus. I planned to go to the neighbouring town to visit their Vodafone shop. Today would be the day that I would buy a disposable phone. With cash of course.

Today, I didn't buy a phone. I ended up with an electronic tablet that incorporates Wi-Fi; contains built-in memory card slots and boasts a screen resolution so sophisticated that it can play back crystal-clear videos in formats that have yet to be invented. I also was on the hook for a leather case and a new home broadband package that includes free landline calls.

We don't actually have a landline anymore. I can only imagine the misery in store for me when Laura discovers the new direct debit.

Vodafone was crowded when I stepped through the doors, and I quietly slipped amongst the customers. I examined the various offers, trying not to draw attention to myself despite dragging a braced leg and having a cast on one arm.

I picked up a smartphone attached by a cord to a stand. It was perfect. It was internet enabled and could be purchased on a Pay As You Go basis.

I could see myself handing over the cash at the counter.

I could see myself bent over the screen on the bus home, seeking fool proof methods of introducing anaphylactic shock. Were dry roasted peanuts as potent as the salted variety? These were questions made for Reddit.

Despite attempting to remain stoic, I felt myself beaming. Then a voice interrupted.

'That's on special offer, sir.'

I knew it was on special offer. It was under the signage marked "Special Offers". That said, I was lucky that the wording was so prominent. In truth, the Vincent De Paul charity shop glasses were somewhat distorting and the world before me was a blur.

'I'll take it.'

'A good choice, Mr Devaney,' the voice said. 'I have one myself.'

I froze and felt a bead of hair dye form, roll out from under my cap and slide down my forehead. I peered at the sales assistant. The distortions of the lenses meant that all I could make out was that he was wearing an orange top and had a big head.

'You don't recognise me, sir?' the voice asked, cheerfully. 'Why would you? I was wearing a different uniform then. You learned me English. So you did.'

'Well, I'm glad to see you too—'

'Hector,' the man said cheerfully. 'I set fire to your briefcase once.'

Sadly, that did not narrow it down too well, but I knew my cover was blown. Suddenly he had a newer smartphone out of its box and swirled it about under my nose. I was half afraid a drop of Clairol would drip onto it.

'I can of course give you a much better deal than the Athlone branch,' he said slyly.

The bastard. He knew damn well where I lived and was churning through possible scenarios.

'Present for the wife?' he asked innocently. He grinned and watched as my forehead grew further stained from droplets of dye. My list of people that I wanted deceased grew longer. He probably assumed that I was going incognito to buy something for a mistress.

Like I can afford one on a teacher's salary.

'Yes, it's a present,' was the best response that I could muster.

Hector smelled blood in the water. 'A present?' Hector's voice faltered. 'Not sure, if she'll be impressed with this knockoff.'

Did he not just say that he had one himself?

'Your wife deserves the best does she not?'

I had to say that she did.

'Also,' he said, looking at my battered body, 'We have to look after those with disabilities.'

Somehow, I was sucked into banter. It turns out that Hector also felt that the granite island in my kitchen was a fad that was sure to pass.

He opined that Liam would eventually settle.

Hector winked when he rang through the purchase. Of course, he could not let me go without reminding me of the screen protectors and the accessories that I'd require to protect my valuable purchase.

I probably would have given him a pint of blood if asked just to get out of there. As it was, I was grateful to stumble out of the shop with plastic bags dangling from my plastered arm.

I threw my spectacles into a bin on the bus and unboxed my new device as the countryside passed by outside the windows. Hector had outlined all the functions until my eyes, tired already from the glasses, began to glaze over. This tablet was more than an internet-enabled device, it was a calculator, it was a games device. It was connected to an app store. It would not surprise me to learn that it could get up in the morning and cook breakfast.

One aspect did barge its way through the cloud of data on gigahertz, bandwidth and refresh rates. It was the built-in card reader.

I cracked open a SD memory card and slid it into a port. I understood the implications. Not only could I carry out my research anonymously, but I could write out my plan and save it on the memory card. What better way to study it and refine it as required? When the deed was done, the card could be destroyed with no evidence left behind.

I wiped away a streak of hair dye and ignored the other passengers lost in their own devices. I removed the stylus, created a note, and entered my first word, a word that signified that the countdown had begun.

"Prologue."

Liam

71

Liam forked sausages directly from the frying pan into his mouth. Music played faintly from his earbuds. He wore a waiter's uniform that was at least two sizes too small. He had grown into a tall, lanky chap and I supposed the hotel had nothing smaller that could fit him, either that or he just couldn't be bothered to obtain one. I noticed that the name badge, pinned to his waistcoat misidentified him as 'Joseph.'

He hadn't noticed me entering the kitchen from the garden. I'd spent the morning in my workshop typing up my notes and daydreaming of Brenda. He spotted me at last plugging in the tablet to charge. He nodded.

'So you are going to work?' I said.

He read my lips as he ate. 'No.'

The communications course was paying for itself.

'You're wearing your uniform,' I said.

He lowered the music volume by sliding a finger over his smartphone. 'What?'

'I was saying you're wearing your uniform.'

He sighed. 'Is this like bonding, yeah? Okay, Martin. FYI, I'm wearing the uniform because I was helping with the breakfasts. Ergo, I'm not going to work as I've been. Anything else you wanted to clear up?'

He gulped back a sausage. He reminded me of a seal swallowing a fish. There was an egg-stained plate beside him. I had filled the fridge with high calorific items to play fast and loose with Laura's cholesterol levels and it appeared that I had also inadvertently been preparing her son to survive a famine or give him options should he wish to hibernate for the winter.

He spooned more food into his mouth and unbuttoned his waistcoat to make more room for his stomach.

'I thought they provided meals at work?' I said, alarmed at the amount of food he was downing.

'I wasn't hungry then,' he said.

'You will put the dishes away, I hope. No maids here,' I said.

I saw that the bin was brimming with rubbish. It was like a game of Jenga where the objective was to pile on as many leavings as possible without them toppling to the ground. With my good arm, I carefully eased out the bin liner before tying it off and dragging the sack out the back door. Liam must have then sauntered over to the pedal bin and scraped the rest of the contents of his dish into it before placing the plate on the countertop.

I re-entered the kitchen and rummaged under the sink for a fresh bin bag.

Liam watched me as he fingered the earbuds deeper into his ear canal; no guilty thoughts clouded his face.

A notification alert pinged on his phone, and he looked at the message. He smiled and swiped on the screen. 'We chat later, yeah?' he said to me and held out the phone to show me a profile picture of a pouting young woman. 'What do you think?'

'Very pretty,' I said. 'What's her name?'

'Name?' he asked in a puzzled voice, like I'd asked him a trigonometry question. He threw on a backpack, stepped towards the back door, and turned to me. 'I'll be sure to ask her for you.'

'You do know that we have a dishwasher?' I called out to his back as he closed the door behind him. Through the window, I could see him strolling out the side gate. He hadn't bothered to change from his work uniform. Not even a good jumper. That's how it is now, I said aloud with a trace of envy.

I stood on the bin's foot pedal and the lid popped open. I held out the bin liner and saw congealing leftovers dripping down the sides of the bin.

'Oh for crying out loud.'

I swore. After Laura had gone to her just reward, I'd leave it a week before changing the locks. When a new lion takes over a pride, he often kills all the cubs from the previous male. I could see why. They haven't the option of farming them out to an Airbnb.

Laura screamed upstairs.

My face shot skyward. Surely her arteries had not snapped shut that quickly? Those eclairs I'd left on her vanity table must have tempted her after all.

I charged awkwardly up the stairs, my leg, confined by its brace, made running a challenge. Sadly, CPR was beyond my capability. I would truthfully tell the paramedics that it is almost impossible to deliver chest compressions one-handed. I stepped onto the landing and was surprised to discover Laura standing there, clad only in a robe and still damp from a morning shower.

'You all right?' I asked.

She pointed to the bedroom.

'Yes,' she said. 'Sorry about that.' She made a sign of the cross.

My head poked in through the doorway and found nothing out of the ordinary bar the weighing scales in the centre of the floor. Realisation dawned.

'Never mind,' I said. 'It's hard to lose a few pounds when you hit our age.' I munched on a square of chocolate. I'd wasted away on hospital food and was eager to return to my fighting weight.

It had only been a few weeks since I'd started on her new "diet". I had insisted on accompanying Laura to Lidl and loaded up the trolley with foods that would make a dietician lose the will to live. The fridge was filled at the beginning of the week and was as empty by the weekend as a Mayo All-Ireland trophy cabinet.

'I know,' she said. 'But I did it.'

She stepped tentatively onto the scales and eyed the LCD with trepidation. A smile confirmed the bad news.

'What?' I pushed further into the room, eyes on the LCD trying to read it the right way up.

'A full kilo!' she said triumphantly. 'Aren't you going to say something?'

'Well done,' I stammered. 'I knew you had it in you.' She also had several thousand calories in her, so I was more than a little taken aback by the revelations. There were households of active marathon runners that had fewer calories coming in through the door. Surely, they weren't all slipping down Liam's gullet?

She stepped on and off the scale to check that there was no glitch and smiled before vanishing out into the hallway, rooting through the airing cupboard for a towel.

There was always a possibility that the scales were malfunctioning. I stepped on the scale and the LCD displayed ninety-eight kilos. I recoiled in horror but then realised that the scales also took into account the weight of the plaster cast and my shoes.

My corduroy pants also.

I stepped off and back on again.

The LCD stuck to its lies. Revisiting the chocolate gateaux clearly was counterproductive. It did not help that I had an arm bound in plaster making exercise a challenge. It's difficult to jog when you have the appearance of a teapot.

The irony of the situation hit me. The idea of downsizing the number of people in the household was intended to benefit my financial situation.

The only thing gaining weight was my credit card printout.

I would not dismiss this high-calorie approach yet until I got to the bottom of Laura's weight loss. I'd allow the diet to take its course or until the weekly shop bankrupted us.

'You all right?' Laura asked, re-entering the bedroom, towelling her hair.

'I was just thinking that I can't wait to get back exercising. Soon as I get this plaster off.'

'You're up a bit then?'

'I'd say that the plaster adds a few kilos. I should weigh the cast.'

'You might weigh that belly hanging over your belt at the same time.'

'That's not nice.'

'Trying to motivate you.'

'Oh,' I replied. 'You're motivating me all right.' She had no idea how well.

She reached into a cupboard and pulled out a pair of running shoes. 'These are yours, yes? One careful owner.'

'I'll be in them the moment they take off the brace.'

She smiled. 'You know that I'm a nurse, yes?'

It was a rhetorical question, and I knew no good would come from any answer.

She pursed her lips and edged closer, blocking the sole exit to the room.

'Yes,' I said, a sense of foreboding washed over me. 'I know this.'

Suddenly she was reaching for the Velcro straps of the leg brace.

'Wait,' I gasped.

'I know what I am doing,' she said and before I knew it, she had the brace whisked off me. 'You won't need this anymore.'

I had no choice as it dangled from her hand.

I tentatively put weight on the injured leg. 'Not so bad,' I admitted.

'Happy to hear it. You know they've opened up the Greenway?'

The Greenway was an old rail track that had been converted into a pathway for leisure use.

'We have a Greenway?'

'Funny,' she said. 'And you're soon going to know every bit of it.'

'I shouldn't rush into things.'

I had ruled out cycling as an exercise option. Lycra was not a good look for me. A sweating, middle-aged man, bent over handlebars was unlikely to be picked at random for a *Vogue* cover.

'Martin,' she said, 'you've got bigger boobs than I do.'

'I don't think so.'

'You need to exercise. Now get your pants off.'

'Can we close the door at least?' I said.

She pushed me back on the bed and quickly stripped me of my shoes and trousers.

'You're right,' I agreed. 'I need to burn off some calories.'

I lay back on the bed as she rummaged in the wardrobe.

'What are you putting on?' I asked.

She produced a pair of men's shorts.

'Those are mine aren't they?' I said, puzzled.

'Let's see if they still fit, shall we?' It dawned on me that she wasn't proposing some kind of role-play game.

She bent over me and slid them up my hips.

'Just about,' she said. 'Not for much longer though if you stay at the chocolate.'

I felt like protesting at the insinuation that I was not minding myself. Those bars contained dairy milk.

'I don't know what you're talking about.'

'I'm sorry if I've offended you. I mean you do still have a six-pack,' she said, slipping my feet into the running shoes, and tying the laces.

That was more like it. Abs lurked somewhere under this sweater.

'The trouble is, they're in the fridge in your man cave.' She burst out laughing.

No jury in the world would convict me.

'You can start with a walk around the estate.'

She waited for a response.

'No time like the present,' I said slowly, 'although I hear it might rain.'

It was imperative of course that the cast remained dry.

'Well, then you can learn to run,' she said and left the room.

Sean's Bar

70

Sean's Bar is not only the oldest pub in Ireland but is said to be the oldest in the world.

The bric-a-brac on the wall adds ambience, while the sawdust-strewn floor probably dates from a tradition formed when burly jobbers mixed with the British cavalry officers stationed at the nearby castle.

Nowadays the clientele comprises locals and tourists. The dark smells of Irish stout intermingle with the aromas of cologne and French perfume, while the scented flavours of e-cigarettes drift in from the purpose-built smoking area out the back.

Irish pubs have been smoke-free since 2004 with smokers dispatched to allocated areas outside. These areas might have a roof but are otherwise exposed to the elements which mean that come the winter, only the most hardcore of smokers remain.

These spaces also happen to be the prime pulling spot for those in the mood for love or a quick feel in the back of a car. It's not uncommon to hear a young buck's opening gambit include a reference to the flavour of an electronic cigarette.

I could envisage myself out there someday, in a warm cardigan, of course, primed and ready to make small talk about the merits of vanilla scents versus scented pine.

After my marital status changed.

Until then, I must park the idea of learning to vape and must instead focus on the matter at hand.

I adjusted the arm sling, and got comfortable in the dark cubby hole at the back of the pub. I had set out in my running kit, as promised but then a bus had come along. I interpreted this as a sign that I should ease into my exercise regime. Thankfully, I'd stowed the tablet in a backpack along with a water bottle and protein bars.

Timmy, the owner – no one thought it at all confusing that the owner and bar's name didn't match – had just placed a pint on the table in front of me, careful not to spill anything on my tablet. I turned it on, and its screen lit up.

Sean's Bar may be the oldest pub in the world but its Wi-Fi is twenty-first century.

I scrolled through a website devoted entirely to chocolate desserts. Who knew that "Death by Chocolate" is a thing? I sipped my drink and glanced around. This was a perfect spot for subterfuge. These walls could tell many a gruesome tale if they could talk.

I imagined years of lowered conversations being held in these corners; the furtive peeks of revolutionaries towards Red Coats at the bar while all sucked tobacco smoke down the stems of clay pipes.

I was a conspirator of one. I'd chosen this location for its privacy and the hope that hundreds of years of clandestine conversation could be channelled into a working plot.

I skimmed through a recipe for double chocolate pudding without enthusiasm. It didn't make any sense. I'd left treats scattered around the house; Laura should not be losing weight.

Maybe she had a wasting disease?

I'd better not count on it. I'd just have to figure out an alternative method of achieving bachelorhood.

Then I'd have to grieve. Brenda would just have to wait until I finished mourning.

I had thought of using a firearm for my mission but quickly ruled it out. Guns are restricted in Ireland. Farmers are permitted the use of shotguns, but the background check is so extensive that it practically extends to cavity searches.

You would think that one of the Irish Republic's founding fathers could have borrowed from the American constitution when framing the Irish version. De Valera was born in New York, after all. However, perhaps Dev recognised that the right to bear arms could have unintended consequences. After a session in a pub, a domestic argument involving an overcooked chicken might not be resolved without body bags.

Irish law also forbade everything from crossbows to Samurai swords. You could still kill someone in Ireland with other sharp implements. Bread knives and razors were, for example, not banned.

The downside was that murder weapons are confiscated by the authorities and taken away in evidence bags. This ruled out anything in the kitchen. We had some nice cutlery from IKEA and I didn't want to break up the set.

With inspiration lacking, I idly scrolled through the internet on my tablet. I flicked through a survivalist site whose devotees rated the best homemade weapons that could be manufactured during the apocalypse.

One DIY flamethrower seemed like it would be more lethal to the user than to the zombie hordes.

I stared at a centuries-old painting of a grim-faced man on the wall, appealing for some inspiration, but was ignored.

I powered off my device and pushed it aside.

It was going to be one of those days.

I sipped at my stout and eyed an abandoned newspaper on a corner of the table. There was a picture of the local member of parliament, TD Tim Fagen, on the front alongside the headline "Taoiseach appoints new Minister".

I skimmed through the article about the new Minister of Justice and then randomly turned over a page.

My eyes widened.

Serendipity was alive and well as I drank in the article about a shop worker unpacking bananas.

I grinned and raised my glass to the portrait.

Maybe it was my imagination, but I could have sworn that the man in the painting winked back.

Alex

69

Pet Kingdom is a cacophony of sounds intertwined with an array of pungent scents. Birds sing, hamsters burn calories on noisy wheels, and meaty animal food odours combine with the aroma of dampened straw. I'd say if you had zero allergies, it would be a wonderful place to work.

I pushed a trolley with my good hand, avoiding the display cases of arachnids, and meandered between pallets piled high with dog food and bird cages containing colourful specimens that ignored me. Perhaps they had access to my credit report.

A woman dressed in the blue uniform of the store approached.

'Hi there, Martin,' she said in a faint Polish accent.

I turned. 'Alex,' I said.

She stared at my cast. 'Oh you poor thing,' she said. 'You still have it.'

'Not long now,' I said.

'Do you remember that I pop in and see you?'

'You did?'

'You told me that you loved me.'

'I'm sure I would have remembered that.'

'You also said the same to the nurse, I think you proposed to the caterer.'

I shook my head. 'It must have been the stuff they pumped into me.'

'A pity. The caterer said, "yes." We have another day out, yes? I get a big hat.'

'I'm not sure that Laura would be thrilled.'

She hoisted up my cast and pointed to an inky scrawl. 'See, that was me.'

'I didn't doubt you for a bit.'

'Hold on,' Alex said and raised her finger to me. She swivelled and stared towards some knee-high enclosures divided into sections, containing various rabbit breeds. A girl aged about eight held up a struggling bunny by its ears while her father snapped a picture with his phone.

'That's so cute, love,' the man said.

'Can I have it, Dad?' the girl asked and squeezed the rabbit to her chest, like a cuddly toy.

'Of course, sweetie,' the dad said and snapped another picture for his camera roll. 'Think of it as an early birthday present.'

Alex stepped forward, all smiles. 'Actually, that's not just a rabbit, it's a Dwarf Hotot, a very mischievous breed.'

'There you go,' the dad said. 'Perfect.'

Alex peeled it from the girl's arms. 'Unfortunately, this one is not for sale.'

'What?' the girl said. 'I love it.' She then pointed to another. 'I'll take that one then.'

'I'm sorry,' Alex said, 'but that one's not for sale either.'

Both dad and daughter looked stunned as Alex popped the rabbit back into its enclosure.

'Martin,' she beamed, turning back to me. 'I have to tell you, that you look amazing to me. So hot.'

'That's very nice of you to say, Alex.'

'Are you working out?' Alex asked and squeezed the bicep of my good arm.

'I've been running as it happens,' I said.

'You can so tell,' she said.

I sighed, not in the least bit fooled by her flattery.

'I have tickets so you can knock it off.'

Alex grinned. 'In truth, you look like you are up a few kilos.'

'It's the plaster,' I said.

Behind her, the little girl tugged at her father who grew more and more irate.

'Ah, that would do it. I'll tell you, Martin. Your All-Ireland is the one thing that keeps me from climbing up onto the rooftop with a rifle.'

Alex had moved to Ireland a decade previously and embraced all things Irish. She loved the rain, the green fields, and the sound of Uilleann pipes at a pub session. She relied on me to obtain tickets for the biggest game in the Gaelic Athletic Association calendar – the All-

Ireland. I carried out some youth coaching and this entitled me to an allocation.

'I'm bringing a teacher from school, he's American, he's never been.' I held up my plastered arm. 'You're driving.'

'No problem,' Alex said. 'I know it's asking a lot…'

'I've a pair of tickets for you as usual.'

Alex grinned. 'Amazing.'

'Excuse me,' Dad said, interrupting. 'We were talking.'

Alex nodded. 'And then we finished, yes?'

'Here now,' Dad said, more than a little bit confused. We all watched as an assistant picked up the rabbit and slid it into a pet container on the shop counter. A teenage girl paid with her phone app.

'I thought you said that the rabbit was not for sale?'

'Yes, I did. I did say exactly that.'

We all watched as the beaming teenager scooped up the pet carrier and walked out the door.

'Hello, I'm still here you know,' Dad said.

'Hello, sir, what can I help you with today?' Alex said to him, all smiles.

'I wanted to buy that rabbit.'

'What type is it?'

The man was about to turn towards the signage in front of the enclosure but was interrupted by Alex wagging her finger.

'No peeking. I only just told you,' Alex said.

'It's just a rabbit!' the man said in exasperation.

'And I said that it was not for sale. To you.'

'What?' Dad said.

'Daddy!' the girl said, her voice rising a note. Some meerkats began to pop their heads up in our direction.

'I'll not sell you anything that you can't look after. It's not a bike that you leave outside.'

Dad's jaw dropped open.

Alex glanced toward me. 'Glupek,' she said in a low voice, her eyes rolling.

'What was that?' Dad hissed. 'You are this close to negative feedback. Don't think I won't post.'

Alex sighed. 'You want something free, do you?'

Dad's face curled. 'I have followers you know. Many, many followers.'

Alex had admitted to me once about how she repeatedly broke into a high-security bio-lab to free laboratory rats, a lab guarded by Dobermans especially bred with attitude problems. She literally had fading scars to prove it. She, therefore, was not the least bit intimidated by someone armed with a smartphone.

'I know who you are.'

Dad grinned. 'You've read my blog?'

Alex shook her head. 'No, but I bet you've had some Polish labourers working on your house.'

'I'm sorry but no,' Dad replied, smirking.

'You've maybe had nannies, yes?'

'You mean like, Magda?' the girl piped up, intrigued.

'You see, I do know you. You've heard such words many times. Am I right?'

Glupek was Polish for "moron" and Dad probably had Googled the word to discover it wasn't a term of affection. He glowered; his eyes bulged. He looked like he was going to give Vesuvius (79AD) a run for its money. He reached for his phone and quickly tapped in something. He raised his phone into the air and shoved it almost into Alex's face. His thumb hovered over the touchscreen.

'You think you're so smart. "One star," who's laughing now?' he snarled. 'What do you say to that?'

'I'd say, much chance of you raising an animal when you can't raise a child.'

'What?' Dad said.

'She is in the piranha pond,' Alex said and pointed to a shallow, plastic pool. His daughter was sitting in it up to her chest.

'Piranha pond?' Dad repeated, his eyes bulging. He shrieked and scampered over to the pond before yanking his daughter out.

'You have piranhas?' I asked.

'Our franchise has a policy of not stocking animals that can eat you. Piranhas prefer fish or fruit to people. Don't believe everything Hollywood tells you.'

We watched as a seething Dad carried his soaked daughter out the door.

'You know that you could make a lot more money if you actually sold animals. It is after all a pet shop,' I said.

'I know, but this is more fun, besides, I'm selling animals not appliances, sometimes it's not about the money.'

Alex ran the franchise but made a living selling feedstuff, and animal toys, and accessories. She adored animals and was a lapsed vegetarian who ate Sunday roasts with reluctance but who never ordered second helpings. She somehow reconciled the fact that some animals she sold, like mice, were fed to other creatures like reptiles. If she were a planet, she would have required a massive gravitational pull to resolve all the contradictory forces at play.

Alex stretched. 'Now, can't stand about all day, anything I can help you with? You're here for some kibble for Barney?'

'He likes the duck stuff.'

'I'm sure he does but I'm selling you the low-fat variety.'

'Are you now?'

'Barney is too heavy. I wonder if you should even have a dog.'

'Take it easy, Alex,' I said. 'I'll take the low-calorie option.'

I had visions of Alex rolling up in the middle of the night, ninja style, to rescue the dog.

'No problem, sir,' she said.

I waited for a beat. 'By the way, any interesting drop-offs?' Alex was the local go-to person for illegal pets that had either outgrown or terrified their owners. She'd take them in temporarily and every month or so bring them to Dublin Zoo or the National Exotic Animal Sanctuary. She once had a caiman handed in by an owner on his way back from the hospital, minus a few of his fingers.

What could go wrong in petting a cousin of an alligator?

Alex smiled. 'Oh, I have the usual, a scorpion, some reptiles. You want to see?'

'Love to,' I said. 'Just no spiders mind,' I shivered. 'Only good place for them is on the bottom of my shoe.'

'They're a part of nature,' Alex said.

'So are sea lice and I'd not want to spend quality time with them either.'

Michelle II

68

The glass-fronted terrarium fitted snugly between the sitting room chimney breast and the wall. I peered inside.

Who knew that you could buy a fake rock with a built-in heating coil?

Behind it, a plastic mound of rocks contained a pre-built cave. I read that reptiles get stressed if they do not have a place to hide from potential predators.

They're stressed? They've never had the pressure of standing in front of an ATM with a queue forming behind, as you find your salary hasn't hit your account.

I was pleased. It was like I had created a little corner of Arizona, but in our good room.

The Kerry shop worker had given me the idea. Michael McDermot had been unpacking bananas at the back of the shop when he noticed something uncoiling at the bottom of the pallet. He'd never come face to face with a snake before but knew exactly what to do. He reached for a nearby broom and beat it to death. This would be rapidly followed by a two-day bender when he discovered that the correct course of action was to run quickly, at great pace in the opposite direction. His wife reminded him that he was on minimum wage and that his job specification was to unload goods inwards and sweep out the dock. Indiana Jones he was not.

It appears he had been within moments of meeting his maker. One bite from the fangs of a Gaboon horn-nose viper could mean death within two hours.

Michael knew little about snakes because it was not something that he was realistically likely to encounter. Ireland is famously free of serpents. One account says it's because Saint Patrick banished them;

others say that given the option of a damp Connemara landscape or Mediterranean sunshine, the snakes vote for the Med every time.

The article mentioned that it was not illegal to own a venomous reptile in Ireland. Of course, the owner must take precautions because one consequence of living on an island with no natural snake population is that there is no national stock of anti-venom.

The newspaper quoted the National Poisons Information Centre which stated that if a person was unlucky enough to be bitten by such a reptile, then the specific anti-venom would have to be flown in from the UK.

Laura entered the house and noticed me on my knees through the open sitting room door. She stepped into the room and instantly spotted the glass case.

'Tell me that's a tortoise,' she said.

'Not exactly,' I said. 'More like its cousin.'

'And you got this thing without asking me because?'

'You know how I've long since had an interest in reptiles?'

'Guessing the right answer to a question on *Who Wants to Be a Millionaire?* does not make you an expert on herpetology.'

'It was the thirty-six-thousand-pound question!'

'Well, maybe you should apply to be on it then. In the meantime, our finances are more unhealthy than a toddler raised on chips. I thought we said that we'd leave the credit card for emergencies.'

I smiled. 'Actually, this won't cost a penny and it's only temporary until Alex collects enough strays to warrant a trip to Dublin. I said that I'd mind some in the meantime. She brought me home with the tank and our houseguest.'

Her gaze dropped down to the case and I sensed the rare feeling of a battle fought and won.

'So you're like fostering it?'

'Pretty much. Think of it as Airbnb but for the unloved.'

'So what is it?'

'Some kind of viper. Alex wanted her off the premises in case she somehow got mixed up with the petting animals. You can imagine how that might turn out.'

'So she's dangerous?'

'Let's just say that she has an attitude problem. She will literally bite the hand that feeds it. If she could, she would take your credit card, max it out and shag your best mate. I've named her Michelle.'

Laura scrutinised me. 'After your ex?'

'There's a passing resemblance, yes.'

Laura's face softened. She'd been suckered by a Life Pro Tip. A husband must always criticise his ex. There are no exceptions to this rule.

'And you couldn't like opt for a fish tank? Like a normal person.'

'It's a focal point.'

'So is my mother's *Child of Prague* statue but that doesn't come with a health warning.' Laura bent forward and stared through the glass.

'So where is she?' she asked.

'In the cave, I think they only venture out at night.'

We stared some more but the snake remained a dark maw in the rock.

Laura tapped on the glass.

'Maybe she's dead?'

'We'll see in the morning if she has finished her snack.' I pulled on an oven glove and picked up a live mouse from a cardboard box.

'You have got to be kidding me,' she exclaimed.

'What? Did you think I was going to feed her waffles?'

'Like we don't have enough mice in the house. The attic is like party central with them.'

I carefully slid open a small hatch on the roof of the terrarium and dropped the rodent in. I quickly slid the hatch closed.

'Remember to always keep this shut,' I said.

The mouse settled on its haunches and viewed us with untroubled eyes.

It yawned.

Laura scowled. 'If you ever find the snake, make her a sandwich. I'm going to visit Brenda and tell her that my husband has lost his mind.'

She stormed out the front door without looking back. I slipped in some cheese through the hatch, and it dropped down beside the mouse. The least I could do was give it a decent last supper.

I felt like apologising to the creature for Laura's attitude, it was nothing personal. Then again, using it as a snack for my houseguest wasn't going to win me any friends in the rodent community.

I swear the mouse shrugged.

I guess it was resigned to being at the bottom of the food chain.

I knew how it felt.

Laura

67

The plastic minnow gleamed as I polished it with a clean rag. A blue streak on top replicated the colour of its living equivalent. In the water, the lure could be made to twitch and jerk in a way that could fool the most discerning of predators. The treble hooks along its underside could ruin a pike's entire day.

I examined it carefully to ensure the barbs were rust-free and ready for the next outing. I opened a tackle box with difficulty as one arm remained almost useless in the cast. The tackle box comprised individual compartments for the hooks, spinners and assorted lures. I carefully placed the minnow back in its slot.

The workshop was a converted shed. Laura sometimes called it my "man cave". I refused to rise to the bait but admittedly, I was doing myself no favours by installing a mini-bar, a flat-screen TV and connecting a WC into the drains. It was foremost a workshop.

A half-repaired net hung from the ceiling.

Workshop!

A rack of freshly cleaned rods rested against a wall.

Workshop!

A workbench with a working lathe took up the centre.

Workshop!

A large noticeboard occupied one wall. The various documents a fisherman might require such as a rod licence and boating permit were pinned to it. There were posters for forthcoming angling events like the International Lough Ree Pike Fishing competition.

The healthy food plate leaflet somehow had found a new home there.

Pride of place on the wall was occupied by a newspaper cut out from *The Westmeath Independent*. It featured a yellowing picture of me holding up a metre-long pike. I'd come third in an angling competition but was now local and therefore merited a decent write-up.

The same pike had been stuffed and displayed in a small cabinet on a shelf to the side of the notice board. Laura refused to let me have it in the house. The taxidermist had replaced the eyes with fakes which Laura claimed, followed her around the room.

I peeked through the workshop window but saw no one. I placed my tablet on the workbench and pressed "play" on a documentary.

The video depicted a tribe that had very little exposure to modern culture. A lot like some of those in 2A in my school. Semi-naked hunters with violet-painted chests and faces glided through the jungle.

A tribesman slowly raised his blowpipe to his lips to line it up on a Howler monkey sitting on a branch. The tribesman puffed, and for a few seconds, nothing happened. Suddenly the troop of monkeys screamed, as one of their members flopped forward, before plunging through the jungle canopy.

As the video played, I removed a tube of caulk from a shelf and carefully cut the red plastic nozzle off with a knife, creating a small cone.

I jolted upright as the shed door burst open revealing Laura.

'Mind if I come in?'

I felt pain and realised that I'd somehow cut a finger. 'You could have knocked.'

I paused the video with my good hand.

'Sorry,' she said, stepping in. 'Want me to have a look at that?'

'It'll be fine,' I said dabbing the wound with a handkerchief.

She surveyed the workshop.

'I was beginning to think that you had another woman stashed away in here.'

'As you can see. No one else here.'

'Of course, she'd have to like damp. And the ghosts of dead fish.'

'Did you want something?' I barely kept my breathing under control.

'Is that the same mouse in the terrarium?' she demanded to know. 'If so, he's gained weight. He loves it in there. Why wouldn't he, you've been giving him leftovers haven't you?'

'Maybe the snake's hibernating or is just not hungry,' I said. In truth, I had been throwing scraps into the terrarium, I wanted the mouse to be eaten, not starve to death. I'm not a cruel person.

She idly picked up a narrow, two-metre length of copper pipe, string wrapped around the middle forming a handhold. By coincidence, her posture matched that of a tribesman in the paused video, holding a blowpipe.

'Maybe the snake's a vegetarian,' she said. 'Knowing you, that's what you got.'

I watched in relief as she placed the pipe back on the workbench.

'So you came out here to look for a fight?' I asked.

Her head scanned the workshop, angling towards the tablet.

'Maybe you could put something on this,' I said quickly and held up my finger, now weeping blood.

'Fine,' she said, her voice softening. 'It's nothing I haven't seen before.' She reached up to a shelf and grabbed a first aid kit, not noticing the transparent plastic case that had been hidden behind it. The case contained several neatly packed darts the length of a pencil made with wire tips and red cone tails.

She unwrapped an alcohol wipe and took hold of my finger and swabbed it. 'You'll live,' she said and began to apply a plaster.

She took her time.

'Everything all right?' I asked.

She cast her eyes downwards. 'You spend more time in here than in the house. Certainly more than the bedroom.'

'I'm banged up,' I said. 'Did you not notice the plaster cast? Hard to sleep when I've an arm sticking out like I'm looking to arm wrestle.'

'I know you're under a lot of stress,' she said.

True. I'd been run over by a river boat. It was not fun on any level.

'I mean, there are the bills.'

'There are a lot of bills,' I agreed.

'We're under a lot of pressure.'

I nodded.

'I'm under a lot of pressure with work,' she said.

I saw where this was going. 'You want to drop to a four-day week?'

'Would that be a problem?' she replied after a brief pause.

'I don't know. How do you feel about surviving with no power when they cut us off?'

She smiled ruefully. 'I know. We're sailing close to the wind as is.'

She let go of my finger. It was expertly wrapped.

'Was there anything else?' I asked.

'I thought we should talk.'

This seemed serious. Was Liam moving someone in? Someone with an even greater appetite.

'Okay,' I said, bracing myself. Maybe I had got it backwards. Maybe Liam was moving out and taking his stomach with him. I'd have to feign disappointment, say something about fledglings leaving the nest.

'Hello,' she said. 'You listening to me?'

'Sorry,' I said.

'You zoned out there.'

'I'm all ears,' I said. With Liam gone, the room would need repainting. I'd strip it back first. How exactly did one sign up for Airbnb? I kept nodding, as she liked when I paid attention.

'I haven't been myself lately,' she murmured.

B&Q had a paint sale now. I could get a deal on a lilac matte.

'Ahuh.' Maybe beige. That goes with everything.

'I need to know that I have your support.'

I registered the pause in dialogue and jumped straight in. 'Don't worry,' I said. 'He's always at the end of a phone. It'll be tough on you, I get that.'

'What?'

'Are we not talking about Liam moving out?'

'Liam's moving out?'

Maybe not.

My phone rang.

Laura rolled her eyes. 'You don't have to answer that.' I held up the phone. The caller ID indicated that it was my boss.

'It's Chris,' I said.

'Call him back,' she snarled.

'It might be important.'

'This is important,' she snapped back.

'You want to cut back on work and you want me to pee off my boss? I don't get you sometimes.'

She shrugged, and it was like watching a hot air balloon collapse. 'He will only want something from you.'

'He might want to know how I am.'

'Here now. This is Chris we are talking about. He always has an agenda.'

'Not true,' I said, prompting my internal search engine to pop out an example of his selflessness, but this just returned a "page not found" image in my mind.

'Remember when he asked Moira Healy out for a drink?'

'To be fair, she was single at the time,' I said.

'Technically yes, still it was a bit awkward seeing as he was supposed to be one of her husband's pallbearers.'

The phone ceased ringing.

'I take your point.' My internal Google refreshed the search but the same results were displayed.

The phone rang again.

'I'll not answer it then,' I said.

It rang and rang.

She gave up. 'Oh, go ahead.'

I answered the phone. 'Ahuh,' I said listening to Chris. I repeated this a few times before disconnecting.

'What was that about?'

'He wanted to ask how I was.'

'Sure he did.'

'What can I do? He is thinking of retiring this year.'

'He says that every year. He keeps that promotion dangling over you.'

'This year it could be different.'

'Fine. Not like we can't use the money but I'm not holding my breath.'

'Don't worry,' I said. 'I'm going to stand up to him. In the meantime, will you give me a lift into town?'

'I knew it,' she said triumphantly. 'He wants you to talk to Suzanne.'

'Well, if you're passing…'

Suzanne

66

Suzanne's offices might be advertised as conveniently located in Athlone's Bridge Street, but convenience is relative as the nearest parking was several streets away. It shouldn't have mattered to many of Suzanne's clients as they were prohibited from driving, but that did not stop some of them. More than one, had half-parked on the pavement outside, while protesting to Suzanne that they should not have been banned, despite the accumulation of double-digit penalty points or being legally blind.

Suzanne thrived on a combination of conveyancing fees, small claims and criminal cases. She had a particular talent for finding the inconsistencies in a prosecution and more times than not could get a conviction reduced or waived. She believed in the innocence of her clients, no matter what the evidence might indicate. She once obtained an apology for a client caught upstairs in a house at five a.m., claiming that he was lost, and that the kitchen window was already broken.

I walked into the reception area of her practice, a pair of polished brown leather shoes dangling from my good hand. A receptionist, a young man in a shirt and tie, waved me towards the conference room when I identified myself. His muscular physique appeared cramped behind his desk. I guessed that he was the type of person for whom happiness involved a bench press.

'So who's the new lad?' I asked after Suzanne strode into the conference room and kissed me on the cheek. She smiled and removed her glasses and sat down on the opposite side of the table. She did not require spectacles, but she felt that they gave her a certain gravitas. She wore a formal pants suit. At work, she was the personification of prim and proper. After work however, she explored a wild side that was illegal in many countries.

'What can I say?' she said. 'A woman has her needs and he does type forty words per minute.'

The Iron Stomach competition was part of a week of dubious college entertainments. Students competed to finish anything that was put onto a plate before them. I'd breezed through the dog food round before attempting sheep's eyeballs. Suzanne and I met throwing up in the Buttery toilets. We'd been firm friends ever since.

I had travelled over to Dublin from England as the favourable sterling exchange rate meant I could survive happily on my university grant. I had intended to stay until I'd obtained my degree, but I had met Michelle and instead settled in Dublin, teaching.

In hindsight, the marriage was always destined to fail. My then-wife appeared happier being tied to a tree (to prevent illegal logging) than going to the cinema. The final straw was when she decided to picket an American air-force base in England. We were just too different. She set out to prevent World War Three while I focused on protecting our credit rating.

The end came abruptly. I had been waiting for Michelle at Dublin's arrivals lounge, with flowers in hand, when my phone pinged. She'd texted me to say that she was sorry, but it was all over and that an American GI "got her." She also confessed that she'd shagged my best man but that it meant nothing. Also, a groomsman. It just took less than one hundred and sixty characters to destroy the life I knew. Suzanne had answered the phone after I'd been escorted by security out of the airport. Tears and meltdowns were common occurrences in the departure lounge but less so in the arrivals hall. I recall fearful glances. There were rumours of a plane crash.

Suzanne had told me to pack my things and get out of Dublin. Come stay with me, she'd said, meet my fiancé, Chris. Chris who was the principal of a local secondary school.

A school with vacancies.

Suzanne glared at the pair of shoes I had placed on the floor beside me.

'Chris asked me to pick them up while I was in town,' I said.

'Seriously?'

I edged them away from her with my foot.

'So this is not a social call?'

'He can't come himself because he's not entirely sure he'd make it out alive.'

'But I'm only little,' she said coyly.

'He says you were spotted buying a five iron. He's worried.'

'That's nonsense,' she said.

'He has a right to be concerned. He figured you spray-painted his car.'

'Oh yeah? What makes him say that?'

'You signed it.'

Suzanne laughed. 'It's just that when I see him, this red mist washes over me.' She paused. 'Tell him, I'll try to be good.'

'I agree that he's a weasel,' I said.

'As if there is any question about that.'

'Agreed.'

'He humiliated me, Martin. On the morning of my wedding day. Who does that?'

'I know and I'm not here to defend him.'

'I have a right to be pissed off,' she continued. 'I went on honeymoon with a bridesmaid.'

Suzanne had been determined to carry on with the wedding despite developing a vacancy in the groom department. She insisted on enjoying her big day out regardless. She said, everything is paid for. Besides there are only two chances of getting refunds at this late stage and Slim just left town.

It was however beyond awkward when she walked down the aisle with her father between rows of guests who did not know where to look. She intended to remain aloof and sail through it all, but Suzanne is not someone who can rein in her emotions.

She bawled every step of the way; tears and snot speckling her corsage. Somehow her parents were persuaded to renew their vows to fill in the gap while the priest ad-libbed an impromptu marital rite. Unfortunately, trigger words like "love" or "marriage" would set Suzanne off once more. Words that, it turns out, appear all too frequently in wedding ceremonies.

She bawled through the official wedding photographs.

She bawled through the reception.

I'll tell you, trying to deliver a best man's speech for a groom who's gone AWOL, with a bride sobbing inconsolably beside you, is not something I ever want to repeat.

No one told the band that the groom was somewhere out on the lake. Their call for the happy couple to come to the dance floor was met with even more crying that eventually faded when Suzanne became dehydrated.

'You know, I'm doing very well here,' she said indicating her office with a hand. 'I just have a weak spot with that bastard.'

'You'll get through it.'

'Of course,' she said. 'What do they say? The best way to get over a man is to get under another.'

'Do they say that?'

'All right, Martin, I'll try and lay off. I'll do it for you. I promise this time.'

'You and your promises.'

'I've known you since college, Martin. You know I'm a woman of my word.'

'You said, "try and lay off," not that you will,' I replied.

'So I did. So what else is on your mind? I know you. This could have been handled in a phone call.'

'I suppose.' Suzanne could see through me. 'I just wanted to pick your brain for some free legal advice.'

'As always. Go on.'

'A student was asking me about law of the land. A civics class. How would someone fare out in a divorce who—'

'You and Laura are getting a divorce?' she interrupted.

Suzanne was quick. It was important to explore if I had other options. Murder should not be the default position in any dispute otherwise, for example, the local multiplex would be the scene of weekly bloodbaths as couples argued about whose turn it was to pick a movie.

'I never said divorce.'

'Do you think I was brought up yesterday? There are no secrets between us.'

'If it ever came to that, how would I fare?'

'You're in a worse position than when your first marriage broke up. You sold your house at a loss and carried that negative credit report for years. A report, I might add, that was more toxic than a shed full of influencers.'

'I know that,' I said. 'That was then.'

She sighed. 'You could try and force her to sell the house and split the proceeds. You might get the deposit for a flat out of it. However, she still has a dependant in the house so she could drag out the process. Financially, your best option would be to split but remain there.'

'So we could be separated but living under the same roof?' I said.

'You'd be surprised just how many couples do that. They can't stand one another but they can't afford to move out either. Some use tape to divide the house into zones.'

'Not great prospects.'

'It's like being married only without the sex.'

That summed up my marriage already.

'That narrows down my options,' I said. In more ways than one.

'Just telling it as it is.' She paused. 'If you want to take a time out, I've a spare room you could use, if it came to that.'

'Thanks, Suzanne.' I stood up and picked up the shoes. 'So you'll keep away from Chris.'

'I'll do my best.'

It would have to do.

We hugged and I moved to the door. I nodded to the corner where a golf club leaned against the wall.

'I thought you said you never got a golf club?'

'I denied getting a five iron. That's a wedge.'

If I ever ended up in court. I'd want Suzanne in my corner.

65

Laura's car was gone when I entered the house but that did not mean that the house was empty.

'Are you there, Liam?' I shouted up the stairs but there was no response.

I went into the utility room and retrieved a sports bag that I'd stowed there and placed it on the kitchen island.

I pulled out some gloves, a slim glass vial and a short length of tube with a noose at the end.

The idea of a blowpipe appealed to me as it had a long reach. I was not a man built for close-quarter combat. However, a blowpipe is not designed to kill. It's merely a mechanism for delivery. Tribes use a dart to deliver a dose of poison to some creature that they want for supper; anaesthesia is used if something is required to be tranquillised. It's an important distinction, as it's vital not to mix up the doses. It would not do, if say China lent you a panda that subsequently climbed out of its enclosure and you then accidentally euthanised the animal.

South American tribesmen used poison obtained from the skin of the less than imaginatively named blowpipe frog. I did not have access to one but I had the next best thing in my sitting room.

I donned the gloves, placed the vial in my pocket and holding my 'snake pole' entered the sitting room.

I sighed in disbelief. The snake's intended lunch remained inside the terrarium, running on the plastic wheel that I'd bought for it. I'd provided it with water, bedding, and several last meals. It turns out that I wasn't a bad host, if you excluded the fact, I'd housed it with a roommate that was supposed to kill it.

Maybe, Laura was right, and the snake was vegetarian.

Was everyone in this house on a diet?

My phone rang but I ignored it. Time to focus on the task at hand. I was nervous. I had lived my whole life and never had the need to milk a snake before. Milking a snake is very much unlike milking a cow. Snakes don't have tiny udders for one thing. Milking a snake refers to the process of holding a snake's mouth open and forcing it to bite on fabric stretched over the top of a container. The snake's poison then drips down from its fangs for collection. I'd watched several YouTube videos on the topic and decided that I could do it.

How hard could it be to milk a snake?

Milking a snake is very hard.

Especially when one arm is in a cast.

I slid open the lid on the terrarium. I slipped the rod inside with the coil of thin rope attached and slid it into the dark gap in the rocks using the hand in the cast. I felt movement and pulled the loop closed with my other hand. I managed to snag the snake on the first attempt. That was easy, I thought.

However, the snake had other ideas when it dawned on it that I wanted more than to show it views of my sitting room. She fought and squirmed angrily as I hauled her out. It was a lot like trying to get Liam, as a child, up and out of bed and dressed before school. At one point, the snake squirmed free and bit down on my glove. In reflex, I lashed out and the lid of the terrarium flew off. We fought more. The terrarium tipped and the mouse shot out like it had been launched from a catapult. It rolled on the floor, dusted itself off and slid underneath the sitting room door, no doubt en route to join its cousins in the attic. The snake and I fought on until I grabbed it behind the head. Minutes later, I possessed a vial that contained precious drops of venom.

I dropped the limp snake back into the terrarium and shoved the case back into place. The snake must have been as exhausted as I was, as she had given up the fight. I retrieved the lid and leaned in close to seal the tank when the snake suddenly launched itself upwards at me. What else should I have expected from a Michelle? In reflex, I slammed the lid shut and stumbled backwards, rolling against the curtains; my good hand grasped the curtain cord and ripped one end loose. Unbalanced by my cast, I somehow twisted about, wrapping the cord around my neck. Thankfully, my feet remained planted firmly on the floor.

I gasped as the cord tightened around my throat. I froze, terrified that the slightest movement might lead to me accidentally hanging myself. I slowly and methodically began to untangle myself.

Just then Liam, wearing a bathrobe, sauntered into the sitting room, yawning. He held his phone in his hand.

'Liam,' I said struggling for breath, 'you were here?'

'I live here too, you know,' he said.

He surveyed me as I remained partially trussed up in the curtains.

'It's your house, I don't judge, you mind keeping it down. Some of us are like night owls.'

His eyes remained untroubled.

'Mam is on the phone,' he said.

He held the phone against my ear.

'Martin?' Laura said.

'Yes?' I said, struggling to maintain some dignity despite the appearance of auto-erotic asphyxiation.

'You weren't answering your phone.'

'I was a bit busy,' I said.

Liam smirked.

'I forgot to tell you that you're supposed to get the cast off this afternoon.'

Like she couldn't have mentioned it before? Like I wouldn't have appreciated the full use of both limbs today?

'Will you be able to make the appointment? It's at two.'

Liam put the phone to his ear.

'He's well able,' he said. 'And you two really should have a talk.'

He clicked off the phone and left the room.

Paul

64

Plastic curtains enveloped my cubicle in the Outpatients annexe. I sat on a bed and waited for someone to attend to me.

I flexed my arm under the cast. I could hardly wait until I had the use of both arms as I would be twice as lethal. That was still kind of depressing as I had made no substantial progress in advancing my ''til death do us part' plans. Swapping Laura's low sugar substitute with the real thing was fooling no one. And, while I could now bake a chocolate meringue in my sleep, Laura was not biting. At this rate, the only way I'd appear in *True Crime* would be if they incorporated a food supplement.

The curtains swept back with a flourish. A young man entered. He wore a blue jacket that I'd seen around the hospital. I'd long since given up trying to figure out what each uniform denoted. I guessed that he was unlikely to be a gynaecologist and therefore I was in safe hands. He opened a moulded plastic container and pulled out what appeared to be a modified angle grinder, with a power cord at one end and a small circular blade at the other.

'Ready for some DIY?' he said brightly and plugged it in.

I nodded. He appeared vaguely familiar. Maybe he'd been at our wedding? There had been a lot of nurses.

'You could do serious damage with that,' I said.

His brow furrowed. 'What do you mean?'

'Sorry,' I said. 'No offence meant.'

'This is a cast saw,' he said holding up the device. 'Perfectly safe. Designed to only cut through plaster or synthetic casts.' He thumbed the "on" switch and it buzzed menacingly.

'Let's see shall we.'

The buzzing saw dropped onto his bare arm.

'Oh my god,' I uttered in horror, expecting to be sprayed with arterial blood.

'See,' he said. 'Want to see that again?'

'No,' I said quickly.

'So I'm Paul. I'm a care assistant. Wait, you knew that, right? You know I'm not a physio or a nurse?'

'Of course,' I said.

'Our uniforms are almost identical,' he said and slid his hand down a seam of the jacket as if he were on a catwalk and emphasising the finer details of the design. 'I mean, the times I've been asked if I was a nurse, you wouldn't believe. Last week I was asked to deliver a baby. I didn't of course. That would be unethical, yeah?'

'I'd say that might be considered as crossing boundaries.'

He stared at me.

'So which arm is it, again?'

I tentatively held up the one with the cast.

'We have to ask you know.'

He thumbed the switch again and it buzzed into life.

'I'm just going to slice into the plaster,' he said, smiling. He raised the saw over my arm and the machine roared into life. He eyed the plaster cast. 'It shouldn't hurt.'

'Shouldn't? You have done this before?'

He leaned down and held my arm firmly. 'Oh yes, just never on a real person.'

The saw buzzed into life, and I froze. He rested the oscillating blade on the cast. It sank into it easily. He surveyed the incision. 'That wasn't too bad,' he said, before leering at me. 'Who knew what I would end up doing? I'd high hopes of being a Guard.'

I grunted. Too nervous to stir a muscle.

He ran the blade down one side of the cast.

'Sometimes,' he said, 'your future often comes right down to your grades.'

I was there.

'I taught you?' I said.

'Back in the day,' he said. 'I looked different then. Different uniform. Big glasses. I wear contacts now, at least I would if I didn't go and forget them.'

He squinted and held onto my plastered arm and twisted it around. 'All I needed was a few more points and I could have got in,' he said, 'however, you never gave me them. So here we are.'

The Irish educational system dived into unknown territory in 2020 during the viral pandemic. The national state exams were cancelled, and student grades were ultimately decided by a combination of algorithms, in-house tests and teachers' recommendations.

'I'm sorry if we did not give you the grade you wanted.'

'You're sorry?' he said, and the saw buzzed into life.

'Nurse,' I yelped.

I recalled him now; he had been the subject of a teachers' conference. He'd missed more dates than he attended. Assignments were handed in late, if at all. The benefit of the doubt can only extend so far. His French teacher, for example, could hardly award him an A when she had never met him.

'It wasn't just me, it was the algorithm,' I squawked.

'You don't like cats, do you? Not everyone does.'

I was confused by the segue.

If I wanted banter, then I'd have booked a haircut.

'Sorry, am I missing something?' I asked.

'I just said that you're not a cat person.'

'I wouldn't say that.'

'You ran over one.'

Could I for once not be reminded that I had once backed over a cat?

'That was an accident and how would you even know that?'

'It's a small world,' he said. 'My auntie lives next door to you.'

'Mrs Keena?'

He nodded.

Why was I not surprised?

'I love my auntie,' he said.

'Of course you do,' I said, resigned to my fate.

He revved up the saw and dropped it abruptly down onto the back of the cast, instantly filling the air with plaster dust.

Tom

63

The sun beamed down through a cloud-free sky. Despite the open window, the workshop sweltered as heat penetrated the galvanised roof.

Laura's sunbed was directly in my line of sight, across the lawn, on the patio.

I noted activity in my peripheral vision.

Mrs Keena sat in a deckchair next door, while a pair of cats dozed on her lap. Several gardens over, someone mowed grass. Earlier, I'd spotted Mary Reilly at her upstairs window that overlooked our garden, cleaning the glass with a cloth and spray. There was the sound of children splashing in blow up pools. Barbecue smells drifted over fences.

Laura emerged from the house wearing a pair of shorts while leaving her bra on as a top. Laura liked nothing better than basting under a warm sun on a day off.

Heaven for her was dozing on a lounger while an unread novel slipped from her fingers.

She sat on the edge of the lounger and rubbed lotion onto her legs. She then unhooked her bra and leaned forward, chest down on the lounger, a book folded open on the ground beside her.

I reached into the small fridge under the counter and pulled out the vial before carefully peeling off the protective top. I reached for a dart and carefully dipped the needle into the vial, coating the tip. I repeated the process for a dozen more darts. One would do, but it was no harm to have spares if I missed. I was thankful that I now had the full use of both hands.

The choice of using a blowpipe was risky but it was better than allowing the snake to roam free when I knew Laura was alone. There was no guarantee that the snake would opt for the intended victim, and as much as I disliked the television licence inspector, I didn't see much merit in polishing him off.

I peered out the open window of the workshop.

Laura was already sound asleep. Thunder wouldn't wake her. I placed the blowpipe onto the bottom edge of the window frame and slid the tip of the pipe out.

With luck Laura would experience a small pinprick and assume it was just an insect, that's if she noticed anything at all in her slumber.

This could all happen right under the noses of the neighbours, and no one would suspect a thing. I had a neighbourhood of witnesses, but none could place me directly at the scene. I'd slip out and retrieve the dart, of course, after Laura drifted away.

I loaded my blowpipe and sighted it at Laura. She stirred slightly as she slept. I had a moment of indecision; Did I really have any other option? And then I recalled the gas bill that was in the process of being handed over to a collection agency.

I lined up, inhaled, and blew hard. The dart shot out of the end of the tube in a direct line towards Laura. My aim seemed perfect.

I admit I gloated at the cleverness of it all. The detectives would write it up as a tragic accident, I planned that they would find an empty terrarium and therefore they should conclude the snake had escaped. I mean who in their right mind would try and kill someone with a blowpipe? Certainly not a schoolteacher. They could canvas the neighbourhood all they like but they'd not find a single tribesman living here.

In my mind, I was throwing myself onto the floor as they broke the news, but my reverie was interrupted by Laura sighing and turning on the lounger.

I poked my head up and peered through the window. The dart lay forlornly on the grass, just outside. I realised that the dart must have faltered the moment it left the tube and plopped straight down.

I tilted the blowpipe to get some added trajectory in my favour and offset my aim to account for the curvature of the earth.

I puffed but the next dart was blown off course by a gust of wind and plunged into the ground beside Tom, one of Mrs Keena's cats who had wandered into our garden for a poo. It leapt up into the air, startled but then resumed defecation. It simply refused to comply with any attempt to keep it out. That's cats for you, the Karens of the animal kingdom.

I tried again and this dart fell short.

I guessed that South American tribesmen had larger lungs than their diminutive stature would suggest. They could easily hit a monkey twenty metres high up in the tree line. I was no South American tribesman, but I was motivated by something they'd never faced— a vulture fund mortgage loaded with terms and conditions that loan sharks would be embarrassed to be associated with.

I quickly prepared more darts. I huffed and I puffed, and I blew hard into the mouthpiece. Another dart shot out.

Miss.

I tried again. Same result.

And again.

Before long, I'd used up the venom and my stock of darts and was experiencing symptoms of mild hypoxaemia.

I collapsed onto my chair, gasping for air. My heart raced. This was a whole lot harder than it looked on YouTube.

Outside, my feathered efforts peppered the grass but Laura slept on, blissfully unaware that I'd been attempting to use her as a dartboard.

I would write on my tablet about how the blowpipe proved effective, but it was not much use if I did not have the puff to propel the darts any great distance. I mulled over a developing idea of attaching the mouthpiece to a compressor.

I gloved up, stepped out of the shed, not worried about who might see me now and began carefully gathering up the darts, mindful of the tips in case there was any residue of venom. To any observer, I was just tidying up twigs on the lawn. I froze when I noticed something at the rear of the workshop and groaned.

I'd need to fetch the spade.

I tamped a small patch of soil down with my boots just as Mrs Keena walked out into her garden.

'Psst pst,' she called. 'Here kitty, kitty. Here kitty, kitty.'

Kitty was not responding.

Neither was Laura who snored on.

Mrs Keena popped her head over the fence. 'You haven't seen, Tom?' she asked.

Laura stirred.

'What's wrong?' she asked, sitting up.

'Tom's missing,' Mrs Keena said.

'I'm sure he's not gone far,' Laura said.

'I agree,' I said, standing on a corner of disturbed earth that was now for ever feline.

Mrs Keena wasn't convinced.

'You can set your clock by him. Something is wrong. I feel it,' she said.

'You want me to help look for him?' I asked.

It was the least I could do.

Several hours had passed by the time I finished stapling to a tree, the last poster depicting Mrs Keena's cat.

Michelle II

62

Upstairs, Liam practised solos on his drum kit and the kitchen ceiling vibrated. I gazed upwards at the faint cracks that had spread across the plasterwork. I longed for the day that I could retire my tub of Polyfilla and filling knife. An LED on the iron clicked green. I picked up the iron and began to run it over my football jersey just as Laura entered the kitchen with a bag of groceries and began putting the contents away. I watched apprehensively as she lifted leafy vegetables from the bag. I stifled a groan as she produced a carton of low-fat milk.

'I thought we agreed that I'd help with the shopping?' I said stiffly.

'It's just a few bits,' she said taking out some tins of tuna.

I forced myself to focus on the ironing before I burned the fabric.

Laura watched me.

'I never met anyone who can find their way around a laundry basket better than you,' she said. She picked up her uniform hanging on the back of a chair.

'You did a great job,' she said.

'I've time on my hands and you'll need it tonight,' I said.

'I'm not working but thanks anyway.'

Everyone has particular chores in a household. Mine included ironing and housework. Laura's included DIY and causing said housework. I'd begun finding teacups in the airing cupboard. It was like she'd shrug off her considerable organisational skills with her coat whenever she entered the house.

Liam had an indeterminate role as he was left to focus on his studies, sometimes he left out the bins. Sometimes even on bin day.

There was a buzzing noise outside. Through the window, we could see a drone hovering over my workshop.

'Mrs Keena is still missing her cat,' I said.

The drone abruptly soared into the air and skimmed over nearby gardens.

I slid the iron along the sleeves of the Gaelic Athletic Association jersey. My father loved the GAA and would be glued to a UK television on match day, no matter who was playing. I'd be in the crowd in the meantime and would wave at the TV cameras on the off chance, he'd see me. Laura would also watch the game on the television. Her county was in the final and she could no more miss the game than a junkie would pass on a round of cocaine. Tribalism is such a part of being a GAA fan that it should be listed in Wikipedia.

I unplugged the iron and folded the jersey over the back of the chair. 'I'm heading for an early night after this,' I said.

'All right granddad,' she said smiling.

I sniffed. 'I remind you that I'm not long out of hospital. I'm surprised that I can manage all that I've been doing.'

'You only broke your arm,' she said. 'It wasn't open heart surgery.'

'I'd like to see you doing cartwheels after being run over by a boat.'

'You're never going to let that go, are you?' Laura sighed.

'It wouldn't have happened if you had filled the car with petrol,' I said.

There was the sound of a drumroll overhead.

'And I said, I'm sorry,' Laura said, pursing her lips.

'Maybe we can get John Bonham up above to lay off for a while,' I said after a moment.

'I'll have a word,' she said. 'He's heading out anyway so he won't disturb you tonight.'

'Good.'

A thought struck me.

'Isn't this your night on?'

'I've taken some time in lieu,' she said, 'but I'm still going out. The Barony of Eplaheimr needs me.'

She referred to the name given to the Irish Midlands by the Society of Creative Anachronism.

'I don't know why you bother,' I said. 'You spent all that time recreating illustrations on parchment and scarcely got a mention in the newspaper.'

'That isn't the point,' she said. 'Did I tell you that we've moved onto medieval combat?'

'You could lose an eye,' I said.

'At least I won't drown,' she said.

'I was wearing a lifejacket,' I shot back. She was reminding me of the time when my dingy overturned out on the lakes.

We both withdrew from the battlefield.

'I'll stay in Liam's room,' she said, 'if it turns into a session.'

'I'll see you in the morning then,' I said and edged towards the door. She nodded.

I plugged the tablet with my updated notes into the charging station in the kitchen. It would have been deeply suspicious if I hid the device. My manifesto was hidden in plain sight. Password-protected, of course.

'Martin,' she called out as I left the room. I turned around and saw her sitting at the island, her hands clasped around a mug of tea.

'Did you have anything to do with the disappearance of Mrs Keena's cat?'

'Why do you ask?'

'You flattened her last one.'

'Why must everyone keep bringing that up?'

'It's just you didn't seem yourself yesterday, out in the garden.'

'Could I just not be concerned about her cat?'

'You hate cats,' she said.

'Only the ones that defecate in our garden. I've nothing against cats. I'd feel the same way if the bishop dropped his trousers out there.'

'And you're dying your hair,' she said.

I had scoured my hair when I'd returned from purchasing the tablet, but a residue of colour had remained. Laura missed nothing.

'I'd thought it was shampoo,' I said.

Laura nodded slowly.

'Now, was there anything else?' I asked, tersely.

'Nothing,' she replied. 'Goodnight.'

'Goodnight to you too,' I replied and headed upstairs.

I slept fitfully and woke up on my back, staring at the ceiling. It was still dark. I flicked on the bedside locker lamp and the room filled with light. It must have been after two a.m. The house had that kind of silence to it. I felt at peace. I had the house to myself once more. Liam was out while Laura's side of the bed remained empty. Perhaps her medieval group had become the epitome of excitement as they recreated a long-lost pigment. Perhaps they just went back to a house and partied like it was 1399. Maybe she had just slipped into Liam's room as she'd promised.

I yawned, still in half a dreamlike state. I glanced downwards, spotting my erections in the bedsheets. I probably should get up to use the toilet. I debated in my mind if I could last until morning. My eyes started to droop and then somehow my brain logged an incoming alert. My eyes shot open.

Erections?

I was instantly wide awake. I stared down along the bed. A familiar shape pushed upwards under the duvet to create a small tent-like structure. However, another tent had formed just below it. As I watched it grew higher. My mind was trying to process what I was seeing. The object rose higher until it towered several centimetres over my manhood.

I heard a hissing sound due south of me.

There are corpses that moved more than I did. My bedfellow shaped up against my stiffie. This is not the way I wanted to go. I forced myself to think of Mrs Keena next door, slipping into some lingerie. My hard-on gave up the fight and collapsed. Mrs Keena, however, refused to leave and lurked in my mind. I might never become aroused again.

Time passed, until at last I felt the snake slide down through the bedclothes before it grew still. I slowly eased one foot upwards before edging it to the side of the bed. Carefully and stiffly, my other foot joined it and kept inching out of the bed until they both found the floor. I tugged the duvet cover back and in a smooth movement rolled out of the bed. I backed to the bedroom door, opened it, and stepped out into the hall. I slammed the door closed and opened Liam's door, shouting for Laura to wake up but there was no sign of anyone. I turned and fled downstairs. I grabbed oven gloves and the snake pole.

I returned quickly and carefully pulled the duvet back to reveal… nothing. My houseguest, like the prisoners in *The Great Escape*, had escaped.

I spent the rest of the night feeling like an army sapper checking for booby traps. My anxiety levels surged as I gingerly opened cupboard after cupboard. I had checked every crevice in the house by the time dawn broke. My hands shook with adrenaline-fuelled nerves. My former detainee could well be on his way to the county boundary for all I knew. As a last resort, I let Barney sniff a rock from the terrarium and he shot out the front door into the garden before barking triumphantly at a patch of geraniums.

I followed without much enthusiasm and, using the snake pole, moved the flowers aside. I peered at what lurked underneath.

I retrieved a tennis ball.

I should have known better. Barney might have had a pedigree but was bred for looks not IQ, a little like a New Orleans debutante.

Mrs Keena stepped out her door, wearing a house coat. Did the woman ever sleep? No one else in the estate was surely up. 'Looking for something?' she asked.

What did she think I was doing? Teaching the dog, the Latin names for the shrubbery?

'We lost something.'

'The snake?'

'Yes.'

'How did you do that?'

'We were taking it for a walk and it slipped off the leash. What do you think?'

'There's no need for that attitude.'

'I'm sorry,' I said. 'It's been a long night.'

'I know how you feel, my Tom is still not home. I checked the wheelie bins you know,' she said, 'after the last time.'

'Well, I'm sure you were wasting your time.'

'What do snakes eat anyway?' she said ever so slowly.

'I didn't feed your cat to Michelle, Mrs Keena if that's what you're suggesting!'

'Who's Michelle?'

'The snake, Mrs Keena.'

'You named your snake, Michelle?'

'I'm going back in,' I said.

'You'll have to be more careful in the future,' she said.

She was right. There'd be hell to pay if the pizza delivery guy wound up as collateral damage. I'd have the whole estate reaching for pitchforks and tripping over themselves in their haste to assemble into a mob.

Importantly, my current plan to obtain widower status had been knocked back. I guess I was tempting fate by naming the snake after my ex.

It wouldn't surprise me to go back into the house and find my wallet missing.

Cora and Kyle

61

Laura walked in the front door, dropped her keys on the hallway table and moved to the kitchen. She held a long canvas holdall in her hand and placed it gently on the floor. She hesitated for a moment when she saw me sitting on a chair on top of the kitchen island. I wore several layers of clothing, both oven gloves and held a yard brush in my right hand.

'Good morning,' she said and poured water into the kettle before plugging it in.

'I was about to send a search party out for you,' I said.

'I didn't realise the time,' she said. Her hand shook and I suspected that her history group once again 'researched' mulled wine.

'Tea?' she asked. She reached into the fridge for some milk.

'That would be nice,' I said. 'Aren't you going to ask?'

'Ask what?'

'Like why I am sitting on a chair *on* the kitchen island?'

She looked me in the eye.

'The snake got out, yes?'

I shrugged. 'Apparently so,' I said.

Laura's facial expression did not change. 'There's a surprise.'

'What do you mean by that?'

'When's my birthday?'

I hesitated; she'd not want me to check my phone diary. 'September,' I said confidently.

'When?'

'The middle?'

'It's the nineteenth, Martin. You should know, as that's the night you normally sleep on the sofa.'

In my defence, it was only twice that I'd forgotten. The second time was when the phone battery died, taking my annual electronic reminder with it.

'If you can't be bothered to remember to take me out for dinner one time a year, how can you expect to remember to always close the lid on that tank properly?'

She had me there. Had I secured it? I was so exhausted that I could not be sure about what I did.

'Maybe,' I conceded.

'Where was it last?' she asked.

'In our room,' I replied. 'Under the duvet.'

'Good job Liam has gone off somewhere.'

'Because he's safe?' I said, sulkily.

'No, because I'm going to use his bed. Let me know when you find it.'

'If I find it. I looked everywhere,' I said. 'We found a tennis ball.'

'Unless you're thinking of signing up for the tennis club, then that's not what I want to hear. You should have asked me if I minded sleeping under the same roof as something that could kill me.'

'You'd have said no.'

She gestured with her hand indicating the house. 'You can see why!' she said, her voice rising. 'You should have bought a fish tank. A goldfish isn't going to escape and hunt you down.'

She was interrupted by the sound of a car pulling up to the front of the house. A car horn honked.

'That'll be Alex,' I said. 'And the boys.'

'You're forming a posse?'

'It's the All-Ireland,' I replied. I toyed with the idea of prostrating myself on the ground in front of her.

'There is that,' she said, weakening.

People seldom get married in Ireland on Sunday. Mainly, I suspected, as it might clash with match day.

'Maybe I shouldn't go,' I said, gambling on Laura doing the right thing.

I slowly climbed off the kitchen island.

Laura shook her head.

'Go on. It's only once a year.'

'And the snake?'

'If I find it, that's your supper sorted. Now go on and don't be annoying me.'

'If you're sure,' I said

'I'll be fine. I'll sleep for a few hours, put the fire on and watch the game. She'll not come for me if she knows what's good for her.'

She unzipped the holdall and pulled out a long sheath with the handle of a weapon attached. She slid out a sword and gripped it expertly in her hand.

'Excuse me?' I demanded. 'What's that for?'

'Hand-to-hand combat if you must know.'

She waved the sword and posed in a fighting stance.

'I thought you were recreating medieval parchment?'

'I believe I mentioned combat.'

'I didn't think you were serious.'

'Relax, Martin,' she said. 'I've yet to sharpen it.'

'A heads up would have been nice if you're bringing weapons into the house.'

'Martin.'

'What?'

'I've a sword in the house, just so you know.'

'Funny,' I said and backed out of the room. One obscure rule of fighting. If the opposition has a sword and you've lost your only snake: they win.

I peeled off my layers and slipped on my jersey. I said goodbye, opened the front door and stepped out. Alex's game car was parked in the middle of the road. Whenever we would go to the final, Alex would purchase a clunker that was no more likely of passing the National Car Test than I was of being called upon to model for *It* magazine. The car would be crudely hand-painted by Alex in the colours of one of the finalists. She had stencilled, "Up Galway" on the side panels. Maroon ribbons hung from the aerial and a teddy bear in the county colours was taped to the roof. Passing aircraft could have identified which county Alex supported. We did not worry that the car lacked central locking. No self-respecting Dublin car thief would be seen dead in it.

Alex waved at me from the driver's seat.

'You took your time,' she called.

I'd decided to not say anything about the absentee houseguest at the moment. Alex might feel that she was somewhat responsible for lending it to me. Besides, there was no way she'd go to the match knowing one of her charges was on the loose.

As it was, we had to leave early in case we had to stop and assist wildlife crossing the motorway, an activity, we found, that did not come without risks.

'All set,' I said.

I wandered over and pulled open the passenger door. The teacher that I had invited, Kyle, was squeezed in the back. He was the ex-Marine who had come to Ireland to meet a girl he met online. Romance blossomed and they were married within weeks. The separation happened within less time. He had idly asked her how many lovers she'd had before him and during a momentary lapse of attention, she'd told him.

'I didn't expect that I would be her first one,' he'd confessed to me. 'Who knew but we're talking double digits here?'

I hadn't the heart to say that there wasn't a soul in the county that did not know, proving once again that Einstein was wrong; some things, like gossip, can indeed travel faster than light.

He also did not realise that he was about to be let go. Chris had agreed that HR should take care of it and thought the match might keep him onside should he not react well to being downsized.

Kyle had a pleasant manner about him but the rumour around the staff room was that he could handle himself. They said that he'd been cornered in a house with a malfunctioning M16 during a firefight, and that he'd killed two Taliban fighters with a butter knife he'd found. He was reluctant to speak of it but eventually admitted that the story was kind of true. It wasn't a knife, he explained to me. It was a spoon.

'Hello, Kyle,' I said. 'And who is this?'

A woman in her forties was sitting in the rear seat beside him. She also wore a football jersey. Her face appeared vaguely familiar.

'This is who I invited,' Alex said. 'Patrol Inspector Cora Halligan.' She swivelled her head to Cora. 'I get that right?'

Cora smiled. 'Cora is fine,' she said.

'Sorry,' I said, 'I didn't recognise you without the Garda uniform. You gave a talk in the school.'

'Was it any use? Anyone commit any crimes?'

'I hope not, they are only about twelve.'

'I'll still count that as a result.'

Alex told me later that the problem dad who had been refused a rabbit, had returned seeking trouble. Cora had responded to the call. She never questioned how the customer had ended up hog-tied. Alex had offered her the ticket as a thank you.

Alex waved at Laura who stood in the doorway. Cora also waved and greeted Laura. As a local Garda, she'd know everyone.

Alex pressed a button and the driver's side window dropped a few centimetres before jamming.

'Don't worry, Laura,' she shouted, through the opening. 'We'll have him back safe and sound.'

'At least return the jersey,' Laura said and turned back into the house.

Croke Park

60

Croke Park on All-Ireland hurling final day is a sea of heaving colours as fans stream towards the gates. Hawkers selling county flags vie for space with desperate fans seeking one of the eighty-thousand tickets. They might travel the length of the country to stand outside the stadium on the off chance that they could get lucky and find a tout with a ticket or ideally someone with a spare who would sell it at face value. It rarely happened. Fans would postpone surgery rather than give up a match ticket.

I felt bad that Laura could not join me. She was a Galway girl through and through and this year her team was in the final.

She had been overcome with emotion in the Hogan Stand during a nail-biting game a few years ago and dashed out onto the field, hurling abuse before being forcibly restrained by the linesmen.

I had joked that they'd removed the posters of her and that the restraining order had long since expired, however, she could not be persuaded to attend. In truth, I think she would prefer to be dressed up in the maroon colours of Galway and remain at home during the game. She could then say what she liked, and drink what she liked, without being wrestled to the ground.

We found our seats overlooking the pitch and attempted to educate Kyle about the game of hurling as we tucked into soft drinks and popcorn.

Alex explained how hurling is one of the fastest games on grass and it is also one of the oldest. She mentioned how there are references to the game as far back as 1272 BC.

I added that very little has changed since then. Fifteen men armed with hurls (think flattened clubs) line up on one side of a pitch to face an equal number on the other side. The object is to score by driving a sliotar (a small ball) travelling up to a hundred and eighty kilometres per hour into a goal or over the bar for fewer points. If it bounces off an opposing player's torso en route, so much the better.

Kyle frowned. 'So if it's that physical, why not wear something?'

'Like the armour your American footballers wear?' Cora had said.

'Exactly.'

'I think that they don't, as they'd be laughed out of town,' I said.

The annual clash of the ash (the wood that hurls are often made from) can lead to injuries, however, there is no diving like in soccer. A player would need to be beaten unconscious before a free is given and even then, he might be slagged by his *own* side for being a drama queen. The fact that they used so-called, "blood substitutes" to replace injured players encapsulates their attitude. It's all the more remarkable to note that players do not earn a cent for playing as it's an entirely amateur sport.

The modern game has, however, been dragged into the twenty-first century. There is a requirement that players wear lightweight helmets, with shin guards being an optional extra.

Alex claimed that this was a cultural thing. She said that the ancient Irish warriors, like the Gaesatae, used to charge into battle stark naked. This practice began to die out when better armed and fully dressed opponents fought back, while no doubt averting their eyes.

The game began with a brawl but then moved into a fluid series of exchanges. The sliotar would be carried up the field, balanced on the bas – the rounded end of the hurl – by a sprinting player before the ball was hand-passed to a teammate or pucked up over the heads of the opposition. The ball might be intercepted in mid-air and volleyed back in the opposite direction. Hurls would rattle off one another as one team tried to gain the upper hand, before driving the ball into the back of the net or over the crossbar.

I texted Laura several times and she responded almost instantly. She complained of referee bias or expressed anxiety whenever the game paused for the Skyhawk video referee to decide which side of the uprights the ball skimmed past.

If we were not shouting encouragement at the players, we were throwing sarcastic comments at the other team's supporters sitting beside us. Stands are never segregated. Supporters rarely threw punches at each other, but they had no issue in suggesting that their opponents enjoyed sexual congress with a parent who was not the father.

The game was nearly over and Galway had it in the bag. I punched Laura's number on the phone.

'Hello,' I yelled above the deafening roar of the crowd, as I heard it connect. 'Can you believe it, Laura?' I shouted before realising that I was listening to her voicemail message.

I wondered about our houseguest. I had not found her in my searches but snakes have spent millennia learning how to conceal themselves.

I replaced the phone in my pocket as the final whistle blew. Alex gave me a thumbs up, beaming.

'Some game!' she shouted and hugged Cora. Alex was beyond happiness. She then hugged the man beside her, all glum, wearing the colours of the opposition.

'Better luck next year,' Alex said.

'Ah, feck off,' he replied. He had a long drive home ahead of him.

'We got a result,' Alex said again.

'Yes,' I murmured. 'It looks like we got a result all right.'

Ella, Sam, Julian

59

We arrived at the estate after night had fallen. Alex pulled up outside my house and hauled up the handbrake. Laura's car was in the drive, but the house was in darkness.

I opened the passenger door, all smiles while wondering what I might find inside the house. The car interior light had clicked on revealing Kyle snoring, his head, now topped with a fake wig in the Galway colours rested on Cora's shoulder. He clutched an empty whiskey naggin to his chest. The car smelled like a distillery. Someone had painted his face maroon.

Alex opened the driver's door.

'You mind if I check in on her?' she said.

'Why?' I said too quickly. 'She might have gone for a walk.'

'The snake,' Alex said.

'Oh, right,' I said.

'And I need a wee,' Cora said, 'if you don't mind,' and opened the rear door to step out after struggling to extricate herself from underneath Kyle.

'I suppose you'd better come in,' I said as the two women stood beside me on the front step.

I placed the key in the front door, opened it and was met by gloom. I stepped inside and switched on the hall light.

'The downstairs loo is there,' I said pointing to the under-stairs toilet and Cora brushed passed me.

Blue light from the television flickered beneath the closed door of the sitting room.

Alex started to move around me, but I blocked her.

'Maybe put the kettle on first,' I said. 'Let me see that the room's tidy.'

'Okay, fine,' Alex said frowning. 'Should I be worried? Tell me you're not feeding her takeaways. If I go in there and see McDonald's wrappers then I know what the snake will be fed next.'

'Just give me a minute,' I said.

Alex shook her head slowly but walked straight into the kitchen and picked up the kettle.

I took a breath, turned the handle to the sitting room and swung the door open. I poked my head inside.

The TV had the volume turned down; a movie played in silence, partially illuminating the darkened room.

Laura lay on the floor, her open eyes staring vacantly at the ceiling. The sword lay beside her. She looked like a medieval knight laid out in a tomb. I shuddered; she was the personification of serenity. I felt a sob bubble up from somewhere. We'd almost twenty years together under our belts, after all. I would have to be made of stone not to have felt something.

I backed out into the hall and closed the door behind me.

A toilet flushed and I turned to face Cora, closing the WC door.

'You all right?' she asked gawping at me.

'I'm not sure,' I stammered. My opening remarks were woefully unprepared.

Alex strode towards us. 'I was right, wasn't I? Are we talking Burger King wrappers?'

'What?' Cora said.

'I know this man, years,' Alex said pointing at me. 'I know he is lying to me.'

I found it hard to speak. My heart pounded.

'No, no,' I said.

I slowly pointed to the sitting room.

I opened the door behind me.

Cora and Alex leaned their heads in and out again.

Cora threw me a perplexed look.

'You know I have the exact same sofa,' she said.

I turned around and my momentum carried me into the room. There was no sign of Laura but the connecting double doors to the kitchen were ajar. Cora and Alex followed me into the room. Alex stepped right up to the terrarium to peer inside. Cora however remained close behind me as I continued into the kitchen.

Laura, eyes half closed, was pouring water from the kitchen tap into a glass.

She noticed the two of us staring at her.

'What?' she said, her voice groggy.

'I saw you on the floor,' I said.

'Asleep until you came barging in. I'm still wrecked after last night.' Laura sipped at the water.

'You offering anyone a drink?' she said to me. And threw a side-look at Cora.

'I'm fine,' Cora said.

Alex appeared beside us. An annoyed expression on her face.

'I knew something funny was going on. Can anyone explain to me why the terrarium is empty?' she demanded.

Laura smirked. 'You're in trouble,' she said in a sing-song voice.

'About that,' I began.

'Hold on,' Cora interrupted and raised her hand.

No one spoke.

We heard a muffled shout, and what sounded like heavy furniture falling over. It emanated from the party wall that separated our home from Mrs Keena's.

There was a scream.

Streetlights illuminated a pair of paramedics wheeling Mrs Keena down her front path on a gurney. Swollen limbs poked from beneath a blanket. They pushed her onto a ramp at the rear of the ambulance. A male paramedic, tall and sinewy, pressed a button that raised both he and Mrs Keena slowly upwards.

An unattended Garda car, its light flashing, was parked in front of our house.

A small crowd had gathered in the street. I recognised a local press photographer who snapped away with her camera. Brenda stayed out of the way; she looked gorgeous in a colourful dressing gown that clung to her. I'd overheard her tell a neighbour that she'd rushed out when she heard the ambulance arriving.

The other paramedic, a woman in her thirties strolled over to Laura and me as we huddled together on the street.

The paramedic peered at me, 'You don't remember me, do you?' she asked.

'I didn't teach you, did I?' I replied, peeking at her name tag. 'Ella Byrne.'

'Oh no,' she said. 'We fished you out of the Shannon. That was us that patched you up, brought you in. Myself and Sam.' She pointed towards the open door of the ambulance. The tall paramedic gave a cursory wave as he strapped in Mrs Keena. 'They tell us the anti-venom is on the way. It'll be in Dublin in an hour and the Air Corps will fly it down by helicopter.'

Helicopter? Why didn't I think of a helicopter?

'She's a lucky woman,' Ella continued. 'What are the chances of getting a snake bite and there being both a casualty nurse and a snake expert next door?'

Laura had known exactly what to do. She'd calmed Mrs Keena down, kept the leg with the bite below heart level and washed the wound. Alex had assisted, offered advice, and identified the exact snake to the National Poison Centre on her phone so that they could chase up the correct antidote.

Alex had surmised that the snake must have exhausted its venom sac. It probably had already bitten something, she'd said and hadn't had enough time to properly refill its depleted reserves. Its reduced toxicity may have explained why Mrs Keena was still alive.

I thought of the vial that I had filled with venom.

'Some snakes take weeks to rebuild their toxins,' Alex had said.

'Who knew?' I replied.

Ella was about to turn to walk back to the ambulance.

'That's funny,' I said.

'What?' Ella asked.

'Sam and Ella.'

Ella shook her head. 'Never heard that before.'

She called out to the ambulance, 'Sam and Ella!'

Sam poked his head out the back. 'That's a good one, must remember that.'

As sarcasm goes, the medics were playing their A game.

I noticed Brenda sidling up to us, she shivered slightly in the cool evening air.

'She'll be fine, I reckon,' Ella said.

'That's a relief to know,' Laura said to me quietly.

Mrs Keena called out from the back of the ambulance. 'He did this,' she shouted. 'He did this.' She forced a hand from beneath a strap and pointed in my direction.

'Maybe not,' Ella said.

I grimaced and just waved back.

'He was fooling no one with that hat,' she roared. 'I saw him sneaking out of the estate. Don't think I didn't.'

Ella gazed at me quizzically with raised eyebrows.

I lifted my hand to the side of my head and rotated my finger in the universal, she's crazy gesture.

Sam leaned over Mrs Keena, checking that she was secured. His voice rose and he spoke like he was addressing a three-year-old. 'Don't worry, love, you are safe now. We are taking you away to meet some very good doctors.'

'Don't patronise me, you bollocks,' Mrs Keena yelled.

Ella hurried over but Sam gave her a thumbs up as he took Mrs Keena's arm and strapped her in, extra tight.

Ella climbed into the cab as Sam started writing on a clipboard.

'I'm glad, she'll be okay,' Brenda said, now standing beside us.

'Thank god,' Laura said.

We watched the paramedic as he double-checked that a saline bag, feeding fluids into Mrs Keena was secured.

'I know him,' Brenda said in a low voice to us. 'Didn't he get a medal in the Olympics a few years ago? He ran the eight hundred metres in one forty.'

'I didn't know you followed the Olympics,' I said in surprise. Was there no end to the layers of this woman?

'I don't really,' Brenda chuckled, 'but you know all those fit bods, what's not to like?'

'Oh, Brenda!' Laura said, smiling for the first time all evening.

'So if I'm ever sick, you know who to call,' Brenda said giggling, nodding towards the ambulance. She shivered. 'Anyway, I'm gonna run back inside, the tits are frozen off me. Goodnight.'

She scuttled off in the direction of her house. I watched her go, just to make sure she got home safe. I sensed Laura staring at me. Just then Inspector Cora Halligan, still in her GAA jersey, emerged from Mrs Keena's house, her arms folded behind her back. 'Come on, Julian,' she said.

A fresh-faced Garda stepped slowly out the front door. I would not have been surprised if this was his first posting since attesting from Templemore— the Garda training college. He held a pet carrier at arm's length in front of him. Something bucked inside. He froze for a moment.

'It's okay,' Cora said. 'It's not getting out of there. Now pop it into the boot will you. Now is good.'

Alex followed behind offering advice.

'Mind her now,' she said, 'she's had a traumatic evening.'

'Maybe you should carry it?' Julian said and carefully walked to the back of the squad car.

Mrs Keena, constrained by straps, struggled to sit up in the ambulance.

'You mind closing the door,' she shouted. 'Some Guard you are.'

Cora pulled the front door closed behind her.

Mrs Keena relaxed as the door clicked shut. 'I have it all on camera,' she called out triumphantly and collapsed back onto the cot.

I felt myself go pale. What had she on camera? Could I come up with an innocent explanation for shooting darts at Laura?

Cora's eyes furrowed and I could see that she was about to respond to Mrs Keena.

'Will I get that back, Cora?' I asked quickly, pointing towards the container that Garda Julian was lowering gently into the boot of the squad car. 'I mean the snake's not under arrest or anything?'

Cora glanced towards the ambulance as the rear doors slammed shut. The ambulance drove out of the estate. She studied me for a moment.

'Sorry, Martin. It's going to Dublin Zoo, whether they like it or not. If it comes to it, Julian's leaving it outside the door with a note. For sure it's not coming back into the county.'

Julian gently closed the car boot before sitting behind the steering wheel. The driver's door remained open as Julian peered nervously into the rear-view mirror, as if expecting the snake to burst through the seats.

'Relax,' Cora said. 'I'm sure it's secure.'

'How about you drive then?' Julian said sullenly.

'All right, Garda Julian. Remember who's got the epaulettes,' Cora snarled. Her tone quickly changed, and she smiled. 'I'm off duty, shouldn't even be here, You'll be grand. Think of the overtime.' She slammed his door shut, almost popping every hinge in the car, 'just watch out for potholes.'

Julian bit back a response, started the car and slowly drove off.

Laura turned to me. 'In case you were thinking of it. No more pets. We are so done with them. Return the terrarium and that's final.'

Laura was in a foul mood and there seemed little point in raising the topic of unloved scorpions that might need a temporary sanctuary. She just would not listen.

She waved goodbye to Alex and Cora before turning on her heel and storming back into the house.

'I have to agree,' Alex said, sliding into the driver's seat of her car. 'You only had one animal to mind and look how that turned out." Cora opened the passenger door carefully, mindful of Kyle sleeping in the back seat, oblivious to the evening's drama.

'I'm sorry, Alex,' I said as Cora sat in the car.

Kyle stirred in the rear seat as Alex and Cora closed their doors.

'Are we there yet?' he asked.

Alex ignored him, started the engine, and drove off without looking back.

I watched the car leave the estate. My mind replayed what Mrs Keena had said. What did she mean when she said she had it all on camera? What camera? And then my eyes settled on the bird box mounted on the streetlamp facing us.

A bird box, like others in the estate that no bird ever used.

I moved to Mrs Keena's front door and stood with my back to it. I glanced around but the onlookers had drifted away. I reached down and pulled Mrs Keena's spare key from under the mat. She wasn't the only observant resident in the estate.

I quickly entered Mrs Keena's house which was partially illuminated by streetlights. The downstairs was a mess of turned-over tables and broken vases. It was where she had fought the snake and we had applied first aid.

I slowly moved up the darkened stairs; they creaked at every step. When I reached the landing, I risked turning on the light.

Suddenly a hissing black cat leapt out at me before running into a bedroom.

I recoiled in horror.

It appeared identical to the cat that I had buried.

Maybe Tom had a twin? Was there such a thing as a zombie moggie? I poked my head into the room, but the cat had somehow vanished.

I passed the open door of a bathroom and stuck my head into her bedroom. It had been carefully made up. I backed out and opened the door to what, in our house, would have been the box room. It faced out onto the street.

She had set it up as a home office. A home office that someone in the NSA might aspire to. Several large computer monitors mounted on a modern desk displayed feeds from CCTV cameras.

I sat down at the desk and peered at the monitors. Even in darkness, infrared cameras displayed clear views of the front of her house. I gazed through the window, directly at the bird box. Its concealed lens caught me staring out. I peered closely at the other video feeds. Hidden cameras also captured the windows of houses that backed onto our gardens. I could see Tim Murphy, the owner of number 8, sitting on the edge of his bed wearing nothing but his Y fronts and a bra. I didn't want to judge but neither garment matched. This was Neighbourhood Watch on steroids.

You sly dog, I thought. It explained her interest in ornithology.

I leaned over and used the computer mouse to place a cursor on the camera feed that covered our garden.

I rewound to when I used the blowpipe and saw that I was in luck. The camera was partially obstructed by a tree obscuring the demise and burial of the cat. However, my blowpipe could be seen poking out the workshop window if someone was to carefully zoom in.

I deleted the footage.

I selected the camera feed that captured the front of our house and Mrs Keena's. I clicked on the timeline and scrolled backwards; night became day and then became night again as the recordings flashed past.

I paused the video when I reached the morning when I'd purchased the tablet. I watched myself emerge from the house in disguise.

So much for my plans for going incognito.

I selected the clip and deleted it.

I then fast-forwarded through the clips until I reached the previous evening.

I watched as Laura entered the sitting room with a mug of tea in her hand, before switching on the television and sitting down. I forwarded the video causing her to lurch around the sofa at four times normal speed before standing up.

I slowed the footage to normal speed and observed her approaching the terrarium slowly before staring into it. She glanced upwards as if she could somehow see me sleeping through the ceiling, before peering at the terrarium again.

She stepped back, turned, and closed the curtains.

A few minutes later, I followed her progress upstairs as house lights turned on, one by one.

A minute passed and the lights went out as she retreated down the stairs again.

The front door opened, and she exited towards her car, pulling on a jacket. She peered up at the room where I slept. Her head bowed as she unlocked the car door before climbing in and driving off to her medieval meeting.

I rewound the footage and froze the image; her face happened to face the camera. The video proved nothing. Laura could have just gone upstairs to get her jacket. On the other hand, I did not recall closing my bedroom door.

If I had not left the terrarium lid open, how did the snake escape? Was it possible that Laura had carried it upstairs and released it?

I knew nurses didn't have to take the Hippocratic oath to preserve life but freeing a deadly serpent in the room of a sleeping patient might appear as a blemish on her CV.

I stared at her image. I had motives to kill, but Laura had almost exactly the same.

Had she just tried to murder me?

Would she try again?

This was a woman who performed CPR on a drowning victim, that others had given up on, but somehow brought the swimmer back to life. Laura was not someone who ever gave up. If death could not stop her, then I was in serious trouble if she decided that she wanted to separate but didn't desire the paperwork.

Rambo

58

Laura had encouraged me to exercise after my accident, she'd push me out of the door, and I'd make half-hearted attempts to comply. She didn't know that I sometimes walked only as far as the coffee shop while taking the bus home if it looked like rain. All it took was the suspicion that she might want me dead to get me out jogging.

Maybe they should put that in a motivational video.

I knew that a fitter me would be better prepared for whatever surprises lay in store.

I'd also learned that Brenda had a soft spot for athletic types. Maybe she could be persuaded to gaze beyond my "love handles" but I thought, better safe than sorry.

I, therefore, had several reasons to be dressed in shorts and a t-shirt as I trekked back towards my estate breathing hard. Sweat rolled down my face. Keeping fit was way harder than I remembered it to be. For the sake of appearances, I broke into a run as I turned into the estate. I padded along the pavement, jogging gamely as I passed Brenda's house, on the off chance she was at home and perusing the street. I spluttered to a halt right past her house, sucking in air. I waited until my heart rate slowed, feigning a few stretches in case anyone was watching. As my breathing returned to normal, I heard voices emanating from my back garden. I peered through a gap in the hedge.

An old eight-by-four sheet of plywood leaned against my workshop. Liam was holding flattened cardboard boxes against it as Laura stapled them into place. Laura thanked him and appeared pleased. She glanced in my direction, and I stepped back guiltily.

I walked in through the front door and aimed straight for the downstairs bathroom. I threw water on my face and reached for a towel. I exited into the hall and met Liam sauntering in the opposite direction.

'You all right?' he asked as I towelled my face. 'You want me to ring nine-nine-nine?'

'I'm fine,' I said.

I was sure the redness was fading from my face.

'You should try the gym,' he said, 'if you're serious about doing this fit thing.'

'The pavement is free,' I said.

'Does the pavement have a CPR machine? I don't think so.'

He placed a hand on the newel post at the bottom of the stairs. 'You should go Tuesday mornings. I think that's when they have discounts for aul lads.'

He skipped up the stairs before I could challenge him to some press-ups.

I peeked out the kitchen window and observed Laura painting concentric circles onto the cardboard.

I threw the towel into a linen basket in the utility room and stepped outside.

'How was the walk?' she asked, glancing up.

'Jog,' I said. 'It was mostly a jog, for your information.'

Her brow furrowed.

'That wasn't you that I saw going in the coffee shop then?'

'I needed to hydrate,' I said. 'What's that?' I asked, pointing towards her handiwork.

'What does it look like?' she replied coolly.

'Like you're marking out my workshop for an airstrike.'

'Nothing so modern,' Laura said and scooped up a set of arrows and a bow from behind the patio furniture.

'Hold on. What's this?' I asked as Laura took several steps from the target, the bow, and arrows in her hand.

'I told you how we were researching weaponry. We're making a big thing of it this year.'

She'd gone from close quarter weaponry to ranged weapons in days. At this rate, she'd be testing space lasers in a fortnight.

'I'm not sure that the neighbours will be too impressed if you turn our garden into a firing range,' I said.

'I'll be careful,' she said. 'I'll wait until the children are in their summer camps.'

'Are there no other medieval crafts you could try?' I asked. 'Basket weaving for example. You're not putting anyone at risk when you're bending willow into shape.'

She brought up the bow, notched in an arrow and in one smooth movement, drew and released the string. The arrow flew straight and true and buried itself into the outer ring of the target.

The rear wall of our garden also served as the rear wall of number 15. I could see Mary Reilly nervously peering from her upstairs back bedroom window as Laura lined up the next shot.

'Take it easy,' I said. 'You need to maintain a nice smooth movement.'

'Is that right?' she said, placing the string and a notched arrow to her lips.

'Fine,' I said. I waved surreptitiously at Mary Reilly, warning her to duck down.

'What are you doing?' Laura said. Her eye remained focused on the target, moving the tip of the arrow into position.

'Nothing,' I said guiltily. My hand plunged back to my side.

Suddenly the bow bent before Laura released the string. The arrow flew through the air and landed just off-centre.

'Not bad,' she said.

Mary Reilly waved back. I hope that she appreciated that I could have just saved her life and that her streak of luck couldn't last.

Amazingly, it did.

Laura's next arrow landed dead centre on the target.

As did the next one after that.

'There I was thinking I married a nurse and it turns out it was Maid Marian,' I said.

'And who might you be?' she shot back. 'Friar Tuck?'

She was in a foul mood. It was just what I was afraid of.

She definitely was on a diet.

'So what's the sudden interest in keeping fit?' she asked.

'You inspired me,' I replied truthfully.

She let another arrow fly, but it landed within the outer circle. She squeezed her eyes shut for a moment.

'There was a gust of wind that time,' I said.

Laura sighted along another arrow. 'Isn't there something that you can be doing?' she said.

'I suppose laundry,' I replied.

'Then don't let me stop you,' she said.

She let fly again and scored another bullseye.

Rambo II

57

Laura had her back to me in bed.

'Are you awake?' I whispered.

Laura did not respond.

'You're good at the archery,' I said. 'I'm thinking we'll do okay if the Vikings sail back upriver.'

Perhaps she was asleep, but she wasn't snoring.

My eyes remained open, and I wondered if hers were too. Barney lay between us, the only one snoring tonight. I wondered again if the woman I married had released the snake on me. Would she have known it wasn't that toxic or could she have cared less?

How did my wife turn into Rambo?

Had she guessed that I had already made an attempt on her life?

Unless Dunne's released a range of pyjamas with a Kevlar lining, I might never sleep well again.

'If it's okay with you, I might borrow your car in the morning,' I said into the darkness.

'What's wrong with your car?' Laura asked after a moment.

I knew it. She was awake.

'Chris hasn't returned mine,' I said. 'He's somewhere out on the lakes, god knows where he is.'

Chris lived on his luxury cruiser and spent the summer exploring the hundreds of miles of inland lakes and rivers. He'd arrive at a new town, hellbent on emulating the marauding Vikings of old who had used the Shannon River as their personal motorway. He boasted of his ability to ravish local maidens, no doubt assisted by a Tinder Platinum account.

'Why am I not surprised?' she said, referring to the car.

'Then why did you lend it to him?' I snapped back.

'I did not lend it to him,' she said slowly. 'I only asked him to move your car from the bridge. I was kind of busy, you know, being by your bedside in the hospital and all.'

I thought about mentioning that I wouldn't have been there in the first place if she'd filled her petrol tank, but I didn't fancy my chances of surviving the night if I did so.

'So is that a yes?' I asked.

'You're very hard on cars,' Laura said.

'I'll keep it under the limit,' I replied.

'Have it back by lunchtime,' she sighed.

Alex

56

Alex peered coolly at me from inside Pet Kingdom as the electric security shutters rolled upwards.

I pressed inside as soon as she unlocked the door.

'Good morning, Martin,' she said. 'My good friend. It's good you popped by this way no one sees you get beaten by a girl.'

'I'm sorry the snake got out,' I said. 'I feel so bad about it. I haven't slept.'

'You were supposed to mind it,' she said, not disguising the rising fury in her voice. 'You're lucky your wife was there.'

'For Mrs Keena?'

'For you. I know how to neuter.'

'And I said that I was sorry. And I also think you have to be a licensed vet to carry out that procedure.'

'Who knows what trauma you caused it?' she said.

'I'm quite sure Mrs Keena got the worst of it.'

'I don't know Mrs Keena, do I?'

'I'm not sure that's the point.'

Alex sighed deeply. 'I get that we are supposed to put animals before people but have you met some of my customers? Mrs Keena should never have been placed in that position. Such wild animals should not have been in this country never mind in her house.'

I knew enough to let her calm. She was in the business of animal welfare and would not have taken too kindly to my attempts to transform a wild animal into my personal hit-snake. Alex despised animal cruelty in any form. She'd marched to support a new animal rights bill back in Poland and had been held for questioning about a fur shop in Gdansk which mysteriously burned to the ground.

Once, under the cover of darkness, I helped her load a pair of neglected donkeys into a trailer. Their hooves had curled upwards through neglect. Together we drove them to a sanctuary. Some nights later, the animal's owner awoke to find his shed on fire. It seemed that a lot of buildings combusted whenever Alex was around.

'So what do you want?' she asked.

'Something for Barney,' I said. 'A toy maybe? He's lost some weight now. I've been exercising him.'

'He's down weight?' she said, softening.

'I'm taking him for walks now,' I said.

That pleased her. 'I'll see what we can do,' she said.

'I also want to say again how sorry I was. I thought the terrarium was secure.'

'Well, it wasn't.'

'I know that, it means no more houseguests, Laura has put her foot down, but I do want to make up for what I did.'

Alex studied me. 'You can clean up at the shelter. They always need someone good with a shovel.'

'If I have to shovel dog poo then so be it. I was thinking, I can drive now. I might be more useful dropping off any unwanted animals to the zoo if you'd trust me again. No large alligators though, Laura's car is not that big. Or spiders. That goes without saying.'

She was torn, and she glanced towards the back room.

'As it happens we do need to make a run. Got enough animals back there to wipe out a small town.'

'We can't have that, Alex,' I said. 'Not on our watch.'

With luck, there'd be a spare Bushmaster to be transported. I could settle for a cobra. Right now, Laura was getting more lethal by the day and I needed to replenish my armoury.

I drove fast along the motorway, eager to get to Dublin and back without delay. Pet carriers rattled against each other on the backseats despite being belted in. Alex trusted me and I would not let her down. First things, first though. I clicked on my indicators as I crossed into the next county and swerved abruptly into a lay-by that overlooked a lake. I stamped on the brakes and the car slid to a halt. Cars whizzed by as I got out and retrieved a holdall from the boot. I squeezed into the backseat beside the pet carriers.

I slid on some gloves from the bag and began searching through the containers on the backseat but found nothing promising. There were some scorpions but I'd no idea how to milk one of those. Some containers were labelled, "spiders," with their species written in brackets. I shuddered.

I was not going near them unless it was with the heel of my shoe.

No snakes. Not a single one.

I slipped out of the car and slammed the back door in frustration, catching the edge of a container that rattled against another.

I was annoyed and the views did not help.

I shouldn't have allowed my hopes to build up, she'd assured me that the load was as lethal as a contingent of Attila the Hun's men trying to reach a quota. However, none of my passengers were of any practical use.

I had to force myself to think. I was out of poison and even so an English longbow far outranged a blowpipe.

So, what made the longbow obsolete?

On cue, a farmer crossed a fence in the distance, his shotgun broken open for safety.

I smiled.

Let Laura acquire the skills of a knight.

All I needed was some charcoal and some stale urine.

Excited now, I slid back into the driver's car seat, closed the door, and started the engine.

That's when I realised that the lids on several of the containers had popped open. I sensed movement around me as creatures slithered. A centipede inched its way across the dashboard. A scorpion curled up in the footwell.

I dropped off the containers at the National Exotic Animal Centre. They could tell that I was shaken. I'm certain they were used to Good Samaritans dropping off wildlife that could kill them and therefore didn't pass any comments as I passed over the containers. They could have done a lucrative sideline in sweet teas and hair dyes if they felt inclined. I felt that my hair was already halfway to grey and accelerating rapidly.

I was back on the road as quickly as possible, putting as many kilometres between me and the assorted arachnids and reptiles as I could. I pressed hard on the accelerator feeling the adrenaline rush that accrues when someone drives too fast.

I was therefore halfway home when the centre's volunteers checked the containers against the inventory.

I can imagine the opening conversation.

'Wasn't there supposed to be seven spiders?'

Brenda

55

Laura was screwing a small electronic box into the wall of the utility room when I arrived home.

'You're an electrician now?' I said, through the open door.

'It's a smart meter, it's really not that complicated. Some basic hard wiring into the mains, the rest is Wi-Fi.'

'And we needed one because…?'

'We can turn the heat on and off remotely. The lights too. Make it seem like we are at home.'

'We are always at home.'

'It'll save money,' she said. 'If you're at work you can switch off the immersion using your phone.'

'I love it,' I said.

'So where did you get to?' she asked.

'Just out for a drive.'

'What do you have there?' she asked.

I held a newly purchased plastic bucket in my hand.

'Just something I need for the workshop.'

I was eager to get out there at once. I'd held a full bladder for the last hour.

'You and your workshop,' she said. 'You might have been advised to keep on top of the jobs here first.'

She said this with a straight face; she had to move a basket of laundry to work on the meter, and it wouldn't have been that difficult to empty it into the washing machine. Then again, I shuddered at the memory of the time she left some pink briefs in with my whites.

Laura's phone pinged, and she glanced at the message. She quickly texted a short response. Her expression did not change as she pushed it deep into a pocket.

'Can I have my car keys back, please? I've to go into town,' she said.

'How about I join you?' I suggested, passing her the keys.

'Why would you do that?' she asked stiffly.

'You might need a hand if you're going shopping,' I replied.

'I'm not going shopping,' she said. 'It's a union thing.'

'Maybe I'll just come into town anyway just in case you change your mind.'

'The thing is,' Laura said slowly. 'Barney needs exercise and it's not like you can't afford to drop a few pounds.'

'I've lost weight for your information.'

'Good for you,' she shot back. 'You deserve a reward. You've earned it.'

I agreed.

'Are we talking about a takeaway?' I asked.

'Better. What could be nicer than fresh air and gorgeous views? Belvedere House would be a treat for you both.'

'So not a takeaway then?'

She ignored my response and just stared at me.

'I'll get my trainers.'

'Good man,' she said.

I put on my gym shoes and shorts but not before zipping down to the workshop to urinate into the newly purchased bucket

Laura drove off as Barney hauled me towards the converted stables that houses the visitors' centre for Belvedere House and grounds. Belvedere House is a former hunting lodge with dramatic terracing that drops down to a lake. It is famed for its Diocletian windows and Rococo plasterwork. Importantly, the coffee shop serves a chocolate eclair that is almost legendary.

The dog was beyond excited. The morning was filled with the prospect of new smells and things to urinate on. Laura had said that this would be a treat and she was unaware of how right she was.

Despite my running gear, I was not planning to push myself. The key to getting fit is consistent exercise while incrementally building up muscle mass. Athletes are prone to fractures and infections; it was, therefore, best I eased into it. Maybe I'd build up a sweat queuing in the coffee shop and that could suffice for today.

Barney would remain in a dog pen outside, with luck, he might share an enclosure with a mutt who was open to a friend's-with-benefits arrangement.

We passed through the entrance, and I pulled out my phone to check my device finder. We used an app to locate each other's phones in case they were lost or stolen. Was Laura actually going into town? She seemed not overly enthusiastic about me joining her. I was about to open the app when I almost collided with Brenda striding in the opposite direction.

Her bulldog panted on his leash. Brenda wore a lightweight jacket to protect herself from the wind that could blow across the lake. I guessed from her sneakers and leggings that she had been out for more than a light stroll. She was a woman who liked fitness.

A bit like future me.

Her dog collapsed onto his stomach as we met. Its baleful expression seemed to say, "Don't let her make me do another lap".

'Hi, Martin,' she said. 'What brings you here?'

'Try and stop me,' I said, putting away my phone, I wasn't lying (see chocolate eclair reference). 'I love spending time out in the walled gardens,' I added as I would not want her to think that I was superficial.

'Aren't they closed today?'

'Yes,' I said slowly. 'They are. But there's more to the place than orchids.'

They were bound to have some.

'Speaking of which, I never properly thanked you for the flowers you sent when I was in the hospital.'

'Oh those,' she said. 'Least we could do. Some of the residents took up a collection.'

My enthusiasm waned. I'd seen the same bunch of flowers in Tesco for nine ninety-nine. Fifty houses in the estate and that's the most that they could come up with?

Brenda leaned over and patted Barney on the head.

'Good boy,' she said. 'You're right though, there's more to the place than orchids. I'll bet he loves it here. Not many parks allow you to walk dogs.'

Barney's ears perked up, there were walks here too? If she mentioned that you were also allowed to throw tennis balls. Barney might think he'd died and gone to dog heaven.

I was therefore relieved when she changed the subject.

'So what's it like being famous?' she asked.

I remembered that *The Westmeath Independent* had covered the story of Mrs Keena's snakebite. It featured a front-page picture of her being wheeled out her front door. Laura was quoted about how happy she was to offer assistance while I was pictured inside, pointing dramatically to the empty terrarium. The article was a salutary reminder about the dangers of keeping exotic pets.

'I'm fighting off the groupies,' I said.

'At least Mrs Keena is all right thankfully,' she said. 'The word on the estate is that she's introducing a pet's policy for inclusion into the AGM. No wild or farm animals. I guess that rules me out getting an Alpaca.'

She straightened up. Her dog panted happily, its stubby tail beating.

'You're not going, are you?' I asked. 'I could get a lift back, save Laura a trip.'

Brenda hesitated.

'It's a shame to come all this way and not use the facilities. I can wait.'

'So coffee then?' I said seeing my opening.

'I thought you were here for a run?' Brenda asked. 'You're dressed for it.'

'Of course. I was going to run first but I don't mind having a rest day if you're in a rush back.'

'I'll wait,' she said.

There was no avoiding the run.

'Which route do you recommend?' I asked.

Brenda thought about that for a moment.

'There's the short circuit but the longer one takes you right by the lake, so I'd rule that out. I mean you've not had the plaster off long.'

'It's tempting. You know what running is like when it's in your blood.'

Her face lit up. 'You're really a runner?'

'Well, I am rather stiff after the brace but try and stop me.'

'Tell you what,' she said. 'I'll mind Barney while you go round.'

If truth be told. I'd never actually ventured further than the dog pen out the back of the coffee shop. The lattes here were that good. I peeked furtively over her shoulder searching for signage that indicated the routes.

'I'd not like to put you out.'

'No trouble at all. It's a lovely day for it. We'll wait for you on the lawns.' She took Barney's leash from my hand. Barney's mouth dropped open. We were not going to the pen? His tail began to wag madly. If he had been more aerodynamic, he'd have lifted off skywards.

'Oh, I have a tennis ball by the way,' Brenda said. I swear, Barney almost cried. Perhaps he had dreamed about what lay beyond the dog pens and today he might just find out.

On top of that, there was a tennis ball.

Brenda had concern written over her face. 'I didn't know you had asthma,' she said.

'Oh, not for years,' I wheezed, trying not to bend over double. 'My leg was in a brace for such a long time, it's just cramped up. Normally I could do this run backwards.'

She watched me suck air. 'Should I get you a glass of water?'

'No, I just need to stretch out of it. I took on too much, too soon.'

'Of course,' she said nodding. 'It's a credit to you that you managed… so far.'

I knew she was being kind.

'Impressive, yes?' I gasped, struggling to breathe, gesturing to the ruins that towered above us. I'd rather she faced anywhere than me. Sweat dripped down the crack of my bottom. My torso tottered over knees that barely supported me.

Not a good look.

'Oh that,' she took in the walls that rose several storeys into the air. Carved stone windows punctuated the stonework, and you could imagine a long departed monk staring through them over the lake. Perhaps he then returned to his illustrations as he worked on a bootleg copy of the *Book of Kells*.

However, none of this was possible as the gothic buttresses of the abbey were as genuine as a politician's promise. The so-called "Jealous wall" had been a nineteenth-century addition built adjacent to Belvedere House. It was no more real than a film set.

Brenda smiled. 'It's gas what people do to keep out the neighbours.' She knew her walls.

Lord Rochford had built the wall, supposedly to block out the view of his house from his estranged brother's home further along the lakeside. I searched in my mind for what the leaflets in the coffee shop had said.

'All because he thought Lady Rochford was carrying on with his brother.'

'Maybe he should just have just bought her some flowers,' Brenda said.

'Different times,' I said.

'I feel so sorry for her,' Brenda said. 'That poor woman, stuck out here in the middle of nowhere. Not allowed to see anyone, visit anyone. There are only so many times you can look at the view. I'd go nuts. No wonder, she fancied a ride with the neighbour.'

She reddened.

Before I could respond, snot dripped onto my T-shirt.

I needed to freshen up and at the same time investigate if Belvedere House had a CPR machine.

'Would you mind hanging onto the dog while I splash some water onto my face?'

'Happy to,' she said.

I rinsed my face in the male WC and used soap as an impromptu deodorant. It would have to do.

I purchased some coffees and eclairs and found Brenda sitting on the grass, twirling a tennis ball attached to a short rope around her head before throwing it down the hill. Barney tore off after it. Her dog slept at her feet.

'You didn't have to do that,' she said, taking her coffee and cake.

'It's nothing,' I said, 'Sure it's not like we don't know how to burn off calories.'

She nodded and chewed on an eclair. She didn't speak with her mouth full. She had class.

She finished the eclair in two fast bites.

Even ladies can be famished.

My phone pinged as I sat on the grass. Brenda's dog slumbered between us. I checked my phone, Laura had texted to say that she was running late and Brenda could give me a lift back. I wondered how she knew Brenda was here.

Brenda lay back in the grass, resting on her elbows, drinking in the sun. Her eyes closed, one hand holding the coffee cup and the other idly stroking her dog.

'I think if I was reincarnated,' I said watching her dog enjoying the feel of her fingertips, 'I'd like it to be as a dog. It doesn't take much to make them happy.'

Shouting interrupted me. Brenda's eyes popped open, and she pushed herself up onto her elbows. A man was running frantically downhill, waving his arms towards a golden retriever. A golden retriever being enthusiastically mounted by Barney.

Brenda threw me a watery smile.

Laura

54

Barney lay sprawled out on the kitchen sofa, dead to the world. He yapped in his sleep, dreaming perhaps about the best day of his life.

I could empathise. I was secretly thrilled to share the lift home with Brenda. I bet the perfume she wore was expensive. Something that might be purchased in a pharmacy.

I lifted the lid off the slow cooker and stirred the pot with a wooden spoon.

Bacon simmered in duck fat. It was like a supersaturated anti-personnel mine. I felt calories pile on just by looking at it. The liquified eggs and cheese were inspired by an offering from an American restaurant that said anyone who could eat it in one sitting, without a bathroom break, could eat free for life.

That was clever marketing as the person who could pack this away probably would not be known for their longevity.

Laura entered and placed her car keys on the kitchen island. She noticed Barney, his leg twitching.

'What did you do to him?' she asked.

'He had a great time although I'd avoid Belvedere House for a while. A chap there might be seeking a paternity test.'

Laura smiled at the animal.

'How was town?' I asked.

She looked at me blankly. 'The Union thing,' I added.

'Oh that,' she said. 'The usual, boring.'

Laura was a senior staff nurse and frequently had to advise nurses for disciplinary hearings.

'Anything juicy? Remember when someone left the sponge in a patient?'

'I never should have told you that,' she said. 'And besides, that was a surgeon, not a nurse who did that— she just was afraid to speak up.'

Retained surgical instruments refer to items left inadvertently in a patient's body. It's why there is usually someone appointed during surgery to account for every item used.

I caught her looking at me intently as I stirred the pot again.

'What?' I said.

'Nothing,' she replied. 'I'm just tired.'

'You'll have some dinner?' I asked.

'No, I'm good,' she said. 'If you don't mind, I'm going up.' She walked out of the room and up the stairs. I heard the floor creak overhead as she entered our bedroom.

I seized her phone that she had left behind on the kitchen island and keyed in her PIN.

There was a message from earlier in the day.

"See you in town, looking forward to it."

The text had a familiarity to it that I'd not associate with union business.

She had replied, "OK".

I slid the phone back to precisely where I had found it. I was annoyed at her deceitfulness.

I heard two muffled thuds. I recognised it as the sound of Laura launching her shoes at the back of the wardrobe. It was something she sometimes did when she was on edge.

As unpalatable as the idea was, I must face facts. Laura might have tried to kill me by releasing a snake into the room while I slept but for certain, she was nursing secrets of her own.

Not only that, but she might well be on a diet. The resulting hormonal imbalance could make her lethal on the best of days.

She was also using medieval weaponry at an expert level.

For sure, if she asked me to make tea, I was making it.

And making it quickly.

Rambo III

53

The workshop was beginning to smell like an alley beside a late-night chippie. I grimaced as I peed into the bucket in the corner, the fumes of stale urine wafted up my nostrils. No wonder saltpetre makers in medieval times had been banished to the outskirts of towns.

I wandered out into the garden to enjoy the morning sun and inhaled some fresh air. I gazed at the target leaning against my workshop, its centre punctured with holes. Laura, I had to admit, was good. I wondered, how difficult could archery be?

I fetched her bow and arrows from the kitchen. I examined the bow and drew back the string. I could hit double tops at darts, maybe I was a natural archer?

It turns out that archery is harder than it looks, especially with an audience. Mary Reilly must have been an early bird as I noticed her watching from her bedroom window as I aimed at the plywood sheet. She held a large frying pan close to her body. Thanks for the vote of confidence, I thought.

I drew back the string until the bow arched and the string touched my cheek – exactly as I'd seen Laura do. I released the string, and the arrow landed several centimetres from the edge of the plywood sheet. I tried again and this time it was almost within the concentric circles. I was pleased to see improvement already.

Maybe this time I'd try a shot five metres away.

I fired off some more arrows but only hit the bullseye when I sneezed unexpectedly.

'Don't give up the day job,' Laura called out.

I stiffened and turned around. I'd not noticed her enter the garden. 'I thought you were in bed?' I said in surprise.

She shrugged. 'I was. All right if I take a turn?'

She beckoned with her hand. I reluctantly handed over the bow and the last arrow. We only had six arrows. Four were more or less on target and I was sure I'd find the last one when I searched more.

'I think my arm is still a bit stiff after the cast, but I managed a few bullseyes regardless,' I said handing it to her.

I didn't say that I wasn't quite up to the seventy-metre distance required for Olympic targeting. I'd need to get some practice in first – and perhaps a bigger garden.

'Be a dote, would you?' she said sweetly.

I strode over to the target and pulled out the first arrow. I noticed that the tip remained sharp, it hadn't been blunted by the cardboard layers. I reached for the second arrow, glanced up and noticed that Mary Reilly had vanished from view. I tugged on the third arrow. It refused to budge.

'Hurry up, haven't all day you know,' Laura called out. 'I'm getting old, here.'

I rested one hand on the shaft of the arrow and turned to Laura. 'I don't want to damage them. I only got si— five.'

People say that they feel hairs rising on the back of the neck when they experience jeopardy. I can confirm this to be true. I realised that I was standing in front of a target while Laura stood at the other end of the garden drawing an arrow back and forth on the bow. How did this just happen? A glance confirmed the empty window at Mary Reilly's. My tiredness abruptly vanished as if a treble espresso had just kicked in.

'Ready when you are,' Laura said sweetly.

I felt my hands dampen and yanked the arrow out. I turned around to face Laura, thankfully the arrow was pointing towards the ground. I was not reassured as I knew she could raise the bow and fire off a shot in an instant.

Studies have found that a medieval arrow can cause as much catastrophic injury as the bullet from a modern-day assault rifle. One shot alone can be fatal. It's not like the movies, where a hero can wrench several arrows from his body before continuing in battle. In reality, one hit from those bad boys and he's not only out of the fight but he's crying for his mum.

Laura's expression changed and nodded over my head. I guessed that Mary Reilly had appeared at the window and I felt held breath leave my body.

I hurried to Laura's side as she slowly raised the bow and placed an arrow down range into the centre of the target.

'Not too bad,' I murmured.

She put the bow down and slid the remaining arrows into her quiver.

'You should relax, Martin. You know me. I wouldn't hurt a fly.'

'That's good to know,' I said slowly.

She wore her poker face well today.

She bit her lip and then smiled abruptly.

'Tea?'

'We're out of milk though. I had the last of it,' I said.

'Don't you have some in the man cave?'

I had some in a small fridge but that would mean going down range from an armed woman on a diet.

'I'm out,' I said quickly.

'You'll be a pet, will you? Get some milk. Take my car,' Laura said as she sighted her arrow, 'since Chris hasn't bothered to drop yours off.'

'As it happens, he texted me its coordinates.'

'That was big of him.' She glanced at me. 'And get some doughnuts from Gerry's,' she added.

I brightened.

Things were looking up. If she was off the diet, then I might make it through to the end of the week.

In the meantime, my chemical soup was burbling away nicely in the workshop.

Maggie

52

My mood had dramatically altered as I drove fast down the dual carriageway, overtaking car after car. Gerry's home bakery sold the finest cakes in the area and although he was located outside the town, he was never short of customers. I wondered as I changed lanes, how my potential victim had channelled her inner Hawkeye from the Marvel Cinematic Universe. She was proving to be remarkably uncooperative in my quest to become a widower.

Laura's car's engine roared in protest as I accelerated, I guessed that if I pressed too hard my feet would push on through the rust at the bottom of the foot-well. I checked my watch as I braked and was forced to slow down behind two articulated lorries which occupied both lanes. I began to doubt that I could make it to Gerry's before he closed for lunch. I decided to select option B, I swung the wheel hard and veered across the motorway, horns blaring behind me as I took the exit ramp. I reduced speed as I became caught up in town traffic. Minutes later I turned into the shopping centre, thinking of the deli inside. Not as good as Gerry's but needs must. I drove quickly down a lane between the car parks.

I suddenly noticed Maggie Geraghty-Philbin hesitating on the pavement in front of a bric-a-brac shop. She'd recognised our car and peered intently to see who was driving.

I groaned. Her appeal to return Ruairi to school remained on my desk, gathering dust. Could I pretend not to have seen her and make a handbrake turn?

I pulled down the sun visor, convinced that I could bluff this one out, I just had to avoid eye contact.

I avoided eye contact with Maggie but instead found myself staring into the eight eyes of an Australian jumping spider hanging from the visor.

I froze, then roared and then realised that the car still had momentum. Maggie filled my car windscreen.

Her expression went rapidly from triumph to puzzlement to shock as I bore down on her. I stamped roughly on the brakes, but it was too late to stop in time. I glanced left and right. The choice was to swerve into a group of girl guides or a bunch of nuns sharing a cigarette. I only had a split second to make a decision – none of them palatable but all of them involved paperwork and possibly the future of my immortal soul.

Maggie understood in an instant that I was going to run her over. I braced for impact as she launched herself forward onto the bonnet. Our eyes met as her fingers scrabbled at the paintwork. Her face was a smorgasbord of hateful expressions such as the glower a father gives to his daughter's first boyfriend alongside the glare a woman throws out when corrected.

I wrenched my eyes away and noticed that the shop was selling scented candles at half price for today only.

Good value, I thought, just before Maggie and I plunged through their plate glass windows.

Paramedic Ella rolled Maggie into the back of the ambulance. Maggie's eyes remained locked on mine. If looks could kill, then I'd require an undertaker and not a paramedic. I was assured she'd recover "just fine" but they were taking her in for tests regardless.

Sam sidled over.

'I feel that we should be taking you out to dinner or something. We're getting to know you so well.'

'It was an accident,' I protested. 'There was a spider.'

He held some gauze to my forehead. I was sitting in the rear seat of an open Garda car, my feet on the ground outside.

'Last time there was a snake, wasn't there?'

'Doesn't the service have any other paramedics?' I asked gruffly.

'Why, you want them to practise more as well? Believe you me, we're busy enough without your help.'

'It's just a coincidence,' I said.

Ella approached. 'I'm seeing you more than my husband. I probably should thank you.'

'We were wondering,' Sam said, 'if you broke any mirrors lately?'

'Any black cats crossed your path in the last day or two?'

'You know we don't offer frequent flier miles?'

I grimaced. 'Shouldn't you bring Maggie to the hospital?' I asked.

'I hear you trying to be considerate, but you did run her over,' Ella pointed out.

'I had no choice. There were nuns.'

'I can't force you to go in but I'd have the head looked at if I were you, in case of concussion,' Sam said.

'Normally we'd say avoid driving,' Ella added, 'but in your case, that advice is too little, too late.'

She scanned my wife's car as a weakened shelf of cosmetics collapsed onto its roof.

They turned back and climbed into the ambulance. Sam wound down the window. 'See you soon!'

Strobe lights began to flash, and they were gone.

I shuddered, if I had lost control on the dual carriageway at speed then I might not have required the services of an ambulance crew. The job may have fallen to a County Council worker with several buckets and a shovel.

Did Laura know about the spider? She certainly knew I'd freak out if I got up close and personal with one.

A uniformed Inspector Cora approached and stood over me as she flicked through her notebook.

'They're right,' she said. 'You have been seeing a lot of them.'

'Sorry for the inconvenience,' I said as I tried to stand, 'it was an accident,' and I collapsed back into the seat.

I was seeing two of Cora and began to think that concussion was indeed likely, either that or Cora had a twin.

'And you didn't know Maggie was going to be here?' Cora asked, peering at me.

'No. How could I?' I replied, slurring my words slightly. I was in a fog and barely knew my name.

Cora watched as the corner of a shop sign "Maggie's EuroSavers" dropped a few centimetres.

'She's a bit of a pain in the hole. Made threats,' Cora said, turning to me.

I was groggy and responded without thinking. 'She is the very definition of a pain in the hole. I could wallpaper my office with the demands she's made to reinstate her son. You know she grabbed me when I was in the hospital?'

Cora didn't miss a beat. 'I'd say you were very upset.'

'Of course I was.'

'Did she get you down below?'

My stomach heaved. 'No. My leg actually.'

She nodded in sympathy. 'You felt violated all the same.'

'In a sense.'

'All in all a good motive for running her over. Who'd blame you?'

'Exactly,' I said and realised that Cora could maintain eye contact and scribble notes at the same time. 'No. Hold on. I never said that.'

'Said what?'

'Please stop writing,' I demanded. 'I never said, what you just suggested I said.'

'That you ran her over on purpose?'

'Exactly.'

She pored over her notes. 'That's what she says.'

'There was a spider. A big one.'

'Which we can't find.'

'It was the size of my hand.'

'I'm sure it was. Still, it would have been very convenient for you if you'd just been going a little faster.'

'It's not like I've not had to deal with problematic people before. I've chaired Parents' Association meetings. Let's leave it at that.'

'Don't get me wrong, Martin. I sympathise with you. She'd do anything for Ruairi. Claiming that you ran her over on purpose could help her case to reinstate him. She might say that you were being vindictive.'

'I'm not a vindictive man, Guard,' I said.

'Are you sure? You said that she grabbed you and not in a special way. Maybe it all built up inside until you felt compelled to run her over and demolish her shop.'

Cora's words registered. Of course, Maggie owned the shop that I'd now parked in.

'I only wanted pastries, Cora,' I said quietly.

'So you're sticking with the "I was scared by a spider" story.'

'It's what happened.'

'Regardless, I'm just saying, person-to-person, forget the uniform. You just gave her even more leverage.'

I slumped back in the seat. I was thinking that I should have opted for the nuns.

'Is Ruairi worth this?' Cora asked.

I was beginning to wonder that myself. Ruairi was in Maggie's blind spot. She saw a young man who had been hard done by. She did not see that indulging his every whim would have consequences. I could bring the boy back into the school but that would have resulted in a teacher walkout. Even a blind man could see that Ruairi's future involved a street gang followed by a stint in Mountjoy Prison, that is unless the gang formed a quorum and decided to remove him for ungentlemanly behaviour. It was likely that he would be too psycho even for them.

Cora surveyed the write-off – formerly known as my wife's car – now taking up residence in Maggie's shop, as Garda Julian emerged from the wreckage.

'I didn't think that they were turning the EuroSaver into a drive-through,' he said.

'Very good, Julian,' Cora said. 'You mind putting up a bit of tape? If it's not too much trouble.'

Julian grinned and rolled bright yellow tape with Garda Síochána written on it, across the entrance to the shop.

'Julian can manage here. Can I give you a lift?' Cora said to me.

'That would be great,' I replied. 'As long as you put that notebook away.'

'Least I can do seeing as you're keeping us all in a job,' she said grinning.

Julian paused as he finished unravelling the Garda cordon tape. He surveyed the ruins of the shop.

'Does anyone else smell smoke?'

Rowan

51

I carried a drink and a scone into the sitting room. Laura sat on the sofa while Liam slouched in an armchair. Both had matching trays on their laps. Liam sipped at a beer (mine) and had a pile of snacks at the ready. Laura seemed satisfied with a juice carton and a small bag of popcorn. She had refused the chocolate cake I had offered. The window of opportunity to break her diet had passed. I hoped that she'd change her mind. The cake was homemade and contained more fat content than an American truck stop.

The room was lit by the television paused on a British satellite news channel.

I sat down stiffly. I don't know how James Bond did it, he could roll off a cliff and shake it off without complaint. I had been thrown about in the car crash and still felt it in every joint. 'Okay,' I said getting as comfortable as I could. 'Let's do it.'

Liam lifted the remote control and pressed "Play".

The news report unfroze. A news anchor spoke down the lens of the camera. Behind her was a Picture-in-Picture map graphic depicting the centre of Ireland.

'One hundred and forty people are out of work today,' she intoned, 'after a fire gutted a popular shopping centre in the very heart of the Emerald Isle.'

The graphic cross-faded to a file picture of Golden Island shopping centre.

'Here we go,' Liam snorted. He had his phone in front of him and double thumbed its keys.

'There was panic as firefighters evacuated shoppers and employees of the centre. Dramatic footage captures the moments as fire engulfed the building.'

Cue mobile phone footage of smoke rising from shop fronts intercut with shots of people scrambling out the exit doors with fire engines arriving with lights flashing. Real cinema vérité.

It was dramatic stuff. It edged out a report of a factory closure in Liverpool as the image of a padlock and chain over an entrance gate just did not have the visuals.

'The blaze appears to have started after a car crashed through the window of a shop.'

'And you're up,' Liam said. His phone pinged.

'The car driver is reported to be local vice principal Martin Devaney.'

Liam cheered as mobile phone footage showed me sitting on the rear seat of the Garda car with Sam standing close by. Blood seeped through the gauze on my forehead.

I understood why I had made it into the headlines. As newsroom mantra dictates, if it bleeds, it leads.

'It was an accident,' the on-screen me said. 'There was a spider.'

'Damage is estimated to be at least six million pounds,' the newscaster said.

Liam whistled. He entered something on his phone.

A screen grab taken from our school website showed me smiling foolishly. It was out of context. Our school had just won the all-Ireland debating tournament.

The announcer continued with the script. 'This is one teacher who hopefully… has learned his lesson.'

They had to go there.

Liam's phone continued to ping. He paused the TV. 'Guess who's trending on social media,' he said.

'Can we watch the rest of it please?' I asked.

Liam pressed "Play" and the broadcast resumed.

'If confirmed then Martin's car insurance will exceed the previous world record for a pay-out that was held by comedian Rowan Atkinson.'

Cut to a picture of Rowan.

'And his McLaren.'

Cut and hold picture of a wrecked sports car poking through a hedge.

Liam pressed pause and the screen froze as I appeared again. A graphic underneath contained the caption "World Record Car Insurance Pay-out".

'There goes your no claims bonus,' Liam said.

I sipped at my drink. A vodka and tonic but without the tonic.

'It's lucky I didn't go for those cakes,' I murmured. 'If I panicked on the motorway then I mightn't be here now.'

Laura glanced over.

'The benefits of giving up sweet things are well known,' she said.

Our eyes locked for a moment.

'Maybe it will teach you to slow down.'

'The spider was massive,' I said.

'It was probably more afraid of you than you of it,' Laura said.

'I don't know about that,' I replied.

Laura smiled. 'On the plus side,' she said, 'you're alive and haven't you always wanted to be in *The Guinness Book of Records*?'

I resisted an urge to reach for a butter knife but remembered that she had a sword stashed somewhere in the house.

'You'd better get your car back,' Laura said, 'or we are all going to be taking buses.'

'I'll get right on it.'

'I know,' Laura sighed. 'You have the coordinates.'

Maggie

50

Chris's coordinates, entered onto my phone, directed me right to my car parked in a taxi rank.

'Oh, you bastard,' I groaned as I peeled the parking tickets from the windscreen.

I pushed open the lid covering the fuel cap and found my car keys inside, just where Chris had texted they would be. I sat in. I pulled takeaway wrappers from underneath me. In his defence, it was clear that Chris had a social conscience and didn't like to litter the streets. I closed the car door and started the engine. The fuel tank was full. Maybe Chris had filled it for me? I tapped on the dial, and it dropped down to almost empty.

Maybe not.

I picked up an air fresher at the car accessories aisle in the petrol station that doubled as a small supermarket. I dropped it into a basket and added a second. I'd already added upholstery wipes, disposable gloves, and a disinfectant spray. I then meandered to the magazine stand. The top shelf rack used to be stocked with plastic-wrapped *Playboys* until someone discovered that not only was the Internet cheaper – for well-written articles – but you could avoid bumping into a neighbour while you were in mid-reach.

I scanned the magazines. Brenda liked her men fit. She did not yet realise that my BMI masked an inner athlete.

A magazine displayed a fit-looking man on the cover, a headline referred to his tips for an Ironman triathlon. That could be me someday. I just had to maintain my fitness regime, and if there was an internet-sold pill I could take to help, well so be it.

I added the magazine to my basket which also contained some sports drinks. It was heavy but I did not require a trolley. I felt dormant muscles easing back into life.

Suddenly, I heard Maggie Geraghty-Philbin berating someone at the dairy products display. I grimaced. She was out of the hospital already?

'This cheese is off. You shouldn't be selling it.'

I poked my head around an aisle and saw Maggie holding up a block of cheese to a sales assistant.

'It's a best-before, not a use-by date,' the sales assistant said in a bored tone. Her customer service manner could have done with some tweaking as she sighed deeply. Perhaps she was experiencing phone withdrawal symptoms as it was forbidden on the floor to have her phone switched on. Perhaps she was simply losing the will to live. Maggie had that effect on people.

I noticed that Maggie wore a neck brace.

I backed away slowly. I had already offered my apologies. I had called by the hospital to visit her with Laura. Coincidentally, Maggie had occupied the same bed as Mrs Keena. I'd brought chocolates for her as well but Mrs Keena had told me to shove them up my arse.

At least we were on speaking terms.

Maggie had said much the same thing. Laura had to explain to the nurses that I didn't make a habit of sending people to the hospital. At least not until recently.

'Ah,' Maggie said loudly to the shop assistant. 'I don't think that's good enough, do you?'

'Blame the EU for those labels,' the girl said. 'Besides, cheese is basically milk that's gone off anyway, so I don't see what difference it makes.'

'Don't take that tone with me, young lady.'

'Whatever,' she said shrugging, before calling out, 'Jenny. A little help here!'

I could sense a scrum forming around Maggie as management was drawn in. It was like witnessing a black hole that absorbed everything about it.

I hoisted my basket onto the checkout counter at the other end of the store. A sales assistant scanned item after item, triggering loud beeps as the barcodes were read. The noises seemed to echo through the shop. He added the cost of the fuel before asking,

'Do you want a bag?'

I nodded eagerly, seized the offered plastic bag and avoided eye contact. Eye contact meant the possibility of conversation and delay.

I quickly packed the bag and ran my debit card through the card reader. I bolted out the automatic door.

I hurried to my car parked alongside a fuel pump. That was a close call. I unlocked the car with the remote on my key fob, popped the boot and dropped in my purchases. I pulled out a wad of Chris's detritus at the same time, scurried to a nearby bin and shoved it inside.

I returned and sat in the front seat.

Mission accomplished. I sighed happily.

'We need to speak about Ruairi,' Maggie said from the passenger seat.

'What?' I did a double take. 'Mrs Philbin?'

'Geraghty-Philbin,' she said frostily.

'What are you doing here?' I asked.

'Not giving you a chance to run me down again for a start.'

'I explained already that there was a spider.'

'And burned my livelihood to the ground.'

'Quite a big spider.'

'So you say. Do you know how many messages I've left for you about Ruairi?'

'You left messages?' I said feigning innocence.

In truth the school secretary, Peggy diligently wrote down the messages before filing them in a wastepaper basket.

'I left messages and e-mails. You were to get back to me.'

'About Ruairi?' I said, buying time.

'Of course, it was about Ruairi,' she barked. 'He's been out of school for the last four months and I need this issue resolved. Term is starting soon.'

'I thought we'd cleared this up,' I said gently. 'Ruairi has been indefinitely suspended.'

She was having none of it. 'Ruairi is entitled to an education.'

So was the lad he put in casualty. The incident had featured heavily on social media. Ruairi was in the centre of a group, laying into a young chap half his size who was begging him to stop.

'You know he has ADHD?' Maggie said. 'You can't discriminate against children with disabilities.'

Try me, I thought. Doctor Maguire had unethically rung me up to say that Maggie and Ruairi had burst in and had intimidated him into writing up such a diagnosis. He said that he would have diagnosed Ruairi as having ADHD, OCD and PMT, if necessary. Anything to get them out of the surgery while it was in one piece.

'That lends a whole new complexion to the matter,' I said. 'I'll get onto the Department at once.' (Well, when school started anyway).

'And in the meantime?'

'In the meantime, Ruairi unfortunately, must remain at home. The Department will continue to have a teacher calling into him after the holidays.'

'Yes,' she snarled. 'Much use they are. He went through three different ones in a fortnight.'

There's a surprise, I thought. He tried to grab the breasts of one teacher and threatened another – a Gaeilgeoir (native Irish speaker) for correcting his Irish vocabulary. I never knew why the last teacher, a former paratrooper, quit. He was last seen driving out of town crying. Rumour had it that he'd given up teaching to become a mercenary.

The consensus was to draw the matter out until Ruairi was eighteen and legally an adult when the Irish Prison Service would likely have jurisdiction. However, Ruairi was just twelve which meant that we would have to be on our A-game when it came to red tape.

In the meantime, we would keep feeding him teachers as he was our failure and our responsibility.

We could have transferred Ruairi to one of the many other secondary schools in the town but that would have meant an inevitable push-back. The Teachers Union of Ireland has a long memory and transferring the equivalent of a pre-teen Genghis Khan to a new school would never end well for the principal signing off on it. One of our history teachers pointed out that our sister schools always did very well at the annual

Young Scientist & Technology Exhibition in Dublin, and we shouldn't risk it.

'I wouldn't put it past them to build a siege engine,' she'd said. 'They'd sling dead cats over the school gates.'

I told her that she was letting her imagination get the better of her.

Maggie locked eyes with me. 'I'm not giving up. You know I will do anything for Ruairi. Anything.'

Feelings of nausea coursed through me. If she lunged over the hand brake to give me a blowjob, would I be allowed to flatten her with the Tefal frying pan that I'd purchased on special offer?

'There's nothing more you can do,' I said.

'That's where you are wrong,' she snarled.

'Look, you know I'm only the vice principal,' I said. 'I'll do my best but my hands are tied.'

'Chris says otherwise.'

Of course he did. The weasel.

I had to be charitable. Maybe she was holding him hostage.

'Chris says a lot of things,' I said. 'By the way, how did you get into my car?'

She ignored my question.

'I hope you're looking forward to going back to school,' she said and stepped out of the car. She leaned in the open doorway. 'I might just show up.'

'It's a free country.'

'Believe me, Martin' she said. 'You have no idea what I'm capable of.'

'Are we talking about some kind of petition?'

'The gloves are off now. You ran me over. Spider indeed.'

The door slammed shut.

I groaned. Only six years to go before the little terror and his mother were no longer our problem.

Laura

49

Laura, wearing thick rubber gloves, popped her head into the study, AKA the converted box room that served as a home office. I was continuing my research on how others carried out murder most foul. There's no point in reinventing the wheel, after all. I was reading a book on the Borgias. What a family! Their crimes included murder, incest, theft, bribery and selling church property. Loosely speaking, more than a few comparisons to people I knew when I taught in North Dublin.

'So, you busy?' Laura asked.

'Maybe,' I said as I sensed a job pending. I surreptitiously put the book down and replaced it with a book on gardening.

'Did you contact the gas installer?' she asked.

The ancient boiler was long since overdue a service, but other priorities pushed it to the back of the queue. It would have to wait until the winter.

'I'm getting right on it. Just have to pay a few bills first, like food.'

'It needs a service, you said you'd take care if it.'

'Why can't you have a look at it? You'd be well able. It would save us a few bob.'

Laura could have serviced the boiler, but it was illegal for an unqualified person to do so.

'Just do it,' she said and pursed her lips. 'How are you feeling?'

'What do you mean?'

'Down there?'

'Again, what do you mean?'

'We need to boil everything. Liam's got a dose,' she said.

I felt an urge to scratch.

'Only warts this time,' she added.

'Lovely.'

'But the lotion does wonders,' she said.

'It's a tranquilliser he needs,' I said. 'Or maybe it would just be cheaper to take away his bus pass.'

'Be that as it may, I suggest that you use the gel I left out for you in the shower.'

'So this is what's been on your mind?'

'What do you mean?'

'I've noticed that you've not been yourself lately.'

'What have you noticed?'

'You're off your food for one thing.'

'And that's what you noticed?' she said. 'It's not like I can't afford to lose a few pounds.'

'I never said that you were fat,' I replied tersely.

The room went cold.

'Fat?' she said quietly.

I felt thankful that she hadn't the broadsword to hand.

'Let's put a pin in this conversation,' I said.

She nodded. 'Are you using your car? I'm only asking as you burned out mine.'

'There was a spider. The size of a plate.'

'I'm sure there was.'

'What do you want my car for?'

'Does anything I ever say to you register at all?'

'I'm not likely to forget genital warts in a hurry,' I said. 'Or ever use a towel of his again. So some things stick.'

'It's the fayre. I told you about it.'

'That's on again?'

Every year, Athlone Castle holds a medieval fayre. It features exhibitions; musicians playing medieval instruments and Laura's history group enthusiastically revelling in aspects of medieval life. Who can forget the "open arse" food demonstration? This medieval medlar fruit, known by its colloquial name due to its shape, also had the dubious distinction of only being palatable when rotten. Some things are best lost to history.

'What are you doing this year? I hope you're passing on the authentic food stalls. There is a reason why stuffed swan vanished from our menus. If it was any good it would be served in Tesco.'

'We're not focused on food this year,' she said, 'as you know.'

'You know they didn't use forks in medieval times,' I said. 'Just knives and hands.'

'I'm on the committee,' she said. 'And I told you about the forks.'

I knew enough to back away from further discussion. She was the only one in the family who not only knew how to use a broadsword but actually possessed one. She also was an accomplished archer. All in all, the type of person that ensured muggers could no longer venture out alone at night.

'Just so you know, Brenda is there this year,' she said.

'Why?'

'She's a stall. She asked me to pick stuff up from her house as she's running out of stock.'

'I didn't know you had a key to her house?'

'You don't know everything, do you, Martin?' she said sweetly.

I rose from the desk. 'Sure, I may as well give you a lift. What are neighbours for, eh?'

'If it's not too much bother,' Laura said. 'First though, hit the shower.'

'Fine.'

'Don't forget—'

'The special gel. I know, I know.'

Laura went downstairs as I stepped into the en-suite and turned on the shower. I picked up the plastic bottle of the gel that Laura had prepared. I baulked as I removed the cap. It smelled like the love child of apple cider vinegar and chlorine, but I had no choice but to lather it on. I knew Brenda liked her men fit but dosed with genital lesions – probably not so much.

Laura

48

I carried a box of fabric through the main gate of Athlone Castle and entered thirteenth-century Ireland. Throngs of tourists and re-enactors dressed in fighting tunics, armour or pleated dresses milled around the courtyard. A musician using small wooden hammers tapped on the wires of a dulcimer; its notes echoed off the walls. An area in front of the keep was roped off from the crowds for fighting demonstrations. Stalls sold artisanal food and medieval-themed merchandise.

Smelling of detergent, Laura and I pushed our way through the crowds, mindful of the plastic swords wielded by children upon one another.

We passed a small group dressed in medieval clothes, standing beside a humanoid figure constructed from straw and held together by twine. The group gripped bows and arrows in a scene that could have stepped straight from a medieval manuscript. The illusion was somewhat marred when one man pulled out a phone from within a tunic before calling, 'Selfie!'

They huddled in for a snap and then one woman noticed Laura.

'Hi, Laura,' she called out. 'Didn't expect to see you today. You going to join us?'

One man bowed his head towards her.

'Sorry, lads,' Laura said, shaking her head as she passed them. 'I am sure you can manage.'

'Aren't they part of your medieval group?' I asked her.

'You mean the ones dressed in tunics, breeches and wimples?'

'You have a real flair for sarcasm sometimes,' I said.

'It's a gift. I've won prizes for it.'

'Really?'

'No,' she said.

We carried on through the throng. She spotted Brenda waving to us. She was surrounded by mannequins dressed in colourful, flowing dresses.

'Greetings to ye, simple towns folks,' Brenda said to us in a faux-medieval accent, as we approached. She indicated where I should drop the box and hugged Laura.

'How's it going?' Laura asked.

Brenda shrugged. 'I can't keep up. They're flying out. I'm almost down to just taking orders.'

I could see the attraction. Brenda was a better advertisement than any mannequin. She wore a bodice that exposed more cleavage than might be seen on a Saint Tropez beach. I didn't know where to look but I caught the look of amusement that Laura and Brenda exchanged as I examined my feet.

'While we are here, you want a hand?' Laura said.

'That would be great,' Brenda said. 'If you're not too tired.'

'I'm fine, Brenda,' Laura said stiffly.

'In that case, we need to get you into something a little less comfortable,' Brenda said and held a dress against Laura. 'What do think?'

'I love it,' Laura replied, beaming.

'You can change in the loo,' Brenda said pointing to the visitors' centre.

'What about you, sire?' Brenda said, turning to me. 'Wouldst thou be a peasant or methinks a knight? I have a box of stuff there you can try on.'

'I'm good,' I said.

'Oh, don't thou be such a crooked-nosed knave,' Laura said. 'Of course, he'll do it.' She threw me a smug look. 'What are neighbours for, eh?'

Brenda reached down into a box. The decision had been made.

Laura and Brenda were busy hawking their merchandise when I eventually emerged from the visitors' centre. Brenda nudged Laura and they both laughed. I wore leggings, and a long-sleeved tunic that did not quite reach my crotch. I had stuffed a handkerchief in there, but it only served to give the appearance of an enlarged testicle.

'So what do you think?' I said.

'You look amazing,' Brenda said, and I found myself blushing. 'Doesn't he, Laura?'

'Quite the coxcomb,' Laura said. 'Maybe wear it home later. I might fancy a good ravish.'

Laura and Brenda burst out laughing.

There was a blast of trumpets and a man's voice called out, 'Hear ye, hear ye, come hither. Bring ye close upon me for the display of bravery and swordsmanship.'

The crowd cheered. The man dressed in a leather tunic and leggings continued to address them.

'Who among ye… is prepared to duel with…' he paused dramatically before introducing, 'ye Black Knight!'

The crowd cheered. A dozen children raised their plastic swords. The crowd parted to reveal a knight in a studded leather tunic, a metal helmet enclosing the head.

A pair of steely eyes peered out through a slit in the helmet. He held a dagger in one hand, while his gloved hand, held the hilt of a sword, its tip resting on the cobbles.

The knight's head slowly surveyed the audience. There was menace there and the plastic swords dropped out of sight. He drew the knife and held it out in front of him, before slowly tracing an arc in the air. It paused at a man in the crowd who ducked down. The knife continued and then slid to a halt.

Some poor sap is in for it now, I thought. The eyes of the crowd followed the line of the dagger and heads turned towards me. I looked left and right, wondering on which side of me the victim stood. I noticed people edging away. A large, bald man, licking an ice cream grinned in my direction, enjoying my discomfort.

Dawn broke.

'You are having a laugh,' I muttered.

The man in the leather tunic appeared at my side. He addressed the crowd as he gripped my arm, raising it. 'We have a challenger!'

'No, we certainly do not,' I muttered to him.

He dropped his voice. 'You'll be grand,' he said. 'It's just playacting.'

The crowd began a slow clap.

'Oh, go on,' Brenda said. 'It'll be great craic.'

Brenda and I should have a talk. Her idea of a good time diverged from mine. However, if she thought a real man was someone who could disembowel a wild animal, then so be it. It's not like knife play was a skill required in the twenty-first century, some Dublin flats being a possible exception.

'Go, sire, and defend my virtue,' Laura added.

Yes, right. That ship sailed a long time ago. I felt myself being propelled towards the roped-off enclosure. A helmet was placed on my head. My arms were slipped into a chainmail vest.

'You'll be great,' the man said. 'And don't worry, you can't do any harm.' A sword was thrust into my hand. 'Merek of Turlough House is the real deal.'

'He's a time traveller then, is he?'

'Just make it look good, it's all for show.'

'All right,' I said. The man slipped behind the rope. I raised my sword. It was heavier than it looked but I could do this. Didn't I play Marcello in a school production of *Hamlet*? There was a fight scene, albeit with wooden swords. I waved the sword, letting my arms feel its weight and letting muscle memory kick in.

The man bellowed again.

'Greetings, gentle ladies and squires of honour. You are about to face an example of true and mortal combat. The swords they use are real.'

The crowd cheered, hoping for blood.

'Alas, the Health and Safety Authority has asked that we use blunt edges.'

The crowd booed. I even noticed Laura laughing and giving a thumbs down.

'However,' the man said. 'The HSA began in 2007 but we're not in 2007, are we?'

The crowd cheered. The prospect of blood had them glued to their camera phones.

I whispered to the man, 'This is all part of the act, yes?'

'We're in 1216!' the man roared, and the crowd went wild.

Another voice cut through the cacophony. 'I am Merek of Turlough House,' The Black Knight said. The voice somewhat muffled by the closed visor seemed familiar. 'Today, these stones will run red with the blood of this charlatan.' The knight tipped up the mask visor revealing a face. It was Paul – the Care Worker from the outpatients clinic.

'Hi, Martin,' he said. 'Fancy meeting you here.'

'You,' I said, nervously. 'It's all acting, remember.'

'You really should have given me the points,' Paul said, and snapped his visor shut.

He turned to the crowd and shouted out, 'I will take this challenger on and may God have mercy on his soul.' He raised his sword. 'To the death!'

The crowd cheered; phones held out. There was a feeling that a social media meme was in the pipeline.

The battle began.

There was some clashing of swords but mainly it consisted of me running about the enclosure and getting smacked hard by Paul's sword. He landed blow after blow using the flat side of the sword (using the pointy end might have had implications for his public liability insurance) but maybe he was gearing up for a big finish.

In my peripheral vision, I could see Brenda and Laura holding silk scarves against one another's throats. They appeared not to notice that their knight was struggling to maintain empty underpants.

I rolled clear as another blow landed on the cobbles where I had been curled moments earlier. I scrambled backwards; all semblance of dignity lost. I found myself backed up against a canon, cobblestones pressed against my bottom. *This is it*, I thought. Paul approached and raised his sword over his head for a death blow.

'I would have been an excellent, Garda,' he hissed.

'Stay, now, good knight,' a voice called out.

In unison, we both swivelled our heads to the side. Laura had pulled on a leather bodice, and she had a sword gripped firmly in her hand.

'This vassal is mine,' Laura said. 'I decide his fate, not you.'

'He is not worthy of you,' Paul called back. 'He is hedge-born and should be put down like the dog he is.'

'Here now,' I said. 'There was no call for that.'

'Do you accept my challenge?' Laura said.

'So be it,' Paul said as he swirled and rounded on Laura.

I almost felt like warning him.

Almost.

Swords clashed as the bout began.

Paul lunged and Laura parried.

Paul struck out and Laura blocked the blow. Suddenly, she moved sideways, raised her sword, and brought the blade down in a vicious swing.

Paul's helmet rolled across the ground towards me, settling at my crotch. The crowd yelped.

I screamed like a toddler refused ice cream and scrambled to my feet.

Laura handed her sword to someone while Paul looked at his helmet in astonishment, no doubt thrilled that his head was no longer inside.

Brenda

47

Night had fallen and the last of the tourists had gone. All that remained were the re-enactors and the stall holders disassembling their stalls and drinking unsold mead. The gates were closed, and we had the castle to ourselves. It was time to party – medieval style. A musician was lost in the strings of a harp while emboldened by drink; squires flirted with maidens at picnic tables.

Paul, aka Merek, was chatting up Brenda.

'When not here, I work in the healthcare sector,' he said, his voice slurred with ale.

He had one foot on the bench where she sat, all the better to show his codpiece. He swivelled around, pulled an arrow from the mannequin, and handed it to her.

Brenda giggled as she placed a tankard of ale on the bench and picked up a bow. She was barely able to walk, which should have indicated that she was in no condition to use lethal weaponry either.

Of course, there wasn't a Health and Safety Authority in the twelfth century.

She notched the arrow and pulled back on the string. She turned to the hangers-on who ducked down.

'What do I do again?'

'That way,' someone said, pointing in the correct direction.

She sighted more or less correctly on the straw target.

Laura sat alone on a bench but was comfortable without company. She watched Brenda and the others with an intense look. She drank in the sounds of laughter and music under the night sky. Her hands trembled as I watched her pop a sizzling tablet into a tankard of water.

She was heading off a hangover, I guessed.

She drank deep and held the tankard with both hands, watching.

Laura had played me. I was the nominated driver leaving everyone to drink what they liked. I sipped on something that I hoped was squash.

Brenda pulled back on the bow and released the string theatrically. The arrow sailed over the target and vanished over the battlements into the darkness.

'You have another?' Brenda asked.

Paul giggled and took the bow from her.

'You shouldn't be using a bow. In your condition.'

'At last,' I said.

I was sitting on the steps of the keep.

Paul picked up a crossbow and said, 'Maybe this instead.' He also picked up an apple and held it on his head.

The woman sitting on the steps beside me said drunkenly, 'we should call someone.'

'You think?' I said.

'We should kick them out. Someone get the person in charge. The curator will sort them.' She reached drunkenly for a phone and began tapping at the keys.

'Much good that will do,' I said.

'Why you say that?'

'You are the curator,' I said.

'Only kidding,' Paul said and put the crossbow down. He picked up another apple and a third before attempting to juggle.

An apple fell to the ground. Someone laughed.

Me.

Paul shook his head sadly and picked up the apple. I almost felt sorry for him.

It turned out that Paul's initial clumsy attempts at prop manipulation was just an act, as moments later, fruit sailed into the air in a circular motion before being expertly caught and thrown higher.

Brenda began to gently clap.

I shook my head in disbelief and noticed Laura looking at me over the lip of her tankard.

Paul threw the apples high into the air and caught them one by one in a big finish. He then bowed and handed one to Brenda. She took a bite and giggled. I wanted to interject and say that at no point had I seen the fruit being washed. They clearly still inhabited a century where hand hygiene lay far into the future.

Laura banged her tankard on the table.

Voices grew silent and she banged it again.

And again.

The rest joined in one by one, forming a rhythmic beat as they pounded on tables with their fists or tankards.

As an Englishman in Ireland, there had been times when I felt excluded from the conversation. It could have been a chat about a local politician or the retelling of a historic event. This was one such time.

Laura began to sing in Irish.

'Thuirt an gobha fuirighidh mi

S thuirt an gobha falbhaidh mi'

Her voice echoed off the walls.

'S thuirt an gobha leis an othail

A bh' air an dòrus an t-sàbhail

Gu rachadh e a shuirghe.'

Everyone but me joined in the chorus while maintaining the primitive beat. It was a scene that would not have seemed out of place at a campfire, aeons ago.

'Si eilean nam bothan nam bothan

Eilean nam bothan nam bothan

Eilean nam bothan nam bothan.'

I escorted Brenda and Laura down the steps of the castle, holding each of them upright under each arm as they had lost the capacity to walk unaided. They giggled at a parked car. An arrow stuck out of the bonnet.

Try explaining that to the insurance, I thought.

I fumbled through my jacket and produced my car keys.

'Thanks for this,' Laura said, as I strapped her into the front seat. 'I'm so tired.'

'That's the job I signed up for,' I said.

'You can be so lovely when you want to be,' she said.

'Thanks.'

'But that was then.'

'I don't know what you mean,' I said.

Her eyes lost focus.

'What was that song about?' I asked.

'A blacksmith goes courting,' she murmured, her eyes shutting. 'Seeking true love.'

I closed her door and opened the rear door. Brenda swayed like she was caught in a gale. I held her with one hand as she was about to fall.

'Yes, you are so lovely,' Brenda said and leaned forward to plant a kiss full-on my lips before falling into the car, giggling.

She strapped herself in with difficulty as I stood, stunned, outside.

Did that just happen? So what if her breath smelled of ale and a trace of vomit? I stood there, savouring the moment.

'Oh, go on,' Brenda said to Laura. 'Show us your bosoms, wench. I'll get mine out too.'

I was back in the car in an instant.

The girls giggled.

Laura's eyes remained shut.

'Home, James,' Laura said.

'Isn't she amazing?' Brenda said. 'Say, what's with all the burger wrappings back here?'

'She is one of a kind,' I said. 'And that's not my mess.'

'I'm going to miss her.'

'I don't know what you mean,' I said. 'She's not going anywhere.'

She sniffed. 'But no one stays forever, do they?'

'No,' I said.

'We must carry on.'

'We must.'

'Thou art very good.'

I gently accelerated away into the darkened streets. I did not want to disturb Laura who was on the verge of sleep.

'You know, Brenda,' I began. 'Tonight was fun.'

I glanced at her in the mirror.

Brenda began to sob.

'Are you all right?' I asked.

'Yes,' she said. 'I'm thinking of Liam.'

'Liam?' I said. 'What about him?'

She reached over and squeezed my shoulder urgently. 'Will he be okay?' she asked.

'They're just genital warts,' I said. 'He had a right dose but he's responding well.'

She released me abruptly. 'Warts?' she asked.

'What else did you mean?'

She spoke with difficulty. 'You know in medieval times; they'd rub a piece of meat into a wart and then bury it. The meat I mean. Not the wart.'

'If I find the leg of lamb is missing then I'll know who to blame.'

Brenda giggled.

'Why were you asking about Liam?'

She did not reply. I wondered if she was overwhelmed with sexual tension after that kiss.

She snored. I guess not. The moment was lost. I shouldn't have been surprised.

Venereal disease is the ultimate party pooper.

I resisted the urge to press on the accelerator and instead took my time driving through the dark streets of Athlone, throwing fleeting looks in the mirror at Brenda. Something made me glance over to the passenger seat. Laura had her eyes open but appeared to be watching the street passing outside.

'You okay, love?' I asked.

She nodded and wiped her hand over the side glass, removing moisture.

Laura

46

The tablet was booted up on the workshop bench. I was updating my notes and tapped with two fingers on the virtual keyboard. I entered:

"She nodded and wiped her hand over the side glass, removing moisture."

Suddenly there was the sound of an arrow ploughing into the sheet of plywood leaning against the workshop. Dust floated down from the ceiling as another arrow hit the target.

Each impact resonated loudly throughout the workshop. More dust fell as another arrow landed. I reached for an old World War II British army helmet that was hanging from a nail. I slipped it on. The straps tucked under my chin kept it in place. Another bang and another. Each impact rattled the workshop. More dust fell. She must have ordered more arrows. The single bare lightbulb from the ceiling swayed. I'd just have to wait out her target practice.

Suddenly an arrow flew in through the open window – missing me by millimetres.

'Are you okay?' Laura called out, a few moments later.

'I'm fine, darling,' I said.

The shaft of the arrow quivered. Its head was embedded dead centre in the picture of me holding up the prize-winning pike.

'Sorry about that, love,' she said. 'Wouldn't want any harm to come to you.'

Another arrow crashed into the plywood.

I rolled onto the floor and peered through the gap in the open window. She lined up another arrow and fired it in my direction. I ducked as it smashed against the plywood.

That's the way you want to play it, I thought and pulled a cloth from over a metal pipe mounted on a wooden block and a set of wheelbarrow wheels.

She remained in the Longbow era but some of us had leapt centuries. I'd sifted the stale urine to create saltpetre before mixing in some charcoal and sulphur to enter the age of gunpowder.

The workshop shook again as another arrow connected. I reached into a drawer, pulled out a jug of the black gunpowder and poured it into the mouth of the cannon. I removed a lead sphere, that I'd cast, about the size of a tennis ball, and dropped it into the barrel of the canon before shoving the ball deep into the barrel with the handle of a sweeping brush. I rolled the canon forward on its wheels along the worktop, until the tip of the barrel protruded through the open window.

I kept my head down, sighted it in Laura's direction and pulled open a drawer revealing a box of long matches. I struck one, it blew out. I struck another and the flame burned brightly. I grabbed a pair of ear defenders, threw them on and grimaced as I touched the fuse sticking out of the rear of the cannon. It burned quickly, the flame vanishing into the body of the cannon and then… nothing.

I must have miscalculated the exact proportions of the ingredients.

It became oddly quiet outside. I contemplated waving my handkerchief from the end of a stick.

Laura called out.

'I'm getting tired, Martin. Do you want to come out? We can have tea.'

'Sure,' I said evenly, 'I can think of nothing better.'

I rose to my feet and slowly pushed out the workshop door and stepped into daylight.

Laura stood before me at the top of the garden, one arrow held limply in the bow faced down. Her hand pulled gently at the string. Had I found myself at the business end of a firing squad?

Suddenly Mrs Keena popped her head up over the garden fence.

'Have you heard about the robberies,' she said. 'Churchwood was done last night. Three houses were broken into.'

'They'd better not come near here,' Laura said in a voice that registered red on the annoyance scale. She gestured with the bow and arrow. 'Not unless they fancy being converted into a pin cushion.'

'I think the Guards would prefer if we didn't turn into vigilantes,' I said.

'I don't know about that,' Mrs Keena said. 'I don't think they'd want the paperwork.'

'It might be harder than you think,' I said. 'To shoot someone. Harder than a paper target.'

I stepped from the meagre protection of the shed and walked towards her.

'You reckon?' she asked.

'Even trained soldiers can find it hard to kill someone.'

'How do they know until they try?' she said.

'What do you think, Mrs Keena,' I said. 'Could you kill someone if push came to shove?'

I kept stepping forward slowly until I was level with Laura.

'I reckon I could,' she replied.

'Really?' Laura said.

'I don't think a judge would convict me, do you? I'd bring biscuits.'

'So you would do it because you think you would not go to jail?' I asked.

'I don't make a habit of breaking into people's houses. I expect the same courtesy. They come in through my windows and they get what they deserve if you ask me.'

I guess everyone's a liberal until they wake up in bed to hear the sounds of their downstairs back door being jimmied.

'I'm heading into town,' Mrs Keena said. 'I might pick up some bamboo.'

'You thinking of adopting a panda?'

'It's for the burglars. I'd like to see them try.'

'You're going to make them a basket?' I asked.

'I'm going to sharpen them and put them into the bottom of a hole. Some shite on top, of course. Like the Vietcong did to ambush the Yanks.'

I kept edging towards the house. Mrs Keena took her Neighbourhood Watch job way too seriously. I'd better warn the gas meter reader.

I stepped, with relief, behind Laura.

'I've some news,' Mrs Keena said and peered over the fence. 'Tom's back.'

'Tom?' I said.

'Covered in dirt, he was, whatever he was up to. Found him at the back door.'

Laura looked at me and I shrugged. I guess I'd only stunned Tom. He had not responded when I tapped him with my foot, which for me is one indication of death. I hadn't checked him for a pulse, I mean, how does one check a cat's pulse anyway? I had somehow recalled that a rectal temperature below thirty-seven degrees for a cat is a warning of impending death, but no way was I using our good thermometer.

'I guess that's good news,' I said.

Mrs Keena threw me a filthy look.

'No thanks to you,' she said.

'Didn't I put up posters?' I replied.

'You leave us be,' she said. 'Be thankful I warned you about the bamboo.'

She turned and vanished back inside the house.

'You know what she's talking about?' Laura asked.

'She should be in a home,' I replied.

'And you had nothing to do with her cat's disappearance?'

'I love cats,' I said.

'It shits in our garden.'

'Maybe not all cats then,' I admitted, 'but I didn't have anything to do with her cat vanishing. Maybe it went on a cat bender? We may never know.'

Laura raised the bow suddenly and fired off a shot. The arrow landed outside the concentric circles of the target.

The bow dipped. It looked like she was going to cry.

She tried again and this time the arrow barely landed on the edge of the plywood. I was a better shot than this. I felt an urge to offer her archery lessons.

'Martin,' she said. 'I'm so tired.'

'You want me to make you tea?'

She turned abruptly, fury on her face. 'I don't want tea.'

'What then do you want?' I asked. She had mentioned tea just moments earlier. It was hard to keep up.

'You can stop lying for one thing.'

'Is this about the cat? I can explain.'

She burst into tears. 'I don't know who to believe.'

'Who?'

She wiped her eyes.

'Are you trying to kill me, Martin?'

'I don't know who's been talking to you but I'm not trying to kill you.'

There must have been a slow-burning fuse because at that precise moment the mini cannon exploded and blew out the windows and roof of the workshop.

We watched glass and debris shower down.

'It's not how it looks,' I said at last, but Laura was already inside.

I sighed. At best, I'd be sleeping in the spare room tonight.

Part II

The Gunpowder Age

"All is fair in love and war."
William Shakespeare

Maggie

45

I drove towards the front gate of the school, weaving through the chaos of double parked parents dropping off children and students crossing the road, while glued to mobile phones. I was exhausted, I'd attempted sleeping while wrapped in several army blankets in our spare room— the poorly built annexe that could double as a walk-in freezer. We'd tried to rent it out once. Our mistake was listing it during the winter. We'd shown it to a student who had been put off by the icicles.

I'd spent the night shivering, contemplating the injustice of it all. How dare Laura say that I was trying to hurt her when it was I that was experiencing a seemingly random set of accidents. I didn't want to voice my suspicions that she was somehow involved while she didn't want to talk at all. She did say she needed space to think and claimed the bedroom. I heard her quietly lock the bedroom door in the night. There was no lock in the annexe and I pushed a chair against the door, although that did not stop me from sitting bolt upright every time someone took a step on the upstairs landing.

I discovered Maggie Geraghty-Philbin standing outside the entrance holding up a placard on which was written "Education for All".

Two other women from the Parents' Association stood self-consciously beside her. Paula Daly gripped a sign emblazoned with the words, "Justice for Ruairi," in coloured markers. Jackie Bourke carried a clipboard. She kept her head lowered as she'd been cursed with bad genes and two eyebrows that met in the middle.

'Justice for Ruairi,' Jackie said aloud without conviction in between asking passers-by to sign the petition.

'What's this about, Maggie?' I asked after rolling down my window.

'I said that I'd welcome you back,' she said.

'And you couldn't just buy me a cake?'

'We'll see who will have the last laugh,' she said.

'I'm sorry for running you over,' I lied.

'Not so sorry that you'll take Ruairi back.'

Too true. I could not see how Ruairi could return unless we issued PPE gear for the staff. Already, the Department was desperately trying to organise home-schooling for Ruairi but word soon got out about his proclivity for violence and intimidation. No teachers could be found locally who would take him on. His reputation was the talk of education message boards. In desperation, the Department had flown in a teacher from Syria just before term started. He lasted a week before claiming refugee status. His last text claimed that he didn't escape a civil war in his home country to face another.

'We're not leaving until we get justice,' Maggie snarled.

'Hang on,' Jackie interrupted. Her clipboard dipped. 'You only booked me until eleven?' She lowered her voice, 'I'm getting my eyebrows done.'

There were already signs of a schism.

Maggie placed her placard down, stepped back to the school gates and reached into a hold-all.

I waved to Paula who held her sign listlessly at an angle above her head.

'So why are you here, Paula?'

'Justice for Ruairi,' she said without enthusiasm. Her voice lowered. 'Plus I'm kind of afraid of Maggie.'

There was the sound of a chain rattling. Maggie looped a chain around a pedestrian gate on one side of the main entrance and snapped a padlock shut.

Students continued to stream past her. I guessed that without sufficient manpower, she'd opted for a symbolic protest as all she'd managed to do was delay traffic.

'I'm not going to go quietly,' she said.

'Fair enough,' I said.

'We're going on hunger strike, you know,' she said.

'We're what?' Paula asked nervously, someone who probably could benefit from the consequent reduction of calories. She clearly didn't maintain enough social distancing from the fridge.

'I'd make yourself comfortable,' I said. 'Not bothering anyone here.'

Maggie grinned. 'I said I was going to do whatever it takes,' she said.

'And you think that it will help?'

'I've the *Topic* on the way. They'll take pictures. And, *The Westmeath Independent*. Also, Virgin Media are sending a TV crew for *Lunchtime Live*.'

'Tell them to make sure they spell our names correctly,' I said.

I saw both Paula and Jackie blanch. I guessed that they hadn't been told that they were being set up for a newspaper spread and television stardom.

'*The Independent*?' Jackie said nervously and rubbed at her unibrow. 'I told you I have an appointment with the beauty therapist.'

'Doesn't TV make you look more fat?' Paula added.

'You'll be fine girls,' Maggie said.

Her followers were not convinced, one perhaps longed to get bits of her plucked, while the other wished for a pair of Spanx.

'They'll want to know why you won't let a choirbcy back to school,' Maggie warned.

'Ruairi's in a choir?' I said, astonished.

'He will be by the time that they get here.'

'They fact check you know.'

'They can check all they like, but I'll tell them that he knows every word of *Nessun Dorma*. That the bishop says he has the voice of an angel.'

Jackie and Paula began crying out, 'Justice for Ruairi,' as a car pulled up and a photographer stepped out.

The potential PR disaster didn't bother me too much. The voices would decrease by a third at eleven a.m. when Jackie left for her appointment. I was confident that Paula would scarper by lunchtime unless Maggie had organised catering.

'I hope you know what you are doing,' I said.

'I'll do anything for my son,' she said. 'I did warn you.'

She then abruptly waved me through. I put my foot on the accelerator and drove in through the gap. In my rear-view mirror, I could see that her eyes never left me as I parked in the vice principal's space.

Maggie's glower abruptly changed into a smile before she turned to face the press photographer.

That was weird, I thought. I felt like she was sending me a message. One that didn't arrive fully formed in my inbox. I tried to shake off the growing suspicion that there was something larger in play. I switched the engine off and stepped out of the car.

Students outside the school entrance leaned over mobile phones. Some elbowed others when they saw me, and their giggles increased. I pulled my briefcase from the back seat and slammed the car door shut just as two second-year boys approached, heads down, preoccupied with their phones. An alien invasion could have commenced, and they'd remain oblivious to it all.

I heard a familiar voice.

Mine.

'Boys,' I said.

They froze in their tracks. Their heads jerked about like they'd been shocked to find themselves in this reality.

'Sir?' one of them said.

I put out my hand. 'Do you mind?'

He handed over his phone. I sensed that he was on the verge of a panic attack. His phone withdrawal symptoms were already kicking in.

I held up the phone and pressed the play icon. The video featured a block of flats collapsing in a controlled explosion, followed by an inserted clip of me saying, 'It was an accident. There was a spider.'

I handed back the phone before he needed CPR.

'Go on,' I said. 'In with you.' They scampered off into the school.

I noticed that Chris's BMW was parked alongside my car. His was so new that, if it was a child, it would still be in nappies. Mine on the other hand would be old enough not only to be in secondary school but would be actively trying to get someone pregnant. The gleaming chrome finish of his car however was marred by a spray paint design that didn't originate in Bavaria.

'Bastard,' was written in florid lettering.

I guessed that Suzanne was once again demonstrating her flair for artistry.

In fairness, she'd not used the golf club.

Then I saw the off-side mirror.

Peggy

44

Peggy, the school secretary, bumped into me in the hallway. She was dressed in a long skirt and a cardigan that she constantly adjusted when nervous. She clutched a bundle of papers to her chest.

She was close to retirement but was holding out as long as she could because she enjoyed being a thorn in Chris's side far too much.

She point blank refused to do anything for Chris. She said she'd pull her fingernails out before she'd as much as photocopy a piece of paper for him.

Chris had broken the heart of a cousin of hers and she made it her mission to ensure that he got some payback. Chris had talked about sacking her until I pointed out that Peggy alone knew all the computer passwords and buried the notoriously complex records required by the Department of Education in random computer folders, buried deep within other folders. Hackers would find it easier to break into the Pentagon's servers than Peggy's databases.

'Welcome to the madhouse,' she said leaning upstream against students flooding past her.

The first full day back after the summer break was always frenetic. Padlocks for lockers wouldn't lock; something would break down; parents would have to be escorted off the premises after taking endless selfies with their mortified children.

'How's everything on the front lines?' I asked.

'Hanging in there,' she said. 'Chris is in. I'm as surprised as anyone else. I thought we would have to text him in case he'd forgotten the address.'

'Anything else?'

'All quiet on the Western Front,' she said.

This would change when the students settled in. Soon there'd be a queue of them sitting on chairs outside my office, dispatched by teachers for wearing shortened hemlines, swearing or arson.

We cracked down on indiscipline straight away for a school is very much like a nuclear reactor with an unstable core. Several hundred hormonal teenagers crammed under one roof are perpetually on the brink of a chain reaction. Our role is to moderate adolescent fission and avoid the educational equivalent of Chernobyl.

Our history teacher had already confided to me by text that he was already back on the anti-depressants. He said that he was beginning to see merit in the Roman ancient practice of decimation whereby they'd punish rebellious legions by slaughtering one in ten of the soldiers. I replied that I would bring the idea to the next departmental meeting but I'd not hold out much hope.

Just then a black, Kerry calf bounced passed us, mooing loudly.

'I'll get this one,' Peggy said and chased it down the corridor.

Many of the students were from farming backgrounds and often set up elaborate pranks using farm animals. Once Peggy entered her office and found a llama.

I caught the eye of Dervla Kennedy who was heading downstream. She was not happy. Her brood was not about to increase this year.

I wondered if she'd need an orientation.

'Martin,' she said stiffly.

'Dervla,' I said guardedly. I recalled how she'd been less than impressed with my comments while I was under the influence of anaesthesia.

'How are you doing?'

She sniffed. 'Dennis is out of work because of you.'

'What do you mean? Wasn't he a manager in the sho—' I interrupted myself. 'Oh yes. He worked in the shopping centre.'

'He did until you decided to burn it to the ground.'

'It was an accident,' I said. 'There was a spider.'

'We've mouths to feed,' she said peevishly.

I wanted to say that it all could have been avoided if she had gotten Dennis the snip. Then it occurred to me that over one hundred and forty families probably felt the same as Dervla. I'd have to be extra diligent when crossing the street.

'I'm sorry to hear that,' I said.

The door to the principal's office swung open. Normally, I dreaded meeting Chris but this time I was more than happy to see him.

'Sorry, Derv, love,' he said, 'can I grab him if you don't mind? You're looking fabulous by the way. Love the blouse, it really emphasises your—.' He interrupted himself when he caught me glaring at him. 'And you look good too, Martin in that suit,' he added trailing off.

I pushed him back into the office before he could trigger another harassment lawsuit. I closed the door behind me as Dervla stormed off.

'What did we say about personal comments?' I said gruffly. 'We discussed this. Did you not listen to a word I said? Does hashtag "MeToo" mean nothing to you?'

Chris nodded sheepishly as he retreated to his desk and sat down.

'I know, Martin,' he said. 'I was just being nice.'

'You were being you,' I snarled. 'And no one wants that. And, for the love of God, will you stop calling staff "love" or "pet."'

He nodded, chastened, his head bowed.

I took a breath.

'Thanks of course,' I said, 'for the rescue, I thought she might be about to challenge me to a fist fight. She blames me for the fire.'

Chris wasn't interested. The centre didn't sell Paul Costello suits and therefore he could not care less.

I sat down in the chair opposite him.

The desk between us was strewn with unopened envelopes and documents. He had long since given up on the paperwork. If it was that important then I'd be expected to resolve it, which wouldn't happen until the envelopes started having *Urgent, Immediate Attention* or *For Fucks Sake Give to Martin* stamped on the front.

'What are we going to do about the protest out front?' he asked

I sighed. 'We'll sympathise and say we're doing all we can. You know what to say.'

'I think that you can handle this one.'

'You want me to do it?'

Normally Chris would scramble over anyone to get his face in the paper. He adjusted his tie. He seemed flustered. He appeared as if he had slept in his tailor-made suit. The top button on his shirt was undone. He could have done with a shave.

'It's a relief to see you in,' he said. He beamed warmly and this set my antennae quivering.

'What do you mean? I was in last week for the first-years induction.'

'Oh, right.'

Chris had rung in to say he'd be working remotely from his boat and obviously, he'd not checked the roster since.

'I saw your car,' I said. 'Someone tagged you.'

'Oh that. It'll wash off.'

This was a shock. He spent hours keeping it polished. He claimed that there was nothing more beguiling than the aroma of expensive leather. It did ensure that he struck out with the vegan community, but he said that he'd expect no good luck with anyone perpetually hungry anyway.

'You all right?' I asked.

He nodded and I guessed that he didn't really hear me.

'Thanks for letting me borrow yours while you were out,' he said.

'Don't mention it, although the fuel tank was a little fuller when you got it.'

He pulled out an embossed red leather wallet from his jacket, slid out a hundred euro note and handed it to me.

'This cover it?'

This was a first. I never even knew he owned a wallet. He glanced over and caught my look of astonishment.

'What?' he asked.

'Are you okay?' I said sympathetically. I could see that he was in the office in body only. I didn't want to pry, perhaps his worst nightmare was coming true, and he was coming to terms with erectile dysfunction.

He nodded too enthusiastically. 'I think I have flu. What's so strange in me paying my way?'

'Last time you dipped your hand in your pocket, velociraptors walked the earth.'

Suddenly his phone rang with an Ed Sheeran ring tone. He had chosen it as he felt that it not only indicated that somewhere in his chest cavity lurked a heart, but that it suggested that he was woke and current. He picked it from his desk, glanced at the screen and placed it face down.

We listened to the phone play and vibrate for a few moments until the caller cut the connection.

He buried his head in his hands.

'I'm sorry,' he murmured.

A long silence rolled in.

Outside, I could hear the faint sounds of mobile phones playing back memes that ended with me saying, 'There was a spider'.

I decided to seize the initiative. 'If you are worried about Suzanne, I can run into her after work. Ask her again to ease off on the tagging.'

'Cheers,' he said without any enthusiasm. His face remained buried in his hands. 'You think I'm a bad person?'

I thought about it for a few moments. 'On balance,' I said, 'I'd have to say yes.'

'Someone's been at the truth jar,' he said, raising his head to observe me.

I was tired from trying to sleep in rough army blankets, and my patience was wearing thin. Nightmares all too frequently interrupted my sleep. I'd dream of snakes squirming under the duvet or Laura chasing me with a broadsword. Exhaustion had reduced my ability to dissemble.

'You're not exactly Mr Popular,' I said. 'Husbands hate you, the Department wants you gone and it's only a matter of time before a member of the female staff chemically castrates you. I assume the threat of which is the only thing that's causing you to behave. So, on balance, I'd say yes, you're a bad person.'

'I guess there's a fair few that have it in for me. Suzanne, I mean, of course,' he said somewhat forlornly.

'To be fair, you stood her up at the altar.'

'Not my finest hour, I must admit. We all make a mistake or two.'

'Maybe you shouldn't have done it by text.'

'I think I know that now, Martin,' he said. 'I'd like to think I've grown as a person.'

'What's going on?' I asked. I hoped that he'd not ask me about anything remotely located near his prostate.

'It's nothing,' he replied. 'I said it must be the flu.'

He dolefully contemplated the mess that was his desk.

'I was thinking,' he said. 'Maybe we should do the right thing by Ruairi? I hate seeing that commotion outside.'

'Are you serious?' I asked. 'You think there's a commotion now? Wait until the entire teaching staff are on the picket lines. Bengy talked about self-immolation on his turn and I'm not entirely sure he's joking.'

He nodded. 'So there's no way?'

I cleared my throat.

'I'm confident that hell would freeze over before the TUI would agree to have him back. We may not see eye to eye at times but the teachers here really do want what's best for the kids we have.'

He nodded. 'You're right of course.'

'Okay, so I'm presuming you are actually feeling guilty about the salary the Department is paying you,' I clicked open my briefcase. 'If you want to step up, we might look at the curriculum. The Department has some new ideas coming down the line.'

'That would be magic,' he said without enthusiasm. 'I could think of no better thing we could be doing.'

He reached over and fumbled with some documents, although I could tell that he'd have no intention of reading them. His heart was just not in it.

'Is there anything that I can do?' I asked, wondering if I should anonymously slip him a few leaflets on proctology.

'Well, funny you should say that. There is one thing,' he said, his tone slightly brightening.

Here it comes, I thought.

'You probably saw Kyle's car in the staff car park.'

Kyle was the former marine slash teacher who was supposed to have been let go.

I shook my head. 'I can't say I did to be honest.'

'Well, it is. He's up in the science lab as we speak.'

A wave of nausea washed through me. Now we were getting to it. 'You mean no one told him that he was laid off?'

Chris shuffled paper on his desk. 'There probably is a letter in here somewhere for him.'

'Which was not posted?'

'Apparently not.'

'How did this happen?'

'In a funny way, it's kind of your fault.'

'What?'

'It's something that you would have been all over if you had been here.'

'I almost died, Chris,' I said. 'I was run over by a boat, remember?'

'We can bounce blame around all day but in the meantime, we are where we are and he's up in the lab mixing chemicals.'

'So you want me to tell him?'

'You are best of friends, are you not?'

'I shared an All-Ireland ticket with him because I felt sorry for him. That doesn't make us besties.'

Chris shrugged and shuffled some more papers on his desk. He opened a thick, bound departmental publication and peered at it. He picked up a ballpoint pen and clicking on the thrust button caused the ballpoint tip to repeatedly appear and disappear. 'So if you wouldn't mind taking care of it,' he said, glancing up from his desk.

I watched him for a moment. 'I see you reading up on the junior certificate examination,' I said.

'What about it?'

'You do know that they phased that exam out years ago.'

Chris had the grace to look guilty. 'It's more than just the flu,' he admitted.

I crossed my fingers behind my back. I hoped Chris wasn't about to show me a scan of his undercarriage.

'I'm thinking that I'm not cut out for this job,' he admitted.

Like this was news.

'I'm thinking that early retirement might be the way to go.'

He'd dangled this carrot before. I tried to not get my hopes up.

'Are you serious?'

'Yes, I think so.'

'When?'

He placed the pen back on his desk and buried his head in his hands once more. 'Soon, I promise.'

I'd not seen him as distraught before. It wasn't even a patch on the time when he'd heard that Louis Copeland's store for men had burned down.

'He dressed Pierce Brosnan,' he had sniffed, '007 himself.'

'I'll do your dirty work,' I said, 'as long as it's for the last time.'

Chris popped his head up, his face brightening slightly. 'If you're sure?'

He made a sign of the cross that almost caused me to change my mind.

'You know he's killed people?' Chris reminded me to make sure I knew what I was getting into, probably for insurance purposes.

'Not recently as far as I know,' I shrugged. The part of my brain that presses the alarm button must have been on a tea break. I'd filled the void with the image of my name on the office door.

Chris pulled out his hip flask. 'If this helps…'

'I hope I won't need that.'

The part of my brain that operates the alarm button returned from its break asking, what did I miss?

Chris saw the doubt in my face. 'It's probably not true that he killed anyone with a butter knife, you know,' he said.

'He told me he didn't.'

'Well, there you go then,' he beamed.

'It was with a spoon.'

'Take the flask,' he said, and I did.

Kyle

43

I leaned forward over my desk and scrolled through websites on my tablet. I enjoyed being lost on the Internet as it distracted me from my cramped office that also doubled as a utility cupboard. Textbooks and noticeboards lined one wall. The other comprised shelves of cleaning products. If I spent too long in here, I smelled of Dettol.

My mind was unfocused, and I was unable to retain one iota of information about garrottes. I had the families of one hundred and forty former employees of the Golden Island Shopping Centre who would glare at me the way Greenpeace activists view fishermen setting off to club baby seals. I was about to add a trained killer to the list. It wasn't even eleven a.m.

There was a knock on the door.

'Come in,' I said, and Kyle strode in. He sat down on the chair in front of my desk. He idly stirred a mug of coffee with a teaspoon. A metal teaspoon. I wondered where he'd gotten it from as I'd surreptitiously replaced all the staff cutlery with plastic alternatives.

I was acutely aware that he now blocked my exit, the alternative was a two-floor dive from the window behind me onto the asphalt of the school car park.

'Kyle, I thought I asked Peggy to arrange a chat at lunchtime, in the staff room,' I said. There was method in my madness; there were plenty of exits and I could perhaps count on some teachers, hanging around the kettle, to jump in should he start bludgeoning me with Department issued furniture.

I could not help noticing that Kyle's muscles fought to free themselves from his shirt. He had been the subject of several unprintable comments by some of the female staff. I would not be surprised if he jogged five K before breakfast after a session on the bench press.

'She did,' he drawled, 'only I was planning to buy some essential oils during lunchtime. Also, I was kind of hoping to duck out early today.'

That I could help him with.

'I suppose you are wondering why I asked for a chat?' I asked.

'Is it about the PTSD? If so, I can explain.'

Kyle, our soon-to-be former Science Teacher, had only been with us for a year but it was enough to surmise with some certainty that he was going to end up behind bars. Apparently being pinned down by the Taliban can result in anger issues. He'd shoved a parent halfway out a (thankfully opened) window after the man remarked that there were too many blacks in his son's class. I'd warned Kyle that we couldn't put our hands on parents, even if some of them had the mental acuity of a bluebottle but with worse personal hygiene.

Kyle received a second warning after he subbed for a class and was asked how to kill someone. He explained in graphic detail the lethal capabilities of bare hands. He was never asked back to the first-year girls' Civics class.

We thought the matter had blown over but then the judge's son had passed a comment about one of the girl's flat chests. The doctors said that he was minutes away from losing a testicle. The judge looked for Kyle's head until I pointed out that we had caught the incident on security cameras, how his precious son had mocked the girl remorselessly before she lashed out. He only backed down when I told him that I could make the footage go away but I'd hold on to it for safekeeping.

'Explain what exactly about your PTSD?' I asked somewhat apprehensively.

'To be straight with you, Rosie is still not returning my calls and the breathing exercises can only do so much. I have a *Yoga Master* DVD though and I honestly think it's helping.' He breathed in and out deeply. 'I understand that I have many steps before achieving supreme, immutable bliss and sometimes there may be leakage and I apologise for that.'

'Leakage?' I asked.

'I make fists.'

He raised a hand that was squeezed into a tight fist. 'It's a sign to exhale and let the bad energy out.'

He breathed out deeply and his fist uncoiled.

'So I'm telling you, Martin. I'm good. At least I have this job. We all need a purpose that gives us something to cling on to.'

I felt my chances of leaving the office alive dip below fifty per cent.

'I'm delighted that you are getting your life back in order, Kyle,' I said. 'Maybe you'd like some time off to focus?'

He stiffened.

'Are you shitting me? The term has only just begun.'

His body language shifted menacingly, and I began to worry about the teaspoon that he stirred his coffee with.

The silence sat between us. I felt like showing him a picture of Liam and emphasising how I needed to support him.

'You saying this is a done deal?' he said at last.

'Out of my hands, I'm afraid. They think that you and the chemistry lab are a bad mix.'

Kyle nodded. 'I get the way things are,' he said, 'but I would have thought you would have fought for me. As they say here, you're a blow-in as well.'

'I did fight for you,' I said, exaggerating slightly. (I had pointed out that he'd be missed, but I'd said it while frowning.)

'Yeah, right. Like nothing happens here without you signing off on it.'

'I'm sorry,' I said.

I was sorry. Kyle was a good teacher; however, the school had lobbied for a new sports hall before commencing a toxic relationship with a planning official who seemed hell-bent on delaying the build. The man now demanded an environmental impact study, claiming there might be rare newts on the site. It was the same person that Kyle had shoved out the window. It was clear that sacrifices had to be made.

Kyle stood up. I could see his knuckles whiten and he breathed deeply.

'Has this anything to do with Michael Barnes?' he asked.

Michael Barnes was the name of the planning official.

I shrugged. 'It might have been better if you had just tossed him out entirely,' I said.

'A part of me expected this, you know,' he said, visibly calming. 'I have to think of Rosie, what she might think if I suddenly went postal.'

'And I'm sure Rosie would be pleased that you are taking the news like a man. Just like my stepson Liam who thinks the world of me. I can show you a picture of him if you like?'

'Doesn't mean that I'm not pissed,' he said. 'I also know you could have found a way if you put your mind to it.'

I sighed. 'Michael Barnes is a bigot and a moron, and even turned down an offer for his son to travel for free for the school trip to Paris. He really believes the world is flat. He's an engineer. How can I negotiate with someone like that?'

Kyle stared me down until I averted my eyes.

'You shouldn't have given up on me,' he said.

He turned abruptly and left the office without looking back.

That went well I thought. If the situation had gone pear-shaped then I'd have applied field dressings to myself. I'd rather bleed out than face Ella and Sam again.

The morning break was awkward. I entered the staff room and was greeted by abrupt silence. A gaggle of the female teachers had gathered around Kyle, forming a tableau of anguish. A pair were hugging him. Dark expressions were thrown my way. I was clearly at fault for depriving them of their eye candy. Some of the male teachers viewed Kyle enviously. Some wanted to be him, some I suspected wouldn't have thrown him out of bed for eating biscuits.

I thought about protesting and telling them about the newts and how we'd all benefit from the new sports hall. However, I knew that no one would listen. Emotions were high and reasoning with a mini-mob was as pointless as trying to persuade a teenager to donate his phone to the homeless.

I poured tea in silence. Chatter rose behind me as I walked back out the door, mug in hand. I could hear teachers wishing him well. One said, he could call by anytime he liked, I don't think she meant to the school.

I stood at the window of my office and stared out.

Maggie remained at the gates being interviewed by a TV reporter. A camerawoman peered into the eyepiece of a camera recording them, while a sound operator dangled a boom microphone over their heads. Paula was applying lipstick, while Jackie stared forlornly at a pair of shackles that padlocked her to the gate, one hand held up covering her unibrow. I wondered if Maggie had slipped them onto her to prevent her from escaping to the beautician.

A few passers-by dawdled and watched the interview. A man, around my age, stood nearby but appeared to have no interest in the newsmakers. Instead, he stared towards the school.

He wore a beanie hat pulled low over his ears. His padded jacket was worn and white insulation pushed through a cut in the seams. He seemed like someone who slept on the streets. I wouldn't have passed any notice if he hadn't appeared to be staring directly at me.

As I watched, Kyle appeared in the car park below me. He must have moved his car while I was hiding in my office, as it was now parked beside mine at the staff entrance. He placed a box of books on the back seat of his car. He sat in and glared up at my window before I could step back. He waved at me although his face was hardened. This, no doubt, was the last image some Taliban saw before they went to meet their virgins.

Kyle then grabbed hold of his steering wheel, squeezing it tightly until his knuckles whitened. Suddenly his hands came free and he pounded the steering wheel. I guessed exhaling wasn't cutting it this time. The car horn sounded loudly and then remained jammed on, a blaring, several hundred decibel beep. It was so loud that it rattled my windows. The noise seemed to bring him back and I could see him breathing in and out as he regained control. In the meantime, the staff car park began to react spontaneously as car alarms were triggered. Lights flashed in one car after another.

Kyle smiled, visibly calming as he noted the activity about him. He punched the centre of his steering column sharply, silencing his car horn. He accelerated out of the car park, wheels screeching.

Maggie glanced back. The camerawoman's head popped out over the camera eyepiece.

My gaze dropped to my car as its hazard lights began flashing and its alarm kicked in.

'Beep, beep,' it wailed.

I fished in my pocket for my keys.

The man in the beanie hat seemed oblivious to the mayhem and continued to stare at me.

My car then did something that has never happened before during my twenty-plus years of driving.

It exploded.

Cora

42

Inspector Cora Halligan breezed into the car park in a squad car as the fire service blew a layer of foam over my car. She stepped out of the car beside me, and I noticed that she was squeezed into a too-tight hi-vis jacket. She appraised the scene.

Her colleague Garda Julian joined her.

'You again,' Cora said to me, her eyebrow half raised.

We gazed at the ruins of my car.

'We seem to be meeting quite a lot lately,' she said, pulling out a notepad. 'So what happened and please this time, don't blame it on a spider.'

'I sacked someone and I don't think they took it well. A teacher.'

Cora diligently wrote, "Teacher" into her book.

'So which of your teachers would do such a thing?'

'Kyle Gaffney,' I replied. 'He's got the skills and I'm not sure if he's all there.'

I could see the pencil freeze in mid-sentence.

'You need to talk to him,' I said.

'The Yank?' she said, her voice rising in pitch.

'We went to the All-Ireland together.'

'I know who you mean,' she said. 'I was there.'

Garda Julian paused in the middle of taking a selfie with firefighters and the ruins of my car in the background.

'Is he the same one that took six Garda to get into the van in Bundoran?' he piped up.

I hadn't heard of that. It helped explain why Chris made a sign of the cross when mentioning him.

'Ah well, you see. I'm due off shift soon,' she replied. 'And an Armed Response Unit isn't due in town.'

'He might have planted something,' I said angrily and pointed to the smoking wreck. 'He had the morning to do it.'

'You saw him did you?'

'No.'

'So now we're entering the area of speculation, Martin,' Cora replied, somewhat frostily.

'He's got explosives experience. He could create a device based on any number of household chemicals and kitchen appliances.'

Cora shrugged.

'If we find a toaster anywhere in there. We'll let you know. It's a job for forensics. No question.'

'You have to speak with him,' I said.

'I'll have one of the lads look into it,' Cora said and nodded towards Julian watching the last of flames die out.

'In your shite you will,' Julian said in a low voice, as he caught her look.

'We might start with a letter,' Cora said. 'In the meantime, we'll box up what we can and send the lot to Phoenix Park ourselves.'

She was referring to the location of the Irish forensics' laboratories.

'So no CSI then?' I asked.

'We don't call them that here,' she replied. 'They're Scenes of Crime Officers and that would mean calling Dublin. Why do that when we might just be looking at faulty wiring?'

She reached down and picked up a piece of glass at her feet that still had a yellow National Car Test sticker attached.

'See this is well out of date. You were overdue a service. The NCT catches these things all the time.'

'So you reckon a faulty fuse or something caused this?' I asked incredulously.

'I'm saying not to jump to conclusions,' Cora replied.

We watched as the camera crew filmed us.

'They were quick,' Cora said.

'They were already here,' I said. 'Maggie was protesting at the gates. It was all caught on live TV.'

'I know. I was watching. She wanted to make the news, I guess she got her wish,' Cora said thoughtfully. 'Still a bit of a coincidence that she was here.'

Cora turned and noticed a pallid-faced Chris sitting nearby on a chair. Some teachers gathered around him. Someone thrust a mug of tea into his hands. A blanket was thrown over him.

'I wasn't told there were casualties,' she said.

I shrugged. 'Chris is having a panic attack. He gets stressed deciding which tie to put on. Having explosive devices go off on the premises is well outside his comfort zone.'

'What do you think, Guard?' Chris called out. 'No chance it was just an accident?'

Cora glanced at the car engine that sat smoking on the roof of the school.

'Too soon to say,' she answered. 'We'll put it down as suspicious until we know more.'

An ambulance pulled into the yard. Ella and Sam stepped out. They saw me and exchanged glances. Ella rolled her eyes. Sam handed her a ten-euro note.

I pointed listlessly towards Chris.

They trundled a gurney past me without comment.

'So do you know of anyone else who might want to hurt you?' Cora asked.

'Apart from Kyle?' I replied.

'Apart from Kyle,' she said.

A nagging doubt started to grow somewhere in my mind.

There was a growing list of suspects. Maggie would do just about anything for Ruairi. She could decide that the intimidation route might be worth exploring as haranguing was getting her nowhere. Could her appearance just be a coincidence as Cora said?

I watched as Ella and Sam attended to Chris.

I'd put one hundred and forty people out of work.

My wife had developed an interest in lethal weapons.

'You might need a bigger notebook,' I said.

Cora reached into a pocket and slid a card into my hand.

'That's my number if you have anything to add. I could tell you that I've no problem in you ringing me any time but I'd be lying unless a crime is in actual progress.'

'Office hours then.'

'That's it. Julian will take a statement off you.'

Cora walked over to the smouldering car and bent down to examine it closely, poking debris with the tip of a pencil.

Ella turned to face me.

I braced for the onslaught.

'Say, Martin,' she called out, 'can I ask you a question?'

'Go ahead.'

'Will you be around next week? It's only like, Sam and I were thinking of taking a few days off.'

Sam grinned and fed Chris some oxygen via a mask. 'You might text your movements in the meantime,' he said. 'We could be circling the block.'

Ella laughed and entered something into a clipboard.

'Don't forget, Martin, the number's still nine-nine-nine,' she said.

I turned my back on them and faced the crowd that had gathered outside the main gates, gawking at the smouldering wreck of my car. The one exception was the man with the beanie hat who stared directly at me.

'Hello,' a voice wailed out. Heads turned. Jackie held up her chains. In the excitement, she had been forgotten about. 'A little help here,' she said. 'I have to wee.'

I looked back but the man in the beanie hat was nowhere to be seen.

Suzanne

41

As a newly designated pedestrian, I took the bus into town. My car was in more pieces than a Pamplona china shop that had left the door open. I hadn't spoken to Laura yet. I had written off her car and now mine had blown up. To paraphrase Lady Bracknell, to lose one Toyota, Mr Worthing, may be regarded as a misfortune, to lose both looks like carelessness.

I was about to step through the front door of Suzanne Mulvey & Co Solicitors when some instinct made me turn around. I hesitated in the doorway as pedestrians streamed by me. I noticed the top of a familiar beanie hat getting closer in the crowd. I waited; people passed revealing the hat… was worn by a man whom I'd never seen in my life before. I guessed the manufacturers made more than one.

I rolled my eyes. I was being paranoid.

I felt stupid. I should just go home. I shouldn't have rung Suzanne to tell her about the car bomb and that I wanted to chat.

Then again.

My car had blown up.

How many people are on first name terms with the crews of the ambulance services?

It's not paranoia if they really are out to get you.

That's when I caught a reflection off the plate glass window of a man standing across the street.

The man in the beanie hat, from outside the school, held a takeaway mug of coffee in one hand and made no effort to break my gaze.

He grinned at me as I quickly stepped through the office door.

Suzanne met me as I entered and was about to greet me when I put my fingers to my lips, silencing her.

I walked straight into her conference room.

She followed me, a bemused expression on her face as I hurried across the room to stand with my back to the wall beside a window.

'Look,' I said. 'Outside.'

I stayed hidden from the street and pulled on the cord that opened the blinds. Suzanne moved to stand beside me and peered out.

'What am I looking at?' she said.

'There's someone following me,' I said. 'He's out there now. Drinking coffee.'

'Who? Oh, I see,' she said.

'You see him?' I said, pleased at having a witness.

'Oh yes. Very suspicious. The whole black look and all. The perfect cover too.'

I slowly raised my head and peered out. The stranger was gone. A priest stood on the pavement speaking into his mobile phone, a coffee in his other hand.

'So you think Father Delaney is out to get you?'

'Don't be stupid,' I said.

'You think this goes all the way to the Vatican?' she said grinning.

'I know what I saw,' I said.

'Okay sit down,' she said, and I did.

She poured me a whiskey. Heck, I was not driving and I needed something. My hands trembled. What if I had driven out of the school with the device attached? What if the device had been planted earlier? I shuddered at the number of potholes that I'd driven through to get to work. I recalled stories of RUC officers who had driven around with faulty bombs attached to their vehicles for weeks.

I had filled in Suzanne on the phone about the explosion and how I needed some advice. She came straight to the point.

'You don't actually think Kyle had anything to do with this?'

'He could have. He has the skills and he was more than a little pissed off at me for showing him the door.'

'But you don't just feel it.'

'I guess that's it. I had thought of Maggie Geraghty-Philbin. She has a knack for getting into cars and I would not put anything past her.'

'So you think that she'd go this far, just to get her child back into mainstream education?'

'I'd not rule it out,' I replied. 'The woman is mad at me enough. She told me that she'd be welcoming me back – maybe this is what she meant?'

'And that was before you ran her over and demolished her livelihood.'

'It was her or the nuns.'

Suzanne sighed. 'I wouldn't be surprised if she takes it personally. Of all people to run over, you had to mow down Ginger Reagan's cousin.'

I felt the blood drain from my face. 'She's Ginger's cousin?'

I'd forgotten that there was a connection. Ginger was a dissident Republican with fingers in many pies. He was rumoured to be involved with everything from diesel laundering to arms smuggling. Everyone knew that a car dealership in the town was owned by him. No one missed a car payment there. Ever.

The decision to avoid running over the Girl Guides was beginning to seem ill-judged.

'I forgot that she was connected,' I whispered.

'However, it can't be him,' she said.

'Why not?'

'He is still abroad, for one thing. Spain, I hear. Has to stay under the radar. Money from a cash-in-transit robbery vanished into thin air and he was in the frame for it. He would end up in jail if he reappeared in the town.'

'That's reassuring.'

'Besides, it makes no sense for him to do this. It's too public. A car bomb? Really? It would be like skywriting the IRA is back and the peace deal is over. The Garda would crack down, big time. Anyone who looked at them funny would end up on remand. No one would be able to shift a litre of dodgy diesel without a tail from Special Branch. Jail would be the least of his problems, as some dissidents might take it into their heads to deal with him, quietly in-house, with the matter settled on waste ground. Only a madman would rock the boat.'

'Maybe it was only meant to let everyone think it was the IRA?' I said slowly.

'I see where you're going with this. Some Loyalists and dissidents would love it if the Troubles kicked off again,' Suzanne mused aloud.

She picked up the whiskey bottle and placed it on the conference table in front of me, before sitting down on the other side of the table. I poured myself a glass.

'Oh that's wonderful that is, so I might have Loyalists *and* the IRA after me,' I said.

'What it boils down to is this. Why you?'

'If I knew that, you'd be the first to know.'

'You're English. You'd tell me if you were MI5?'

'Yes, Suzanne, I've spent all these years in the centre of Ireland because it's a hotbed of political activity.'

'So that's a "no" then.'

'What do you think?'

'It's my job to ask the tough questions,' Suzanne said.

'I'm not a spy, all right.'

'So who was that following you?'

'You believe me now?'

'I never said I didn't.'

My head was wrecked.

I'd come to Suzanne for reassurance and now discovered that those with grudges against me could potentially include terrorists. And not the good kind. 'I don't know,' I said. 'I've never seen him before until today.'

'Anyone else, apart from the Golden Island workers you put on the dole, have any grudges against you?'

She'd almost asked the same question as Cora. I bit back an urge to mention my dear wife. It would be more than suspicious to mention her name and then for her to come to a sticky end.

'There's a care worker who has it out for me. Although I think a throwing knife is more his style.'

I told her about the disgruntled former student of mine.

'I think that's the extent of it,' I said.

Suzanne scribbled something into a legal notepad.

I drank a shot quickly and Suzanne poured me a refill.

'Let's narrow it down,' I said. 'What does Ginger look like? Do you have a picture?'

'You're thinking of the man you saw?'

'Yes.'

'I don't have a picture to hand, but Ginger Reagan does have one distinguishing feature.'

'Which is?'

She sighed. 'That H-Dip you got for teaching, you didn't download it, did you? His actual name is Peter. Ginger is his nickname.'

Dawn broke.

'He's got red hair,' I said, catching on.

'Exactly. Bright red. You could make him out from a mile away. In fog. Does the man that followed you have red hair?'

'I don't know. He was wearing a hat.'

'Which means nothing.'

'Or the opposite. If his hair was as bright as you say, would he not cover it?'

'True.'

I was back to square one. I had no clue who might be after me. I knew we'd fallen behind in the Credit Union loan, but they tended to write form letters and didn't yet branch out into improvised explosive devices.

'I'd remain careful but you have one thing going for you.'

'What do you mean?'

'Those devices are very complex. You're certainly talking about some wiring, maybe electronics, maybe even a mercury tilt switch. That takes a certain set of skills. Which narrows the list of suspects down. Find the person with those skills, there's your bomber.'

'Fair point.'

'It's good that I don't charge you.'

'Why is that?'

'I'd have to insist on payment in advance.'

'Not funny.'

'Maybe just a little.'

Laura

40

Laura was standing on a small step ladder in the hallway when I entered through the front door. She adjusted a brass light over a framed picture, pulled a cordless screwdriver from her tool belt and fastened the light fitting to the wall.

'That should do it,' she said, and vanished back into the utility room off the kitchen. 'I'm going to throw the fuse. Give me a shout if it's working.'

I heard a click from the utility room as she flicked a switch on the fuse board.

'Nope,' I said. 'It's still off.'

She reappeared and pulled a drawstring that dangled underneath the new picture light. The light flickered into life, illuminating a framed photograph of her secondary school class in 80's era dresses, and tuxedos for a graduation ball. It had been carefully snipped from a local newspaper and contained the headline *All Glammed Up for Athlone Debs.*

'There,' she said. 'That's saved us a few bob. It was on special offer in B&Q and it just begged me to take it.'

'Good job,' I said.

'How was work?' she asked and retreated to the kitchen. She unhooked her utility belt and pushed it into a cupboard. She snapped the stepladder shut and carried it into the utility room.

I entered the kitchen.

'I sacked Kyle which means we might get a sports hall this century. Oh, and my car blew up,' I said.

She wandered back in from the utility room.

'What was that?'

'I was telling you about work.'

'Hold that thought,' she said. 'Be a love and put on the kettle. I'm going to have a quick shower and change. Brenda wants to go out and she needs a wingman.'

Was Brenda sending me an oblique signal? Her patience must be running out. She wasn't going to wait around forever.

I nodded as Laura stepped into the hallway and ran up the stairs. I followed and stopped at her latest handiwork. 'Sure,' I said, staring at the picture light. It was a neat job.

I pulled the cord, and it turned off, pulled again and on it came. *Very professional*, I thought.

I admired the workmanship of the installation. A neat job indeed.

Laura sat opposite me fifteen minutes later on a high stool at the kitchen island. She looked good in a dress; her love handles had vanished without a trace. She wrapped her hands around a mug. I also had a mug of steaming tea in my hand. Nothing separated us but a packet of digestives.

'Car bomb?' she said after I repeated the news of the day.

'I'm going out on a limb here, but the car exploded.'

She thought about it for a moment. 'Who would want to do that to your car?'

'I don't think that was the point. Everyone likes a Toyota. They run forever.'

'Everyone likes them except maybe Volvo or BMW,' she said.

I threw her a filthy look. 'I think that whoever planted the device,' I said, 'is unlikely to be the board of Volkswagen or General Motors. Someone hoped that I'd be in it.'

She nodded. 'If someone wanted to kill you then they'd have fitted a device hooked up to a mobile phone, waited for you to get in before calling the number.'

'You seem to know a lot about the subject.'

She shrugged. 'What can I say? I read a lot on nights. Certainly, a trembler, which is motion sensitive, is rather indiscriminate. What if you gave a lift to the local bishop or a set of orphans? I'm saying that if I was to do it, I'd use a remote.'

'That's reassuring,' I said. 'On no level whatsoever.'

'You wouldn't want to see clergy or children die, would you?' she asked.

'Or me. So we're looking at a bombmaker with a social conscience?' I replied.

Laura sighed. 'Maybe we are getting ahead of ourselves. You don't look after cars. Maybe it was just a fuel leak meeting a discarded cigarette butt.'

She made a lot of sense. Ireland has no-smoking regulations within the workplace. Our teachers did have an outdoor area to smoke but many would just sneak a quick ciggie outside the staff entrance.

'And if it was deliberate,' she said, gazing at me, 'who would want to do that to you?'

I told her what I'd said to Suzanne. Spoke of the hundred and forty shopping centre employees now signing on. Added Paul the care worker. I even mentioned the Loyalists.

She dunked a digestive.

'Well?' she said. 'Waste not, want not.'

She nibbled on the dampened biscuit, and I lifted my mug to take a sip.

'At least, I'm not on your list,' she grinned.

'Should you be?' I asked innocently. 'I'd say you could have put a device together, you've the skills. You also seemed to have thought it through which is kind of a red flag in my book.'

'It wouldn't be that hard,' she admitted, 'but wouldn't the spouse be the number one suspect?'

'Statistically, you might be right.'

'All it would take would be for forensics to match a thumbprint of mine to a partial on a circuit board and I'd be bunched.'

'True,' I said.

'On the other hand, if I'd found that spider and didn't warn you, and you had lost control at speed, now that could have been put down as an accident.'

'It could have been the perfect murder,' I said slowly.

'That you brought on yourself.'

Had Laura just confessed?

'It was never going to work,' I said. 'Too many things could go wrong. Like me getting off the motorway and slowing down.'

'It only has to work once,' she said, a dark expression crossing her face.

'It was a stupid plan,' I said.

'Says the man that blew up his shed, and almost himself with it.'

'That was an accident.'

'Exactly, accidents happen. Even bizarre ones.'

She smiled again. The picture of innocence.

As the years of wedded bliss rolled on, I thought I'd figured out how to tell when Laura lied to me. I was no longer so certain. I thought again about all the reasons for wanting her gone. The insurance, the pay-outs. She had the same motives.

'What are you thinking?' Laura asked.

'That you could do with another top-up,' I said as I raised the teapot and she thrust out her mug.

'You know me so well,' she said.

'I thought that I did.'

'I see that you used the teapot,' she said.

'I just saw it there,' I replied, 'thought we might as well use it.'

I wasn't drinking anything she was not drinking.

She smiled. I so wanted to believe that she had nothing to do with my car learning how to fly.

She pulled on her coat and glanced at her watch.

'I'd better head,' she said, 'seeing as I can't borrow your car.'

'Speaking of which, what's the story with yours?' I asked. 'The insurance come through yet?'

'I wouldn't hold my breath. You filled in the policies. I asked you to make them comprehensive, but you knew better.'

I'd expected her to throw that jab at me but there was no malice in it. In fact, she appeared like she couldn't be happier. Maybe she was thrilled that I hadn't been transmogrified into a red mist when my car exploded.

'Third party was cheaper,' I said but still, she didn't turn on me.

'Don't worry about it,' she said.

That was easy for her to say. I was the one facing the prospect of heading to work on a school bus.

'I may have this mess sorted,' she said.

'How do you mean?'

'It's a surprise,' she said as she grabbed her handbag and walked towards the front door.

'What do you mean?'

'Of course, I could tell you but where's the fun in that?'

I watched her through the kitchen window as Brenda pulled up in her car. Laura jumped in and they were gone.

I poured the rest of the tea down the sink and approached the bin to dispose of the teabags. I removed the lid of the teapot and placed my foot on the bin's pedal. I froze and stared at the bin.

I gulped, feeling like a rookie soldier who'd just placed his boot on a landmine. I pressed down gently on the pedal and the lid swung open.

Mrs Keena

39

The sky had begun to darken when I pulled our wheelie bin down the side of the house and pushed it out onto the road. The estate streetlights flickered on. I glanced about. It was time that I faced Mrs Keena.

I walked up her path and raised my finger to push the doorbell, but the door swung open before it made contact.

'What do you want?' she demanded, revealing the former Late Tom curled up and purring in her arms.

'I came to ask about your cat,' I said.

'He's very upset if you must know,' she said and raised him out in front of her. He snarled at me and extended his claws before throwing a fast swipe at my face.

'Oww,' I exclaimed as I felt my cheek for the tell-tale signs of blood.

'I knew that you had something to do with it,' she said triumphantly.

'That proves nothing,' I said.

'Cats don't lie,' she said.

I was certain now that she had nothing but suspicions. I had fortunately remained in the dead zone of the garden cameras when burying her cat.

However, she seemed to believe whatever the cat had to say.

I wondered if cats could be bribed. And the response came in an instant. Of course, they could. Cats are much like teenagers in that way, their loyalty is short-lived and transactional. I'm not sure if Liam would walk over my dead body to turn on a light switch, but I'd be less certain if he required my car keys.

I felt I could win Tom over. I'd just have to add tins of tuna to the shopping.

I decided I had better be honest. Maybe she had images of me from a satellite.

'I thought he was dead,' I admitted. 'He wasn't moving when I found him. I wasn't sure what to tell you.'

'So an accident was it? Another one. Maybe you just hate cats.'

'I don't hate cats,' I said.

'So go on then, apologise,' she said after a moment.

'I'm sorry,' I said.

'Not to me you moron.'

I bent down and looked the cat in the eye, glad that there was no one to witness this.

'I'm sorry, Tom,' I said.

'For…' Mrs Keena added.

'For burying you?' I finished.

'For not taking him to the vet,' Mrs Keena snarled.

'That too.'

'It's not me you should be addressing,' she said and held the hissing cat out towards me.

'Sorry for not bringing you to the vet,' I said. 'Next time—'

She yanked Tom quickly back.

'What do you mean by that?'

'I meant that I know what to do if anything else happens and I am sure it will not.'

Mrs Keena nodded uncertainly. 'What are you up to, Martin?'

'I don't know what you mean,' I said.

'I have my eye on you, you know,' she said. 'It's not just what you're up to in the shed—'

'Workshop,' I interrupted.

'Whatever, you're up to something. Why else would anyone be watching you?'

I felt a chill run through me. 'Excuse me?'

'You think I don't know what's happening in this estate?'

I was thinking of the man I had seen standing outside Suzanne's office.

'You saw a man? Was he wearing a beanie-type cap? About my height.'

Mrs Keena shook her head. 'There's someone else after you as well? And you wonder why cats don't like you.'

'Who are you talking about?'

I wanted to add, you crazy old witch but that probably would just end in Mrs Keena's door being slammed in my face.

'If you are running a crack house then no good will come of it.' She held out her cat again and he snarled. 'Tom's got good instincts, you know.'

I tried to remain calm and direct her back from crazy town.

'Who do you mean, is watching me?' I said through clenched teeth.

'I'm not taking names. Lord God. What are you into, Martin?'

'Please, Mrs Keena,' I pleaded. 'Who have you seen? Can you describe him?'

'It's not a him.'

'A woman?'

'It's not a woman either. It's two men.'

'Two men?'

'That's what I said.'

'And you didn't think to tell me?'

'I don't like to stick my nose in,' she said.

I resisted the urge to commence a murder spree there and then.

'Can you describe them?'

'And besides, you buried my cat,' she continued, 'so you're not exactly someone that I'd throw myself on a grenade for.'

'And I've apologised. To you, to him. I apologised,' I shrieked.

'I'm not sure that I like your tone,' she said about to turn. 'And for sure, Tom doesn't appreciate it.'

'Mrs Keena and *Tom*, I am truly sorry for any offence caused,' I said.

She hesitated.

'I'd watch out for that thin one,' she said.

'Thin one? What thin one?'

'The one in charge. Tanned, foreign I'm guessing '

'Foreign?'

Beanie hat man was pale.

'The other man has a bandage on his head. Works out, but it's more gym muscle than real muscle, if you know what I mean. I don't want to cast aspersions but I'd say he's on steroids.'

I realised that Mrs Keena was not focusing on me. Her gaze was directed over my shoulder.

'They're here now?' I said, my voice dropping an octave.

'They've been here since 18.25.'

The sudden chill down my spine dropped a few more degrees.

I slowly turned around. I followed her eyeline and saw a silver Toyota Avensis parked up the street. Two men sat inside the darkened interior, hunched down. There were white number plates on the front that began with letters. Number plates in the Irish Republic began with numbers denoting the year of registration. This suggested that the car was from Northern Ireland or mainland Britain.

'They went away for an hour,' Mrs Keena said. 'Maybe it was their dinner time.'

'You sure?' I stammered. 'Maybe it's a television licence inspector waiting on Joe Dealy.'

'Nonsense,' she said. 'That's not how it works. Besides Joe paid off his licence in full last Thursday.'

'I'm not even going to ask how you know that,' I said.

'There's been a lot of robberies, lately,' she said. 'Willowpark and Bloomfield were both done last night. Someone has to take this job seriously.'

'You don't seem that worried?' I said.

'Why should I be? It's you they want. My house is well secure, I'd like to see anyone try a break in.'

It was true. I had discovered that her home defences were modelled on Fort Knox. In the event of a zombie apocalypse, then I'd be knocking on her door (with cat food).

Part of me wanted to run up the street, wrench open the car door and demand to know what the men wanted. The other part of me saw that scenario ending up with me being slapped.

Or them just laughing a lot.

The car engine abruptly started and the car reversed at speed, did a U-turn and drove off out of the estate.

'I guess they're not on your cameras?' I asked,

Mrs Keena shook her head. 'Clever so and sos,' she said. 'They always park just outside their range.'

'It might have been useful to get the registration number.'

'Who says that I haven't their number?' Mrs Keena said and held up her phone. 'Don't I have them on this?'

I nearly kissed her – nearly – very nearly.

Laura

38

Every passing car in the estate shook me awake. I dozed in an armchair that I'd dragged to the sitting room window. My hands tensed on Laura's bow and arrow firmly gripped on my lap. If someone tried to break in then I hoped that I could impale one intruder, if they were slow enough then I might have time to reload. I'd used the card that Cora had given me to ring her, but she hadn't answered. I left her a message about my stalkers and asked her to call me when she clocked in.

Liam was staying over with some girl he'd met online leaving me alone in the house. I'd given up on sleep and instead spent the night standing guard. Dark thoughts occupied my mind. Was the purpose of Laura's night out to create an alibi? Was this the surprise she referred to?

I watched the sunrise, but there was no sign of the men in the Toyota.

My eyes had closed by the time I heard a car pull up into our front yard. My eyelids shot open like roller blinds on an industrial spring. I eased the curtains slightly apart revealing a new Honda SUV in our driveway. I ducked back and held an arrow to the string of the bow. I heard the car door open and close followed by footsteps that crossed to the front door. I slid into the hallway, keeping my back to the wall, the bow and arrow held in the at-ready position. I would not go quietly.

I heard a noise. Someone was quietly fiddling with the lock.

I tensed the string on the bow and eased the drawstring back.

Suddenly the door swung open revealing Laura.

'Hello,' she said in surprise. She noticed the bow in my hand. 'Here now,' she said. 'Don't even think of using that thing indoors.'

'I couldn't find the sword,' I said.

My arrow drooped.

'I thought you were someone else,' I said.

She yawned. 'Can't I enjoy just one girl's night out without you getting all weird on me?'

I walked back to the window to examine the car.

'Is that the surprise you were on about?'

She followed me into the room and nodded.

'It's unreal.'

'What do you want me to say, it's nice? Want to return it before the owner finds out it's missing?'

'Thanks,' she said. 'However, I'm keeping it.'

'What do you mean?'

'I've never owned a new car in my life until now.'

'Did you win the lottery or something?' I asked. 'You know the oil tank needs filling? Or were you planning on driving south for the winter?'

'Relax, Martin,' she said. 'I traded in my car.'

'The one I parked in the shop? The one that burned up like the rest of the shopping centre?'

'There was a scrappage offer and I took it.'

'How could you have traded that in? It gave junk a bad name.'

'What can I say, the garage thinks highly of front-line workers.'

'That was generous since it had the driving potential of a paperweight.'

'They put it through as having one careful lady owner. Which is not exactly a lie. It meant that I got a great deal.'

'So nothing underhand there at all.'

'So they exaggerated. Maybe we should break a few rules? How has it worked out for us so far by playing nice?'

She had a point.

'How can we afford it?' I said, shrugging.

'It's a finance offer. It's cheaper to run than the yolk I had; it won't break down every five minutes. I know that I'd need to make a final bulk payment after five years but sure a lot can happen between now and then.'

'You might have told me,' I said as I fell back into my armchair.

'Life is for living, Martin. I realise that now.'

'You mean after my near-death experience?'

'It was a consideration.'

'So do I get to drive it?'

'Ah well, you are not insured yet. Also, your record lately has not been the best so I'd not hold up much hope – at least not until I get the actuary to stop laughing.'

'I take your point.'

'You want a look?'

She vanished back out the door.

I struggled back out of the armchair and followed her outside.

The car gleamed. A sticker on the rear window read, "Another Happy Owner – Reagan's Sales & Service" followed by the dealership phone number.

I could see Mrs Keena lurking on her side of the hedge, no doubt surmising that the brand-new car was purchased on the proceeds of my activities in a cartel.

'Brenda gave me a lift out to collect it this morning, once she was sure she was sober enough to drive. I followed her home. We're going for a spin.'

'I'll get my coat,' I said.

'I meant Brenda and me,' she said as Brenda appeared on the path.

'Hi, Martin,' she said, but she only had eyes for the car. 'Isn't this amazing?' She pulled open the passenger door and sat into the cab. 'This is bigger than my first apartment.'

Laura smiled at me. 'I'll take you out later but I promised Brenda.'

Brenda pressed the car horn and almost blew out my eardrums.

Birds flew from distant rooftops.

'Come on,' she called out. 'We have to cruise down Main Street, check out the talent.'

Laura spoke up. 'Or we could just go shopping.'

'Yes,' Brenda said, 'that too.'

Laura climbed into the car.

'Catch you later,' she said and started the engine. It roared into life. She slammed the car door shut and backed quickly out of the driveway. With another roar of the motor, she drove out of the estate just as a Garda car arrived from the opposite direction.

Cora

37

Inspector Cora Halligan settled into my armchair.

'Was that Laura I saw on the way in?' Cora asked.

I nodded.

'Nice wheels,' she said.

'Better than that last thing she was driving,' I said.

'Let me guess, insured it for ten times its actual value? I've seen it before.'

'No,' I said, although I wondered the same thing.

'People don't realise that insurers only pay out for the book value so good luck claiming your junker is equivalent to a new Porsche.'

'I'll remember that,' I said. 'So to what do I owe the pleasure?'

'I got your message,' she said and sat back in the seat. 'About the lads you saw. We're following it up, trying to figure out who they are and what they are up to. Next time try to get a better picture.'

Mrs Keena's photographic skills wouldn't leave Annie Leibovitz feeling threatened. The men were barely more than dark silhouettes in the screenshot that I'd forwarded to Cora.

'The number plate was nice and clear, though.'

Cora smiled wanly. 'Would you believe we thought of that?'

'Well?'

'We got a match,' she said milking it for all it was worth.

'Okay?'

'The number plate belongs to a vehicle owned by Ed Sheeran.'

I didn't see that coming.

'The singer? What? Why?'

'Maybe you pirated his *Zero* album, and he doesn't like to work for free.'

In fact, there was a copy on my computer upstairs. Pop stars really took piracy seriously.

'Relax,' Cora grinned. 'We are fairly confident whoever was here used false plates.'

I nodded. 'That also makes sense.'

'On the other hand, if Ed's crew is stalking you, call me at once. I saw him playing in Dublin and Galway and I'd love an autograph.'

'I don't think you're taking this seriously.'

She sighed. 'If it makes you happy, I will make sure a car passes up here a few times a day. It's a small town, we will find them.'

She was probably right to rule out a multi-award-winning singer as my potential stalker but regardless, I was deleting my *Zero* and *Multiply* copies.

Cora's smile faded. 'The results came back about your car. It was a bomb.'

'I've some first-years who could tell you that.'

'What can I say, Martin?' she said. 'The job I'm in is all about saying nothing until someone signs off on the paperwork.' She leaned forward. 'We found parts of a device that are not supposed to be there. Certainly, nothing that Toyota ever made.'

'Don't look at me,' I said. 'My insurance is void if I modify the vehicle in any way.'

'This is more than some go-faster stripes and a snap-on exhaust.'

I could tell she wanted to tell me something but was limited about what she could share.

'So are we talking about something like a mercury tilt switch, Semtex?' I asked.

As someone who had grown up in England, I was more than familiar with newspaper and television coverage of The Troubles. I knew the language of violent death and how some had met their maker.

'I don't think I can answer that,' she said.

'No phone parts then?'

'Maybe. Why do you ask?'

'Someone told me that it would be less discriminate if it was remotely operated.'

'They would be right but that's no excuse. It went off anyway, didn't it? Someone could have been killed.'

'So you did find a phone?'

She nodded faintly. 'I can't comment officially,' she said. 'But let's say that the device has some Republican hallmarks, although the remote components are a new development that seemed pure Afghanistan.'

'So I was targeted by an IRA-Taliban combo?' I said, sitting bolt upright.

'No, that's not likely. There's a peace deal, remember. It might be an attempt to throw suspicion on dissidents.'

The remark was similar to what I'd told Suzanne.

'But why me? Wouldn't they go after a politician?'

'I'm afraid I can't help you there. Unless there's something you're not telling me, we're at a dead end.'

I did not want to mention how Laura had skills and motives. Cora might dig deeper and wonder at the half-pounder cannon that I had built.

'I've racked my brain and can't think of any reason for someone to come after me.'

'You sure?'

I shrugged. 'I refereed the Gerald's versus the Park under fifteens match and not everyone agreed with the outcome.'

'Hardly justifying a car bomb?'

'You know how passionate the Park lads are about their GAA.'

'True, but I think we can safely rule them out.' Cora leaned in close. 'I can tell you that you have Harcourt Street burning the midnight oil.'

'What do you mean?'

'That's where the CSB— the Crime & Security Branch is located. You're on their radar it seems. Unofficially.'

'What would the CSB want with me?' I asked. 'Barney's dog license is out of date but it's surely not that big of a deal.'

'Between ourselves, the Department of Foreign Affairs called in the British ambassador and demanded to know if they were running any covert operations in the county.'

'What?'

She leaned back. 'They denied all knowledge, but of course, they would.'

I whitened. 'They think I'm MI5?'

Spies in Ireland rarely lived to obtain their pension. When Ireland was under British rule before independence, spies were unearthed regularly. That's what you get when you train British agents in spy craft for years but then employ local sympathisers as secretaries, who required no more skills than the ability to steam open top-secret envelopes.

'Suzanne asked me the same question,' I said. 'I also told her the same thing; you are out of your mind if you think I am working for the security services.'

'For what it's worth, I don't think you're a spy.'

'Thanks,' I said, somewhat disappointed that she didn't think I had it in me.

I remained worried. When I eventually replaced my car, I'd be forever nervous about switching on the engine.

'So are the CSB watching me?' I asked.

'If they are, you'd never know it. However, I don't think so. The powers that be recognise the benefit of having eyes on the ground. I grew up here. I know where the bodies are buried.'

I shot her a baffled look.

'Not literally I hasten to add. I am just doing some fieldwork. No doubt we'll solve it and no doubt someone else will get the credit. We can't get too excited; it has the potential to be political. No one wants to throw petrol on that particular fire.'

I nodded. I got it. Peace deals were a fragile thing, there would not be a security blanket thrown over the town. It explained the apparent lack of interest when my car blew up and why no detectives had called by. There was no question of any exhaustive investigation. I was on my own.

'No one wants to rock the boat,' I said.

Cora shrugged. 'I've been instructed to consider this as a local matter. Our newly elected minister wouldn't be impressed if his hometown was found to be a hotbed of Republican activity.'

'I do hope that if I'm whacked it won't embarrass anyone. Heaven forbid.'

Cora had the grace to appear chastised. 'Our esteemed member of the Dáil has threatened fire and brimstone on anyone breaking the peace deal on his watch.'

'So I'm safe?'

'We'll keep an eye out.'

That wasn't the response that I wanted to hear.

'Thanks,' I said, thinking that I'd need to get way more arrows if I had to face off against a pair of dissidents armed with AK47s.

'To be honest, we're running into brick walls on this. I mean you've no enemies really, apart from Maggie Geraghty-Philbin.'

'We all know she's nuts.'

'Maybe so but turning her shop into a car park and then burning it to the ground hasn't played well with her family. She could have reached out for help.'

'You mean Ginger Reagan? We can rule him out. I heard that he was in Spain.'

'Except...'

I could see that she was struggling. 'Except. The National Surveillance Unit doesn't think he's in the wind. There have been possible sightings. He might be back after all.'

'You mean back in Ireland?'

'Just rumours and conjectures at this stage. However – you've never met him – it's not like he has anything against you personally. That is unless Maggie asked him to ramp up the pressure.'

'A bomb seems extreme.'

'Her petitions and letters got her nowhere. Are you convinced that she's not brought it up to the next level?'

I recalled the way that she watched where I parked. How she said that she'd do anything for her son. Maybe the bomb was supposed to go off without me in it as a warning?

'I'd not rule her out, I guess.'

'Best to keep an open mind.'

'When was he last seen?' I asked.

'Someone matching his description was spotted a few days ago, in Dublin. He was gone by the time the ERU kicked in the door.'

'So how long was he in the country?'

'He doesn't file his travel plans with us, Martin. Be assured, it makes no sense for him to come here. He knows we're looking for him and that if we catch him that he will be back on E Landing, Portlaoise before he knows what hit him.' Cora stood.

'I meant to ask you, did Laura ever mention Ginger in passing?'

'She mentioned years ago that the garage in town was in his name. Everyone knows that.'

I recalled Reagan's sales sticker on the back of her new car.

'Is that it?' she asked.

'What do you mean?'

Cora contemplated me for a moment. 'You didn't know?' she asked. 'She went to school with him.'

I closed the door when Cora left and stepped towards the picture light in the hallway. I reached for the attached cord and tugged it. The fluorescent light illuminated the faded newspaper picture of her secondary school class, all dressed up for their graduation ball. I examined it carefully.

The picture portrayed several rows of beaming young men and women dressed in a variety of 80's-style suits, tuxes, and dresses, mugging for the camera. Some students sat on a line of chairs, while others stood behind them.

An older woman I took to be the head teacher sat awkwardly in the middle. I ran my finger along the students and found a youthful Laura standing at the back in a blue dress.

I tracked my finger downwards to a list printed below the picture, naming the students left to right as they appeared in the photograph. I quickly identified "Laura Carty" – her maiden name. I noticed a familiar name printed alongside hers, "Peter Reagan". I ran my finger back up the picture and found him standing beside Laura. He was a bearded young man whose head sported a mass of red curls. His scarlet hair popped right out of the picture despite the quality of the newspaper print from the time. The picture was several decades old, and I tried to envision what an older Peter might look like without a beard. This could well be the man in the beanie hat. All I knew was that Peter had his head twisted slightly. The moment in time captured him gazing at Laura.

Kyle

36

The bus drove off leaving me alone on a quiet road lined with bungalows. I hoisted a small backpack over my shoulder and checked out the traffic. No one appeared to follow. I cut down a narrow track bordered by thick hedgerows that led down to the lake. I trudged onwards until I arrived at a small cabin on the lake shore.

'Can I help you?' Kyle said from a small speaker in the front door. My hand had paused in mid-knock. His voice had emanated from the doorbell that I guessed doubled as a surveillance device. If Kyle had no trouble wiring up a smart bell to his phone, it would not be a stretch to imagine him activating, remotely, a smart device under my car. Didn't Cora think there might be an Afghanistan connection?

I held up my backpack.

'I come in peace,' I said.

'I'm around the back,' Kyle said.

Kyle had created a homemade gym at the back of the cabin. Rocks doubled as weights. He lay on a bench press heaving a large rock into the air, listening to tunes on earbuds. His phone was propped on the ground beside him. Metres away, waves from the lake gently lapped against the stony shore.

'Sorry for interrupting you,' I said as he heaved the rock up and down in an almost effortless rhythm.

It seemed like his t-shirt had been shrink-wrapped while he was still wearing it. It clung so tightly that his muscles threatened to burst through. He dropped the rock and rolled upright, scooped up a bottle of water and drank deeply. He gestured to a garden chair.

'So what's up?' Kyle asked.

'I wanted to say sorry about letting you go,' I said, sitting in the chair. I held out the backpack and peeled back the top. 'I bring biscuits. The good ones we keep for visitors,' I said.

He sat forward and glanced inside. 'If I didn't know better, I'd say you were trying to waste me. I'm getting diabetes just by being in the vicinity.'

'You want me to run to the shop for a salad?' I asked.

Kyle took a breath. 'I'm sorry. I know, my firing wasn't just up to you.'

I shook my head. 'I had no significant input into it at all.'

'I'd prefer if you were straight, with me, Martin. You had input.'

'I took the minutes,' I admitted. 'That's about it. Oh, for your information, Chris and Suzanne know that I am here.'

'Point taken,' he said, an amused expression crossing his face.

'I just thought I'd mention it in passing.'

'So why the cookies?' he asked.

'I said that I can go for a salad if you prefer.'

'What do you want, Martin?'

'I'd like to think that we could let bygones be bygones.'

Kyle smiled. 'You suspect I booby-trapped your car?'

'It crossed my mind. You are a trained ex-Marine. Don't tell me you can't make things go boom if the inclination took you. Also, you served in Afghanistan, you could have picked up a few tips.'

'True. And yet here you are. What's to stop me from finishing the job?'

'I refer you to the fact that numerous people know that I am here.'

Kyle smiled. 'Sure they do.' He leaned forward. 'Seriously, you think I'd need explosives to take you out?'

He flexed an arm.

'I take your point,' I replied. I didn't want to say that Suzanne and I had considered that the car bombing was a diversion to pin it on the IRA.

'I may be wrong, but I don't see your motive in targeting me. I think that you've a lot to lose by blowing up your employers. That kind of thing doesn't look good on a CV.'

'Like what would I lose?'

'Like whom? Rosie.'

His face clouded. 'What about her?'

'She liked that you were settling down, didn't she? That you had a job, that you weren't throwing anyone out windows.'

Kyle leaned back on the bench and began pumping rocks above his chest.

'What do you want, Martin?'

'I was thinking that a good reference would help you out. I do have some influence.'

Kyle continued his workout.

'The thing is, it's not much use if I don't live long enough to write it,' I said.

Kyle said nothing.

'I need help,' I said. 'Imagine how heroic Rosie would find you if you dealt with my stalkers.'

There was a hesitation in his rhythm.

'Stalkers?' he asked.

'Yes, there is more than one, yes.'

'You need to get Cora to help you. That's what the cops are for. She seems solid.'

'If it's political, then her hands are tied. I can expect minimal help from the authorities. There's a growing list of people out to get me but she's paying no heed. She even dismissed Ed Sheeran as a suspect out of hand.'

Kyle stopped pumping the rock.

'The singer? He's involved?'

'Nonsense of course.'

'Rosie loves him.'

'But you never know,' I added quickly. 'We can't rule anything out.'

'She'd love tickets,' Kyle murmured. 'But the whole tour's sold out.'

'I'm sure we could work out something. He wouldn't want this to get out. There must be comps.'

Kyle paused his workout.

'Did I ever tell you how I met Rosie?' he asked.

He appeared to settle into an almost trance-like state as the rock rose and fell.

'Yes, you did actually,' I said.

Kyle paused in his workout.

'Wrong answer,' I said. 'Go on.'

'Man, she was something else,' he continued. 'We were taking rounds once, but I just couldn't put the phone down. Even when the mortars started coming in, I just had to hear her out. She told me the Loch Ness Monster was Scottish. I never knew that. Did you?'

'I think I heard something about that,' I said.

'So when I got out, I met her in Dublin Airport before finding the nearest hotel. Let's just say, that we spent a heck of a week there before I stepped outside again. And when we did, we were married.'

I was quite sure that while the hotel probably had a chapel, marriages took far longer to arrange. This was Dublin and not Vegas.

I did know that their honeymoon in Donegal didn't last twenty-four hours. One thing that can dampen a marriage is if a groom is led away in handcuffs on the wedding night. Their mistake was to pick a hotel with a fibre broadband connection. He'd wondered about the best wishes from the county hurlers and realised that she'd personally thanked each and every one of them for getting to the final. Some of them twice.

Kyle sat up and threw the rock aside.

'She means the world to me,' he said. 'We're now back on the texting stage. We're thinking of bringing it to the next level. Video calling.'

'So that's progress.'

'Sure. She's happy to hear that I'm keeping fit. The workouts and running help bleed out my demons and I'm taking to the quiet life out here on the lake. I'm learning to chill. She's liking the new me.'

'Glad to hear it.'

He shook his head. 'I don't think you are. I can't get involved. I mean you've got stalkers. Rosie wants to hear that I'm jogging and walking through fields of flowers and shit like that. I'm taking up an aromatherapy course. If she thought I was using skills from my old life, you know what she'd do? She'd block me. Sorry, man. I'm invested.'

Kyle appeared as immovable as the Rock of Gibraltar.

'Will you at least put it to Rosie?'

He pumped some more rock. I waited.

'Fine, I'll ask,' he said, his eyes closed. He pressed on his phone and sighed happily as tunes flowed through his earbuds.

I stood up. 'I'll leave you to it then.'

The meeting was over.

I trudged back up the track as dusk fell. I would have been happier if he said he would help, perhaps even happier if he had denied trying to blow me up.

Rain fell on my face as I arrived at the bus stop. I sighed as I saw a bus fading into the distance. The rain began to bucket down. I made a decision and popped out my thumb as car headlights rounded a corner.

Despite the water streaming down my face, I slapped on my friendliest smile to demonstrate that I was no psycho. The car passed me, but the brake lights snapped on as it began to abruptly slow to a halt. My luck was in. I'd escape the clutches of pneumonia after all. I hoisted up my backpack and jogged towards the car, eager to reach it before the driver considered the effects of a waterlogged passenger on his seating.

In the gloom, I noticed the illuminated yellow number plate on the rear of the car.

A number attributed to Ed Sheeran MBE.

Without breaking my stride I swerved left and dove through a roadside gap in the hedge. I veered off at an angle and bending double, sprinted parallel to the road, keeping hedges and garden walls between me and the path on the other side. I heard the sound of car doors opening. Muffled male voices snapped orders to each other. Breathless, I dropped down and pressed myself against a garden wall. I peeked through a gap and spotted a big bald man, wearing an army-style sweater with patches on the elbows. He had the physique of someone who used their fists for a living. I'd not be surprised to find out that his other job was collecting debts from gangsters with attitude problems. A large bandage was wrapped around his head. A memory stirred. I recognised him, he'd been at the castle licking ice cream. His companion brought no such memories, he was a slender man who wore a well-fitting suit. Together they clicked on torches as they searched each side of the road. Thankfully, they moved away from me.

I felt held breath leave my body. I was wet but downpours were the least of my worries. I noticed that I was in a front garden, illuminated by lights from the rooms of a house. I exhaled again. A nice dormer, I thought. And did they never think of curtains, then again, we were outside the town and occupiers could reasonably have expected some privacy. I stiffened as I noticed a woman in the upstairs bedroom. She was either trying on a bra or taking it off. All I knew was that she had both straps stretched out behind her. Dervla Kennedy's face slowly turned towards the window.

I stood straight up and vaulted over the garden gate, stumbling onto the road just as a car screeched to a halt, illuminating me fully in its beams.

The window slid down on the driver's side. Kyle popped his head out.

'Are you insane? What if I couldn't stop in time?'

I ran around to the passenger door, fumbling with the handle as Kyle slowly reached down to press the unlock button beside him. I yanked the door open and threw myself in, but Kyle it appeared, had all the time in the world.

'I spoke to Rosie, I was dead against getting involved but she said I should hear you out.'

'I like Rosie,' I said quickly, 'can we just go?'

I twisted around in the seat and saw the two men approaching.

'You honestly think there could be tickets? Rosie said to make sure I asked.'

'Please, Kyle,' I said.

He could see the two men in his wing mirror bearing down on us. He also saw Dervla, in her bra, staring out of her bedroom window.

Kyle sighed and accelerated away.

'So what was that all about?' Kyle said as we drove towards town.

'You saw those men. They were the ones I was telling you about. Some of them.'

'There's more?'

'A guy in a beanie hat if you must know,' I said.

'And this has nothing to do with you spying into women's bedrooms?'

'No, Kyle,' I said. 'I was hiding, that's all.'

He shook his head. 'I should have stayed out of it.'

We drove on.

Kyle drummed his fingers on the steering wheel.

'I saw your wife last week. In a coffee shop. I had run in for a juice.'

'So?'

'She was with some guy. I can't tell you who he was. All I saw was the back of his head. I get the vibe that they knew each other. He had his hand on hers.'

An urge to kill arose somewhere inside me. Laura had said she was at a union meeting.

I breathed in.

'Laura, she's free to talk to whomever she wants. I don't own her.' I was aware that I spoke without conviction.

Kyle glanced over at me. 'He wore a beanie hat.'

'See, I'm not making it up.'

'So why is the world and his mother after you?'

'I don't know. I wish I did.'

We approached our estate.

'Just one thing,' I said at last. 'You didn't happen to notice the colour of his hair?'

'Why?'

'Maggie has me in her sights. It so happens that her cousin knows his way around Semtex. He also went to school with Laura. He has bright red hair. It's possible beanie hat guy and Ginger are one and the same.'

Kyle nodded. 'I see where you're going with this, but I couldn't tell you either way what his hair colour was under that cap.'

We pulled up outside my house, just as Laura was entering from her car. She struggled in through the door as she carried large bags in either hand.

'So you think Laura is somehow mixed up in all of this?' he asked.

'I don't know what to think anymore,' I admitted. 'I'm beginning to wonder if I know my wife at all.'

'Let me look into this,' he said, 'but one thing: if I find you're some kind of peeper. I'll not protect you.'

'Thanks,' I said. 'I'm grateful.'

'Don't thank me yet,' he said. 'If I don't like what I find out, you won't even see me coming.'

35

Trails of water dripped from me as I entered the kitchen. Laura poured hot water into a mug from the kettle.

'I'm only just in,' Laura said. 'Brenda and I made a day of it.'

She noticed water pooling around me.

'What happened to you?'

'Rain,' I replied. 'I got caught out. I'll have some tea if you're making it.'

'Sure,' she said and poured hot water into a mug.

'Cora was here.'

'What did she want?'

I explained about the men spotted outside the house. I left out the possibility that Ed Sheeran had us under surveillance. I didn't mention my visit to Kyle.

'Okay,' she said, sliding onto a high stool. 'Why would they be after you?'

'I don't know.'

'Cora also said that she identified a person of interest who may have blown up my car.'

'Really? Who are we talking about?'

I locked eyes with her.

'Ginger Reagan.'

'I don't believe it,' she said in surprise.

'She says that he might not be in Spain. He was seen.'

Her hands clasped her mug. 'Seriously?' she said evenly. 'Where?'

'You tell me?'

Her eyebrows arched. 'How should I know where he is?'

She spoke with righteous indignation in her voice. It meant nothing. I recalled the time she denied speeding until the penalty notice arrived in through the letter box. It contained a clear photograph of Laura staring through the windscreen.

'You do know Ginger Reagan,' I said.

'I never denied that,' she said. 'He sat beside me, so I was bound to know him.'

'You can see how I might wonder how you did not connect a wanted terrorist with a device placed under my car.'

'He was out of the country so why should I? I could equally have listed Al-Qaeda who also know a thing or two about how to create IEDs, but they're not in Ireland either.'

I decided to remain focused.

'What if he's here now? He's got skills in the blowing up department.'

She was thrown.

'I still don't believe it.'

'Perhaps it might suit him if I was out of the way?'

She laughed. 'Now that is beyond fiction. You do know his wife still lives here? Just out the Tullamore Road? The big house with the Palladian pillars?'

Kate Reagan never followed her husband out to Spain. Some said that she remained in the country to raise their son Gerry and did not want to interrupt his education. Gerry had only just moved to London, studying architecture and (it was rumoured) the floor plans of the Houses of Parliament. She was the epicentre of the Midlands cultural movement. She was also an artist whose works hung on the walls of local banks. Banks that were never robbed.

She also owned the main dealership in the town for new and used cars. At least, her name was on the letterhead, but everyone believed that it was Ginger who managed the business remotely.

'What if Ginger had an epiphany, get rid of me to get to you? I saw the way he looked at you in the class picture.'

Laura burst out laughing.

'I thought I heard it all. You are saying that my ex-boyfriend wants to whack my husband?'

'He was your boyfriend?'

My theories began uncrumbling. Would they wait for a decent interval after my funeral, before shacking up?

'That was a more innocent time,' she said. 'When the height of romance was holding hands on the way to school.'

'So he's not after you?'

She shook her head.

'Maybe back in the day but that was before he met Kate.' She smiled wistfully. 'If you knew Ginger as I do, you would know that there is no one else except Kate.'

'What do you mean?'

'A woman could go a whole lifetime without experiencing the look that Ginger gives her.'

'She never followed him out though?'

'Maybe she likes the damp of this country. Maybe she remained to mind her father who's been dying for years now. She also didn't want to mess Gerry about; she was adamant about keeping him in the same school.'

'So if he did come back after all these years. Why now?'

She shrugged. 'You'll have to ask him.'

'Sure,' I said. 'I'd slip into the conversation; Say Ginger how was your flight? Oh, and by the way, did you try to blow me to bits?'

'Let's knock that idea on the head straight away,' she said.

'What?'

'Ginger never tried to kill you.'

'How can you say that?'

'Because if he tried, you'd already be dead.'

I shuddered.

'So that wasn't Ginger that you met in town? The day that Brenda kept me busy at Belvedere House.'

She glowered. 'If I don't know better, I'd say that you were stalking me.'

No good could have come from confessing to accessing her phone, at best I might end up with a barring order, at worse she might claim that I backed into her broadsword.

'Kyle said he saw you,' I said.

Laura rubbed her face.

'I meet lots of people, Martin,' she said. 'Don't spoil my good mood. Just when I was about to tell you that I have good news and bad news.'

'Go ahead.'

She sighed. 'There's a problem with your insurance. They told me we're not covered by Acts of God, war or terror-related incidents.'

'Tell me that you are joking.'

'They said that bombs generally fall into the act of terror category.'

'So what am I supposed to do?'

'Funny you should say that,' she said and lifted a large plastic bin liner onto the kitchen island. She rubbed her hands.

'I give you. The good news.'

She rummaged in the bag.

'You know how I refused to allow Liam get a motorcycle?'

'Ahuh.' I tried not to get excited. I could see where this might be going.

It just took one tour of the spare parts ward (a term the nurses used to refer to the rooms containing motorcycle accident patients) to dissuade him.

In my mind's eye, I saw myself on a Triumph. I thought it would be a good look for me.

'So what changed your mind?'

'Who says I did? It's still dangerous but needs must.'

So, a motorbike was too dangerous for Liam but not for her doting husband?

She pulled out a gleaming motorcycle helmet from the bag.

'I picked this thing up in A&E,' she said. It was a top-of-the-range, full-face motorcycle helmet. 'The owner no longer needs it. I popped out the dent.'

Okay, I thought, trying not to think too much about the provenance of the helmet.

'You need to get to work so I thought we might introduce an interim measure.'

'I couldn't agree more.' I'd have to buy leathers, of course.

'Mary Clancy's husband owns the motorbike shop.'

So she did get me a bike. I could see myself sporting a nice set of shades. I'd probably need to learn how to spit tobacco. As a Briton, the dream, of course, was a Triumph or a BSA.

She pulled out a set of long leather biker gloves.

'Look, matching gloves. One careful owner. Not. You will have to thank Brenda. She spent the day working on them. She sewed them back together as we had to cut them from the body.'

I took them from her apprehensively and examined them closely. Brenda had done an excellent job. You could scarcely notice the handiwork of the triage staff.

'Thanks,' I said.

'This doesn't mean you're out of the spare room,' she said crisply. 'You're clearly going through some weird kind of mid-life crisis.'

Said the woman who more or less admitted that she'd sent me out on the motorway with an eight-eyed spider.

'Can we get it first thing?'

'No need,' she said. 'You'd be surprised what fits in my car when you drop the seats.'

Thoughts tumbled through my mind.

Unless her SUV had TARDIS options so that it was far bigger on the inside than it appeared on the outside, then there was no way a Norton Commando Roadster would fit inside.

Beanie Hat

34

The sun beamed down the next morning as I rode out. The helmet smelled faintly of disinfectant. My newly stitched gloves were designed to keep hands insulated from cold winter breezes. In my case, the gloves might never have to cope with more than a brisk draught.

I buzzed along a residential street on the outskirts of Athlone; the scooter sounded like I was riding an angry sewing machine. I ignored students pointing at me as I passed them. It's important to develop a thick skin as a teacher. It should be the first lesson plan in teacher training college. New entrants should be roasted as they enter the premises. Every blemish called out; any imperfection mocked. Survive that and you are halfway there to giving your first sex ed class.

I kept an easy pace with the cars in traffic. Suddenly my phone buzzed, I tapped the side of the helmet and the built-in headset connected wirelessly with the phone in my pocket.

'Martin,' the voice said.

'Kyle,' I replied, slowly moving forward in traffic. 'What is it?'

'I'm in town,' Kyle said. 'Getting some lavender and cardamom, and guess who I'm looking at? The man Laura met in the coffee shop. He's walking up the town.'

'I've a feeling that Laura is going to meet him,' I said.

'How do you make that out?'

'Call it instinct.'

'You're stalking her?'

'Stalking is such an ugly word.'

Laura's car was several vehicles ahead of me. All had been slowed by a tractor in the distance. I wasn't that worried about losing her, I had my phone charged with a tracker app installed. It meant that we could find each other's phones if they were misplaced. I wasn't stalking my wife, I was stalking her phone.

'We just happen to be going in the same direction,' I said. 'She told me that she was getting her hair done.'

'And you don't believe her?' he asked.

'Let's just say that I'm developing serious trust issues.'

The traffic started to move on as vehicle after vehicle overtook the tractor.

'Got to go,' I said, I paused. 'You mind?'

'Fine,' Kyle replied. 'I'll follow him. Let me know when you are in town.'

I killed the connection and bent down over the handlebars; I needed every bit of aerodynamic advantage I could muster.

I overtook several cars until nothing separated me from Laura's car but a van. I peeped out from behind the van and could see Laura with her phone to her ear. Didn't she know that she was committing a motoring offence? She put the phone to her side and accelerated as the traffic opened up in front of her. She indicated and overtook the tractor. I hummed along behind the van, hoping that the slipstream might pull me along. We kept moving towards town. Whenever we paused at traffic lights, I checked my phone. If she made an unexpected turn, I'd know all about it and could fall in behind her.

Later I worked out that while I was closing in on Laura, a different set of dramas was taking place in town.

The man in the beanie hat watched a boat on the Shannon, as it passed under the town bridge. Kyle observed from a doorway. The man checked his phone and then turned on his heel, waving in Kyle's direction. Kyle pushed himself deeper into the doorway, but the man just shook his head and gestured for him to step out. Kyle knew he was made and stood out onto the street.

'You're not very good at this, are you?' he called out.

Kyle shrugged as he approached. 'It's not my thing. I can shoot expertly at a thousand metres and can fast rope off a Blackhawk. Some skills just don't translate into civilian life.'

Laura's indicator blinked on as she took the dual carriageway on-ramp. She wasn't going into town after all. I groaned as I followed. I accelerated past the, "No L driver" signs and the warning signs prohibiting access to the dual carriageway by vehicles under 50cc. I gulped and drove after her down the ramp anyway.

Kyle and the beanie hat man shared a bench overlooking the river.

'So do you want to go first or shall I?' the man asked.

'How about you first?' Kyle said. 'What were you doing with Martin's wife?'

'Martin's wife?' the man said, and his face seemed to stiffen.

'AKA Laura,' Kyle said. 'What's going on between you two? To be honest I don't see this as you both doing the nasty. No offence, but you smell rank.'

'The hostels I stay in don't tend to feature much in Trip Advisor. What about you, Kyle? You working for Martin?'

'I don't work for anyone. I'm just looking out for him.'

'If you say so.'

Kyle decided to dispense with the foreplay.

'So why are you here? I was thinking executive summary,' Kyle said. 'I've not paid for parking back there and can't afford to be towed.'

The man nodded. 'We'd planned to meet for a chat. Right here. The views are nice.'

A cabin cruiser motored past, disturbing some swans.

'Only she's not coming,' the man said.

'What happened?'

The man pulled out a bag of meal and began throwing it into the water to the intense interest of ducks who did a U-turn.

'You know that you are not supposed to throw bread to waterfowl,' the man said. 'Very little nutritional value in bread.'

They watched the ducks sieve the grains before swallowing.

'There was a change of plan,' the man said. 'Three's a crowd and four is the makings of a dinner party which I'm not exactly dressed for.'

'You're going to start making sense soon?' Kyle said.

'Laura's not coming. She tracked Martin on her phone and reckoned he was following behind. So we called it off.'

'She tracked him?'

'I told you. You're not very good at this, are you? He can track her; it works the other way too.'

I groaned as the pace of traffic on the dual carriageway picked up and Laura accelerated until she was out of sight. I had no option but to keep going and resolved to turn off at the next exit.

Garda Julian stood beside his patrol car parked up on a small ramp reserved for Garda vehicles. He dropped his speed gun, a look of astonishment on his face.

I tried to remain dignified as I slowly buzzed past him. I was fully aware of the eighteen-wheeler heavy goods vehicle tailgating me and the convoy of haulage vehicles, vans and cars following bumper-to-bumper behind.

The radio later referred to the substantial tailbacks on the dual carriageway. They didn't have to mention me by name, but they did anyway.

Kyle was waiting for me as I drove down behind Athlone Castle to the cobblestoned street on the bank of the Shannon.

I had rung him to say that I was delayed and not to bring up the topic of penalty points. I tugged the scooter onto its stand and slid the helmet off. 'This is where you lost him?' I asked.

Kyle nodded.

'He'd too much of a head start.'

'I rang Laura. She said that she had forgotten her purse and decided to go back home. Maybe I'm letting my imagination get the better of me.'

'You and I are going to have a conversation,' Kyle said.

'Like the one we are having?'

'You know how I feel about predators. Be straight with me or I walk.'

'What do you want to know?'

'Are you trying to kill your wife?'

'What makes you say that?'

'A, you're following her and B, I don't hear you denying it.'

I felt my shoulders sag. 'No, you didn't.'

Kyle

33

I hunched down in my all-weather oilskins. The line from my rod vanished into the water of the lake. The boat rocked gently. Kyle sank deeply into his jacket, hands shoved into pockets. His rod poked over the bow.

'To be honest, I'm not seeing the appeal,' he said.

'It grows on you,' I said.

'So where are all the fish at?'

'It's not guaranteed,' I said. 'It's not really the point anyway.'

'Ahuh,' he said. 'Getting back to nature is good for the soul. I get that.'

The Hodson Bay Hotel reflected perfectly in the still waters of the lake.

'I come out here,' I said, 'not for the fishing but to clear the head. It's like a whole other universe.'

Faint cheering filtered down from his end of the boat.

'Are you on your mobile?' I asked.

'Sorry,' he said and pocketed the device. 'The highlights of the game. What were you saying?'

I shook my head. 'The point is to get away from all that.'

He tried to dig up some enthusiasm. 'So you were saying that out here you can chill. I think I read that on a Fáilte Ireland leaflet.'

'So you were listening?'

'Sure, was I supposed to take notes?'

Kyle had me half convinced that he had nothing to do with the loss of my no-claims bonus when my car blew up.

I reminded him of the men that I'd seen with the flashlights. How one had the darker skin of someone brought up abroad.

'Bear with me,' I said. 'If he was Spanish then there might be a connection between him and Ginger – who was hiding out in Spain.'

'And the other dude is the local muscle.'

'You'd need a driver from here,' I said. 'You know what these roads are like. Random signposts. Towns written in Irish.'

'To do what?'

'I know how this may sound. I find it hard to ignore the fact that my car exploded and that my wife knows a convicted terrorist. You tell me he could not create such a device in his sleep? Maybe he planted it himself. Maybe he franchised the job out to Tweedledum and Tweedledee as he has every guard in the country looking for him.'

'Or they could be following you,' Kyle said. 'Hoping you'll lead them to Ginger, to take him out.'

'Cora did say something about that. Anyone setting off unsanctioned car bombs would be likely to end up on waste ground, or under it.'

'So where does beanie hat dude fit into this?' Kyle asked.

'I don't know that yet. Laura denied she met Ginger. Said it wasn't him. Surely even Ginger isn't crazy to show his face in the town?'

'So a lot of complicated moving parts,' Kyle said.

'I'm thinking that maybe it's actually quite simple. Don't they say that the main motivation for crime is sex or money? If anything happened to me then the house would be paid for. The Credit Union and bank debts would be wiped out. There's a few bob payable on the life policy as well.'

'So that's a motive,' Kyle agreed. 'I still don't see your wife at the back of it, asking Ginger for a favour that can't be traced back to her. She's a nurse for crying out loud.'

'Jeffrey Dahmer was a medic and worked in a chocolate factory. Shipman was a doctor who doled out lethal injections like flu vaccines.'

'You seem to know a lot about killers,' Kyle said slowly.

'I know enough to understand that they could be anyone,' I said. 'Even me,' I added to throw him off the scent. 'The alternative is that Maggie is the one pulling the strings. Everyone benefits if I'm gone. My replacement might be more amenable to letting Ruairi back.'

'This seems out there. You've no proof for any of this.'

'What would it take? Me showing up dead?'

'You still haven't answered my original question?'

'Am I trying to kill Laura?' I breathed deeply. 'Yes, I thought about it.'

Kyle stared at me.

'Think of it as self-defence. Would anyone blame me for getting my dig in first?'

Kyle shook his head. 'Man, marriage counselling was made for you two.'

'You believe me, right?'

Kyle mulled it over. 'What if the car bomb didn't explode prematurely and was triggered by a remote, what better way to throw people off the scent, and have yourself as the victim? You blew up your shed, did you not? You can make things go loud if you want.'

I admitted that he had a point.

Kyle stared out across the water.

'Frane Selak,' he murmured after a few moments.

'What is that?'

'It's a who not a what. Frane Selak was a Croatian. He was on a train that crashed into a river, he was hit by a bus, and he was blown out of a plane. His car exploded too. Now *that guy* was unlucky. So shit happens to some people. His luck changed after wife number five when he won the lottery.'

'So you're saying that all that's happening is down to bad luck and coincidence?'

'Let's not rule it out,' he sighed. 'Despite some reservations, I'm going to watch your back.'

I smiled. I needed his skills. It would be easier to take out Laura if I wasn't being hunted. He could help remove my stalkers from the board. I was delighted, I'd recruited my first henchman.

'On one condition.'

'Name it.'

'No one kills anyone.'

I wasn't sure how that was going to resolve my ultimate problem.

'Who knows, maybe you're wrong?' Kyle said.

'About what?'

'About all of it. What if it was me who blew up your car?'

'Stop messing,' I said. I had a flash of *The Godfather II* and how a boat trip on Lake Tahoe didn't end well for Fredo.

I half thought of diving over the side and doggy paddling to shore.

'I'm not doing this for free, mind you,' he said.

I was hoping that he'd not drop hints about Ed Sheeran tickets.

'I've been building up to asking Rosie out again. We said that we would start slow, have a date night, and maybe have sex afterwards, however, she likes a man who can pay his way. I'd be expected to provide the rubbers.'

'Are you looking for your job back?'

'What did I just say?'

I didn't want to mention that Chris had already replaced Kyle. He'd hired someone with a degree in physics, and a PhD in biomechanics engineering. I'm not sure if Chris had read that far into her CV. He'd not got past noticing that she had modelled in college. He'd offered her the job there and then.

'I'll do my best, but the board of management think you're a lawsuit waiting to happen.'

'Is this about the self-defence classes?'

'Our first-year girls could take out a SEAL team, so yes, there is that.'

'I could tell them I was sorry.'

'Are you?'

'No. Not in the least.'

'I'm making no promises, but I'll see what I can do. As I said, a reference could go a long way.'

'I am happy with that school.'

'My hands are tied.'

He looked across the lake.

'Oh yes? One thing I've learned about this country, there's always wriggle room.'

He was right of course. A case in point was the Good Friday Agreement which still held since 1998. The peace deal was a surprise to many who did not think it would ever happen. Generations of grudges had built up, but former American President Bill Clinton had leaned in while British and UK leaders staked their reputations on getting it across the line. If the IRA could be persuaded to cease shooting at British soldiers and vice versa, then surely Kyle could be accommodated. The country now had a history of realpolitik where the past did not dictate the future. If the worst came to the worst, perhaps we could just hint to the board of management that Kyle knew where they each lived.

A low throbbing filled the air. The boat began to rock violently. A large cruiser appeared around the bluff. Music blared from speakers.

'Well, ahoy there!' Chris called out.

He throttled back on the upper deck of the cruiser. He wore a set of aviator sunglasses and a captain's cap. The *Lady of the Lakes* had been his big Lotto purchase. A top-of-the-line, live-aboard cruiser with a galley, berths, a master cabin, and dual steering. He said it was like having his own mobile knocking shop.

The boat edged alongside us, and we rocked alarmingly. It towered above us as it drew alongside. The only chance of catching a fish now would be if they passed away from a coronary and floated to the surface.

'Hi,' Chris called out. 'I thought I recognised your boat.'

Chris peered first at Kyle and then at me.

'I see you have company.'

Perhaps he wondered why I was with a man who may have planted a device under my car.

'That's right,' I replied. 'Just enjoying the lake.'

'Me too,' Chris said, and cracked open a beer.

Kyle eyed the cruiser longingly. There was the smell of pancakes emanating from the galley. The boat even had a toilet.

'I hope you're not thinking of jumping ship,' I hissed.

'I'd invite you up, but you know,' Chris said. He made a thrusting motion with his hips and pointed to the cabin.

A hand slowly slid a curtain over a porthole that faced us. A woman's left hand. There was a glimpse of the back of a ring on her index finger. Chris was not married, however, his passenger appeared to be.

'We know how it is,' I said.

'Maybe next time,' Chris said and shoved the throttles forward. The cruiser engines roared into life, water churning at the stern as the cruiser slid off leaving us bouncing in its wake. He was exceeding the five K speed limit for this part of the lake, but such niceties never phased him. He roared off.

The lake returned to silence once more.

'What's the story, Captain, if I need to take a whizz?' Kyle asked.

I pointed over the side.

'Back to nature, huh.'

I grimaced, watching the cruiser vanishing from view. The water continued to churn in muddy swirls. There'd be nothing caught today. I really hated Chris sometimes.

'I've two things that I'm advising you to do,' Kyle said slowly as the water calmed.

'What are they?'

'First, try and mend some bridges with Maggie, maybe it's not too late for her to back down if she's involved.'

'I think we're too far gone for that. The look she gave me at the hospital spoke volumes. This was before I ran her down and burned her shop to the ground.'

'It's not too late until it's too late.'

'And what's the second thing?'

'You need to speak with your wife.'

'I think I'd have better luck with Maggie.'

'Speak to Laura, maybe all that's happening is some kind of misunderstanding. Maybe she can help.'

'And if she is involved? I'd just be tipping my hand, that I'm onto her?'

'And maybe she'll just ask you to get on your knees and gift flowers.'

'I'm not convinced.'

'I think, you might be approaching a tipping point, Martin. If you don't let some air out of the tyres, your whole world could slide sideways.'

'I don't know, Kyle.'

'Alternatively, do as you're doing. How's everything working out for you so far?'

'Fine.'

'Let me hear you say it.'

'I'll mend bridges.'
'And? I still need to hear you say it.'
'No one kills anyone,' I sighed.

Cora

32

I drove off from the boat slip on my scooter and buzzed toward home. I'd only gone a few metres when I noticed a squad car fall in behind me. The light bar mounted on the front grill began to strobe.

Laura

31

Laura dropped two tablets into a glass of water as I entered the kitchen, removing my helmet. Bicarbonate caused the tablets to fizzle in the glass. Laura's hands shook. I guessed that she had been spending too much time with Brenda.

Laura waited for the water to cloud over and knocked back the drink. Tension washed from her face.

'All right?' I asked.

'I am now,' she replied. 'Any news?'

'Cora pulled me over.'

'And?'

'She told me that the two men who were following me walked into the station.'

Laura rinsed out her glass, but I could tell that she was listening.

'Go on.'

'She says that they had a chat. They claim that they're tourists. She ran their IDs through their Pulse system. One of them is Spanish. Roberto something or other. Cora feels he's ex-Military. The other is from Belfast. He's served time for assault, bank robbery. He's Republican connections.'

'So what were they doing around here?'

'They told her that they were here for the lakes. They said that Fáilte Ireland was running a tourism campaign and they bought into it. They said they were thinking of hiring a Shannon cruiser.'

'So there was nothing she could do.'

'They went to report some vandalism. Someone had swapped their plates, they claimed.'

'Nonsense of course,' Laura said. 'They hadn't anticipated Mrs Keena spotting them. It was only a matter of time before they were caught.'

'Cora told them that she had zero tolerance for vehicle registration offences and that she'd have no hesitation in issuing a five thousand euro fine for a lack of compliance.'

'So they didn't take the hint?'

'They said that they will be more vigilant in the future and were going to explore Ireland's Hidden Heartlands regardless.'

'Sounds like they plan to stick around.'

'That's what Cora says. She thinks there is something in the air, but she wouldn't explain.'

'So you think that these lads tried to blow you up and are waiting to finish off the job?'

'It's a possibility.'

'Why you? You're just a teacher. What have you done to deserve this?'

Laura smirked.

'Maybe you gave someone an F once and they never got over it.'

'It doesn't matter why,' I snarled. 'Do you think it would be some comfort to me to be sitting on the edge of a dock, my feet in a bucket of cement while one of them outlines my offences?'

'I can see you're upset,' Laura said. 'So what do you want to do about it? Apart from moan about it.'

Kyle had urged me to make peace with my wife. I could see the merit in his approach. Maybe I should just shake the tree and see what fell out.

'I have an idea.'

'Okay, spill it.'

'I've got Kyle involved and he's willing to help. He's also an ex-Marine. Perhaps if we turned the tables on the two lads following me. Ambush them. Tie them to chairs. Maybe use white noise and some sleep deprivation. Get them to confess or back down.'

'You've really thought this through.'

'I'm fine-tuning the details at the moment. For waterboarding, we just need a basin, which we have, and old towels, which we also have.'

Laura nodded. 'I see. So we kidnap the pair following you and get them to rat one another out?'

'It could work,' I said.

'You really think so?' she said. She picked up her jacket and slid her arms inside.

'What are you doing?'

'No time like the present,' she said and scooped up the car keys.

'You're going with my plan?'

'Does any of it involve you getting into the car with me?'

I had thought she'd be a good lookout. She could be part of the team. We could get some kind of matching outfits.

'Yes,' I said.

'We'll do that bit.'

'And the rest of the plan?'

She shook her head.

'No. We won't be doing any of that.'

Kate

30

Laura climbed into the cab of her SUV, and I slid into the passenger seat. I pulled an electricity bill from underneath me.

'What's this doing here?' I asked.

'It's paid, isn't it?' she said as she buckled herself in. She started the engine and checked the mirror before backing out of the drive.

'I'm glad that something I said is sinking in.'

I pointed to the sticky note on the dashboard.

'Check fuel,' was written on it.

'Don't want you diving off any more bridges,' she said and accelerated towards the estate exit.

I scrambled to click on my seatbelt as she swung the wheel in the opposite direction from town. She accelerated and almost instantly braked hard.

I bounced my head off the windscreen.

'What's that all about?' I said, rubbing my head.

She'd stopped on the road and appeared oblivious to the cars following who had to overtake her. She hauled up the handbrake and slid down the driver's side window.

'That's the car you were on about, yes?' she said.

Sure enough, a car with Northern plates was parked outside the pub that faced onto the entrance to the estate. The two men that it belonged to paused in mid-step, as they saw us. They'd been on their way out of the pub. I guess even thugs were entitled to dinner breaks.

'I'll ring Cora,' I said and reached for my phone.

'And say what? Nothing illegal going on here that I can see.'

She was right.

'Did you try the homemade burger and chips? It's to die for,' Laura called out through her open window.

The thin man nodded. I noticed that the bulky one had a smaller bandage wrapped around his forehead. He fumbled for his keys.

'What are you doing?' I stammered. 'Wind up the windows.'

'We're heading out the Banagher Road. Just so you know,' Laura said pleasantly.

I thought about wrenching the wheel from Laura and leaning over to stomp on the accelerator.

'The Banagher Road,' the thin man repeated in a Spanish accent. 'They say it's nice out there.'

'Clonmacnoise is in that direction,' Laura said. 'People come from all over to see the ruins.'

The bulky man scratched his head. He probably was more comfortable at ripping people out of cars against their will than exchanging tourist tips. He found the car keys and waited.

'It's on the bucket list,' the first man said slowly.

Laura released the handbrake and drove off, while the two men scrambled to get into their car.

'What did you tell them that for?' I demanded.

'It's time for sense to prevail. If you want a hive to leave you alone, you don't go after the drones. You go after the queen.'

'Ginger is the queen?'

She shook her head. 'I wonder at you sometimes.'

Laura kept within the speed limit and drove onwards. I could see the two men following in their car.

I felt my palms sweat. What was I thinking? If Laura wanted me gone, had I just handed myself to her and her crew? Had I willingly joined a convoy where my next ride was in a long black car?

'I was thinking that straying away from public areas might not be the way to go,' I said.

I fumbled for my phone and saw I had no mobile phone coverage.

Laura ignored me. We travelled in a mini convoy for a few kilometres before she clicked on the indicators once more. We turned in through an elaborate set of gates and drove up a long, gravelled driveway that ended in Ginger Reagan's house.

It was a two-storey mini-mansion that was rumoured to have been built on the proceeds of laundered diesel. No expense had been spared and multiple architects had been involved. It partially explained why the main house looked like the bastard love child of a Mississippi mansion and the Arc de Triomphe. It was like a footballer's wife had walked into a yard sale of Egyptian relics and declared, 'If two Palladian columns are tasteful, then eight are four times as good.'

A black Mercedes was parked in front of the portico. The driver, in a neat suit, stood leaning against the car door. A separate saloon was parked behind it. It contained two men. I noted the presence of a pair of aerials mounted on the roof— it marked them out as being part of a Special Detective Unit. The men following us had halted on the side of the drive behind us when they saw the cars.

Laura's plan involved us going to Ginger's house. A house with only one way in and out. Laura probably should stick to nursing instead of dealing with the criminal underworld. I was wondering how it would look if I threw myself on my knees in front of Ginger, begging for my life. Would Laura lose the tremendous amount of respect she had for me that I'd accrued through the years? I was relieved though at the presence of the gardaí.

We parked and walked past the Mercedes driver. I noticed the corner of a handgun poking out of his jacket. The Irish police force was not armed but there were exceptions. Special armed units for example and protection details could be tooled up to their eyeballs.

We nodded to each other in greeting.

Laura leaned on the doorbell and waved me forward. We did not have to wait long as the door was swung open by Ginger's wife, Kate. She wore a thin gown, belted at the waist and some slip-on plastic shoes splattered with paint. She had long hair and an angular face with a streak of paint on her cheek. She examined us carefully.

'Laura,' she said smiling. 'Long time no see.'

'Hello, Kate,' Laura said.

Kate looked at me with a bemused expression.

'And Martin. You're both just in time.'

She turned on her heel and we followed her into the hall that rose to a ceiling high above us. I'd never stepped inside before and took a moment to take in the artwork that dotted the walls. Reproductions depicting the gables of Belfast houses were squeezed between paintings of gunmen and Saracen armoured cars. Former Republican leaders were featured in life-sized portraits.

Kate walked onwards into a large room that had been converted into a studio. There were easels, paint-spattered sheets on the floor and an expensive camera mounted on a tripod. The centre of the room was made to appear like a wooded glade. A large artificial boulder was surrounded by real plants and ferns. A drop-down backdrop showed gnarled oak trees. Lights slung from bars sent beams of "sunlight" across the scene.

A tall middle-aged man stood beside the set. He wore a tailor-made suit. I recognised him from the television.

'Hello, Minister,' I said.

Local TD Tim Fagen had benefited from a cabinet reshuffle and was now the newly appointed Minister for Justice.

'Hello, nice to meet you, Martin, isn't it? And Laura, of course,' he said, his face forming a well-practised grin. 'Thanks for the tour,' he said to Kate, 'but you will excuse me, I have to dash.'

He shook Kate's hand and walked to the door, adjusting the top button of his shirt. He opened the door and stood there for a moment as Kate sidled up to him.

'I'll see you there,' she said firmly.

'I don't know,' he said in a low voice that Laura and I strained to overhear, 'a man in my position. It's about the optics.'

Kate murmured. 'I don't care,' she said.

Laura and I exchanged side glances.

Laura made a grinding motion with her hips.

Tim Fagen hurried down the steps and sat in the rear seat of the Mercedes. The driver closed the door for him before quickly sitting in the driver's seat and starting the engine.

Kate waited until the Mercedes and the Special Detective Unit car had driven off before closing the door. The car with our two followers remained parked at the gate.

Laura and I showed a keen interest in a painting as Kate walked back in. She beckoned to Laura.

'Would you be a dear?' she said and pointed to the camera facing the sofa. 'I'm having problems with the remote. Press the button when I say?'

Laura stepped up into position.

'Okay,' Laura agreed. 'Kate, we want to ask you something.'

'I am always happy to oblige,' Kate said. 'but first I need a cherub. I had high hopes that Tim would have obliged but he's above all that now.'

She eyed me up and down.

I started to protest but Laura cut me off.

'Martin, we haven't all day.'

I began to undo my tie.

'Quite right,' said Kate and stood before the chair.

She pulled at a cord and the robe fell to the floor. She was entirely nude. She sat down on the chair, pulled a beret on her head, and pulled out a replica M16 from underneath a bush. Or at least I hoped it was a replica. She held it out, posing theatrically, the weapon partially obscuring those bits of the anatomy normally hidden from sunlight, and waited for me to join her in the woods.

Kate, wearing her robe, entered the sitting room, carrying a tray containing mugs of tea and biscuits. She plonked them down on a coffee table and curled onto a deep, leather armchair.

'I take it that the car is going well,' Kate said.

'I love it,' Laura replied, taking a cup of tea and sipping it. She sat on a long sofa with intricately carved legs.

Kate nodded as I entered the room, tucking my shirt into my trousers and sat down on the sofa beside Laura.

'I hope I don't get any body paint on this,' I said, patting the sofa. 'I think I got most of it off me.'

I took a cup of tea from the tray.

'I hope not,' Kate smiled, 'as we'd have to fly in a specialist cleaner from London. The insurance company would insist.'

I carefully held the tea cup away from me and the sofa and bent over the cup to drink.

'So what brings you out here?' Kate asked us.

I explained that where I came from; car bombs were considered the height of rudeness.

'And you think Ginger had something to do with it?'

'To be fair,' Laura said, 'it's not like he'd need to look up a manual.'

'Ginger's out the country though,' she said coyly.

'I heard that he's missing the weather here,' I said.

'Maybe so, but I heard that he was in Spain, having dinner with the local mayor when your car blew up.'

'He's very lucky with his alibis,' Laura said.

'Didn't he show up at Athlone Garda barracks looking for a passport, at the exact same time that an ATM in Belturbet was being removed from a wall?' Laura added.

'Coincidence,' Kate said smiling.

'And the time he went to apply for the dog licence. The Balla Post Office was robbed if memory serves me correctly,' Laura said.

'Coincidence?' I asked.

'What can I say?' Kate said. 'It's lucky he happened to be in the barracks at the time.'

'Of course.'

'But why would Ginger have you whacked?' Kate asked.

If it was to clear the way to Laura, then it wasn't something that I was going to bring up with his wife.

'I don't know,' I replied.

'Maybe you've other enemies? I mean – a pub burns down. Ginger gets the blame. A loss-making business mysteriously catches fire and Ginger again. He's the go-to guy whenever something goes wrong in the county. Maybe he is being set up.'

I found that hard to imagine.

'So Ginger is the victim here?'

'It might be the case. He's been out of the country for years and he still gets blamed for anything that happens.'

'Regardless,' Laura said interrupting. 'I would ask you a favour of one woman to another.'

Kate nodded and put her hand on Laura's. 'If Ginger happens to get in touch. I'll have a word. That's all I can do.'

'Thanks,' Laura said.

Kate stood up. 'Now is that everything? I'm up to my eyes getting ready for my exposition and I want to push on before I lose the light.'

She ushered us to the front door.

'What about the chaps outside?' I asked. I was thinking of the men guarding the driveway.

'Who do you mean?' Kate asked and swung open the door.

The driveway was empty.

Kyle

29

I stood at Maggie's door with the largest bouquet that Dolan's had in their shop. They'd put a little of everything in it as I had no idea what Maggie might like. Mrs Dolan called it a fusion; I just called it expensive. Regardless, if it kept Maggie off my back then it was an investment worth making.

Laura had echoed Kyle's words and had advised me to mend some bridges. I would agree to almost anything that would keep my followers off my back. It's beyond frustrating when plans for murder are interrupted by bona fide murderers.

Maggie's house faced directly onto the street. A ground-floor window was half open in front of closed curtains. I guessed that Maggie had not noticed the potential for burglary. Then again, who would rob anything from a relative of the Reagan's?

I knocked on the door but there was no answer. I eyed the flowers and the letterbox. Perhaps I could feed them through one stem at a time?

I did not want to leave the bouquet on the street, nor did I wish to repeat the journey, where I'd learned why florists use vans for deliveries and not scooters. Most flowers had arrived with petals more or less intact, and I wanted to keep them this way. I viewed the half-open window and made a decision.

I slid the window up slightly and passed the flowers and a box of chocolates through a gap in the curtains and onto the floor. I then closed the window all the way, pleased that I had done my bit for Neighbourhood Watch. I was hopeful that Maggie would thank me later.

Feeling somewhat thrilled with myself, I drove off on the scooter. Almost straight away the phone rang.

'It's me,' Kyle said when I tapped the side of my helmet and answered.

'What's up?'

'I'm on overwatch. At your house.'

'Don't let Mrs Keena see you. Or Laura.'

'You know I trained for this? I'm not on the street.'

'Where are you?'

'In a hide.'

'In a what?'

'I'm in the field opposite your house.'

'Why?'

'You asked me to.'

'I asked you to watch my back, I don't think I mentioned the word, "field" in there.'

'Just covering the bases. I can stop if you want me to. Back off.'

'What?'

'Sorry, talking to some sheep.'

'I don't see the point?'

'You will when I show you the pictures I've taken.'

'Of sheep?'

'Someone's just left your house.'

'Liam?'

'No, he left this morning. This man came afterwards. Stayed for half an hour.'

'Was it Ginger?'

'No.'

'How can you be so certain? Was he wearing a hat?'

'I'm telling you it wasn't Ginger.'

I pulled over to the side of the road.

The silence lingered between us.

'You know who he is?' I said.

'Oh yes, I certainly do. We both do.'

I grimaced.

'I'll see you at your place. I don't want to go near home until I've seen what you have.'

'I can meet you in town.'

'If I'm going to have a meltdown – it ought not to be in a public place. I'm hanging up now,' and I did.

I looked at the phone and scrolled down through my contacts and dialled. Laura picked up at once.

'Hi,' she said. 'Did you drop the chocolates over to Maggie? That'll be one less worry if she backs off.'

'Better than that. I added flowers as well.'

'Flowers? We never said flowers.'

'I thought I'd go the whole hog.'

'As long as you didn't go overboard,' Laura said uneasily. 'Maggie is basically allergic to summer.'

'What do you mean?'

'Whenever the pollen count is high, she normally doses herself with a bucket of antihistamines and dozes off in the room farthest from the garden.'

The room that faced the street.

'Oh, right.'

I had an image of Maggie napping in a room that I'd thoughtfully filled with a handpicked selection of asters, roses, and chrysanthemums.

'It's the thought that counts,' I said.

'I'm sure that she'll appreciate them.'

'Any news?' I asked innocently.

'No,' she replied. 'Just putting up a shelf.'

'Did Liam go to college?'

'Yes, I feel that he's going to make it through this time.'

I listened to her breathing on the phone.

'Was there anything else?' she asked.

'I just rang to say that I'm popping over to Kyle's,' I said.

'That's nice. I'll leave something for you in the microwave. Bye now.'

She cut the connection.

She'd not mentioned anyone else popping by.

I twisted the throttle all the way. The front wheel of the scooter would have raised itself in the air if it had the power, instead it just accelerated, quite quickly.

Kyle

28

Kyle stepped from his car just as I buzzed in on the scooter.

'I'm impressed,' he said. 'You must have found an extra gear to get here so fast.'

'I was motivated,' I said, 'plus I got a tailwind.'

'We could have had this out in town.'

'I don't care much for crying in public,' I said. 'Here is as good as any coffee shop. You've got coffee. And biscuits too. I know as I brought them.'

'Okay,' he said and stepped onto his porch. He rattled his keys, unlocked the front door, and pushed it open.

'Come in,' he said loudly.

'I'm not deaf you know,' I said, following him.

The door opened directly onto a living room and kitchenette. A pile of laundry, neatly folded, sat on a small table. A remote control for the flatscreen TV was centred precisely on a coffee table. Kyle, if anything, was a neat man. The only thing out of place was a camouflaged army jacket that hung from a doorknob. He gestured to me to sit on a sofa and took some tumblers out of a cupboard.

'Nice place,' I said.

'I like it,' he said. 'Great views and a spare room should Rosie kick me out for snoring.'

'So you're back on?'

'Not exactly. We've moved beyond texting though. We're exchanging pictures of genitals.'

He held up a bottle of whiskey and I nodded. He poured a large measure into each glass. He produced a miniature jug of water and he poured a tiny drop into each drink.

'So who are we talking about?' I said taking the glass. 'Who left the house?'

He pulled out his phone, opened a camera roll app and scrolled back a few pictures. I took the phone and stared.

This wasn't Ginger Reagan. It was a man I recognised. I scrolled back and forth through the images, and it gave the appearance of him backing in and leaving the house. I'd recognise the face anywhere.

I should since I served as his best man.

Our drinking continued on the lake shore at the back of the cabin. The lake was a dark hole in the night. Occasionally car lights on the other side of the lake flickered between trees.

'He's such a dick,' he said.

He stirred logs in a burning pit between us.

'True. You know I was his best man?' I slurred warming my hands near the fire.

'Does it count if the ceremony falls through?'

'I should have known; he tries to sleep with everything with a skirt. Why should my wife be the exception?'

'To be fair he could have just swung by to leave a message.'

'That's what phones are for.'

'I guess.'

'Why didn't Laura say anything? Or mention him?' I said aloud, startling some swans somewhere out on the lake.

Kyle shrugged.

'Maybe that was her on the boat,' I said sitting up, furious. 'She's never come out on my boat. Not once. All the times I asked her.'

'Let's not jump to conclusions,' he said. 'That way lies chaos.'

'I could kill him for what he's done,' I said before I could bite back the words.

'It takes two to tango.'

I raised a glass.

'For sure. I've rolled over too long for him. That promotion should have been mine a long time ago.'

'And of course if he's sleeping with your wife.'

'That's adding insult to injury,' I said angrily.

'So how would you do it?' he asked.

'I'd mow him down in that fancy car of his.'

'You need to think this through. Jacob in Glenowen is a magician with bodywork. He can knock out the dents, and remove the blood spatter, but he wouldn't thank you for it.'

'You're right. I couldn't do that to him,' I said, slurring. 'Maybe I'd run Chris through with an arrow, Laura has plenty.'

'You could do that?'

'He'd have to be standing perfectly still,' I admitted.

Even though the drink was talking, my mind retained some degree of sense. I was no archer and as it turned out, also not much of an alchemist either. I sighed. I was over complicating the matter. 'Maybe I'd just push him down a lift,' I said.

'It's not like the county is falling over with high-rise buildings. This is not New York.'

I saw the futility in what he was saying.

'We could go to Dublin.' But such a trip left me cold. 'That wouldn't work. There'd be tolls. And don't let me get started on the parking.'

I felt a warmth towards Kyle. Perhaps it was the whiskey.

'No,' I said. 'I have a better idea.'

The part of my brain that triggers alarms was trussed up by Power's Gold Label in a corner. I knew I shouldn't be revealing plans, but Kyle was such a good listener.

'I'd planned the perfect murder.'

'Oh yeah?'

'Ideally, you'd get a dart frog.'

'A what?'

'Columbian natives use them. To bait the tips of their blowpipes.'

'Really?'

'However, they are very hard to get now. They've a bunch of them in London. How hard could it be to break into a zoo? You got the skills.'

I giggled at the idea.

'And if we could find such a frog and bring it back in our hand luggage. What then?' he asked.

'Trust me, you'd not pick up this chap too quickly with your bare hands.'

I was aware that I'd been rabbiting on.

The part of my brain that triggers alarms had managed to escape from its bonds.

'You're not drinking,' I said.

'I am,' he replied. 'Just not as much as you.'

'Oops,' I said, 'I'd better be going before I say something I regret.'

'I'm not sure any one of us in any condition to drive.'

'Speak for yourself,' I said, annoyed. I stood up and approached my scooter in the darkness.

'You can crash on the sofa,' Kyle said, picking up a torch and illuminating the pathway.

'I'm fine,' I said. 'The fresh air will clear my head.'

I seized the handlebar with one hand but struggled to find the scooter power button.

'I might need a push,' I admitted.

'Much good that would do you.'

'And why not?'

The beam of his torch moved from my face to between my legs.

'That's a lawnmower.'

Maggie

27

Students played basketball, exchanged gossip, and surreptitiously glanced at phones that they were not supposed to have during school hours. I stood out in the playground on supervision duty oblivious to all about me. My mind was elsewhere and short of a full-blown riot with hostages being taken, I left the students to their own devices.

I wore the clothes I had slept in last night and my head pounded. I had woken up on Kylie's sofa in a deserted cabin. I'd let myself out and drove the scooter straight into work.

I stood gazing at a plot of rocky waste ground adjacent to the yard. Signage indicated it was a "Protected Habitat" with a picture of a newt underneath captioned, "Lissotriton vulgaris (smooth newt)".

I could believe Chris trying it on with Laura, but I could not be more surprised that she had responded. Then again, I never thought when I married her that she could become so adept at armed combat that I half expected a cold call from the CIA asking for her resumé.

I stepped forward.

A child ran past, chasing another with a stick.

'Stop running,' I muttered, without enthusiasm.

I found myself standing at the wooden sign that marked a parking spot. "Reserved. Chris O'Donnell. Principal" was written on it. I noticed that the sign was crooked.

Chris was not in. I wondered if his car was parked alongside Laura's SUV.

I nudged the sign with my foot, and it straightened up but slid back again.

The child who had chased another ran past; this time the other child had a bigger stick.

I let them go. Sometimes, revenge takes many forms.

I nudged the sign again, and it slumped back. I tapped it with my foot, and it plopped back. I kicked it harder and then harder.

I sensed activity in the schoolyard grind to a halt as students paused to watch me kick and stomp the living daylights out of the sign.

The school bell rang.

Playtime was over.

I was shaking when I unlocked the door to my office and was surprised to find Maggie Geraghty-Philbin not only sitting in the chair opposite my desk but that her head seemed twice its size. Her eyes were slits in her swollen face.

'Maggie?' I asked, unsure who it was for a second. 'Are you all right?'

'Nothing would stop me,' she snarled.

'You get my flowers?' I said. Then hesitated as I put two and two together. 'Clearly you did.'

'I think my allergies are well known,' Maggie said. 'It's why I disappear for a few weeks when the pollen count is high.'

'I was just trying to say sorry for what happened.'

'A funny way you have of showing it.'

'I didn't know you had allergies,' I said.

'So you say.'

'How did you get in, by the way?' I asked.

'I needed a seat,' she said.

'Maggie, you really can't just show up here without an appointment.'

'You mean the appointment that's in your diary for now?'

Maggie was chair of the Parents' Association. Her pursuit of the position became clear as it meant increased access to school management. She'd driven off several competitors for the post with veiled threats. I checked my work diary that lay open on my desk.

'So you're here to talk about the Christmas panto then?'

'Of course,' she said sweetly as I took my place behind the desk. 'We concluded that there should be one.'

'Oh good.'

'Now that this is settled. I see that we've time on our hands.'

I knew what was coming.

'Would this be about Ruairi?'

'What do you think?'

'I told you what you needed to do. I gave you the forms to fill in.'

'Much good it did.'

'I agreed. It's all out of my hands.'

I felt a surge of malice creeping in. What loyalty should I have to Chris when he had none to me? I'd shielded him long enough.

'You see my powers are limited, I wish I could do more,' I lied. 'The person who makes the ultimate decision is not in this office, I am afraid.'

'You mean Chris?' Maggie said, a hint of a smirk trickling over the corner of a lip.

I sensed she was leading me into a trap. It was hard to tell. She had the ultimate poker face.

'You might want to make an appointment with him. Peggy can do that for you if you like?'

'I can make my own appointments.'

Clearly, she could. Maybe she could plant a bomb under Chris. I thought, would it be bad of me to offer my services as a lookout?

She rose from her seat.

'We all know that Chris couldn't find his way around the school without a map. It's you who does his dirty work.'

I wasn't sure if she was insulting me or paying me a compliment.

'What do you mean?'

'Chris and I already had a conversation.'

Something about her tone bothered me. I suspected that she'd have thrown me a smug look if her face hadn't been so swollen. She was no more capable of expressing emotions than a Botoxed starlet.

I felt a scene of foreboding.

'What did Chris say?'

'Chris also feels that Ruairi's past should not define him.'

I was aghast.

'You are saying that Chris agreed for Ruairi to come back?'

'That's why I am here. I wanted you to be the first to know.'

No wonder Chris was absent. He would be in dire danger of being trampled to death in the staff walkout.

'He was supposed to be here to sign off on it,' Maggie snarled. 'He promised.' She moved to the door. 'Mark my words, he'll play ball.'

I almost felt sorry for the man but that feeling passed in an instant. If what she said was true… What was he thinking of?

'You're planning to go to him now?' I said surprised. 'You know where he is?'

'People should not make promises without delivering on them.' Her lips pursed with difficulty due to the swelling. 'By the way,' she said. 'You're not off the hook.' She pointed to her face. 'You did this to me.'

'I said I was sorry.'

'I spent the day in the casualty department of Portiuncula Hospital,' she snarled.

I wanted to mention that they also have an excellent plastic surgeon on call but remembered that Maggie might have access to illegal weapons.

'You haven't seen the last of me,' she sneered. 'In the meantime, you'd be well advised to print out Ruairi's book list.'

She slammed the door behind her.

The ever-vigilant Peggy knocked on the door of my office moments later and entered after I told her to come in.

'Good morning,' she said, and noticed my whitened face. 'You all right?'

'Maggie was just in,' I said.

'I saw her run out the door,' Peggy said.

'She tells me that Chris agreed to let Ruairi back.'

'You're joking.'

'I wish.'

'There'll be a strike.'

'I know,' I said.

I jumped to my feet. 'Is he out of his mind? What was he thinking of?'

'Never going to happen,' Peggy snorted. 'Ruairi starts here, and I guarantee there will be a riot. There will be teachers on the barricades. What are you going to do?'

'I'm going to stop him,' I said. The months of pent-up tension accrued from being almost blown up, stalked and run over by a boat were channelled into a fury that surprised both Peggy and me.

'I'm going to go and wait in his office,' I said.

'Much good that will do. He rang in sick.'

'Really?'

'That's what he said.'

I needed time to think. I waved her away and she scurried out the door. No doubt she was en route to co-opt the art classes into making industrial action signs, maybe she'd plans to advise the Chemistry Lab to stockpile Molotov cocktails.

In the meantime, I fretted.

If Chris was not in school, where was he?

He knew my roster. Did that mean the coast was clear for him to call by my house? If I stormed in through the front door and caught the two of them in flagrante delicto, then I'd need to take pictures on my camera phone for the divorce. However, who would care? Knowing my luck, I'd catch the two of them riding on our kitchen island and I'd get done for disseminating pornography.

I picked up the phone and rang Chris but got no response apart from voicemail.

I paced about the office.

A husband in France used to be able to get away with the murder of his wife and her lover if they were caught in their marital home in a so-called crime of passion. The trouble was that we lived in Athlone. The crime of passion law also was abolished in 1975 so even a contrived weekend away in Paris could not achieve much unless I could persuade Jenny Foyne – the smartest kid in the school – to ditch her cancer research and look into time travel.

I picked up my mobile phone and rang home. The phone was answered at once.

'Hi Laura,' I said. 'I think I forgot my calculator. Would you see if it is there?'

'Where is it?' Laura asked.

'Can you ask, Liam? I think he had it last. Is he there?'

'No. They just rang and asked him to come to work.'

'Oh, right. Never mind. I'm sure we have calculators here.'

I cut the line. Laura was alone. Or was she?

I paced some more. I could hear raised voices emanating from the staff room. Peggy must have lobbed in a verbal hand grenade. I could not yet face them. I rang Kyle.

'What's up?' he said. 'How's the head?'

'I've a headache like you wouldn't believe. Chris is not in.'

'So?'

'Peggy says he's sick.'

'Your point being?'

'You're not in the hide, are you?'

'As it happens, I'm in the chemist buying lube.' His voice rose. 'I'll take all you got,' he said to someone. His voice dropped in volume as he spoke again into the phone, 'I'm meeting Rosie. Should I draw you a picture?'

'Never mind,' I said before he went into detail.

I cut the connection and logged into my device locator app. It confirmed that Liam was on the way into town, while Laura's phone remained permanently locked in position at home.

I stood at the window and observed some teachers huddling together on playground duty casting sly glances in my direction, students passed basketballs to one another but there was no enthusiasm in it. The scene reminded me of an article by an embedded war correspondent in Iraq. He described being on foot patrol in a small dusty town, discovering workman's tools hastily discarded by the road, and women in hijabs summoning their children inside. A sergeant said that they had to hustle as an attack was pending.

The school was on edge and Chris was at the back of it.

It was time to stop thinking and start doing.

I strode out the door.

I almost ran headlong into one of the teachers and Union rep, Steven Casey who had been lurking outside.

'Is this true, that Ruairi is coming back?' he demanded.

I brushed past him.

'Over my dead body,' I said without stopping, 'I'm going to find Chris and sort this out once and for all.'

I heard a classroom door open. I glanced back as another teacher mouthed to Steven, 'Is it true?'

I bolted out a fire exit door before I was rugby tackled to the ground by one of the teaching faculty.

I hopped on the scooter as my phone started to buzz. I switched it to silent, twisted the accelerator as far as it would go, bent my head down into the breeze and zipped out of the car park.

I buzzed up the road and half an hour later zoomed into our estate and purred up to the front door. Laura's car was nowhere to be seen.

I opened the front door and found her phone on the kitchen island. Unless a high spec feature of her SUV was self-driving, Laura was not at home. I picked up her phone, entered her PIN and noted that the call history showed an outgoing call to a private number. There were some used coffee cups left out. It was like the Marie Celeste but with a mortgage.

Barney greeted me and wagged his tail. I asked him where Laura was, but he wasn't sharing.

I looked at my watch. I had to get back before the school descended into Beirut circa 1968-1978. I scurried out the front door and jumped on the scooter. I revved the scooter's engine.

I really should return to school, but I was worked up and needed to satisfy an itch. I took off and zipped down back lanes. I wasn't sure what I was supposed to do if I saw Laura's car parked near Chris's boat. Would I drive at full throttle, kamikaze like at the cruiser? Would I knock on the porthole frightfully hard?

I leaned forward to reduce wind resistance and eke out as much speed as I could. I zipped through lanes in the direction of the lake. I buzzed straight through a crossroads on the approach to the marina. I zoomed in through the entrance gates and instantly noticed that the Northern Ireland car was parked on the dock beside Chris's boat. Muscular guy was standing in the stern and eating from a bag of chips. I slammed on the brakes and halted abruptly. He continued to eat his chips, unconcerned. I noticed that he wore blue disposable gloves. I wondered if the Spanish man was below decks with a scrubbing brush. Maybe they'd branched out into contract cleaning.

Suddenly I was not so keen to find out if Chris was at home. I scanned the car park but did not recognise any car.

There seemed little else to do but return to school. I twisted hard on the throttle and drove fast out of the marina, one eye glued to the wing mirror to see if the Northern Ireland car followed me. I bent down into a corner at speed and promptly crashed into a flock of sheep.

26

The class bell sounded as I entered the building. I quickly stepped into the staff bathroom and began to wash my hands. I pulled some twigs from my jacket and slid a hand down my sleeves, but it still appeared like I had decided to take up sheep shearing in a suit.

The school corridors filled with the sound of students bursting out of classes and filing down corridors to the toilets or their lockers. Electronic notifications followed quickly afterwards. They weren't supposed to use their phones in school but we'd long since given up trying to police the devices. Students were expected to keep them in their lockers and every forty minutes in between classes they could check their feeds for updates. The bing of the notifications seemed to drag on longer than usual. Students began calling to one another.

I poked my head out of the WC into the corridor. Students and staff alike stared at phones. This was beyond a joke. The zombie apocalypse was upon us, but the mindless hordes were not the reanimated dead but screen-addicted youth and adults who could not disconnect. A few students huddled in the corridor. One girl was weeping and being consoled by grim-faced school friends. I guessed that word had got out that Ruairi was likely to return.

I felt my phone rumble in my jacket, and I somewhat self-righteously resisted the urge to pull it out of my pocket. Someone had to make a stand. I knew that I had to get on top of the situation before the school descended into anarchy. I could expect union reps knocking down my door. There would be the prospect of a walk-out and other schools closing out of solidarity. Chris had to know that agreeing to Ruairi coming back could lead to the whole Irish educational system grinding to a strike-bound halt. This would go national. I could also expect livid parents hounding me to transfer their children elsewhere.

Just then Peggy burst through the crowd.

'Oh Martin,' she gasped. 'There you are! I was trying to reach you.'

It was worse than I thought. The news would have gone beyond the boundaries of the school. A Department of Education inspectorate was no doubt inward bound. Peggy proved there was no more efficient news outlet than secretarial backchannels. More often than not we'd get a heads up about unannounced visits, and a surprised inspector would roll in to discover that all files were bang up to date, with every roll completed diligently.

'Thank God you're back,' she said. 'The whole school is up in a heap.'

'I can see that,' I said. 'Time we got ahead of this. I'm not sure yet what we'll do. I never found Chris.'

Peggy looked me in the eye.

'You never found, Chris. Okay,' she said and nodded slowly.

Peggy's eyes grew large as she saw the state of my suit. She stared at my white cuffs that were stained red. I eased them up into my jacket.

'That's sheep dye,' I said. 'I ran into a flock of them on the road. Long story but that stuff transfers.'

Peggy pushed me back into my office and in seconds had the jacket off me.

'Hang on,' I said, forcing a smile. 'Can we get the door at least?'

She kicked it shut with her heel and in the same motion had my shirt pulled over my head. She reached into a closet and pulled out a spare shirt. They don't teach you this in training, but spare shirts are crucial as every day you can face upwards of a thousand potential snipers armed with ink-stained paper pellets.

'Put this on,' she said. 'We've not much time.'

I pulled on the shirt somewhat reluctantly. It's not often that I've had a shirt torn off me. In my mind, the scenario had a different ending. And with a different person.

'Thanks, Peggy. You're a star. What time are the inspectors here?'

She ignored me.

'You need to clean up, Martin. I'll have this washed at once.'

'Thanks, Peggy, I owe you. They can't see me like this.'

'I never saw you leave,' she said somewhat cryptically.

'You were probably on a tea break,' I said helpfully. 'Why would you?'

'Work with me here, Martin,' she snapped back. 'Maybe you never left.'

'Okay? Is this like Schrödinger's cat?'

'What cat?'

'It's a theory, where a cat could be both alive and dead at the same time. On a quantum level.'

'You really are not helping on any level. I probably could say I was with you.'

'There was no room on the scooter,' I replied with a sense of foreboding. 'Also I am sure that some of the teachers saw me leave.'

Peggy adjusted my tie.

'They don't pay me enough, you know that,' she said, gave a thumbs-up gesture and vanished out the door with my soiled shirt.

I adjusted my new shirt and my tie. If there was an inspection, bring it on. I'd remember Peggy at Christmas for sure. I took a deep breath and stepped into the corridor and found Mrs Dervla Kennedy staring at her phone.

'Really, Mrs Kennedy? I think you should be more of an example.'

'What do you mean?'

'We have to be professional. Let nothing interfere with the smooth running of the school.'

'Are you serious?' she asked.

'We've a job to do. Let's do it. So I suggest you put away your phone, forget about Chris and get back to class.'

'You callous bastard.'

A cold feeling began somewhere deep down.

'I don't think that's appropriate, do you?'

'I never liked Chris, but I expected more from you.'

I felt like a latecomer to a party where everyone is boozed up and in on the joke. Students and teachers alike were blatantly glued to their phones. A teenager sobbed. The sense of foreboding ratcheted up a level. If this was a movie, crows would gather outside and clouds would roll in fast forward. I guessed the answer but asked anyway.

'What about Chris?'

'He's dead,' she said, her eyes welling up.

'And that's dreadful, of course,' I said replaying my recent exchanges in my mind, considering which passages may or may not be construed as insensitive.

A passing sixth-class student tore her eyes away from her phone and cut across Mrs Kennedy before she could continue.

'We getting a day off then?' she asked.

'I think that it's premature to be asking that,' I said.

'Don't worry,' Mrs Kennedy said coldly. 'We'll return to our classes as per your request. I expect that there will be a formal announcement later over the PA.'

She turned on her heel.

'Of course,' I said.

Students and staff lingered in the corridors. Cigarette smoke wafted from the student toilets. Two students were eating the face of one another. Graffiti glistened wetly on a wall.

'Right,' I shouted. 'Back you go. Now please.'

Reluctantly they complied and the corridors emptied.

I reached into my pocket and drew out my phone. A phone that had not ceased buzzing. A notification appeared on the screen.

'Principal found dead at bottom of lift shaft.'

Part III

The Modern Era

"I have not failed. I've just found 10,000 ways that won't work."
Thomas Edison

25

Peggy and I walked through the hotel doors into chaos. Paramedics Sam and Ella stood beside a trolley chatting. Ella saw me enter and nudged her colleague, rolling her eyes.

Gardaí milled about including Garda Julian holding a clipboard. He was noting the names of people entering the scene cordoned off by tape. Behind him, firefighters stared down the open doors of a lift shaft. A teenage onlooker managed to squeeze the scene into a selfie.

Inspector Garda Cora peeled herself away from a group of Gardaí as we reached the tape.

'News travels fast,' she said.

'I know. Is it him?' I asked.

'You know I can't say.'

'His car is parked out front.'

'There are a lot of cars out front.'

A phone ringtone from Ed Sheeran's *Multiply* album echoed up the lift shaft.

'I wouldn't like to speculate,' Cora said.

'You're waiting for the state pathologist then or what?' Peggy interjected. 'Chris is still there, isn't he? Can we have a look?'

Cora threw me a puzzled glance.

'She gave me a lift,' I said. 'The scooter can only go so fast.'

Peggy was in her element; she operated in a world where gossip was currency and she'd hit the motherlode today. She'd insisted on driving me and I found myself in her car before I could react. Peggy had made the journey in a time that a rally driver would have been proud of, all while applying lipstick using her car mirror.

'As a matter of interest, when did you last see Chris?' Cora asked us.

'Friday but he rang in sick this morning,' Peggy said quickly. Her eyes welled up. 'I can't believe this happened. He had so much to live for.'

I did a double take. Peggy had made formal complaints about Chris. She'd saved his name under "Moron" on her mobile phone. She'd once shown me an online post about Chris after he'd been caught with a married woman. She'd *liked* the comment, "He deserves a bullet in the cock." It seemed a bit extreme even for Sister Mary Sullivan, who posted the remark.

Cora turned towards me.

'What about you, Martin?'

Peggy rounded on me.

'You don't have to answer that,' she beamed. 'I've binged watched *Law and Order.*'

Cora sighed.

'It's just a question. Where were you around lunchtime?' she asked.

Peggy suddenly panicked and reached for my hand.

'He was with me all afternoon,' she said. 'In the office,' she hesitated, 'having sex.'

Cora bit a smile back.

'Anything to add?' she asked, turning to me.

I thought about who could vouch for my whereabouts around lunchtime. Muscle Guy saw me, but he struck me as someone who wouldn't tell the Gardaí the time of day if asked.

'I probably need to talk to a solicitor,' I replied.

Cora dutifully wrote some more.

'So Peggy is your alibi for this afternoon?'

I nodded. 'Apparently so.'

Suzanne

24

Peggy dropped me off at Suzanne's office. I had called Suzanne and said I'd be waiting for her. She said that she was out jogging but could meet me in the morning. I had told her Chris was dead and she replied, 'Now is good. See you in half an hour.'

'So you've had some afternoon,' she said, striding into her office. She wore a tracksuit and runners. 'Forgive the look,' she said. 'You caught me in the middle of a park run.'

'You're all right,' I replied. 'Sorry for interrupting.'

She slipped out of her runners.

'I made some calls. Seems like you're trending on social media. Again. I've always wanted to have a famous client. It does business a power of good.'

'I'm just pleased that I can help you out,' I said.

'Oh don't be such a baby,' she said.

'So what are your sources saying?'

Suzanne was well connected. She offered anyone in uniform a discount; there were few Gardaí in the county that she did not represent at some time or other.

'They're calling it suspicious.'

'You think?' I said.

'It's not like he died in his bed after a long distinguished career.'

I sighed.

'Could it have been an accident? A faulty lift door or something.'

'It's never faulty lift doors,' Suzanne replied. 'Maybe he had something on his mind and decided to take a way out.'

'He was under a lot of pressure. Not least, being the entire teaching staff out for his head. He supposedly agreed to bring back Ruairi,' I said.

'That wouldn't have made him mister popular.'

'Too true but he was distracted lately. He was worried about something.'

'Other than catching the clap?'

'I hadn't thought about it until now, but I think he was seeing someone, the thing is he normally boasted about who he was doing and how many times. I would have to shove him away when he'd attempt to show me pictures on his phone. This time, there wasn't a peep out of him.'

I explained how he looked shattered in his office and how he turned his phone over so that I could not see the caller ID.

'So a married woman?'

I thought of the woman on his boat.

'It's not unknown. But it's never stopped him before.'

'And he never told you who she was?' Suzanne asked.

I recalled how Kyle had pictures of him leaving my house.

I shook my head.

'He never gave me a name,' I said truthfully.

Suzanne shrugged, 'We probably shouldn't be distracted about this mystery woman. It's you I'm thinking of.'

'You think I had something to do with what happened to Chris?'

'Martin,' she said staring directly at me. 'You called me, and I guess it wasn't to chat about the time we knocked back pints in the Buttery.'

I nodded. 'I kind of told Steven Casey that I was going to find Chris and sort him out once and for all.'

'Lovely. Not the most helpful of comments.'

'I didn't find him, Suzanne. I did look.'

'I believe you. It's the jury you have to convince.'

'What do you mean jury?'

'You're worried, Martin. You wouldn't be here if you were live streaming a lunch date with the Bishop when Chris took a nose dive.'

I dropped my gaze to the floor.

'I was at the marina. I hit a sheep.'

'Sheep?' she said. 'That's your alibi? Sure it's open and shut.'

I mentioned the muscular man whom I'd seen.

Suzanne looked at me kindly. 'So you want to put a man, convicted of multiple criminal offences on the stand as your witness? I'd think we'd have better luck with the sheep.'

She pointed to a door to an ensuite.

'You mind if I change? This is not how I want to be seen on TV.'

She slid through the door, leaving it partially ajar, and I heard a shower switch on.

'What do you mean TV?' I called out, rising to stand behind the door, to continue the conversation.

'It's bound to,' she called out over the rush of water. 'It's a slow news day. They'll want to speak to the acting Principal but seeing he's a suspect. They'll have to settle for me.'

I had a thought.

'They can check my phone records. Ping me on the masts.'

'They'll only confirm that your phone was at the marina. Your accomplice could have driven around with it.'

'Accomplice?'

'Maybe you're in cahoots with the beefy bloke. Maybe Peggy? I don't know.'

I slumped against the wall.

'Peggy told Cora that we were having sex,' I said.

Suzanne laughed from the shower.

'I'm asking you to listen to yourself. Imagine I'm a bored juror. I hear about a selfless schoolteacher murdered in his prime. I'd want someone to pay.'

'I didn't do it,' I said again.

'So you say. I mean they catch you out with one lie and it's easy to believe the rest of the statement is full of lies.'

'What did I lie about?'

'So we're not going with you and the school secretary going at it like rabbits,' she called out wryly. 'As a defence.'

'I never put her up to it,' I said. 'She was trying to be helpful. She is thrilled to see the back of Chris. You don't think that Cora would believe her, do you?'

Suzanne walked out of the en-suite in a business suit, towelling her hair.

'You think Cora got to where she is without having a finely tuned bullshit detector? Peggy's going to retract of course when she realises that she could get into trouble. Imagine her on the stand. "Are you having an affair with this man here?" and the prosecutor would point to you. She'd fold. The barrister would then ask the court clerk to read back the transcript. They'll hear again how she covered for you.'

I saw how it might play out. I must be guilty of something.

'The fact is that there was plenty of time for you to get to town and confront Chris.'

I saw where she was going with this. I'd no alibi apart from the sheep and the convicted hoodlum. I was beginning to wonder if I'd like the taste of prison food.

'They won't find CCTV of me in the hotel,' I said suddenly. 'That has to mean something.'

'Absence of evidence is not evidence of absence. The hotel has no CCTV at the lifts anyway. They are famous for their discretion.'

'I didn't know this.'

'The whole town knows this,' Suzanne said. 'I'd not worry too much; Cora has a long list of suspects who will be cracking open champagne at the news of his passing. You are just one suspect among many.'

'I'd have to be very stupid to slip out of the school and confront the man and tell someone beforehand.'

Suzanne raised an eyebrow.

'Half the people I represent do stupid things. It could be argued you were so riled up, thinking that your wife was with another man, that you tore out of the school, your mind clouded with anger.'

I saw her point. I was beginning to doubt myself.

'There's one more thing,' I said, deciding that I'd better come clean. 'Kyle spotted Chris leaving my house the other day.'

Suzanne stood at a mirror, raised a hairbrush but stopped midway.

'So I'm barely thirty-seconds into this and already notched up several motives for you wanting Chris dead.'

She began brushing her hair.

'Do we know why Chris was at the hotel?' she asked. 'I checked and there was a room booked in his name.'

'That's the first I heard of that,' I said.

Suzanne watched me in the reflection of the glass as she brushed her hair. 'Perhaps they could not meet at her house. Perhaps the husband was at home.'

'I guess,' I said in a low voice.

She examined me intently.

'Or the son,' she said.

I shivered. Suzanne was going where I had been all along.

'Liam was supposed to have been home this morning but had a last-minute call to go to work,' I said quietly.

It would have been too late to cancel a hotel booking without losing the deposit.

'There's something else? Isn't there?' Suzanne said and dropped her hairbrush into a handbag before checking herself in the mirror. I realised; she was again looking at me in the reflection.

I mumbled. 'Laura can't swim. We saw someone in Chris's boat, but I don't think it was her. Laura told me she's never been out on the lake.'

'So that might rule out Chris's place to meet and could explain the hotel, but all that being said, this is pure conjecture. I have to ask you; have you been speaking to Laura?'

'She just got home. She rang me when she saw the missed calls. She just said that she was out. I told her about Chris and that I was on the way to see you.'

Suzanne nodded.

'She didn't say where she was?'

'She didn't.'

Suzanne's eyes fixed on mine. 'Sounds like you two need to have a conversation. I can only act for you, you know. If she was anywhere near the hotel, then she'll have to make a statement, about what she saw.'

'So my wife might be the potential witness that proves my innocence?'

'Or…' Suzanne let the word hang in the air for a moment. 'It's not that hard to trip someone.'

I felt my heart rate increase.

'Sorry, Martin,' she said.

'I'll bring it up,' I said. 'Maybe sooner than later. She's waiting outside.'

Laura

23

Laura was parked on the pavement opposite Suzanne's office. I crossed the road and climbed into the cab. I was just in time as a television van pulled up behind us. I slumped in the seat. A news reporter, microphone in hand hopped out of the passenger side and crossed the street before hurrying in through the office door.

'So what did Suzanne say?' Laura asked.

'She said that we can't take it for granted that Chris voluntarily nose-dived.'

'She thinks that?'

'She says that she must be ready just in case. She told me to keep my head down and not to say anything to Cora unless she is there.'

'Good advice.'

We watched as Suzanne, not a hair out of place, emerged from the building, chatting animatedly with the reporter. The reporter beckoned to a camera operator to join them and gesticulated towards Suzanne's offices, seemingly pointing out good angles that included the shop front.

'They got here quickly,' Laura said. 'Like they were tipped off.'

'Someone has to say something about him. How he was a pillar of the community, yada yada.'

'So Suzanne, really?' Laura said smirking.

'I know yes,' I grinned. 'I don't know how she sleeps at night.'

We watched as Suzanne said something on camera, a solemn look on her face.

'Thanks for picking me up,' I said.

'That's the job,' she sighed. 'I've already packed for you.'

'What?' I said.

'Isn't this what happens next? My husband, the fugitive. You always said that you liked South America,' she said, her face breaking into a smile.

'I'm not going on the run,' I snapped back. 'I did nothing wrong.'

'Can you prove it?'

'No. So that might be a problem,' I replied. 'They can't prove I did it either.'

'So that's another positive,' she said.

'What do you mean?' I asked.

'They'll have to make you acting principal which means a boost in salary. When do you think that will kick in, by the way?'

'How can you even think of anything like that at the moment?'

'The bills are still rolling in. So if you're deciding to divert into a life of crime, make sure it's lucrative.'

We watched as the reporter wrapped up the interview. Suzanne's face changed instantly, she stood back grinning and waving at passersby. The camera operator focused on the reporter, recording her nodding sagely. These 'noddies' would then be inserted into the final report as reaction shots.

'You don't think that I've anything to do with Chris's death, do you?' I asked.

'You never liked him. He made your best friend Suzanne miserable, and he blocked you from moving forward. He could have taken early retirement years ago. He just held on, on the off chance he could meet a stacked substitute teacher who had no access to social media.'

'Not liking someone is not a crime. If so then every husband in the county would be guilty of something. I think he liked married women in particular.'

I studied Laura, hoping for a reaction but did not detect any.

She started the engine and pulled out into traffic.

'I would not be surprised if he made a pass at you,' I said tapping into my subtle side.

'Oh thanks,' she said. 'Glad I'm not past it yet.'

It wasn't a no.

'So what would you do if he did?' she asked after a few moments.

'I'd be annoyed.'

'At him or me?'

'Both.'

'Enough to push him down a lift shaft?' she asked.

'Maybe, he had it coming,' I said.

'So there's some passion in you after all.'

I decided to confront her. 'Chris was seen going to our house.'

'Are you following me?' Laura asked.

'No,' I said. I didn't mention Kyle spying on the house.

'There's no point denying it. He will be on Mrs Keena's cameras if they look.'

We drove on.

'He did call by,' she said.

'You didn't mention it.'

'I agreed to say nothing.'

'So why all the mystery?'

'He was in trouble. With a woman.'

'There's a surprise.'

'He wanted my help. He wanted to end it, but she was having none of it. He was afraid of what she might do.'

'Who was it that he was seeing?'

She shook her head. 'I'd rather not say.'

'Why?'

'Just park this for now,' she said. 'I'm asking you.'

We drove onwards.

Her answer seemed too convenient. Chris wasn't around to confirm what she had revealed.

'There are more than men who should be in a line-up with you. There are women too,' she said.

Where was this going? Was she about to confess?

'Like whom?'

'First. Would you report me if I had something to do with it?'

'I don't know.'

'You would. I mean maybe you'd be next. I'd have to keep you silent. Smother you in your sleep.'

'Right, I'll never sleep soundly again.'

'If you're thinking of suspects, Suzanne has got a major motivation. I could see her doing it and I like her and all. Where was she when all of this happened?'

'Jogging,' I replied.

'Or so she says.'

I tried to process what Laura was saying. Chris had messed Suzanne about. Made a real show of her. I mean standing her up on the wedding day, it's hard to come back from such humiliation.

Suzanne had asked to be kept informed of everything, but she was a friend and it was also her job. Could she have done it? If you were to ask me, could she take a putting iron to his car then I'd have said, "no" until she reduced his first car to scrap. How much harder would it have been to give someone a shove at the open doors of a lift? Had she truly been out on a park run?

'I can't see it,' I said.

'Or won't see your best friend doing it,' she said. 'You thought of me quickly enough.'

'I never said that.'

'You asked me if I was seeing Chris.'

'I never used those words.'

'Really? You're as subtle as a brick.'

I sighed. 'You know where I was when it all went down?'

'At school?'

'I popped home.'

'Ahuh,' she said noncommittally.

I watched her face as she focused on the road.

'You weren't there. Your phone was.'

'I must have forgotten it.'

'You'd sooner go out with no shoes than be without your phone.'

'Maybe I didn't forget it,' she admitted. 'It's not like you don't know how to use the phone locator app.'

'What do you mean?'

'It can be used for more than locating a phone lost behind a sofa.'

'You left it behind on purpose,' I said.

She drove on. Seconds passed.

'Turning off the phone would just have made you suspicious, so yes. I left it behind on purpose.'

I perked up. This sounded like an admission to me. Perhaps I missed my calling to work as a police investigator. My heart began to pound faster.

'So you were meeting someone?'

'Yes.'

I'd cracked the case. I'd have to see if there were online forums dedicated to solving cold case crimes. They'd appreciate someone with insights.

I watched the street pass outside the window and realised that we were not heading in the direction of home.

'Where are we going?'

My detective instincts were not yet infallible.

She smiled sadly. 'Maybe, under the circumstances, we should dispense with the secrets.'

'Okay,' I agreed and decided to seize the initiative. 'Who were you going to meet?'

I'd guessed the answer but wanted to hear her confirm that it was the late lamented Chris O'Donnell. I reached surreptitiously for my phone. Perhaps I should be recording this.

'You might tidy yourself up,' she said glancing at me.

I realised that I was still somewhat dishevelled from the sheep.

'Why?'

'Because we're on our way to meet him now.'

I reluctantly ruled out my first guess – as right now, he probably was having a Y incision made by the state pathologist.

Michael

22

Laura parked the car in a space facing the Shannon River. The evening sun shone but the coffee shop on the riverfront was still doing a brisk business. The tables strewn around the pavement were full and a pair of white-shirted servers swooped on down with their notepads, whisking away soiled plates or dropping off orders.

One table was occupied by a lone customer and the other chairs around it remained unoccupied even though a huddle of people waited nearby to be seated.

The problem was the man sitting there – he looked like he might ask passers-by for the price of a cup of tea. He wore a new jacket that fit better than the last one I had seen him in. There were no rips in this one. His beanie was the same, however. Our eyes met. It was the same man that I'd seen outside Suzanne's offices.

Laura joined me, shoving the parking ticket into her purse. She looked to me and the man for a reaction. He raised a hand in greeting – the other clasped a mug. She looked uncomfortable and her eyes darted between me and him.

'This is, Michael,' she said. 'My husband.'

Michael grinned.

'Your ex-husband you mean.'

Laura blushed. 'Yes, that's what I meant, I meant my first husband.'

She sat down quickly at the table. I joined them, thankful that it was a round table otherwise the situation might have become awkward.

She did not shake his hand and I followed her lead.

'This is cosy,' I said, pulling the chair close to the table.

'Very modern,' Michael said. 'That's the way of the world now.'

The silence settled between us. Michael seemed in no rush to fill the gap.

'So you long in town?' I said breaking it first.

'Not very,' he said. 'The question is, am I staying long?'

'Are you?' Laura asked.

'That depends on a lot of things,' Michael said.

Laura turned to me. 'Michael is here for Liam.'

From the look of him, I did not anticipate that he was about to hand over twenty years of paternity payments.

'Really?' I said.

'He's on the verge of flunking out, I've a right to be concerned,' Michael said.

'It might be a little bit late for that. Where were you when he was doing his Leaving Certificate? We were on financial fumes with the extra tutors that we had to find.'

'Lads,' Laura said. 'You want to do this now?'

'Sorry,' Michael said. 'I deserved that. Hands up. I've not been the best parent in the world.'

Best parent? He ranked up there with harp seals. Although at least their mother would stick around for twelve days before abandoning her young.

'So what do you want to do with Liam? Get some bonding in? Take him on a trip? Just so you know, he's never been to Disneyland.'

'I'm not rightly sure what we will do,' he said slowly. 'Maybe it's too late to reconnect but maybe it's worth trying.'

'Does Liam know you are here?' I asked.

Michael nodded. 'He does now.'

Laura threw him a withering look before interrupting. 'We were planning that you would be included in the conversation.'

'That's all so big of you,' I said.

'Don't be a prick,' Laura said.

'It was just a brief conversation,' Michael said. 'He looked me up it seems and recognised me in the street. It's a small town and was bound to happen. Kind of ruined the surprise though.'

A server appeared. Her pen at the ready.

'Would you like to see the menus?'

'I'll have a scone,' Michael said, 'with a regular coffee.'

'Tea, please,' Laura said.

The server's face paled slightly. She'd not likely retire on the commission that she'd make at this table.

'I'll have a Danish,' I said, illustrating that I had sophisticated genes. 'And an Americano.'

She made a few notes and disappeared, whisking the menus away.

Michael was right when he said it was a small town. Kyle had spotted Laura and Michael both together. It was impossible to maintain secrets for too long.

'Just so you know, Martin,' Laura said turning to me, 'I was not expecting this. Michael got in touch to say that he was in town. We met here,' Laura continued. 'I did not think it appropriate for him to come to the house.'

'That was nice of you,' I said.

'I planned to tell you,' she said. 'I didn't know how you'd react. You've not been yourself since being run over by that boat.'

'I might not have put out the welcome mat, but I like to think that I'd have handled it well.'

'Right,' she said. 'So says the man who ran over the head of the Parents' Association.'

'That was an accident,' I said. 'There was a spi—'

Michael interrupted. 'Laura said that you thought you saw someone new in town. She said that you put two and two together but came up with Ginger Reagan.'

'Yes, it seemed logical to think it was her ex.'

'Your ex?' Michael asked, addressing Laura.

I grinned. I felt I'd scored a point.

'Wrong ex, it appears,' I said.

'Will you both stop turning this into my sex life,' Laura said firmly.

'You told me that you only held hands,' I muttered.

'Of course we did,' she said. 'We held hands. A lot.'

I turned to Michael.

'It's like you're everywhere I look lately.'

'I like to get out and about,' he said. 'Catching up on old haunts. The town has changed for sure. That pub on the corner is gone.' He turned to Laura. 'We had some sessions, there eh?'

'It burned to the ground in the winter,' I said. 'Rumour has it that someone attempted to defrost frozen pipes with a blow torch and succeeded too well.'

'Maybe don't do this,' Laura pleaded. 'The trip down memory lane.'

'I was thinking of something else. It's about coincidences,' I said.

Michael shrugged. 'So you're wondering if my showing up and Chris taking up indoor skydiving was related? I knew him from back in the day, he always was a tool, but I never pushed him.'

'Why did you say push?' I asked. 'We don't know the full facts yet. He could have just decided to end it all.'

'Sorry, Sherlock,' Michael said. 'I'm sure it was just an accident. They happen all the time.'

'Around here,' I said, 'using a lift is not generally considered a health hazard.'

'Chris might contradict you,' Michael said.

'Michael,' Laura said. 'Not cool.'

'So where were you then?' Michael said to me. 'When he decided to check out?'

'What are you saying?'

'You think that because you have a job you have the right to accuse me of whatever you like?'

'I never thought that,' I said although I thought that.

Laura stood. 'I'm going to the loo. In the meantime, get your willies out and wave them about if you must but I expect that you shake hands when I return. This is not helping Liam and it's not helping me.'

She grabbed her handbag and was gone.

'Some woman,' Michael said

'Yes,' I agreed. 'We can also agree that Chris was a shit, despite whatever they might say in the newspapers.'

Michael nodded, 'I'll not lose any sleep over him.'

'Me neither.'

'I'm surprised to hear you say that,' he said. 'Don't teachers stick together?'

'Not necessarily,' I said, somewhat hypocritically. Teachers would have no qualms about running over a member of a different union, but we pulled up the drawbridge if confronted by an outsider. We had three months of summer holidays to defend and resisted attacks from all assailants.

'Liam seems to be a good kid,' Michael sighed. 'I want to have a proper conversation with him.'

'He's a good lad,' I agreed. 'Very sociable.' (Laura and I fondly recalled his first STD).

'I missed so much.'

'You did,' I agreed, feeling faintly sorry for him.

'You were good to step up when I was not here.'

'Thanks for saying that,' I said. Michael wasn't that bad.

He leaned in closer. 'You were right to ask me "why now?" Why did I show up now?'

'So why did you?'

'We get all the local papers in London. A few days late, mind, but I know more about what's going on here than you think. Ask me how the local hurlers are doing. Who is in charge of the county council? Whose car got vandalised? Go on.'

'You're all right. I believe you.'

'It's all in the *Westmeath Topic* or *Independent*.'

I could see where this was going.

'If they feature a story on a broken traffic light, you can be sure that a story of a woman being bitten by a snake would make the paper,' he said.

I thought of Mrs Keena being wheeled out.

A woman living next door to us.

The paper had more information. There were column inches to fill.

'By a snake that you owned,' he added.

'I was just minding it,' I said.

'Not much good at it were you?'

'I wouldn't put it like that.'

'How else should I put it?'

'For your information, I almost got bitten. That wasn't in the paper.'

'So you say.'

'It escaped and you know the rest of it.'

The server reappeared with a tray of hot drinks and pastries. She slid them onto the table.

'Enjoy,' she said and was gone.

Michael put his hand over mine and leaned in close. Anyone watching might assume we were swapping racing tips.

'Are you trying to kill Laura?'

I felt the blood drain from my face.

'How dare you!'

My fists clenched but remained pinned down by Michael's hands.

'Settle down,' Michael said, not in the least bit intimidated. 'You know, I've met Englishmen who've made train sets that filled garages, Spitfire scale models that are perfect to the nth degree but not once have I met one who's made a blowpipe, why would someone do that?'

Michael's right hand folded over my wrist. I guessed he was feeling my pulse.

'What has Laura been saying to you?' I said sharply. I wondered if she had sneaked into my workshop and poked about without telling me.

'Very little as it happens. The woman defends you.'

His hands moved off mine and vanished under the table.

My hands remained where they were, knuckles white, as I squeezed my fingers into my palm. How dare he? I sipped from my café Americano as I regained my composure.

His hands reappeared on the table.

'I'm sorry,' he said. 'I meant no offence.'

'I don't appreciate what you said.'

'Sometimes I just come out with stuff. I just need to be a lot more careful about what I say. Then again,' he grinned, and his hand moved off the table revealing the empty but cloudy vial I'd filled with snake venom, 'what am I to make of this?'

'You were in my workshop. You had no right,' I said indignantly.

'So what was this?' he asked.

'Just some stuff.'

'Hope it's not deadly – I slipped some into your coffee.'

I gasped and glanced down automatically.

'Just kidding,' he said, his eyes never leaving me. The vial had vanished.

He leaned closer. 'Just so you know, Laura better not experience any kind of accident. I'm not the forgiving type. It's not like I've to worry about my standing in the community.'

Laura appeared and watched the two of us.

'Are we good?'

'Yes,' Michael said. 'I think we've buried the hatchet.'

'Have we?' Laura said staring at me.

'Yes,' I said. 'He's made his position clear. We agree on a lot of things.'

The server arrived again. 'You want anything else?'

'I think the bill,' I said. I turned to Michael, 'Don't split it. I'll get the lot. My treat.'

'That's very good of you,' Michael said.

The server nodded toward me benignly. 'So you want me to include his lobster?'

I grimaced.

Michael shrugged.

'I got here early and was hungry.'

'Sure,' I said.

Michael had played me. However, I now knew who I was dealing with.

Peggy

21

The soft leather office chair embraced me like a luxurious bed. The late lamented Chris liked the finer things in life, and I planned to savour every one of them. I toyed with a stencilled "Acting Principal" plaque. I wondered how much time should pass before it wouldn't be impolite to screw it on the door.

My new office was much roomier than my old one. I could swing a cat in here or anything else I fancied. Cardboard boxes containing Chris's stuff were strewn around the floor awaiting archival storage AKA a skip. Cora had already nosed around and taken anything that might be useful to her.

There was a tap on the door and Peggy sailed in, a picture of melancholy. She'd taken to keening at the picture of our late principal displayed at the front of the school with the condolences book. I thought the black armband she wore was a little over the top.

'How are you settling in?' she asked. 'It must be some consolation that you got the job.'

'I've big shoes to fill,' I said dutifully, 'and the role is just in an acting capacity as you know.'

She sighed theatrically and pulled up a picture of Chris from a cardboard box.

'He'll be missed you know.'

'I'm sure he will.' I didn't want to be churlish but wasn't this the woman who organised a petition at the staff Christmas party to have Chris chemically castrated?

'Was there anything else?'

She glanced back at the door to confirm it was closed.

'The cops haven't been on to me yet.'

'The Gardaí?'

'They'll want me to make a statement,' she said. 'That's how it goes. An official one.'

'I'm sure that they'll get to you soon enough. Cora is, if anything, thorough. They'll wait for the remains to be released first I guess.'

'You think?' she said. 'Perhaps I'll treat myself to a new outfit.'

'If you like.'

'On that note,' she hesitated. 'I maybe said a bit too much at the scene of the crime.'

'Oh, you think? You could have just said we were updating files.'

'I know,' she admitted. 'I just panicked.'

Some witness for the defence she would be. Suzanne was right. She'd have to walk back her statement.

'Also, we don't even know if there was a crime,' I said. 'Chris was under a lot of pressure. He could have just snapped.'

Peggy looked at me doubtfully.

'He went to a lot of effort to throw himself down a lift shaft. Can you see him doing that to one of his suits?'

She had a point. Chris hadn't changed a flat tyre in his life, the risk of soiling his bespoke suits was too great.

'That's what the AA is for,' he once claimed.

'I'm sure Cora will let us know soon enough,' I said.

She examined her feet carefully.

'What's on your mind, Peggy?'

'If they do suspect foul play, I'm afraid they might catch me out if they start asking for intimate details.'

'What do you mean?'

'If we go for the sex thing.'

'Maybe we won't do that.'

'I don't even know if you are circumcised or not. It might come out. Maybe you should get your lad out and I'll make notes.'

I leaned over the desk.

'Peggy, relax. Just tell them the truth and you'll be okay.'

She nodded eagerly.

'The thing is I haven't slept since it happened. I'm all nerves. I'm chewing Valium like they were sweets. What am I going to tell my husband when he finds out about the affair?'

'There is no affair.'

'And that's what you want me to tell them?'

'Just tell them the truth.'

'If you think so.'

'I think that's the best way, don't you?'

She nodded eagerly. 'Okay, I'll tell them that I think you killed Chris.'

'Hold on, you can't say that.'

She was exasperated. 'Okay, get your lad out or tell me what you want me to say. I'm more than a little confused here.'

'I didn't kill Chris.'

'Okay.' She winked.

'What's that for?'

'Fine. We play it that way. Deny everything. Let them prove it, I say.'

'What makes you think I killed Chris anyway?'

'You mean allegedly?'

'Peggy, you are watching far too much Netflix for your own good.'

'I go where the evidence points,' she said.

'What makes you think I had anything to do with his death?'

She waved her arms about indicating the office.

'There's this for a start. You've had your eyes on this office for years.'

'Okay that's a motive and maybe a very good one.'

'There's the pay rise.'

'True that's a help.'

'He humiliated your friend, Suzanne,' she said, jabbering on. 'And you told Steven Casey that you were going to sort Chris out once and for all before you ran out the door. Steven said there was a mean look in your eye.'

'That's easily explained,' I said uneasily.

'Chris was no help with your references,' she continued.

'References?'

'Whenever you got frustrated at the lack of progress and applied for other principal positions. Ever wondered why they never followed through? It suited him to keep you here as his wingman.'

I had wondered at the lack of positive responses. I rarely even got to practise my interview skills and attributed it to some bias against the English. Some things now made sense. I'd been at a management conference once and one of the principals of a neighbouring school pointedly asked me if I should be drinking anything stronger than Ballygowan over dinner.

'I didn't know,' I admitted.

'I can make a list if you like. I mean these reasons were just off the top of my head.'

I smiled gamely. 'It's true. I had some minor motives to want him gone.'

At least she didn't know about Chris being seen leaving my house.

'Chris may also have been doing the bold thing with Laura,' she added. 'So there is that too.'

I froze.

'I mean what was she doing at the hotel?'

'She was at the hotel?' I gasped.

'Lisa Dooley recognised her.'

'Who's that?'

'She works part-time on the desk. She remembered Laura treated her once for what turned out to be a bad case of thrush.'

'She was sure?'

'Believe me, you'd not confuse it with anything else. You need to knock that on the head. Antibiotics at the get-go is what I say.'

'I mean she's sure it was Laura?'

'Yep. I'll mention that in my statement, shall I? When Cora comes knocking.'

I did not want her on the prosecution side of the aisle.

I did not want her in the country.

I was beginning to wonder if the best option was to show her my penis.

Maggie

20

Maggie Geraghty-Philbin was waiting in the staff car park as I left the building. She stood with her back to me examining my scooter parked square in the middle of the principal's car spot. She turned before I could back away.

'You fell on your feet,' she said, pointing to the "Reserved Principal" sign. Someone had badly scratched out Chris's name. To be fair, I'd waited a day to do it.

'I don't know about that. I got run over by a boat. I've had the worst summer holidays ever.'

'Don't you be looking for sympathy from me,' Maggie said stiffly and pointed to the right side of her head. 'I still can't see out of this eye.'

'Still, you are looking better,' I said. It was true the swelling had receded and she now had more or less, a normal-sized head.

'I could have died,' she said.

'I'm sorry about what happened. I never knew about your allergies.'

I decided that it was best to change the topic.

'So what are you doing here?' I asked, knowing what she was doing here.

I was anticipating some screaming and shouting, maybe the appearance of a cosh from her handbag.

She seemed oddly calm.

'The interview to get the permanent post is, I assume, not competency based. Because sure as hell you haven't the street sense that you were born with,' she said smugly.

'What are you trying to tell me, Maggie?' I asked.

She pointed to the scorched patch on my old parking spot.

'You were never the target,' she said.

Maggie relaxed on the chair in front of my desk. She waited for me to offer her some tea, drawing out the suspense as long as she could.

'Biscuit?' I asked, holding out a saucer of biscuits. She took two from the plate.

'Very fancy,' she said admiring the chocolate covered Kimberlies. 'Someone's putting the boat out.'

I sat down in my seat opposite her.

'So what were you saying about targets?'

'I called my cousin as soon as I heard about your car going ka-boom.'

'Ginger?'

'No, the nun who joined the Poor Clares in Drumshanbo. Of course, Ginger.'

I forced myself to remain polite.

'So what did he say?'

'We talked about the weather first, as you do.'

Remaining polite was hard.

'Maggie, what did he say?' I repeated, gritting my teeth.

'He said it was him. Can I have another biscuit?'

'Are you serious?' I said in shock.

'Yeah I love these,' she said and reached over and grabbed another. 'About the other matter. Course it was him.'

'And you believed him?'

'Why would he lie, Martin, to me of all people?'

So smuggler, arsonist, arms broker but not a liar.

I sat back. I made a show of twisting the seat back and forth on its oiled bearings.

'So he did it but you were saying that I was not the target?'

I think Maggie smiled. It was hard to tell, despite the reduced swelling.

'I was getting nowhere with you lot. I wanted Ginger to help me out, he has some influence in this town.'

I could imagine what that meant. It's not like Ginger was known for writing strongly worded letters to *The Times*.

'No one can tell him what to do but that Kate one has him wrapped around her little finger.'

It was clear from her tone that there was no love lost between them. I wondered why?

'She once called my wee Ruairi a thug,' she said bitterly.

I think I knew the answer.

'There she is in that big house thinking she's somebody. Hasn't worked a day in her life.'

'Be that as it may,' I said. 'Can we get back to the matter at hand?'

She was building up to her moment of triumph.

'I was that desperate that I called by Kate's in July. If I had to prostrate myself before her, then so be it.'

'And?' I said, hoping she'd get to the point quickly and out of the office.

'She opened the door but refused to let me in.'

'I'm sorry to hear it.'

Maggie attempted a smirk. 'She had company. I said to her, "Isn't that Martin's car parked behind the house?"'

'My car?'

She had my complete attention. I stopped moving the chair.

What she said made no sense whatsoever. My astonishment equalled Simon Cowell's on *Britain's Got Talent* when faced with an exceptionally good magician. The trick was impossible but somehow had happened on national television.

'I never stepped foot inside the house until a few days ago,' I protested.

Maggie smiled. She knew this of course.

'Hold on,' I said. 'Last July? I was in the hospital.'

Maggie nodded.

'I didn't say that you were there. Just your car.'

I got it. My car, the one that Chris had borrowed while his was being resprayed due to Suzanne getting in touch with her creative side.

'Chris had my car,' I whispered.

'That's right. He must have parked it there at night for safe keeping,' she sneered.

Maggie knew exactly what she was doing by doorstepping Kate.

'So you and Kate had a heart-to-heart then?' I said.

'Let's say she came around to my way of thinking that Ruairi was entitled to an education, and she promised to ask Ginger to see what he could do.'

'So he blew up my car as a message? He couldn't just like send an e:mail?'

'As I said, no one but Kate tells Ginger what to do.'

'If Chris was the key to getting your son back, why not blow up *his* car?'

'Maybe Ginger didn't know it was borrowed? Everyone makes mistakes.'

'Are you serious?' I said. 'I wore navy and black once, now that was a mistake. Blowing up a car is a whole other level.'

Maggie looked at me with her good eye.

'You don't understand. I have to get Ruairi into a school, and this place has a great reputation. You send loads to university.'

The only way Ruairi was ever getting into university was if he had a crowbar and the ability to shimmy up a drainpipe.

I felt I was getting an inkling of the pressure that Chris was under.

Kate literally had Chris by the testicles; all she had to do was threaten to set Ginger on him if Chris sought to end his sleepovers.

Similarly, Maggie figuratively had Chris by the gonads as well. She could use Ginger as leverage if Ruairi did not get his backside under a school desk.

Chris also knew that if he allowed Ruairi back that it was likely that the whole school would close. It's impossible to teach students if all of your teachers are on a picket line.

Maybe he did take a swan dive after all.

'However, Chris never followed through, he never admitted Ruairi,' I pointed out.

'I know, the little shite.'

'We shouldn't speak ill of the dead,' I said.

'He said it wasn't his fault. He blamed you.'

'The little shite,' I retorted.

'We all know Chris needed a map to find his way around the school. He said his hands were tied if you were not on board.'

Chris had no compunction in throwing me to the wolves. I wished he was alive so that I could have pushed him myself.

Chris was caught between a rock and a hard man but in the end, did nothing. Something had to give. Someone decided to remove Chris from the board.

'You squealed on Chris.' I said. 'You accidentally-on-purpose revealed Kate was entertaining a gentleman caller.'

She shrugged. 'Maybe Ginger just figured it out.'

'And then Ginger decided to rectify his mistake. Enticed Chris to the hotel and we all know how that ended up.'

Maggie shrugged.

'So why, tell me?'

Maggie coughed. 'You claimed that you had no power to intervene on Ruairi's behalf. However, that was when you were a vice principal. You've changed offices.'

'So you want me to reinstate, Ruairi?' I said. 'What if I told you that my hands might still be tied?'

'All I can do is point out the power of family,' she said. 'I mean, I love Ruairi and my cousin love me. I'm going to make the same offer to you as I did to Chris. Do the right thing for my son if you don't want to see the family upset.'

She couldn't have put it clearer if she had placed her message in a large font on page one of the *Westmeath Topic*.

Ruairi was to be allowed back in or I'd need to watch myself around high buildings.

She knew that I had to find a way.

I felt a throbbing in my head.

And they say teachers don't deserve their long holidays.

Despite all she'd said, I knew Maggie was lying.

Kyle

19

Kyle's cabin appeared deserted when I arrived on my scooter. I peered in through the windows. The interior appeared neat. There were tell-tale piles of letters on the floor indicating that no one had been home for several days. The door was securely locked. Kyle's car was gone.

I took out my phone and wandered around the back of the cabin. I rang him but the number connected to voicemail.

'Kyle,' I said. 'Are you about? I'd like to have a chat if that's okay with you.' I paused. 'I'm acting principal now, as you may have heard. I can review your position if you wish.'

Maggie had said her cousin had blown up my car and suggested he had whacked Chris, but I didn't believe her. Kyle also had a solid motive for Chris going to his just reward. If he wanted to win back Rosie then he'd better have a salary and with Chris now off the field, the way was clear in that regard.

I know that I did not kill Chris, but I had no alibi. On the other hand, Kyle, as far as I was aware, had no alibi either. He had said he'd been in a pharmacy and that he was meeting Rosie. What if that was another lie?

I climbed onto the scooter and placed the helmet back on. I hesitated.

If I did not know better, I would say that someone was in the bushes watching.

It was entirely possible that Chris— a man under immense pressure had topped himself but if not, there was only one prime suspect.

'Kyle, you there?' I called out. 'We need to talk.'

I waited, hearing little else but the sound of water lapping at the edge of the lake.

'If you want to meet in a public place then fine.' I held up the phone. 'You have my number.'

Flies buzzed.

If only Chris hadn't fallen down a lift. That's how I guessed that Maggie was lying. It seemed too much of a coincidence that I had discussed this very method of killing Chris with only one person.

Kyle.

A man who was not returning my calls.

Cora

18

Cora waved me into an interview room and pulled out a lunchbox. She gestured for me to sit opposite her at a table bolted to the ground. She tucked into a sandwich as I sat down and discovered that the chair was also bolted to the floor.

'So this is where you bring in the criminals?' I said.

I took in a camera in the corner mounted on a tripod, and a small CD recorder on the table; the bare, badly painted walls.

Cora watched me in amusement. 'You're looking for the two-way mirror, aren't you?'

'No,' I lied. 'So that's not a thing?'

'Maybe in Hollywood,' she said.

She bit into an apple. 'So are you ready to confess?' she asked. 'We know you did it.'

'Did what?' I stammered.

She smiled. 'Force of habit. Everyone is guilty of something.'

'You had me there. I was about to tell you the television licence is long since expired.'

'Really?' She pulled out a notepad. 'Since when?'

'You're doing it again?' I murmured uncertainly.

'We do take Post and Telegraph offences very seriously around here.'

She closed the notebook.

'Yes, I'm just pulling your chain. So to what do I owe the pleasure?'

'I was asking about, Chris. Any news?'

'He's still dead I reckon,' she said and bit into a sandwich. 'The coroner should release him soon although I don't know why they bother sometimes. It's not like we think he was poisoned. Personally, I think it was a fall down a lift shaft that did it, but what do I know?' She hesitated and put her sandwich down. 'And I think I've lost my appetite. Thanks, Martin, you're more motivating than Weight Watchers.'

'Are you thinking that it was not an accident?'

'We ruled that out fairly quickly. The lift doors were opened with an emergency key. I can reveal that as the lift installer is leaking that titbit of information left right and centre. The lifts were in one hundred per cent working order.'

'So Chris, a man under pressure, took the easy way out?'

Cora poised with her sandwich again, giving it a second chance. If she didn't attend a fatal road traffic accident before breakfast, then she probably chalked it up as a good shift.

'No comment,' she said. 'Off the record, Chris didn't seem the type, but you never can tell.'

'And if it was not an accident and if he didn't kill himself?'

Cora smirked.

'You know that I can't comment on an ongoing investigation.'

Especially with a suspect.

I had no alibi apart from a flock of sheep and a convicted bank robber. Neither of which, according to Suzanne would willingly take to the stand in my defence.

'I know you have been here a long time,' I said.

'Here it comes,' she said.

'I wanted to ask you about Ginger.'

'Ginger Reagan?' Cora breathed out deeply. 'Don't say his name too loudly or the ERU will be breaching doors with fingers on triggers.'

She bit into her sandwich.

'You haven't seen him, have you?' Cora asked, munching. 'If you have then I'll need to make some calls.'

I shook my head. 'No chance he found Jesus or anything and reformed?' I asked.

'I doubt it. Why the interest?'

'Maggie his cousin, said she'd sic him on me if I didn't play nice. You told me he might be in the country. So should I be concerned?'

'With Ginger, I'd err on side of caution.'

'What do you mean?'

'Is emigration an option? You could go home to England.'

I paled. 'You serious?'

'It's all settled since the peace deals. The war is over.'

'I sense a but coming down the line.'

'But some had a taste of the finer things in life and found it hard to give up their old ways. If we hear of an ATM ripped from a wall, we don't start rounding up Boy Scouts. What does Maggie want?'

'Ruairi to be readmitted.'

'Some would just roll over and do it.'

'I'm not sure if that's an option. The teacher's union has a stock of strike posters hidden just for this eventuality. Also being involved with a nationwide strike won't exactly help me make my job permanent.'

'Then I'd tread carefully. Anything else?'

'Maggie told me that Ginger had blown up my car but Chris was the intended target.'

'She said that.'

'You don't seem that surprised?'

'Not really.' She hesitated. 'We kind of guessed that you weren't the target. We figured Ginger would have something to do with it. You don't sleep with his wife and get his blessing. I'm surprised at him using a car bomb though. No one pokes that hornet's nest who plans on living. Maybe he just wasn't thinking.'

'She also told me that he was behind Chris taking the plunge.'

'We need more evidence than Maggie's word – which we know she'll deny anyway. We figured he was here for a reason, taking Chris out for the affair makes sense. Just proving it would be the problem. He's wanted for a tiger kidnapping years ago and that's what we will do him for. If we get to him first.'

Tiger kidnappings referred to crimes whereby employees of a bank or an armoured car company were coerced into robbing their employer while their family was being held hostage.

'A member of the public spotted a man in a balaclava smoking outside the home of a security van driver. He put two and two together and made a call. The Emergency Response Unit did their thing and scooped up the whole crew – apart from Ginger who got away through a hedge. There was enough DNA at the scene to place him there. He's been laying low in Spain ever since. The police there made the odd raid, but he's always been a step ahead.'

Spain has an extradition arrangement with Ireland and sunburned Irish criminals were routinely escorted in handcuffs back to Ireland. It was largely one-way traffic however as few Spanish criminals made Ireland their bolt hole, I suppose they missed decent paella.

Cora continued, 'We've tried following Kate, of course, whenever she pops over there but if she can't shake us, she just stays by the hotel pool.'

'If you catch him here, he won't do time for Chris?' I said.

'That's the imperfect world we live in. Sometimes people get away with murder. Remember Al Capone was only ever convicted for tax evasion. He didn't do a day for organised crime.'

'So you'll throw the book at him for the tiger job?'

'That's it.'

'One more thing,' I said turning. 'You said Chris was having an affair with Kate. I never said anything about an affair.'

'Didn't you?'

'You knew?'

'Of course.' She hesitated, preparing her words. 'The war is over, and we are more than happy about that. We would be mighty foolish, though, to be unprepared.'

'You were watching Kate? That's how you knew Chris was seeing her.'

'Let me tell you something,' Cora said. 'I brought in a prisoner once for questioning. He asked to make a personal call and wrote the number on a piece of paper. It was my private mobile number. So yes, we know Kate was seeing Chris. We watch them, they watch us.'

'Am I under surveillance as well?'

'It's Ginger we are after.'

I was beginning to figure out what bait must feel like.

'We're good at what we do,' she added. 'There's no talk of anyone making a move on you.'

'That's a comfort to know. So any other titbits that you can share?'

'I hear you met up with Michael Dwyer,' Cora said.

It was a small town.

'That's true.'

Cora knew about our coffee shop chat it appeared.

'He said he wanted to see his son. I told him that he's leaving it a bit late if he wanted to be father of the year.'

Cora finished her sandwich. 'Did Laura ever tell you why he left in the first place?'

'He didn't want to be tied down.'

'She said that?'

'I assumed.'

Cora removed the cap from a bottle of sparkling water and drank from it.

I sensed that Cora had revealed something important.

'You assumed,' Cora said slowly. 'In my job that's often a mistake.'

'I guess Laura and I need to have a chat,' I said.

'Take it easy,' Cora warned. 'She's been through a lot.'

'Don't worry, Cora,' I said. 'You won't be sitting me down back in that seat in an official capacity.'

'Glad to hear it.'

Laura

17

The kettle clicked off just as I stepped through the front door. Laura waved me into the sitting room and followed moments later with a tray of tea and biscuits and placed them on the coffee table between us. She moved to the kitchen and returned with a single mug of soup and rolls and sat down on an armchair.

I removed my bike helmet and placed it on the sofa beside me as Laura sipped from her mug.

'Is Liam in?' I asked.

She shook her head. 'He's doing a few hours. They called him again, there's a hen night and so it's all hands-on deck,' she said.

'Good, he might not have his hand out for a while so.'

She leaned over her soup, dabbing at it with a piece of brown bread.

It was clear that I had been expected.

'Cora called you?' I asked.

She nodded. 'She gave me a heads up. Said you were on the way home. She said you might have questions.'

I nodded. I picked up a cup of tea. 'She was right. I was hoping for the truth, the whole truth et cetera.'

'Fire ahead.'

'First, can you explain why you were seen going into the hotel before Chris died?'

'I was seen?' Laura asked.

'A woman that Peggy knows saw you.'

'Who?'

'Does it matter? You helped her with a gynae problem. I guess some people don't forget a face or a pair of hands.'

Laura shrugged. 'I never tried to hide the fact I went there. I dropped off some old clothes for Michael and planned to meet Chris after. Chris asked me to help him. He was going nuts and needed advice. He felt that someone had snitched on him.'

'About his affair with Ginger's wife?'

'You knew about that?'

'So does Cora.'

'As it happened, I was just too late. I was barely in the lobby when the alarms started going off. I overheard someone mention Chris's name so I just turned around and left.'

I didn't know if I should believe her or not. As Cora said, everyone lies. I decided to head in a new direction.

'Cora asked if I knew why Michael left town all those years ago. Why would she ask that?'

Laura gazed into her soup. 'Michael was days away from attesting in Templemore.'

'Templemore. The Garda training college?' I interrupted. 'Michael was a Guard?'

'No. He was a recruit. He went on a session. They'd been at a big party to celebrate a councillor being elected Cathaoirleach. That's the head of the county council.'

'I know what a Cathaoirleach is,' I said.

'Long story short, on the way home, they came across a traffic stop. Michael did a fast U-turn, hit the accelerator, and crashed into a ditch. The other recruit was thrown through the passenger window. Some wanted to throw the book at Michael, but no one wanted the headlines.'

Her face trembled. The night was still fresh in her mind.

'The other recruit died,' she said. 'He was the Cathaoirleach's son.'

I studied Laura's face.

'There is more to this, isn't there?'

Laura nodded. 'It was an unholy mess. The toxicology report showed alcohol and traces of coke in the dead man's blood. The newspapers would have portrayed the party as some kind of debauched orgy. The reputation of the Gardaí would have taken a hit. It would have stained the memory of the Cathaoirleach's son and the man himself would be forever blamed.'

'So they covered it up.'

'It would suit the town if the case remained buried. It could end careers, even after all these years.'

I put two and two together.

'The politician went on to bigger and better things, didn't he?' I said.

'TD Tim Fagen,' she said, 'our new Minister for Justice.'

I drank some tea. 'Does Liam know his dad is a killer?'

'Technically it was manslaughter.'

'I'm sure Tim didn't see it that way.'

A flash of anger crossed Laura's face. She took a moment to get in control. 'Liam knows. He asked and I felt I had to tell him. It was years ago now. He hasn't said much since. Then you came on the scene and the rest, as they say, is history.'

'So all these years and no one mentioned it to me?'

'It didn't come up,' she said.

'It's a good job I spoke to Cora then. The topic might never have seen the light of day otherwise.'

Laura threw me a dirty look. 'Cora is not your friend,' she said.

'Maybe yours though. She called you didn't she?' I said. 'To let you know I was on the way.'

She grimaced. 'Doing her duty. Maybe she left out the bit that she was a recruit herself at the time.'

The dots began to connect in my head. Michael and Cora were about the same age.

I knew the answer but had to ask the question anyway.

'So she knew Michael from back in the day?'

'And the recruit that died. Victor Fagen.'

'Victor Fagen?'

'Her fiancé.'

Kyle

16

Laura had left an ironed shirt on the bed. I slipped it on and removed a dark suit from the wardrobe. The late Chris O'Donnell just wouldn't go quietly. I had longed for a promotion, but the post should have come with hazard pay. Multiple people wanted Chris gone and, if you believed Peggy, I was top of the list. I also had the possibility hanging over me of a convicted felon who could take me out if I didn't succumb to blackmail.

I was beginning to think that I should have chosen a safer career, like mine clearing.

I pulled on the suit trousers and noticed that they appeared to have shrunk. I looped a tie around my neck and peered into the mirror that stood on the windowsill. Behind it, a mesh fence bordered the road that separated the estate from rolling fields. Someday there would be houses built there. In the meantime, weeds and hardy grasses struggled to survive on the poor soil. The Amazonian rain forest, it was not. Nothing wilder than sheep lived there. I guessed it was unlikely that the fields would feature in any *National Geographic* special, unless they were having an ultra-slow day at the office.

I sat up straight in the middle of the creation of a Windsor knot. All of a sudden, I felt like a nature walk.

I carefully stepped through the grass, on the uneven surface. I was conscious that my footwear had never been intended for off-road use. I stood in the field and faced my estate. I could see our house through the fence that divided us. I pulled out my phone and ran through my contacts before pressing the call icon. A few metres away a bush started to ring.

'Damn it,' a voice said.

A portion of vegetation rolled back, revealing Kyle sitting on the bottom of a low trench. He wore some faded army fatigues, and his face was streaked with green stripes.

'So how did you figure I was here?' he asked.

'I didn't think you'd skip town and leave Rosie behind. I guessed you'd want to keep tabs on me. I mean, we both know who killed Chris. I figured you'd want to see what I would do.'

'You went to the Guards. Why did you do that?'

'You followed me?'

'As you said, I wanted to see what you'd do.'

'The Guards said that they liked Ginger for Chris's death. Maggie said much the same.'

'So, case closed.'

I watched sheep grazing for a few moments.

'Maybe he had it coming,' I said at last. 'He was not a nice man, on any level.'

An unbidden image appeared in my mind of Chris plummeting past hotel floors.

'So he deserved to die,' Kyle said.

'I never said that.' I looked him in the eye. 'The thing is, is he worth going to jail for?'

'So, let me get this straight. Ginger goes to jail for it, while you get Chris's job. Then we carry on, business as usual?'

'Pretty much. Except you need to be taken care of.'

'What do you mean?'

I could see Kyle stiffening.

'You have skills and I could use you. You could be back on the staff.'

'I don't know, Martin,' Kyle said. 'That's messed up.'

'I think it's a good deal.'

Kyle stared at me and made some calculations.

'I've skills? Blowing up your own car was a nice touch. Did the explosion in your shed give you the idea?'

'Workshop. You think I did that?'

'What better way to throw anyone off the scent? I mean people might figure that someone has a thing against tenured teachers.'

I was shocked. 'What's your game?' I asked.

'You just offered me a deal to stay silent. Not suspicious at all.'

Kyle sat up straight, stretching seized upper body muscles. I noticed he was sitting on a small tarp and had a flask beside him.

'Come on, Kyle. You're the one with the skills. Despite what Cora and Maggie say, I know it was you,' I said.

Kyle almost did a double take. 'Are you nuts? You want to pin this on me?'

We held each other's gaze before I broke.

'Are we saying that the talk about the lift shaft was just a coincidence?'

Kyle's eyes furrowed. 'I guess it could happen.'

'Cora told me that she didn't like coincidences.'

'Me neither.'

On the other hand, coincidences did happen. Didn't the arrival of Haley's Comet appear in the same year that Mark Twain was born and died? Was it just a coincidence that my social media feeds featured advertisements for shoes that, it turned out, were remarkably comfortable?

I shrugged.

'So what we got here?' Kyle asked.

'Some kind of ceasefire for the moment.'

'I'll take that,' I said. I took a deep breath. 'Cora suspects that Ginger was behind Chris's death but she's not exactly beating the bushes to flush him out.'

'What's that about?'

'Cora told me that in the imperfect world we live in, people sometimes pay for crimes they did not commit, in place of ones that they do. I think I get what's going on.'

Kyle poured a hot drink from his flask into a plastic cup, listening intently.

I continued. 'There was a road accident, years ago. Michael was drunk, he killed a man, Cora's fiancé.'

'So no love lost there then.'

'He never served a day for it and never will.'

Cora surely would never have forgiven him for killing her fiancé. Laura, for example, still brings it up that I'd dozed off during Christmas dinner ten years ago and left her to entertain my visiting parents. Would Cora not love to send Michael down, even if was for a different killing?

Wouldn't the father of the victim, our new minister, also love to have some modicum of justice belatedly served? Maybe there was a reason why an inspector and not a detective was investigating the death of Chris. Cora and the minister had Vince Fagen in common.

'Regardless,' I said, 'of who killed Chris, I'd say Michael is going down for it anyway.'

'Rough justice,' Kyle said.

Laura appeared in the bedroom and applied makeup at the mirror. She wore a long formal coat.

Laura hesitated and peered out through the window and noticed me standing in the field. She made a WTF gesture with her hands.

'I'd better go,' I said and edged away, trying to avoid what I hoped was only sheep shit.

Tim

15

Suzanne looked good in black and somehow managed to maintain a sombre expression even though I suspected a part of her danced inside.

We walked behind a hearse that slowly purred along the street. Several dozen of us on foot followed behind. Maggie was obliged to participate in her role as the parents' representative. She appeared bored and glanced at her watch and followed at the tail end of the walkers. Others including Laura followed in cars. A line of students flanked either side of us, looking smart in their uniforms and glad for the day off.

Peggy was inconsolable and had to be assisted by school staff. She recovered a little after we passed the RTE television cameras covering the funeral.

The cortège wound its way through the town. Shops closed temporarily. Crowds lined the street. Chris would have loved it, although he would have been the first to admit that the large turnout was largely composed of people just making sure.

'I lost,' I said under my breath while maintaining my solemn countenance.

'What do you mean?' Suzanne asked, shuffling beside me.

'I'd a fiver that said you'd be wearing a red dress and doing cartwheels.'

'My days of cartwheels are over,' she said. 'However, hold onto your money – you don't know what I'm wearing under this coat. Anyway, I could not but show up?'

'Out of respect?'

'It's part of the job in a small town. Anyone in business has to sponsor a team, employ a local student during the holidays and show up to the removals of the great and the good. It's advertising.'

'Don't even think about handing out cards,' I said.

Several politicians walked alongside us, mindful of the optics. Officially, Chris was one of the pillars of the community and it was important to honour his memory, especially as there was national press and television coverage. Newly elected Minister Tim Fagen, looking distinguished in a long black coat, walked alongside the archbishop directly behind the hearse.

The town had closed ranks. In death, Chris would obtain the respect that he never achieved in life.

Cora, in full dress uniform, waited at an intersection ahead of the hearse, blocking traffic with a squad car. Garda Julian stood alongside her. Cora saluted as the cortège slowly wound its way towards her.

'If I didn't know better,' Suzanne said, 'I'd think we were saying goodbye to a saint.'

'Not everyone gets three priests and an archbishop for a send-off,' I agreed.

'Your homily was good,' she said.

'Ninety per cent Internet, to be honest. I'd have liked to have added a few truthful anecdotes but in the end, the funny story about syphilis didn't make the final draft.'

'Tim was eloquent,' she said. 'You'd think he and Chris were besties.'

Minister Fagen had, of course, also delivered a moving homily. His remarks about the stresses that, "our valued teachers face daily" would copper-fasten the teachers' vote in the future.

Suzanne waved at Cora as we approached.

'Tell me. You trust, her?' Suzanne murmured.

'Why do you ask?'

'Does it not strike you as odd that Michael hasn't been accidentally run over by a squad car? Michael killed her husband-to-be.'

'You're saying that she is a little too calm?'

'I don't know why Michael risked coming back here, that's all.'

Someone bumped into me as I ground to a halt.

The cortège paused in front of the school. We would wait there a minute before we walked to the graveyard.

Cora threw a glance in our direction while she maintained her salute.

Suzanne mumbled to her chest, 'To be honest, the only thing that surprised me was that it was Chris that was found at the bottom of the lift shaft and not Michael.'

'You think she's capable of murder?'

'Wouldn't we all if push comes to shove?'

I threw her a disdainful look.

'Maybe a poor choice of expression,' she admitted.

She resisted checking her watch. The minute of silence must be up soon.

I didn't want to reveal that Michael's days as a free man might be numbered while Cora built a case. Justice might be blind, but it could be nudged in the right direction. Cora had no power when she was a raw recruit, but she was now an inspector. She could interfere with evidence if she desired and put Michael in the frame for Chris's death.

It also occurred to me that Michael was a perfect fall guy for any crime in the town. If anything, also happened to Laura, maybe Michael could take the rap for that too. Who would believe that there were multiple killers in a small town?

I'd need to act quickly before they threw the book at Michael.

Suzanne watched as the archbishop conferred with some priests. 'You hear the Vatican were on. The pope has plans to honour the teachers of the world in an address in Saint Peter's Square. It's odds-on that he'll be singling out our late lamented educator. Our minister has requested an audience.'

'He can bring along my unedited homily if he wants.'

'Peggy's organising a collection.'

'For what?'

Suzanne shrugged. 'A statue, I think. Could be a grotto. I'd no option but to throw some money into the hat. Can't be seen to not support locals up for canonisation. Look what Knock shrine has done for County Mayo? Our own saint would be a godsend to the town.'

'It's a pity he didn't fall down a lift sooner,' I said.

Suzanne smiled. 'It was the only decent thing he ever did.'

There was some unenthusiastic clapping that marked the end of the minute's silence.

Suzanne moved to a man waving to her in the crowd. I remembered what Laura had told me, about me blindly trusting my friend. Kyle must have done it, but could I see Suzanne, in her tracksuit, beside him, keeping watch? Suzanne glanced back over at me, winked, and slid one of her business cards into the man's pocket.

Yes, I could definitely see it.

The cortège moved off again. Minister Fagen slowed and leaned into me and grasped my hand. I had to admire his keenly developed peripheral vision, as he identified the photo-op in front of the school and the TV camera seeking the money shot.

'Terrible business,' he said. 'And congratulations on your new position.'

'I've big boots to fill,' I responded automatically.

'Don't worry,' he said. 'Your elevation is practically in the bag.'

He kept shaking my hand as he waited for a photographer to check her lens.

'I hope so,' I said, for the want of something to say.

The minister grinned as the photographer fired off some shots. He continued beaming as he leaned in a little closer.

'I hope he died roaring,' he said, smiling, and released my hand before falling in again behind the hearse.

My mouth gaped open and then my phone pinged before I could react. A text from an unknown number.

I checked my phone.

"Don't involve crown forces. You know what happens to touts. The Luan. Tomorrow night. 8 pm. Come alone. Tiocfaidh Ár Lá."

The last phrase was a Republican expression in Irish meaning "our day will come". I shuddered. What had I gotten involved in?

The crowd milled about me. Many had phones in their hands. Garda Julian was sneaking a peek at his. Suzanne had joined the cortège, a hand by her side gripped her mobile. Cora stared directly at me, with a poker face that betrayed nothing. She held my gaze before glancing downwards.

I followed her gaze down and noticed that the rear of my shoe was caked with dung.

Ginger

14

It was getting dark as I locked the scooter to a lamppost. I stood on the boardwalk on the edge of the river and apart from car drivers passing on the road, saw no one.

I was worried.

The threat implicit in the text and the Republican slogan suggested that my mystery texter might be none other than the elusive Ginger Reagan, a man who might not respond well to his nephew not gaining access to secondary school.

I could have walked away, could have taken a night boat to England, but I didn't fancy moving into my parents' campervan.

The text had said not to tell anyone, but I had asked Kyle to watch my back. I did not know who or what was going to happen but, for sure, I was not flying solo.

I dolefully approached the Luan art gallery.

This was a modern building built on the riverbank. It incorporated an old hall that once hosted concerts by Count John McCormick, a world-famous tenor in the 1920s. He'd grown up in the town but emigrated, as he probably decided that London and New York had more to offer.

I expected to find the gallery closed as its opening hours normally ended in the late afternoon. However, its windows were filled with light. Somewhat incongruously, a black taxicab was parked outside – a type of taxi typically only found on the streets of Belfast or London.

I walked in through the glass doors and discovered the gallery bustling with activity; men wearing tuxedos and women in designer frocks milled about. I felt under-dressed in my jeans, jacket, and helmet. I wondered if someone might wander over to ask if they should sign for a delivery. I grabbed a leaflet.

It seems I was at a launch depicting the works of Kate Reagan.

I was handed a glass of wine by a server wearing a balaclava – the hooded face covering often worn by terrorists or dissidents (depending on your political point of view). I sensed a theme as other servers wearing the same covering navigated their way between guests. I plucked some canapés from a tray. I'd been counting calories for the last few days, but I was too tempted by these freebies. I was supporting art. It was the least I could do.

'I did not take you for a connoisseur,' a voice said behind me. I turned and almost didn't recognise Cora in a dress.

'I could surprise you,' I muttered. 'I thought you had no life but being a Guard.'

'It's true. I'm never off duty.'

She nursed a glass of sparkling water in her hand.

'Even tonight?' I asked.

'Especially tonight.'

'Oh, right.' I'd regretted the glass of wine. I needed to have all my faculties undiminished by alcohol.

'So?' Cora asked. 'What brings you here? Apart from the canapés?'

I didn't want to reveal the text message.

'It was a text message, yes?' Cora whispered.

She was good.

'How did you know?' I said surprised.

'That's how everyone was told. Imagine, someone is paid to dream this stuff up.'

I got it, I was the victim of some kind of marketing ploy. I felt like another glass. In an instant, a replacement red was in my hands.

'Just supporting local talent,' I said. 'Also there is a faint possibility I might be in something.' I scanned some of the pictures hanging from the walls.

Cora looked at me quizzically.

'You don't know everything,' I said.

I peered at some of the exhibits. I recognised Gerry Adams, the former leader of the IRA's political wing, as well as other Republican leaders. We watched the balaclava-adorned servers pass out drinks.

'Half the people here are undercover,' Cora said. 'You should have smiled on the way in. There are lads out there taking pictures of everyone.'

'I thought the war was over?' I said.

'True, but the cold war continues.'

I slyly looked around. 'So is Ginger here?'

'He'd be kind of dumb to show up, however, you never can be sure.' She clinked my glass. 'To overtime,' she said and stepped back into the crowd.

I sipped at my glass. It was reassuring to know that I was in the midst of the Westmeath Gardaí division.

I noticed that our newly elected Minister for Justice Tim Fagen was soaking up the attention of the press and working the room. He was a rising star in politics. Already there was talk of him being Taoiseach someday and leading the country. He posed for guests' camera phones as a reporter put a question to him.

'I appreciate that my presence here could be seen to condone violence, but far from it,' he replied for the benefit of an audience at home. 'I am here to commemorate a dark time in our history, to acknowledge that there was real suffering on many sides, but let's not forget that lessons have been learned and we are grateful for the peace on our little island. I am also here to enjoy this fine wine.'

He held up a glass.

Guests chuckled.

'And of course, the talent that is Kate Reagan. Optics be damned,' he said catching Kate's eyeline.

There was a smattering of applause.

Kate nodded in approval and raised a glass to acknowledge the praise.

She noticed me watching and I made a show of admiring the painting in front of me, gesturing to it with my glass. I gave a thumbs up and grinned. Her smile faltered and she directed her attention to some sycophants.

I turned and examined the painting properly. It was a full-length self-portrait of Kate wearing nothing but a beret. I quickly stepped to the side and bumped into a server.

'Sorry,' I said automatically.

The man raised his balaclava briefly. It was Kyle.

'No problem,' he said winking. 'Love your outfit.'

I smiled with relief that he was there but was reminded of how dressed down I was. I slipped through a door onto the boardwalk. I felt more comfortable in the semi-darkness outside, mingling with guests admiring the night views of the river.

I sipped my wine.

Good luck to Cora in identifying Ginger, I thought. He could be right beside her, dressed as a server and she might never know.

I leaned over the rail. The dark waters of the river flowed sluggishly underneath. Across the river, a hotel illuminated a jetty filled with cruisers and converted barges. It was pretty, I must admit. Maybe there was something in art after all. I was moved. Perhaps it was the art. The views. Maybe the Cote de Rhône. I felt my phone buzz and peered at the screen.

"Unknown caller".

My eyes swivelled. No one paid me the least bit of attention.

'Hello,' I said after hitting the answer icon.

'Hello,' a man's voice said.

'Who is this?' I asked.

'I'm talking to a dead man.'

'What?'

'Just messing. Do you not know who this is?'

'How would I know that? There's no caller ID.'

The man sighed. 'I thought you were better than that. Who is at the reception?'

'All the great and the good,' I said. 'There are enough TDs to form a government.'

'Many Guards?'

'I'd say there are one or two.' Through glass doors, I spotted Julian in a tuxedo, munching on some cheese and crackers.

'However, not everyone is there.'

I tried to register who was *not* there. It was difficult to focus as the Cote de Rhône was working its magic.

'Don't worry about it,' the voice said. 'Wouldn't want you so distracted that you tripped and fell in.'

I sobered up as I realised that he must be watching I stared over at the hotel. He could be in any room and yet some instinct caused me to lower my eyes to the jetty that sat between us. I peered at a cruiser moored across the river. A man stood on the deck, silhouetted in the light of the hotel. A phone held to his ear.

'You're right that you don't know me,' he said.

'That's what I said.'

Although it wouldn't have taken Sherlock Holmes to guess who I was speaking to.

The man continued. 'Because If you did then you'd know that there is nothing in the world that would cause me to miss my wife's exhibition.'

Cora

13

A corner of the tarpaulin that covered the wreckage of my workshop roof had come loose and so I nailed a wooden batten to secure it. Suddenly there was a knock on the door. I froze and turned with the claw hammer gripped firmly in my hand. There was no point in denying that I was here.

'Yes?' I said, carefully opening the door to reveal Inspector Cora Halligan smiling outside.

She raised her eyes at the raised hammer which I quickly dropped to my side as I stepped outside to join her.

'Bad time?' she asked. 'Only I was just passing.'

I shook my head, not believing a word.

'I was only just getting used to you in a frock,' I said.

'I scrub up when I can. I did ring the bell. I saw Laura's car out front but no answer.'

'She's having a lie-in,' I said. 'Was out late, you know how it is.'

'Tell me about it. I hate night shifts. I'm like the anti-Christ for days afterwards.' She looked at me. 'Don't be concerned. My last all-nighter was weeks ago. So you had a bit of storm damage I see?' Cora said, looking at the roof.

'Nothing that a few nails can't fix,' I said. 'The fishing gear is all right which is the main thing.'

'You getting ready to head back out?'

'I missed the summer season,' I said. 'I'm hoping to salvage something.'

'The fishing festival is coming up, is it not?'

'That's right.'

'The town will be packed. So I guess there must be something to it.'

'It's what helped keep me here over the years.'

'Apart from Laura, of course.'

'That goes without saying.'

Cora nodded. 'I've lived in the Midlands my whole life and I still don't get the appeal of shivering in the middle of a lake.'

'You sound just like Laura. I couldn't persuade her to come out with me at gunpoint.'

'I probably shouldn't knock something without trying it first.'

'Yes, sure,' I said.

'Is that an invitation?'

Had I just been played?

'Of course,' I said. 'Any time.'

'I just might take you up on that,' she said. I saw her eyes flick back up to the tarpaulin that covered the remains of the workshop roof. I'd removed much of the debris but some smoke damage remained since the half-pounder blew up.

Cora's eyeline dropped to mine.

'So any news?' she asked.

I thought about lying but I figured that she'd see through me.

'Ginger rang me.'

Cora acted surprised. 'Why would he do that?'

'He said his wife asked him to call.'

'Let me guess. About Ruairi?'

'That's it.'

'What did he say?'

'He said that I was not to worry.'

'That's it?'

'Pretty much. I get the impression that he didn't trust phones.'

'So what did he mean?'

'Your guess is as good as mine. I'm not exactly on first name terms with wanted criminals.'

'But you're worried?'

'What do you think?'

'Did he say where he was?'

There would be no way that he'd still be on the boat and if it was searched then Ginger might take it personally that I'd pointed Cora in that direction.

A "tout," in his eyes, was someone who shared information with the police and who did not anticipate dying of old age.

'He didn't think to tell me where he was,' I said truthfully.

'That's a pity,' she said. 'It would have been a real feather in my cap if we could have scooped him up.'

'Sorry I can't help,' I said.

'I'll tell the lads to keep a discreet eye out. Get a car to run around the estate every now and then.'

I shook my head. 'You told me that he's a long reach and could get to me from Spain, how easy would it be if he's lying low the next town over? I get the impression that he's a patient man, that he will make his move when he decides.'

Cora peered in through the open door of the workshop. 'You don't strike me as someone who hasn't a move planned yourself.'

Cora was good.

'I have Kyle watching over us now, as it happens.'

'Good to know,' she said and looked towards the field where Kyle lurked somewhere with a pair of binoculars.

'By the way since you know so much. How long do you reckon Michael will stay? You think he's any plans to return to London?' I asked innocently.

I studied Cora's face, but her expression remained neutral.

'Do I look like a travel agent?' she said.

Her manner suddenly changed, and she swivelled around.

'One last thing,' she said and indicated the workshop. 'Can you satisfy something for me?'

'If I can.'

She vanished inside before I could stop her but reappeared after a few seconds, holding a spade in her hand. It was an old tool, but I'd replaced the handle with a new wooden shaft the previous year.

'Can you tell me what this is?' she asked.

I looked at her as if she was an imbecile.

'A spade?'

Cora grinned excitedly. 'You mind holding it?'

She passed it to me, and I held it by the shaft, the tip of the triangular blade rested on the path.

She whipped out a phone. 'I was arguing with Julian. I said that you can't call a spade a spade unless it's a shovel.'

She took a picture of me holding the spade.

'The lad is just out of Dublin. I'd say the only spade he has ever seen is on a pack of cards. This will settle the matter.'

'Glad to be of help,' I said, mystified.

I figured I was of help, but I just did not know how.

She took the spade from my hands. 'Let me put it back for you.'

She disappeared with it into the workshop and was back out moments later.

'Sorry for the hassle,' she said. Cora was about to walk off. 'Of course, if Ginger rings again…'

'You'll be the first to know.'

'If we find him, I'll drop on him like a ton of bricks and your problems will be over.'

'That would be nice.'

If only it were that easy.

'Thanks,' she said, and with one hand in her pocket exited through the side gate.

I gazed at the spade through the open door of the workshop. I noticed that the blade was still dirty from the time I'd used it to bury the neighbour's cat.

I heard a car slam shut and the sound of Inspector Cora Halligan's car accelerating out of the estate.

Suddenly the phone rang.

'Kyle,' I said, answering it. 'Thanks for the heads up. I almost wet myself when Cora appeared.'

'Sorry, man,' Kyle said from the phone. 'Was taking a dump. What did she want?'

'She didn't seem that concerned when I asked if Michael was going to London. Anything about that bother you?'

'Maybe she's learned to forgive. Doing the Christian thing, turning the other cheek.'

'Maybe.' I hesitated. 'A funny thing though.'

'What?'

'She took a picture of my spade.'
'What was that about?'
'Damned if I know.'

Lazarus

12

I had just placed the filled kettle on its power base when Laura's phone rang on the kitchen counter. I picked the phone up. The caller ID showed the call was from "Mags" of the "Irish Nurses Organisation" – the INO. I quickly put the phone back down again as I heard footsteps in the hallway.

Laura, wearing a bathrobe, swept into the kitchen and answered the phone.

'Hi, Laura here,' she said brightly. 'Do you mind holding for one sec?' she folded a hand over the speaker.

'Be a love. Tea, please,' she said to me. She held up the phone and rolled her eyes. 'A union thing.' She thrust the display at me like I'd trust issues, to show who was calling. She slipped into the sitting room and closed the door behind her.

I made two cups of tea and stirred the milk gently with the spoon. I could hear Laura speaking in a low voice. As a union rep for the INO, she frequently had to speak with head office. Then again, it's simple to disguise a contact number as something else. Chris used to store girlfriends' names under "Gardener".

He lived on a boat.

I sidled up to the door with the tea, my head cocked, but I could not make out any of her words. Suddenly the door swung open. She took the tea from me and closed the door. Her words dropped even further in volume.

Without warning, there was a sound of a car horn beeping urgently from out front. I hurried to the front door and opened it. Kyle was in his car and gesticulated at me to come over. I took a step outside. Laura pulled open the front curtains and peeked out; the phone remained glued to her ear.

'Kyle?' I said.

'We have to go. Now is good,' he called out urgently.

'What?'

'Get in the car.'

I waved at Laura and scuttled over.

'What's this about?' I asked.

'Just get in the car,' he said gruffly.

I slipped into the passenger seat and grasped the seatbelt as Kyle accelerated.

'What's up?' I asked, struggling to click the belt buckle home as Kyle screeched out of the estate and onto the main road.

'I thought that we might go and pay our respects,' Kyle said and pushed further down on the go-fast pedal.

'So you turned into a racing car driver now?' I asked. 'Care to share?'

'Let me ask you a question first. Did you notice that Cora walked out with a hand in her pocket?'

'I did. So what? Maybe her belt was loose.'

'She wasn't interested in the spade,' Kyle said. 'What was on it, though, might be a different matter.'

'You have so lost me.'

'I bet that she'll have slipped on a latex glove and scraped off some of the dirt before concealing it in her pocket.'

'Why?'

'You have to get that where I grew up, you expected cops to be corrupt. I watch out for the signs.'

'Cora is not corrupt. She once arrested her own mother for a DUI, as you call it.'

'We all have our price.'

'Her mother didn't speak to her for a year. So yes, no good turn goes unpunished.'

Minutes passed and I noticed the sign for Coosan Point – a spur of land that poked out into Lough Ree. It seemed unlikely that we were going swimming.

Although with Kyle, you never could be sure.

We took the turn. I thought about what lay along the road. A national school, some bed and breakfasts, some big houses. We passed a sign pointing to Coosan Cemetery.

I looked over at Kyle and he nodded. The "respects" word had been the clue.

'Should we be buying a wreath?'

'You'll like this,' he said.

'I doubt it.'

'What do you think of the movement to make Chris a saint?'

'I would have said that people can't be that stupid but on the other hand, I've seen labels on strollers that say, "Remove Child Before Folding."'

'Just think what it could do for the county. Look at Knock shrine. If you got half the footfall they have – the chamber of commerce would be wetting themselves.'

'I hear there's a delegation from the Vatican in town,' I said.

'You heard right. Part of the investigation into his character. The pope is fast-tracking this. Wants a good news story to come out of Saint Peter's, something that distracts from the rumours of his poor health. Chris's timing could not be more perfect.'

'But won't the cardinal clear things up? Tell them about the real Chris O'Donnell?'

'Maybe but having a local saint might do wonders for his own standing, at the next conclave.'

'So Chris could in a way influence who becomes pope? I've heard it all now.'

'Everyone has an agenda; do you not know that by now?'

'Even you?'

'Of course.'

Kyle pulled up on the side of the road adjoining the cemetery. I could see over the low wall that there were a pair of Garda cars parked amongst the tombstones. Cora eased herself out of a car with a takeaway tray of coffee. She walked over to some colleagues and handed out the coffees before bending down to offer one to Garda Julian.

All I could see of him was his head and cap, as he was down in a hole. Julian took the coffee and held his phone aloft. He'd no doubt be annoyed, as the reception out here was abysmal. However, due to the location, there'd been few complaints.

Julian disappeared out of sight. I wondered what was going on. All I knew was that in a graveyard, a hole tended to mean only one thing. I threw Kyle a WTF look.

'I rang Peggy after Cora left,' Kyle explained. 'If anything is going on in the town, the school secretary will have it.'

'I'm not sure if there is any scientific basis for that.'

'She came up trumps, didn't she? She got a call from someone putting some flowers on a grave and noticed some activity. It's not often you see cop cars driving at speed into a cemetery. I mean what's the rush?'

We stepped out of the car and walked through the gates.

Kyle's voice dropped. 'Cora was just getting some soil samples. Dirt is not just dirt. They can tell you almost exactly where it comes from.'

'Comparing it to what? Dirt from here?'

'Now you get it.'

We approached Cora who was standing beside Chris's grave. A cordon of Garda tape surrounded it, encompassing a mound of earth thrown to the side. A Garda drank from one of the coffees. He had a clipboard in his hands, making notes.

'Hi, lads,' Cora said cheerfully as she saw us approach. 'Good news travels fast – but gossip that bit faster.'

'If you must know, Peggy has it on social media. Someone visiting the cemetery noticed all the boys in blue,' Kyle said.

'Did she now?' Cora said and beckoned us forward.

We could not move to the edge of the graveside due to the tape cordon, but we were close enough to see Julian standing forlornly at the bottom of a stepladder.

'That's not something you see every day,' Cora said and pointed to the grave. The mound of dirt obstructed our view, but we could see part of a casket at the bottom of the grave.

'I wonder how this might play for the Vatican,' Cora mused.

Kyle suddenly bent down, 'Stone in my shoe,' he said and stood up a moment later, brushing against me.

He turned to me.

'You're not dressed for this, are you?' he said in a loud voice.

'What do you mean?'

He pointed down and I noticed that there was a streak of dirt on my trousers.

'Hot damn,' he said aloud. 'You probably have mud on your shoes and everything.'

Cora's smile waned briefly.

Kyle turned to me. 'It will explain why there is dirt from here on your things, should anyone ask.'

I got it. Any dirt here could match anything that Cora found.

Cora looked at us keenly.

'So what's going on?' I said. 'Someone desecrated the grave. Last time I was here, it was filled in, with Chris six feet under.'

'Our Chris has surprised us all and only gone and pulled a Lazarus.'

We strained to peer further into the grave.

'You can look as much as you like. You won't find him. Julian is down there and it's not something that even he could miss.'

'He's gone?'

'Appears to be.'

We mulled over this.

'Student prank?' I said.

'Could be but the Athlone lot seldom ventures beyond stealing traffic cones.'

The exception was the one year when several dozen college students dressed up as wedding guests and accompanied by a pair dressed as a bride and groom, arrived in convoy at The Hodson Bay Hotel. The red-faced manager apologised as she rolled out an impromptu red carpet and speed dialled the chefs.

I looked towards the hole, but the vacancy remained.

'Why would anyone take his body?' I mused.

'Maybe he wasn't dead,' Julian said, supping on his coffee. 'Maybe he dug himself out.'

Cora rolled her eyes.

'Not much chance of that,' she said, 'seeing as the last time I saw him, the pathologist had his brain in a jar.'

Laura

11

I used a pair of metal tongs and pulled a Mars Bar from the deep fat fryer. I dropped it on a plate of chips and added a sprig of parsley as the vegetable portion. I left the plate on the counter for Laura. It contained a shedload of calories, but breakfast is said to be the most important meal of the day.

I booted up my tablet and scrolled through a news website with a banner headline "Mystery Deepens". It was populated with pictures of Garda Julian standing beside an empty grave. An insert of Chris was included because he was currently unavailable for a photo shoot. The hagiographic momentum to honour his memory was hitting a few speed bumps. Other headings mentioned how the town council's proposal to rename a street after him was on hold, and that the delegation from Rome could not be reached for comment. Nominees for canonisation had to remain uncontroversial and do little more than stay put if deceased and so Chris's unexplained absence bordered on impertinence.

Suddenly Laura swept into the kitchen.

'They find him yet?' Laura asked.

'Not so far.'

'When they do, they'd better tie him down to be sure.'

'Not very sensitive,' I said.

'If it helps I can take to some keening, as soon as I get my black shawl out of the wash.'

'I'm sure his mother would appreciate it.'

'Mo chroi, mo chroi,' Laura wailed.

'Laura, please,' I said.

She stopped. 'You are right. We have to think on the positive side.'

'Like he'll feel no more pain.'

'That you're getting a salary boost next pay period.'

It felt wildly inappropriate since Chris was only just dead and buried. And unburied.

'It's not going to make a huge difference,' I said. It felt like we had the national debt of a small country. Laura had once joked that we should get Bono in for a fundraiser.

I noticed that Laura was dressed in jeans and a top.

'I thought you were working tonight?' I asked.

Normally, Laura spent the afternoon in bed before a night shift.

She shook her head.

'That shift changed, didn't I say?'

I could not keep track of Laura's shifts. She worked a combination of nights and days in a pattern that I could no longer follow.

'What about your breakfast?' I asked, indicating the food congealing on the hob.

'Thanks,' she said. 'Maybe later but right now I just feel like toast.'

She popped two slices of bread into the toaster and then clicked on the kettle.

I sighed and closed the news windows on the tablet. I examined the plate of food. It would be a shame if it went to waste. I picked up a chip. One chip would do little harm. Two would be plenty. Maybe three if I promised to get a walk in later.

The toast popped up and with her back to me, she spread some jam over it.

She turned around and I noticed that she'd prepared some toast with a side of avocado. I hadn't purchased that. It was a worrying development.

'I do appreciate all the breakfasts that you've been preparing,' she said. 'I think though that I need to mix up my recipes.'

'If you like.'

'What do you think of this?'

She slid a side plate of toast and jam over to me.

I picked up the toast and took a bite.

'I don't mind cooking,' I said.

I didn't want to say how my breakfasts for her consisted of several ingredients from eggs to bacon accompanied by toast dripping with butter. Switching to tea and toast barely satisfied the definition of breakfast unless this was France, but we weren't in France.

'How's the jam?' she asked.

'It's good.'

'Homemade,' she added.

'Very good, I meant,' I said, pleased at dodging that particular landmine.

'So where's Liam?' I asked. 'He never came home.'

'He's a new girl on the go,' she said. 'Want me to draw you a picture?'

No, I didn't particularly want to think about Liam's sex life. I perhaps wouldn't have minded but it reminded me that part of my life with Laura was grinding to a halt. We never seemed in the mood, and I thought the act was not worth the effort. Perhaps it was familiarity, perhaps it was because I thought I should save myself for Brenda.

'Any other news?' she asked pointedly.

Internal alarm bells went off. Her questions had all the hallmarks of a baited trap. There was an expectation of an appropriate response – which could have lethal consequences if answered incorrectly. It was like when I'd won the two tickets for Bruce Springsteen at the sold-out concert in the RDS in Dublin. She'd come down with a bad dose of food poisoning but had said, 'You can go if you like.' I'd seen the trap for what it was. I'd never have been forgiven for abandoning her. I gave away the tickets to what turned out to be the Boss's best concert in years. Instead, I held a basin for puke at the side of the bed.

We weren't long married so it was no big sacrifice at the time. I wondered if Bruce was to revisit the country, what I would do in similar circumstances? I must admit that I'd be right there, in the crowd. I'd use modern technology to remain in touch with Laura, via video calling. It would almost be like I was there for her. It's not as if I wouldn't have left her with plenty of basins.

'No,' I replied.

'No more snakes on the horizon?'

'No, I don't think so.'

'Scorpions? Spiders?'

I shook my head. 'Alex thinks it's a bad idea.'

'It's like your interest in exotic animals was short-lived. Thankfully, for Mrs Keena's sake.'

I bit into the final piece of toast. 'I don't know what you want me to say,' I said. 'No more reptiles.'

'So you liked the jam?' she asked.

I showed her the empty plate. 'What's with you and jam?'

'It was Michael's recipe.'

I froze. 'Michael?'

'He used to love to cook, you know.'

'No, I didn't.'

'He's meeting up with Liam for a proper chat,' she said.

'How nice for them both.'

'Liam's old enough to decide for himself. He's an adult now.'

'He eats like one anyway.'

'They're meeting for a pint.'

'Who's paying? That's what I want to know.'

'I told them both – no pressure. If Liam wants to continue with his father, fine, if he does not – that's fine too.'

'Why are you telling me this?'

'To be fair, you raised him. You are entitled to know.'

I felt a stab of remorse. I had a flash of her walking up the aisle of the registry office towards me. We did have a history that amounted to more than accruing bills. We were good once.

'That's nice of you to say,' I murmured.

'You were always there for him. I would never deny that.'

'We didn't do too badly,' I said at last.

Silence settled between us. I felt a moment of tenderness wash through me. I gauged the distance between us as an urge to move forward and hug her, rose like a tide in me.

I wondered if I should suggest that I move back into the main bedroom.

She looked down at the side plate speckled with crumbs.

'No maids here,' she said.

She stood with her back against the sink, sipping on tea. I rose and put my used cup and side plate into the dishwasher. I wiped the island surface. Laura watched me. Was she checking that I missed something?

I picked up the pepper that she had used on her avocado and placed it in the back of the cupboard. I swear I could feel Laura's eyes boring into me. I closed the cupboard door and hesitated. Something was amiss. I opened the cupboard door again. There was a familiar vial at the back of the cupboard.

It was half full of jam.

I rushed out into the hall and using fingers shoved down my throat, retched into the downstairs toilet.

I wiped my face of vomit and walked back into the kitchen. Laura had remained at her position, leaning against the sink, idly sipping at her mug of tea.

'You're all right,' she said in an even voice. 'I washed that jar out. Besides, venom is mainly harmless if you ingest it.'

'So what was all that about?' I asked.

'I didn't believe it,' she said. 'When I was told.'

'About what?'

'That you were trying to kill me.'

I was about to interrupt but she waved me to silence.

'Please don't deny it. The evidence is all over the toilet in there.'

'Michael gave you that?'

'He did. He said to be careful. I thought he was being an ass. I guess not.'

I didn't know what to say so I said nothing.

'You know, I almost understood it. Felt that this might be revenge.'

'For what?'

'For when I almost killed you.'

'You mean for my accident at the bridge?'

She shook her head. 'Afterwards.'

In my mind I replayed the vision of Chris turning to me in the hospital, asking if I was going to sue. It was followed by an image of Laura adjusting the morphine. 'You overdosed me?'

'Yup.'

'But why?'

'It was accidental if you must know.'

'And work knows?' I remembered the gathering of doctors and nurses around the bed.

Laura smiled. 'Why do you think I've been off the last few months?'

I was taken by surprise.

'What? But I saw you go into work?'

'When? You saw me going out with the girls or Brenda. Sometimes I'd just go for a drive. Sometimes we'd spend the day in Dublin. I didn't know what to say to you. I mean I almost killed you. I don't think I wanted your comments. You're very pass-remarkable when you want to be.'

'You're suspended?'

'On full pay, which is nice.'

'So what happens next, when will you go back?'

'That will depend on the hearing I guess. It may not go well for me.'

I recalled the whispered call from her union representative. The call had not been to do with a different nurse, it had been about her.

'Why now? Why tell me?'

'You tried to kill me, Martin. Do you think I'm entirely stupid? I mean snakes, a canon? You could have joined the tennis club if you were starved for hobbies.'

'It was only one snake.'

'Whatever.'

'Can I explain?'

'I'm tired. I don't want your explanation, apologies or whatever you're planning to say. I'm going out,' she said.

'We are going to talk about this, yes?' I pleaded.

'It might be better for you if you were not here when I come home.'

'What do you mean?' I said.

'Goodbye, Martin,' she said. 'Or do you want me to get Cora involved?'

Laura's mind was made up and there would be no changing it. It was like the time she insisted she was a twelve and squeezed into a dress that, "clearly had the wrong label."

'You won't let me explain?'

'No need. I read your book, Martin.'

I paled. This must be what German High Command might have felt like if they learned the Enigma code had been compromised.

'I took your tablet, pulled the SIM card and copied the file. Liam had the password figured out in about five-seconds. I mean, they tell you to vary your passwords. They say that for a reason.'

I tried to recall how far I'd gotten into my notes.

'I didn't like it when you wrote that you were, "lucky to land Laura". You made me sound like I was a salmon.'

'You read my manuscript and that's the one quote that bothered you?'

She shrugged. 'I liked where you said I was a caring mother.'

'Thanks.'

'You're still leaving, of course. You're not going to sweet talk me into changing my mind.'

I had made so many plans to end my wife.

It turned out that I was already dead to her.

Michael

10

I left the last box of belongings in the lobby of the apartment block. I hadn't brought much as space was at a premium in Suzanne's.

I stepped out to Laura's SUV that I'd double parked outside, its hazards blinking. Laura had agreed that I could borrow it to offload my stuff. It was either that or have me return multiple times, ferrying my belongings on the back of the scooter.

I slammed the boot shut and noticed Michael, leaning against the wall of the block. He sipped from a coffee using one hand, the other shoved deep into the pocket of an old army jacket.

'Where were you ten minutes ago?' I said. 'I could have used a hand.'

'Just passing.'

'I heard the news,' I said.

'About me taking the spare room?'

I froze. 'No, about you meeting up with Liam.'

'That's true,' he said. 'I'm meeting him for a pint after work.'

I was going to say that I presumed he was referring to Liam's part-time job. Michael did not strike me as someone who was on the way to the print shop to make copies of his CV.

'Laura says that I should bite the bullet. Meet him properly. Even if he tells me to go to hell.'

'How about we rewind the tape,' I said. 'What's this about you moving in?'

'Ah,' he said. 'That's a developing situation. I didn't want to overstay my welcome where I was and you've a spare room downstairs. You can see the sense in it.'

'Yes,' I said. 'It's very convenient all right. I should have brought it up myself.'

He smiled and I resisted the urge to hop in the car and reverse over him. I was wound up tighter than a wife who'd discovered that her husband's golf trip had been cancelled but that he'd gone anyway.

'Speaking of convenience. Sure, why not take Laura's car back and save me a trip.' I threw him the car keys and he caught them adroitly.

Michael glanced into the cab of the car. Did I detect a flash of nervousness cross his face? He was normally the paragon of self-confidence.

'I don't think so.'

'You've everything else, why not take it now? Laura's waiting.'

'That bridge is burned,' he said. 'No going back.'

He tossed the keys back and they fell to the ground as I fumbled the catch. I picked them up.

'I'm meeting Liam. Can't drink and drive but thanks for the offer. Besides, I'd be rusty – never needed a car in London. We have this thing called The Tube.'

'I'm familiar with it,' I said.

He shrugged.

'You shouldn't have interfered,' I said.

'The mess you are in is all yours, my friend,' he said, placing the empty coffee cup on a wall beside him, before putting his hands into his jacket pockets.

Something at the back of my mind processed a connection. The jacket that Michael wore seemed identical to the one I'd noticed hanging in Kyle's cabin. This triggered a new thought, Michael was broke, and hostels cost money. Where exactly had he been staying?

'By the way,' I said.

'Yes?'

'You didn't say where you were staying until now.'

'That's right,' he said. 'I didn't.'

'I wonder if you liked living near the lake. A nice contrast from London living.'

Michael smirked. 'It took you long enough to figure out.'

Kyle told me that his cabin had two bedrooms. What if he was there while Kyle and I got hammered?

'I was also thinking that you might have heard me ranting. About how I wanted Chris to die.'

Michael looked hurt. 'Are you suggesting I had anything to do with his death?'

'Kind of,' I said uncertainly.

Michael's expression changed. 'Well, you'd be right. I put him down like the rabid dog he was.'

I stared back. 'Are you serious?'

'Never more so.'

'I could tell Cora.'

Cora was surely planning to pin the crime on Michael, the fact that he was actually guilty could only make the attempt more palatable.

'Be my guest. The thing is, what motive do I have? What proof do you have? You, my friend, on the other hand, are drowning in motives. You want Cora to dig deeper, off with you. Who knows what evidence she could find connecting you to the scene?'

'Connecting me to the scene?'

More dots began to connect.

'You were in my workshop,' I said.

'I took that vial, why stop there? Who knows what else I pocketed?'

Even Cora could not overlook incriminating evidence.

'What do you want?' I asked.

He rounded on me angrily. 'Laura deserves better.'

'What do you want?' I repeated. 'Look at me. You've got everything.'

He turned and walked off across the bridge.

Suzanne

9

Suzanne opened the door to her spare bedroom. I held onto a suitcase and had the prize-winning stuffed pike under my arm. I baulked at the room that was stuffed with boxes of files and bric-a-brac.

'I use it for storage, as you can see,' Suzanne said, 'but yes there is a bed in there somewhere.'

I squeezed in between the cardboard towers and snagged my jacket on the branch of an artificial Christmas tree. I unhooked myself and observed the columns shaking ominously.

I carefully dropped my belongings on the bed. I dared not slam a door in case there was a cave-in. There'd been an earthquake in the Irish Sea the previous year that measured five on the Richter scale. If it were to happen again while I was in bed, and should the epicentre be a hundred kilometres further east, I might not be found without the assistance of the rescue services.

I moved a box from the windowsill to reveal spectacular views of the river. The castle lights were on, and cars passed below me. What Suzanne lacked in space; she made up for in views. The trouble was, views won't kill you, this room however just might.

Suzanne had a bottle of wine open when I eventually managed to find my way out of the bedroom. I'd consider in the future leaving a trail of breadcrumbs behind despite the risk of rodents.

'Thanks,' I said after she handed me a glass.

'You're welcome,' Suzanne said. 'Hope it's not too cramped.'

'Beggars can't be choosers, Suz,' I said. 'It'll do nicely. You'll remember to send in a search party should I not appear in a day or so.'

'I know,' Suzanne said. 'I'm a bit of a hoarder, me.'

'No?'

'It's true, look what else I picked up.' She raised a glass of wine to me.

'Thanks,' I said sincerely. 'You are just a legend.'

'I'm just a people-pleaser,' she said.

'You're more than that.'

Suzanne had literally welcomed me in with open arms. She was the type of person that you could ring at three a.m. and ask for a favour, and she'd say, give me five minutes and I'll get you.

I had told her that she dodged a bullet when Chris stood her up. When Chris reverted to his natural behaviours – which were as predictable as night following day – then the inevitable divorce would be an event destined for a social media meme. I could envisage her cutting a single sleeve from each of his hand-made suits. I could imagine her placing his beloved boat on eBay for a fiver.

In reality, Chris probably should have been grateful that he got away with occasional damage to his car. She did give away his collection of fine wines to the local homeless shelter, but that was his fault for being tardy about changing the locks of his boat.

Suzanne sipped from her wine.

'All right,' she said. 'Tell me again, exactly what Michael told you.'

I repeated how I had met Michael and that he was setting up residence in my house. I told her how he confessed to murder.

Suzanne smiled without warmth. 'I'll bet that he never admits that for the record.'

'So what am I looking at?' I asked.

'Well,' she said. 'I'll say that if Michael killed Chris just to get you out of the picture, that's messed up. He told you he disliked Chris so that made it even easier. However, it all comes down to your word versus his and if he planted evidence… well you are screwed. No two ways about it.'

I knew she was right. I didn't sense he was bluffing.

'Maybe Cora has something already in evidence but has yet to connect you to it.'

'Or she might just be preparing a file for the DPP.'

Suzanne nodded.

I felt an urge to throw up. Michael planned it well. All it would take would be something of mine that had no legitimate reason for being found at the bottom of a lift shaft.

'It doesn't help that I don't have an alibi,' I said.

'He could have allowed for that if he is as devious as you make out.'

'What do you mean?'

'It would just take a phone call to get you out of school on some pretext.'

'As it happened. I made it easy,' I said.

'I'd say that you were just in the right place at the wrong time and Michael's capitalising on it.'

'So now what? Just wait for him to throw me to the wolves?'

'Maybe he'll say nothing, providing you don't make any waves. In the meantime, he has you by the nuts,' she said.

I wanted more wine and handed my empty glass over for Suzanne to top up.

'Maybe he will make his move if you attempt to make up with Laura.'

I recalled the look of disgust that Laura gave me as I left the house with an armful of belongings.

'I doubt it,' I said.

'It doesn't help that her ex is moving in already. That's not normally a good sign,' she said.

I had told Suzanne how Laura also thought that I was trying to kill her. That it didn't help that I was working on a work of fiction outlining how it would be done.

Suzanne then asked if she was in it.

I said we need to get back on topic.

She mulled about my situation for a moment.

'So we may be talking about divorce,' she said. 'We need to put the idea out there. No use in pretending that's not in the mix.'

'Perhaps I can wait it out. Divorce takes time.'

Quickie divorces are not a thing in Ireland, and it could take up to five years to separate legally. I was counting on a long drawn-out procedure, not necessarily with a view to reconciliation, but there were real cost implications to divorce. If something was to happen to Laura before the separation was finalised, then I'd be entitled to any benefits that would accrue with her passing. The mortgage would be paid for by the insurance bond, and I'd look forward to gaining sole title to the house. There'd also be her HSE pay-out.

'I'm not going to kid you, Martin,' she said. 'Divorce can be much quicker than you might think. A crucial factor is determining how long a couple has separated.'

'I was there until this morning!'

'It is also possible to state that a couple could be separated while living in the same house. Would Laura agree that you've spent more time in the spare bedroom than out of it?'

'I don't know what she'd say.'

'She could fast-track the paperwork if Michael is whispering into her ear, egging her on.'

I couldn't dispute the divorce, not while Michael held the possibility of jail swinging over me. It was like a stopwatch had started ticking backwards in my head. A countdown to a legal separation where the only way of winning would be to obtain widower status before it reached zero. That's if Michael decided not to throw a spanner of mine into the works in the meantime.

'Can you explain,' Cora might ask, 'what's this monogrammed ratchet of yours doing at the bottom of a lift shaft?'

Cora may have wanted Michael to go down for the crime but it would be impossible if I had been stitched up efficiently.

There was a knock at the door.

'If you don't mind, I have to get ready,' Suzanne said rising from the table. 'It's date night. We're having a takeaway and a few bottles of red.'

Suzanne was dating. I was so wrapped up in my world that I'd not asked about her current status.

'Is it Mister Right?'

'More Mister Right Now,' she said, applying some lipstick.

I rose to my feet.

'I guess three's a crowd,' I said.

'That's what they say,' Suzanne agreed.

'I'll go to my room. I've a phone and the Internet, what more do I need.'

'Cheers,' Suzanne said. 'You are such a pet.' She moved towards the door. 'One last thing…'

'Go on?'

'The guys who constructed this place didn't go crazy with the sound insulation.'

'Oh, I see.' I thought I could see where this was going.

'The walls are as paper-thin as they could get away with. I certainly hope you are still a sound sleeper.'

'I'll drop off like a log,' I said and was about to step into the bedroom when Suzanne opened the front door to the apartment.

She did not introduce me. She did not need to.

The O'Brien twins were Olympic-class rowers and famous in the town.

Roberto, Brady

8

Sweat soaked my tracksuit as I jogged along the boardwalk that edged the side of the river. I swigged on my water bottle. I had to get the waistline down. I don't know how Brenda felt about love handles but I'd err on the side of caution.

I also didn't want to be the fat guy in prison. Mountjoy might be bad enough without the name-calling.

I was beyond frustrated. Somehow Laura had to be removed from the board before we could get divorced. At the same time, Michael could send me to jail if I fought the separation. I also had a terrorist lurking in the wind whose desire to advance his nephew's education might involve asking me if I was fond of my kneecaps. So life was not too complicated at all.

I paused to get my breath and then an elderly lady jogged past. I swigged some more. I'd let her move on as I didn't want to embarrass her.

I stretched the way I'd observed athletes do in the Olympics and noticed that the car with new Northern Irish plates was idling slowly behind me. I decided that break time was over, abruptly turned and zipped down a side lane that was too narrow for a car. I congratulated myself for my ingenuity as the car accelerated and screeched to a halt at the entrance to the lane. I felt a moment of triumph wash over me but then I ran straight into the Spanish man and despite his lack of bulk, somehow bounced back off him and fell onto the ground. I glanced around to see the muscular man with a band-aid on his head stepping out of the car.

'How's about you?' he said, in a Northern Irish accent.

They'd suckered me. Band-Aid Guy had performed like a gilly and herded me in the right direction.

'What do you want?' I asked and rose to my feet.

'I see you're in a bad way,' Spanish Guy said. 'Maybe you could do with a lift to the hospital.'

'It's just a condition. I sweat easily.'

'Yes, I can see that.'

'You might need to buy a towel?' he said. 'We could bring you to the shops.'

'I wouldn't want to put you out.'

'It's no bother,' Band-Aid Guy said.

'I'm fine,' I replied. 'I have a policy of not getting into cars with strangers.'

'We insist,' Spanish Guy said.

Band-Aid Guy opened the boot of the car.

A voice called from behind me, and we all turned.

Kyle stood there.

'Is this a bad time?'

Spanish Guy stiffened; his feet moved apart. I guessed that he was someone who knew how to mind himself.

Band-Aid Guy shaped up to Kyle.

'This is a private matter,' Spanish Guy purred.

Kyle watched him carefully. 'I'm guessing that you are the Ed Sheeran fan. I mean using his number plates. That was a nice touch.'

Spanish Guy shrugged. 'I saw him the first time in Barcelona. Five times after.'

Kyle nodded. 'So a fan.'

'What's not to like?' Spanish Guy said.

'You wouldn't have any spare tickets? My girl thinks he's awesome.'

Spanish Guy shook his head.

'It was worth asking,' Kyle said.

Kyle then turned to Band-Aid Guy and held out his hand. 'I'm sorry, I was forgetting my manners. I'm Kyle. Who do I have the pleasure?'

Band-Aid Guy was annoyed, perhaps he felt excluded from the music appraisal. It didn't strike me that he was in touch with his creative side. He glared down at Kyle.

'Níl aon Béarla agam.'

Kyle eyed him up and down.

'Okay,' he said. 'You want to go there. Ceart go leor, fadhb ar bith, ach cá bhfuil tú ag gabháil leat an oide, mas mian leat a rá?'

Band-aid Guy's face grew red.

'You want to speak the language, how about you learn it first,' he said.

Kyle had been stationed in Afghanistan when he met Rosie online. He had sought out an Irish member of the Marines to learn more about Ireland. The man had regaled him with images of green fields, leprechauns and talk of Céilí music. To listen to him, you would swear that every crossroad was populated nightly, by locals performing their version of *Riverdance*.

Spanish Guy smiled. 'He got you there.'

'Doesn't mean that I can't twist his head off, Roberto.'

Roberto's eyes rolled. 'And now you've told him my name. Is this, as you say, amateur hour?'

Band-Aid Guy's face flushed.

Kyle pointed to the car. 'You might have considered something with a bigger boot. You haven't thought this through have you, fellas?'

Roberto shrugged. 'Martin has a meeting.'

Kyle turned to me. 'You know anything about this?'

I shook my head. 'Thanks, Kyle,' I murmured. 'I owe you.'

'So what are you waiting for?' Kyle said to me. 'Get in.'

'What?' I said.

Roberto and Band-Aid Guy looked unsure.

'Not in the boot though,' Kyle said.

'What are you doing?' I hissed to Kyle.

'This is not going away,' Kyle said. 'You can't run forever and may as well face it.'

Roberto nodded while Band-Aid Guy held open the rear door of the car.

'So you seriously suggest that I get in with these goons?' I glanced over at Roberto. 'No offence.'

'You want to spend the rest of your life looking over your shoulder? These lads have all the time in the world.'

'I'd rather it not be today.'

Kyle patted me on the shoulder. 'Don't worry.' He pulled out a phone. 'Say cheese,' he said and quickly snapped pictures of Roberto and Band-Aid Guy. 'For the folks back home,' Kyle said. 'I'm still a tourist, taking in the sights.'

'Delete that now,' Band-Aid Guy said snarling.

'Or what?' Kyle said. 'Did I not get your good side?' He held up the camera and took another picture. 'How about now?'

Band-Aid Guy shaped up to him, puffing out his chest. 'I hate Yanks.'

'Thanks for sharing,' Kyle said, 'but I'm warning you, I'm wearing Garda pants. Circa 1980. From the charity shop.'

Kyle was indeed wearing a pair of faded blue trousers.

It did not seem to perturb Band-Aid Guy who stretched his neck from side to side. It was clear, blows were to be exchanged.

'Hang on,' Kyle interrupted. 'What are we talking about here? Boxing, MMA or what?'

'What are you on about?' Band-Aid Guy said, pausing his warmups.

'I mean a boxing round is three minutes, but MMA is five. See where I'm going with this?'

Roberto grinned.

Band-Aid Guy raised a fist but suddenly his feet were swept from under him with a long wooden baton. Band-Aid Guy abruptly found himself horizontal with the tip of the baton resting on his nose.

'Or we could just fight street,' Kyle said.

Band-Aid Guy started to rise but Kyle poked him in the forehead, and he stiffened. The band-aid on his head glistened redly as the wound reopened.

'Did I not say that Gardaí pants from that era had a pocket? It's where they kept the truncheon, hidden inside.'

Band-Aid Guy glowered like he didn't appreciate the filling of a gap in his sartorial education. He held his hand to the bleeding as Kyle pulled out a wallet from Band-Aid Guy's jacket. He glanced at the ID.

'You brought your wallet. Brady, really?' He threw the wallet onto Brady's lap.

Kyle backed away and waved for Brady to rise. Brady grabbed his wallet and stood up, a sullen expression on his face.

'You just cannot get the staff,' Kyle sighed and looked over at Roberto. 'We good?'

Roberto nodded and then threw a look in my direction. 'What about him?'

'Wait up,' Kyle said to me as he spotted me edging away.

I had decided that I'd finish my circuit. The personal best wasn't going to be beaten standing round. I didn't know what to make of Kyle. He said he was helping but he also housed the man who admitted to killing Chris. I knew that I definitely didn't want to go on a car ride with a pair of criminals. I'd seen too many movies, not to know how this could turn out. Lough Ree was not deep – an average of three metres. This was one fact that I had going for me. It meant that I was unlikely to suffer from decompression sickness should I be thrown in wearing cement shoes.

'Time to put a line under this,' Kyle said and turned on his heel before walking away.

Roberto gestured for me to step into the car. The back seat this time, which was progress. Brady muttered to the retreating Kyle. 'I'm going to end him.'

Roberto muttered something in Spanish.

'What was that?' Brady asked.

'I said, shut up.' Roberto said. 'And that you were embarrassing me in front of the victim.'

Ginger

7

The car turned onto the old Mullingar Road. It was a poor relation to the new dual carriageway that carried traffic to Dublin. The road surface had sagged in places meaning a bumpy ride for anyone who chose the route.

I wondered where we might be going. Maybe we were aiming to visit the home of former *One Direction* star Niall Horan? Perhaps we'd visit the ruins of Fore Abbey and its seven wonders, or pop by the studio where the late Michael Jackson recorded songs?

Brady leered at me in the rear-view mirror and turned on the car indicators. We turned off the main road and onto a track that took us onto the Midlands raised bog. The bog stretched to the horizon in every direction. It looked like a flat wasteland of heather but in truth, it was a haven for rare plants and insects. For thousands of years, the peat had been cut by hand and then machine, to feed local fires and later peat-fired power stations. Now the fossil fuel power stations were closing as Ireland reduced its carbon emissions and the bogs were reverting to their natural state. We bumped along the track that was composed of linked potholes. It appeared that the bog was reclaiming the pathways already. We crawled along, the raised centre of the track rubbing noisily off the underside of the car.

'Are we going on a nature walk?' I said but was met by nothing but scowls. We kept driving and bumped our way up a small incline before slowing to a halt. Brady switched off the engine.

Over the ticking sound of the cooling engine, I could hear curlews calling from the heather, insects buzzing and the sound of water trickling along tracks cut in the peat. I wondered if these were the last sounds that I would ever hear.

Beside us, on a raised bank, sods of turf were piled in small mounds, drying in the breeze.

'We're here,' Roberto said as Brady clicked off the child locks. I opened the back door and stepped out onto the uneven surface of the bog. If I wasn't careful, I could trip and twist an ankle.

Brady grinned from the driver's seat. Abruptly a wet sod sailed into the air and dropped to the ground near my feet. Then another sod arrived and another.

Roberto slipped out of the passenger door and began scanning about him. He nodded for me to move forward. I took a few steps and saw a man standing in a trench, just below me, his wellingtons sunk into the wet peat as he adjusted his footing. He gripped a sleán – a flat shovel with a blade on one side – and drove it hard into an exposed part of the bog. He pushed the tool in and tipped it up to free it from the wet peat face, before tossing a dark, damp sod of turf onto the bank beside me.

'Know how to foot?' the man asked, and I nodded. I bent over and grasped the rectangular wet sods and placed them long side up so that they supported one another in a pyramidal shape. This maximised the air circulating around the sod and aided the drying.

The man threw sod after sod onto the bank. It was a practised motion, and he knew what he was doing. He never identified himself. He did not have to. His red hair shone against the dark pools of water that gathered around his boots.

'You've done this before?' Ginger said.

'Yes,' I replied. 'A date took me out, not long after I moved here. Turned out she just wanted to use my body – just not in the way that I'd hoped.'

Ginger adjusted his footing, his boots making sucking sounds in the mud.

'So to what do I owe the honour, Ginger?' I asked, making another mound. The heather roots embedded in the turf rubbed against my hands. A few hours of this and I'd need lotion.

'So you know who I am?' Ginger said, as he worked.

'I met your team,' I said indicating the boys. 'It's not rocket science.'

Ginger sighed and ceased cutting.

'I grew up here, you see. Spent my youth in the bog and hated it but you know, there is something about it that draws me back.'

He stood up straight. Turf cutting by hand was backbreaking work and generations of youths welcomed the invention of a mechanical harvester that could be towed behind a tractor, ripping the turf out and laying it in neat rows. Ginger put the sleán aside and climbed up onto the bank and sat down on the edge. His feet dangled over the muck just below.

He indicated that I should sit beside him, and I did.

He opened a Tupperware container and pulled out a sandwich. He offered me one and I felt that I could not refuse.

'I like to come here when I can,' Ginger said, biting into the ham and cheese sandwich. 'We don't have this in Spain.'

'You do have the weather though,' I said and took a nibble from my sandwich.

'I'm heading back,' he said. 'Thought I'd take a gander out here beforehand. I don't want to wear out my welcome.'

He probably was referring to the ongoing Garda warrant out for his arrest. Equally, he could be referring to some fuming ex-Republican colleagues who wanted to know why he wanted to kickstart *The Troubles II*.

'I hear Maggie is giving you a hard time,' Ginger said.

'That's one way of saying it,' I said. 'Another way would be to just describe it as blackmail.'

'She loves that Ruairi,' Ginger said. 'God knows but he's not the brightest tool in the box.'

'Ahuh,' I agreed cautiously.

'But he is family and that's important.'

I could have stuck to my principles and fought the continued attempts of coercion but who was I kidding? In my mind, I was welcoming Ruairi back to school. He would be accompanied by his mother, smiling sweetly as they walked in triumph through the school gates. Downcast teachers and students would watch in silence as Ruairi's eyes searched the crowd for someone that he'd be relieving of their lunch money.

'However, sometimes you have to cut the umbilical cord,' Ginger said.

The teachers were turning their back on him, and I was reaching to slam the door shut. Maggie's face shifted from triumph to shock.

'What do you mean?' I asked hopefully.

'I mean that Maggie won't be bothering you anymore, at least, she won't be bringing me into it.'

I gripped the school door, slamming it shut in her face.

'The lad has got to learn to stand on his own two feet. Tough love.'

I did not know Ginger could be so woke.

'So I've nothing to worry about?'

'Not from me,' Ginger said. 'Maggie, however, is a different story. She'll make your life a misery, I expect, but not with my help.'

'I could live with that.'

We listened to the breeze blowing over the heather.

'She suggested that you were involved with the new job vacancy in our school,' I said, feeling a rush of blood to the head. Was Michael following orders? I wondered.

Ginger glanced over at Roberto who seemed to be watching all sides of us at once. He nodded, meaning that I was free of recording devices. I hadn't my phone with me as I was supposed to be jogging.

'I never liked Chris,' Ginger said. 'And that was before I heard he was tapping my wife.'

'So you blew up my car, thinking it was his?'

'That wasn't me,' Ginger said sharply and glared over at Brady. 'That was someone taking the initiative. Your car was spotted outside her house, and someone put two and two together and got five.'

I inwardly cursed Chris and then remembered he was now departed and that you are not supposed to speak ill of the dead. You could think it though.

'I had planned to have my little tête-à-tête when I rocked in. Brady's one job was to just swing by now and again to keep an eye on Kate. I didn't think I'd need to assign him a babysitter but what can you do? I never sanctioned a car bomb. You could say that there was a frank exchange of views subsequently.'

I guessed how Brady had obtained his injuries.

No wonder Chris was worried. He'd realised from the explosion that Ginger had found out how Kate was warming the marital bed.

'So did you?' I asked.

'What?'

'Have your little tête-à-tête with Chris?' I was wondering if he was going to confirm that he had set Michael onto him. Michael has said he'd done it, maybe he was just following orders.

'You're asking if I decided to help Chris get up close and personal with the bottom of a lift shaft?'

'You could put it like that.'

'Not my style,' he said. 'That would have been too quick.'

I tried to get my head around this.

'So you had nothing to do with—' I made a plunging motion with my hand.

He shook his head.

'It was a pity that I didn't get in sooner,' he said.

I didn't think consoling him was the way to go.

'So you had nothing to do with Chris's departure from the world?'

'Not a thing.'

So Michael made a solo run?

A thought occurred to me. 'What about Kate?'

His face reddened. 'My wife? You think I'd hurt my wife?' he growled.

I shook my head. I must remember not to antagonise the wanted terrorist.

'I love her,' he said. 'Unfortunately, she is here with her work and I'm abroad with mine.'

'So she's going to be okay?'

'She has her needs, but no one said I'd to roll over and applaud.'

The image of a black widow spider came to mind whose arachnid suitor risked being eaten after copulation. In this case, he might also have to deal with a vengeful mate and a crew who could handle themselves down the docks. Kate must be awesome in the sack to justify the risk. Maybe I should warn Minister Fagen but I guessed he already knew.

'We see each other whenever we can shake the Guards. It's not the life we chose but it's the one we have.'

He closed the lid on the lunchbox.

The meeting was over. I rose to my feet.

'Another thing,' I asked.

'Go ahead.'

'Might you know anything about the whereabouts of the late lamented Chris O'Donnell?'

'They were going to canonise him, you believe that?' Ginger said, a hint of annoyance in his voice. 'That was not right.'

'I have to agree,' I replied.

'He was no saint.'

He pointed to the horizon.

'That way's Meath,' Ginger said. 'The bog goes all the way there and beyond.'

I taught geography on occasion but thought it was not a good idea to interrupt.

'A few years ago, someone from Bord Na Mona was digging in the bog,' Ginger said, referring to the agency that harvested peat for the electricity generating stations. 'And they came across a man that had been buried for over a thousand years. Six foot six he was, nails manicured. He'd probably not done a hard day's work in his life. Irish royalty, they think.'

I could see where this was going. I was familiar with Irish bog bodies. Students lapped it up – the more gore the better.

'Some say that he was a king and that someone turned on him. Stabbed him. Cut off the nipples. That was real hardcore. That was personal. They buried him out here. No monument. They wished him gone in every way.'

I nodded faintly.

'I don't know what he did, but I guess that he was no saint either,' he said.

Ginger picked up the sleán and dropped back down into the trench.

It was clear that Chris would be unlikely to show up anytime soon.

Chris was somewhere out here.

It was ironic because Chris always hated the bog.

Tim

6

Brady pointed to the roof of the car and asked if I saw a taxi sign when I asked for a lift back to town. When I replied in the negative, he said, *that's because there isn't fucking one.* He added, *you're dressed for jogging, jog on.*

Several hours later, I was approaching the outskirts of the town when a dark Mercedes pulled in beside me.

The rear window slid down.

'Maybe you would care for a lift?' Minister Tim Fagen asked.

I pointed towards Suzanne's apartment block.

'Actually, I'm almost back,' I said.

The driver stepped out and opened the rear door. I shrugged and stepped into the back of the Merc and sat beside Minister Tim Fagen. The door closed, and we drove off.

'Where were you two hours ago?' I grumbled. My legs ached.

'It's been an eventful few weeks for the town,' Tim said, ignoring the question.

'You think?' I replied enjoying the soft leather underneath me. 'If I'd been in my car, I could have been the town's first astronaut.'

'Be that as it may. Cora tells me that your car bomb is likely to be a criminal matter and not a political one, which is a relief. That's one Pandora's box that we never want to see opened again.'

'The main thing is that I wasn't in it,' I said sarcastically.

'And we'd all have regretted it of course if you had been,' he said.

'I appreciate the lift and all, but if you wanted to chat then surely you could have just messaged me.'

Tim had something on his mind.

'Ginger will be out of the jurisdiction soon, I hear,' he said.

'We should get him a going away present,' I said.

I suspected that Tim and Cora weren't turning over every rock to find Ginger. Better an escaped criminal behind the car bomb than a captured terrorist. This was rebranding on a whole other level.

Reality must not be allowed to interfere with the official narrative as the peace deal was too precious to risk. However, Tim was playing a dangerous game of his own. He might need every one of his protective detail if Ginger got wind of his wife's new friend with benefits.

I watched the countryside pass by.

'Cora was going out with my son, you know,' Tim said.

'I heard that.'

'Vincent was a good lad. God rest him.'

'I am sure he was,' I replied.

'I don't think there is anything to be gained by digging up the past. You know what newspapers are like when they're short on headlines.'

'I think I know where you are coming from,' I said. 'They did a big spread on me that time when I landed a twelve-pound pike.'

He threw me a disdainful look.

I was exhausted after my trek back into town and was close to my tolerance threshold. I just didn't care what I said anymore.

'I understand that you're still interested in Chris's job?' he said.

'That's right,' I replied slowly. I was mindful that this man could both make and break careers.

'I'm sure I could talk with my colleagues to expedite the matter if you wish?'

'Thanks,' I said, 'but you don't have to.'

Although that's precisely what I wanted him to do.

'We have to look out for one another,' he said.

'I guess so.'

The car pulled to a halt.

'Vincent was a good lad,' he repeated.

The driver opened the door.

I took the hint and stepped out.

I couldn't have had a clearer warning to leave the past alone than if it had been delivered by special delivery.

The Mercedes drove off.

I realised that I was right back at the bog.

'Oh for crying out loud,' I exclaimed.

Suzanne

5

It was dark by the time I fell in through the door of the apartment. I felt like I could sleep for a week but first I needed to quench a thirst built up on the slog back to town. I pulled a can of a fizzy soft drink from the fridge and placed it against my forehead, relishing its coolness. I cracked it open with the tab, stepped out onto the balcony and knocked the drink back.

Below me, the streets were filling with revellers. Young women shivered in micro skirts, while lads risked singing soprano in jeans that a twelve-year-old might struggle into. There was the promise of sex in the air; failing that, the takeaway on the corner did a roaring trade in late-night curried chips.

Above me, I heard giggles. Suzanne was on the balcony directly above. It turned out her dates lived above us.

I heard her being pulled inside and I dropped my gaze back down to the street.

An old Mercedes that had been converted into a taxi pulled up on the street below me. I watched a man and a woman stagger to the rear, and throw open the doors before falling in, giggling. The illuminated sign on its roof switched off and the Mercedes purred off over the bridge. I was in mid-sip when abruptly images that had been hiding in my peripheral vision suddenly slipped into view. I placed the can down and thought for a second about running upstairs to speak to Suzanne, but I gathered from what sounded like furniture being roughly moved above me, that she was occupied.

I skipped over to her filing cabinet and pulled out files.

Suzanne found me at the table peering at old newspapers when she let herself into the apartment.

'You're up early,' she said.

'I had a lot on my mind,' I said.

I told her about my visit with the minister.

'So you are going to take heed then?' she'd asked.

'I can't,' I said. 'I don't think burying my head in the sand is the way to go.'

'So instead of listening to our minister of state, you've been playing at armchair detective.'

'I don't think I've much choice,' I said. 'He as much as promised me the job but what's the point if I'm pushing up daisies.'

'What were you drinking?' she asked.

'Bear with me,' I said. 'First, what do we know? We know Michael did it.'

'Okay?'

I nodded excitedly. 'We know this but why? What if the motive was more than getting me out of the house? I think this started years ago.'

'Okay,' she repeated and sat down. 'Be a love and put the coffee on.'

I shoved a capsule into her coffeemaker and switched the machine on. I then slid some newspaper clippings in front of her.

'These are the clippings from the accident that got Michael fast-tracked out of Templemore.'

'I know,' Suzanne said. 'They're mine. I got them.'

'Look again, would you? I'll make your coffee.'

She sighed and peered at the clippings. She examined one after the other. The coffee maker's green light clicked on and I made her a steaming espresso.

'I don't see it,' she said. 'What has you all so hot and bothered?'

'You see where it says that the recruit who died was thrown through the passenger window.'

'Yes, I told you that.'

'Does it say what car they were in?'

Suzanne bent forward and brought the clipping closer to her face. She studied a picture of the wreck. A familiar logo could be seen on its front.

'No. It looks like an old Merc.'

Since 1987, Ireland's number plates had the year of registration included on the number plate. The accident happened in 2000 while the Mercedes in the picture had a 90 prefix, meaning it was ten years old at the time of the accident.

'Tell me, Suzanne. There weren't that many Mercs around here in 2000, am I right?'

She nodded. 'I suppose. The country was barely scraping along then.'

'So hardly the kind of car the average person would normally drive.'

She examined the clip again and nodded faintly. She got it.

'So who do we know liked flash cars?' I asked.

'Chris,' she said. 'You think the car was his?'

'You know Chris. He liked his cars and would have ploughed any penny he had into one. It was old even then and would have cost a fortune to run. Car tax here was based on engine size, yes?'

'And insurance,' she murmured.

'It would have been his babe magnet. Although I'd say he might use other words.'

Suzanne examined the paper. 'It doesn't say who owned the car. Just that it was stolen.'

'So Athlone was known for its crime waves back then?'

She put down the paper. 'If that was Chris's car. So what? Michael stole it. Does it matter who owned it?'

I smiled. 'Michael didn't drive it that night.'

'What are you talking about? It says it here. He admitted it. They kicked him out of the guards because of it.'

'I don't know everything just yet, but I can tell you that Michael wasn't behind the wheel.'

'How did you work that out?'

'Because Michael can't drive.'

Suzanne looked shocked. 'And you know this how?'

I explained how I had unloaded Laura's car and Michael saw me. How he had looked like a deer caught in headlights when he had the car keys in his hands.

'I never thought too much of it at the time. He mentioned being rusty, about using the Tube in London. I bet that he was covering up.'

Suzanne nodded. 'Michael was a townie. Back then, unless you grew up in the country or had a few bob in the bank, you just didn't drive.'

'So you agree?'

'This proves nothing, but I can make some calls. However, if Michael didn't drive that night… who did?'

I started to pace.

'Chris must have blackmailed Michael to take the fall. Michael lost everything, his career, his marriage. If that's not a motive for murder, then I don't know what is.'

'That's a big reach. I mean what reason could there be for Michael to fall on his sword?'

'It fits though, tell me it does not fit?'

'We have to be careful we don't make it fit. We need evidence.'

'And we need it soon, I'm on the clock here. I don't think Michael wants me digging around in his past, figuring it out. It might suit him if something happened to me.'

'So what are we going to do?' she asked.

'I think that there is only one thing we can do.'

She nodded.

I was delighted. Suzanne could keep a lookout as I dug another hole in the bog.

'I'll start with following up on the driving licence but a licence or lack of one, in itself proves nothing. In the meantime, let's use your phone.'

She lost me.

'What do you mean?'

'I mean that all we have to do is use your recording app. Get Michael admitting what he did. Then let Cora do her thing.'

'Oh, I see.'

'Why? What else did you think I meant?'

I guessed Suzanne, like Chris, didn't much like the bog, either.

Liam

4

It was dark when Suzanne dropped me off at my estate in her car. I had shaved. I even had flowers in hand.

My battle was on two fronts; appeal to Laura's soft side while provoking Michael into admitting what he had done. It seemed that I had little to lose.

I checked my phone, started recording and walked around the corner. I was taken aback by the sound of blaring music coming from my house. Every room was lit up, while laughter mingled with the chatter of people enjoying a party. I baulked. I wasn't expecting an audience but no risk, no reward.

I walked up the path, rang the doorbell and soon heard footsteps approach. I smiled as the door opened. Liam stood there looking surprised.

The kitchen door at the end of the hall opened briefly, revealing people drinking from cans and smoking rollies. Smoking in *my* house. I bristled. A woman in a micro skirt tottered on high heels into the downstairs WC, closing the door behind her. I grimaced at the marks her heels left on the oak laminate flooring.

Liam reached over and took the flowers.

'Thanks,' he said, 'that's nice of you.'

'They're for—'

'I know who they're for,' Liam said coolly. 'I'll pass them on to Mam when she gets back.'

'That's a pity,' I said. 'I was hoping to have a chat.'

'I'm hoping for a First next July but that's probably not going to happen either.'

There seemed no point in sparring with Liam. He had read my notes on the SIM card about me wanting his mother dead. It's the sort of thing that can put a dampener on a father-stepson relationship.

'So when will she be back?' I asked.

Liam shrugged.

We both shared a look at Laura's car sitting in the driveway.

'Her car is here.'

Liam looked at it. 'Yeah, that's it all right. Was there anything else? I need to get back to the books.'

There was a first time for everything but not I suspected tonight.

Liam looked at me. 'I liked you, you know,' he said.

'It's still me.'

'You think I'm stupid, how could you write that about me? Like I was a moron or something.'

Another critic.

'It was just dramatic licence,' I said. 'Based only loosely on facts.'

It was encouraging to know that he could read.

'I don't think you are stupid,' I said. 'I feel that you've a lot going on, that's all. You shouldn't believe everything you read. I mean Laura and I have had our ups and downs but that doesn't mean I really wanted to kill her. I mean, do I look like the type?'

A troubled look crossed his face.

'I don't know what to think. Maybe anyone can be a murderer.'

A voice called out, 'Is that the pizza?'

Michael approached. 'Oh it's you,' he said walking up to the door. He patted Liam gently on the shoulder. 'Go on inside, Liam. Martin and I are due a chat.'

Liam looked at us both.

'Go on,' I said. 'I'm not here to make trouble.'

Liam nodded and slinked back to the kitchen.

'So what's the occasion?' I asked.

'It's for Liam. It's an Erasmus thing. He's going to Glasgow for a term in the morning.'

'So this was Liam's idea?'

'Travel broadens the mind. I'll miss him but that's life I guess. He needs some space.'

'And with him gone and me out of the way, that leaves Laura there for you.'

'Don't go there,' he said.

'It's worked out very well for you, you must admit.'

'So I look like a success to you?' he snarled.

'What would she say if she heard that you had killed Chris? Maybe, no more happy families then?'

He glowered and peered at me intently.

'I don't know what you are talking about,' he said. 'Chris was troubled but if it wasn't an accident, then I hope that they catch the monster who killed him.'

His hand shot out abruptly and seized me by the jacket. His fingers quickly traced the fabric and felt the phone lodged there. He shook his head sadly.

'I spent a lot of time on the streets. You would not survive if you did not learn to read people. When someone thinks that it would be rather fun to piss on you in a doorway, it gives you trust issues.'

He pushed me away.

'You brought this on yourself. Laura wants the fastest divorce that she can, and no amount of foliage is going to change her mind.'

Despite my intention to show a strong outer face. I drooped.

'Oh one thing,' Michael said. 'I'm sure Laura would appreciate a favour.'

'Of course,' I said brightening up a little. 'Anything.'

He reached over and pressed a leash into my hand.

'It's just you know how Barney loves his walks and he's not one for parties.'

He whistled and Barney shot out the door. I turned, mustering as much dignity as I could.

'Thanks,' Michael said and closed the door.

I pulled out my phone and stopped recording. I rang Suzanne and told her that I didn't produce a get-out-of-jail free card. I told her that I had to take the dog for a walk and that I'd take a taxi back later.

I was about to attach the leash to the dog's collar when I thought, sod it, let him at it. I followed him from lamppost to lamppost. Should he take a dump, then I'd not bother with it. I was not living here anymore.

What was the point? I was not sure if Brenda could overlook rumours that I was broke and had planned to kill her friend.

The dog drew me closer to Brenda's home. For the first time, I hoped that she would not appear for a late-night walk. I wouldn't know what to say, I didn't think I could talk my way out of the situation that I found myself in.

Brenda's upstairs light was on. We approached closer and I could see movement in the window. I could not help staring.

Brenda was crying, tears streamed down her face. I felt tempted to ring the doorbell. She toyed with fabric with one hand, a glass of red wine in the other. Brenda turned; her lips moved as she said something. She was not alone. I stood still on the street below, all pretence of dog walking gone. Suddenly a hand appeared on Brenda's shoulder and lingered there. Another arm curled around her. Brenda, smiled and turned into the embrace before locking eyes with Laura.

Barney, for a change, was still, sitting on his haunches looking up at the window. We exchanged a look.

I pulled out my phone and rang a number.

'Hello?' Kyle said when I connected.

'I'd like to call by first thing if I may. I've something that I'd like your help with.'

Kyle

3

I slid the scooter to a halt in the morning mist, kicked it onto its stand and strode up to Kyle's cabin before pounding on the door.

'Hello,' Kyle called out from behind the cabin. 'I'm out the back.'

I trod warily around the cabin and found Kyle standing up to his neck in the lake, a serene look on his face, his eyes closed.

'Are you not freezing?' I asked. I could feel the chill of the lake through my jacket.

His eyes flickered open.

'It's cold water immersion. Great for muscle regeneration. The Finns swear by it.'

'Good for them. You know that we're not in Finland?'

'I do this every morning,' he said. 'Hasn't killed me yet.'

'That's not a benchmark that I'd personally swear by. I like doughnuts, I'm still alive, ergo doughnuts are good for me.'

'The health benefits are well documented, the reduction in stress levels alone is worth it.'

Was he dropping a hint? My stress levels were no doubt pushing the needle into the red zone of any internal gauge, but I doubted a dip would solve my issues. I was putting my money on the purchase of a bulletproof jacket on eBay and never sleeping in an unlocked room again.

'So you're still alive?' he said.

'So far. No thanks to you.'

'I figured that they'd take it easy on you as they'd know that I'd made them.'

'And if you were wrong?'

'Then I'd be really sorry about that.'

Kyle didn't seem to display any guilt about allowing me to get into the car with Roberto and Brady. Maybe he just internalised it.

'Can we talk?' I said glancing around me.

'Fire ahead.'

'Not here.' I was conscious of my voice carrying across the water.

'I'm not done yet,' Kyle said.

'I'll wait for you inside.'

'You're more than welcome to join me.'

'You're all right.'

'I insist,' he said.

'I've no swimming trunks with me,' I said.

'Neither do I,' he said. 'Come on, you pussy. Have to try it before you knock it.'

'I'm quite sure that I won't like it,' I said. 'My instincts are generally on the money in that regard.'

'It'll be good for you. Trust me. Besides if there is someone that's stressing out more than you then I'd sure like to meet them.'

I thought this was a bad idea even as I folded my jacket over a rock. I shivered as the shirt slid off my back. Kyle however seemed to bear it stoically.

I sighed and the last of my clothes fell away. I stuffed my socks into my shoes and placed everything carefully on a flat rock at the edge of the water. I stepped into the lake, moving gingerly over the rocks underfoot. The cold water rose quickly up my legs, then calves. I felt my body recoil. My organs signalled warnings for me not to take one step further. My fingertips puckered up while my scrotum migrated somewhere due north of my appendix. I kept placing one foot after the other. Blood rushed from my extremities to my head. My arms and legs looked like they'd been bleached. I arrived trembling at Kyle. Only our necks poked out of the water.

'You get used to it,' he said

My body, stiff with the cold, begged to differ. My mind ran through the symptoms of exposure, and I was sure that I ticked every checkbox.

'Can't think why I've not done this before,' I said, my voice trembling.

'You'll get it,' Kyle said with a serene look on his face. 'Did I tell you Rosie and I are trying to make a go of it? We're taking it to the next level. Sex in person.'

'That's great.'

'I think so.'

'I guess that she might be planning to stay over then?'

'We're thinking of going full-on tantric. We will spend the first few hours just listening to each other breathing. Then we remove socks. Then breathe some more. So yes we will need time and space.'

'And privacy no doubt,' I said.

'Martin, I like you and all,' Kyle said slowly, his eyelids fluttering open. 'Only you can't watch. It would freak me out and I'm sure it would bother Rosie.'

'That's not what I meant,' I blurted out.

'You sure?' Kyle asked. 'I mean I did catch you trying to get an eyeful of Dervla's bazookas.'

'I'm not a peeping Tom, right.'

We listened to the lapping of the waves.

'So if you're not here looking to whack off to me and Rosie, why are you here?'

'Michael told me that he had to move from where he was staying, it didn't take a huge leap to figure out that he was your housemate.'

'What can I tell you, I'd a spare room and I have a soft spot for veterans.'

Michael was in the army?

'You never mentioned it to me,' I said.

'He convinced me to be careful of you, to keep some cards close to my chest.'

'What do you mean?'

'The whole deal with the snakes. Your sudden interest in gunpowder. Snake venom? I didn't want to believe it at first. I felt that it was better if I was on the inside. If I found out what Michael said was true, then I could have intervened.'

'So I asked you to spy *for* me but you were actually spying *on* me.'

'Pretty much.'

'You're going to have to pick a side, Kyle,' I said, my voice shivering. 'He played you. Michael told me that he killed Chris.'

Kyle's eyes popped open. 'He said that?'

'That's what he told me.'

We watched a pair of swans glide in and land on the lake.

'Why would he do that?' Kyle asked. 'I don't see it.'

'I think that it goes way back to an accident that ended up with Michael getting kicked out of the force – he said that he was driving a car that a passenger died in, but Suzanne checked and there's no record of Michael ever having a driver's licence. I just don't think he can drive. She also found out that the car belonged to Chris who claimed it had been stolen. You don't have to be Columbo to figure out something fishy went on.'

'So why did Michael cop to something that he did not do?'

'I bet Chris had something big on Michael. In the end, he lost his job, his family, tell me that isn't motive.'

'And you have proof?'

'Not one iota. He also mentioned that he has something of mine that he planted at the lift. He said if I make too many waves then I'll go down for it. He was in my workshop; he might have been in my house. God knows what he palmed.'

'You bringing this to Cora?'

'I don't know. Am I to draw her attention to a clue that puts me at the scene? Tell her it's planted? Like she's never heard that before. She also has an agenda, the man that died was her fiancé. It's all connected somehow.'

Kyle looked at the swans vanishing around an outcrop. 'Michael was in your house, all right. I was on overwatch. Laura let him in. It was just before Chris died.'

'You never mentioned this before?'

'You told me yourself that you thought about killing your wife. So forgive me if I was not sharing and giving you more motives.'

'You believe me then?'

'I don't know what to believe. I should add that Cora joined them, she had your Minister Tim Fagen with her.'

'What?'

'They were in the house for well over an hour.'

'Oh very cosy,' I said sarcastically. 'Cora was supposed to be investigating a car bomb and instead, she's chilling with my wife and her ex. And the Minister for Justice is there for what? To make up the numbers for a game of bridge?'

'Cora brought scones,' Kyle said. 'They probably had tea.'

'Tim and Cora had every reason to hate Chris if he had something to do with the death of Vincent. Maybe they met to persuade Michael to do the dirty work.'

'So why was your wife there then?'

'Michael got ran out of town, it broke up her family. She had every reason to hate Chris too.'

'Maybe that's how Michael got the elevator key,' Kyle murmured.

'What do you mean?'

'Do you have an emergency key? I don't. Did anyone ask how those elevator doors were opened? Your fire department personnel would have them, cops too, maybe. Like Cora.'

There was silence broken only by the sound of lake water and distant cruisers.

'You know this is not going to end well,' I said, my voice even, despite the cold.

'What are you saying?'

'It's a big set-up but there is one final move before the game is over. I have to die. Michael is going to kill me.'

'How did you make that leap? You said that he can blackmail you, so what's the point?'

'I'd not think he'd like me out there. There can be no trial. He can't risk a jury not buying into the planted evidence. What if I find an alibi? Also, if I did go to jail, they'd lose the house. No way can Laura keep the mortgage up on her own, even if she keeps her job. Michael hasn't a pot to piss in and Liam's job is little more than pocket money. On the other hand, with me dead, Michael gets his whole family back under one paid-for roof. He could be the dad he never was.'

'People have killed for less,' Kyle muttered.

'I even know the time frame,' I said.

There was something to this cold water immersion after all. Neurones fired. Synapses in my brain found patterns in the chaos.

'Michael told me that Laura was fast-tracking the divorce. It has to happen before that comes through.'

'So you have a few months.'

'Why risk waiting until the last minute?'

'So why not bail? Hide out until the divorce comes through?'

'I could manage to get onto a ferry, go back to England. Thankfully, I don't need a passport, however, that would just trigger a warrant for my arrest as evidence that puts me at the scene of the crime is discovered. If I run, could I look more guilty? No doubt the divorce would be quietly paused until I get caught and fall down some steps in the jail.'

Kyle nodded at my logic.

'I told you,' he said, 'that cold water immersion clears the mind.'

'G-g-g-great,' I managed to say.

'You're feeling less stressed now I bet.'

'I'm not feeling anything at the moment, to be honest.'

'Okay,' he said. 'That's me done.' He began wading out of the water.

'About time,' I stammered.

'Not for you,' Kyle said. 'Give it another minute ' He surged out of the water, and I saw that he was wearing a pair of cut-down jeans.

'I thought you said you didn't have swimming trunks,' I gasped.

'That's right,' he said, 'I don't.' He grabbed a towel and started to dry himself. 'These aren't trunks.'

'Right, very funny,' I gurgled.

'I wouldn't be going skinny dipping, Martin,' he said. 'I mean kids use this lake.'

My heart pumped faster, and I didn't think that it was entirely due to the extra effort required to pump iced-over blood around my arteries.

'There's only one way to stop him,' I called out.

Kyle looked me in the eye. He wanted me to say it. 'How's that?'

'We get to him first. Suzanne can't help me. I need someone with your skills.'

'You sure you want to go there?'

'What choice do I have? I've not one scrap of proof and Cora seems to have thrown her lot in with him. I'm screwed, Kyle,' I said. 'I'm a dead man.'

Kyle rubbed his jaw with one hand as he dried himself with the other.

'I can't do this on my own,' I pleaded. 'Besides, you get to be the next PE teacher.'

'That's still a big ask.'

I sighed. 'He's coming for me,' I said. 'You do know it.'

Kyle stopped drying himself.

'If I'm to believe you, then if I do nothing, someone dies. If I help, someone dies. Man, I thought Afghanistan was fucked up.'

I waited for him to make a decision. I hoped he'd hurry. I'd lost all feeling in my body. He looked up at last.

'So what exactly is it that you want me to do?'

I would tell him the details when I thawed out. I had a plan already in place. I just needed to swap out the intended victim. Laura's turn would come soon enough.

'Don't worry,' I said shivering. 'To start with. All I need is for you to go to the pub while I look for two dead AA batteries.'

Kyle's eyebrows furrowed and he retreated to the cabin.

I left it a few seconds and commanded my limbs to get moving. Fate had other ideas as a flotilla of ride-on kayaks rounded the point. An instructor was followed by a dozen teens dressed in life jackets and helmets intently dipping paddles through the water. They passed by in a line about five metres away.

'Morning, sir,' one of them said.

I grimaced and managed a wave, waiting for either the last one to vanish from view or death from hypothermia.

Laura

2

The workshop had become run down since I moved out. Rain must have seeped through a tear in the tarpaulin. There was the smell of dampness.

I packed my fishing rods into bags, the tackle I'd need, and a backpack containing assorted lures and baits. Everything I required for the Lough Ree International Pike Festival could be just about carried on the scooter.

I closed up the workshop and eyed the house. It should be empty. Laura had said she'd be out with Brenda when I rang to tell her that I was swinging by to collect my fishing tackle. Liam had left for Scotland and Kyle had arranged to meet Michael for an afternoon drink in town. The coast was clear.

I approached the rear of the house when the back door suddenly swung open. Laura stood there, a perplexed look on her face. I ground to a halt. My plan was going pear-shaped already.

'You?' she said.

'Yes,' I said in surprise. 'I rang you yesterday. Told you I was calling by to get my kit.'

'You did?'

Laura's eyes appeared glazed.

'You said it would be okay, that you were going shopping with Brenda.'

Laura nodded. I guessed that she was hungover.

'I must have overslept,' she said and turned on her heel. 'I'm putting the kettle on.'

It seemed like an invitation, and I followed her through the back door.

I saw that her hand trembled slightly as she poured water into the kettle.

'You had a good night then?' I said.

'Yes. We had fun.'

She popped the kettle onto the power base.

'You and Brenda?'

'It's not any of your business but yes.'

'There I was thinking Michael was the competition.'

Her face stiffened. 'You are such a dick sometimes.'

'I'm sorry,' I said sincerely. 'It's been a hell of a few days. And understand that I'm not exactly thrilled about Michael being here.'

She nodded. 'I get that. He is Liam's dad and it's not like he's the money to stay in a hotel. If I kick him out, then I'm separating them all over again.'

I almost felt sorry for Michael. The moment passed quickly enough.

'It's just temporary. We will see what happens when Liam gets back.'

'So what does Liam think about this?'

'I think a few months in Glasgow will do him the world of good. We will give him all the time and space that he needs.'

'Meanwhile, I'll stay in Suzanne's.'

'This is about Liam. Full stop. That's the way it has to be I'm afraid.'

'I guess.'

And in the meantime, Michael could be working his way from the annexe to the upstairs.

'You mind if I get my tool kit?' I asked. 'I'm sorted for tomorrow, but I just need a few bits.'

'You and your fishing.'

'It's not just me. Anglers fly in from around the world for a reason. It's like the World Cup for pike fishing,' I exclaimed.

She shook her head. 'I don't get it but work away.'

She began to pull down some mugs as I retreated into the utility room and reached into a cupboard beside the washing machine to pull out my mini tool kit before stowing it in my inside jacket pocket.

'I don't see it,' I called out. I stepped back and opened the connecting door to the spare room. Men's clothes were scattered about. I recognised the tattered jacket that Michael wore when I first saw him. I guessed he was indeed sleeping here.

For the moment.

I stepped back into the utility room and rattled some cupboards.

'You want me to help look?' Laura called out.

'It's okay,' I said and picked up a broom. I thrust the handle up over the boiler and gave the four-inch flue vent a gentle nudge. It came away easily from the gasket. The duct tape holding the connection together had long since lost its adhesive quality.

'What was that?' Laura called.

'I'm just checking the cupboards,' I said. 'It's here somewhere, I know it.'

I reached into my pocket and retrieved two AA batteries before moving a laundry basket aside.

'The kettle is boiled,' Laura called out.

'I'll be right there,' I said. I glanced at my wristwatch. It was just after two p.m. I'd told Kyle to keep Michael out until at least three o'clock.

A few seconds later, I left the utility room, almost bouncing into Laura approaching.

'I thought that you had got lost,' she said.

I patted my jacket pocket. 'No worries, got it.'

She retreated into the kitchen and indicated a steaming mug of tea. I picked it up. I looked at it.

'Don't worry,' she said. 'It's safe.'

I smiled ruefully. Somehow we had got to this place.

The mug had been a gift. It featured a cartoon image of a fisherman underneath the slogan, "Good Things Come To Those Who Bait."

I peered at it fondly.

'This is my year. The pike doesn't have a chance.' I said after sipping from the edge of the mug.

'You and your fishing,' she said smiling.

'What about you and your archery? Who knew you'd be so good with a broadsword?'

We sipped some more.

'We were okay once, Martin,' she murmured, her eyes misting over.

'I guess,' I said at the unexpected emotion.

'We had some fun.'

'The mortgage and bills crucified us,' I said. 'Not everyone survives that. We just didn't make it.'

She stared into her mug and then looked at me. 'You get everything?'

'I think so,' I said. I had begun to question my resolve. Could I follow through with my plans after Michael was out of the picture?

Abruptly, Laura reached over and touched my cheek.

'I'm just letting you know; you were good for Liam. I want to acknowledge that.'

'Thanks,' I said in surprise. 'It wasn't all bad.'

Laura grinned. 'I'd better go, Shakespeare,' she said. 'You said I promised Brenda that we were going shopping and what girl doesn't like that?'

'Have a good time,' I said sincerely.

'Good luck tomorrow,' she said. 'Hope you land the big one.'

I didn't want to explain that it was the longest, not the biggest that counted.

She turned and vanished up the stairs. I watched her go before I walked out the back door, closing it behind me.

I lay back on the bed. The room shook as Suzanne moaned from her room. Her dates were over and there'd be no sleeping for some time, even if I wanted to. A club was closing for the night, party animals spilt out into the streets. I idly toyed with my wedding ring as I waited, listening to the sounds of laughter from the streets below.

My phone began to ring, and I almost dropped it in my haste to answer. I pressed the connect icon.

'Did I wake you?' Kyle said.

'What do you think?'

'The lights have just gone out,' he said.

There was silence.

'You still want to do this?' he asked.

Kyle's voice shivered; I guessed it was from the cold in his overlook position in the field.

'What choice do I have?' I replied.

I killed the connection and scrolled through the apps on my tablet and found one depicted by a house icon. My finger hesitated over the app and then I pressed it firmly. A new window appeared displaying different categories such as lights, heating, and alarms. I selected a central heating menu and scrolled through some options. I selected a button that simply said, "Start". I could not see it but I imagined the reaction.

Somewhere in the electronic innards of a device in the utility room, a signal would be received causing a tiny light to illuminate, quickly followed by the throaty sounds of the oil burner bursting into life.

Carbon monoxide is heavier than air and is a silent killer; it can't be smelled and there's no taste to it. It would seep through the cracks in the damaged flue, pushing out any oxygen it encountered. Michael would sleep on in the annexe, his body never once recognising that he was slowly suffocating.

Laura would be safe on the upper floors as she normally kept her windows open. Kyle had insisted that he'd call off the hit if they were closed. There could be no collateral damage.

They'd call it a tragic accident.

If only the carbon monoxide alarm didn't contain dead batteries.

Laura

1

I dragged my fishing bags and rods along the dock. I was dressed for the cold and wore layers under my oilskins and boots. The sun burned off the morning mist and anyone sensible was tucked up in their beds. I weaved between other fisherman loading their boats.

There was idle chatter in multiple languages. The Lough Ree International Pike Festival attracted anglers from all over the world. There would be several hundred of us out on the lake. Each of us longing to reel in the monster fish that we knew were within touching distance.

I approached my boat and was surprised to see Cora waiting for me. She was in her civvies and wore a fleece jacket and fingerless gloves to keep out the cold.

My heart pounded faster. Had she discovered a planted tool or button that tied me to Chris's death?

An item planted by the late Michael Dwyer.

'Martin?' she said in surprise, although who else did she expect to find at my boat? I dropped my bags on the dock.

'Hi, Cora,' I said. 'Didn't expect to find you here.'

I looked over to the shore, wondering if there was a squad car behind the trees, waiting for Julian to swoop in on me at a prearranged signal.

'Remember you said that I was welcome to try it out when I asked you what the fuss is all about?'

'Oh yes,' I said completely lost.

'It's not like I've anything on today,' she said.

'Oh, right. Will you join me?' I asked hesitantly.

'If you don't mind?'

'No bother,' I said. Having the local inspector as a passenger and an alibi could be of use.

'Lovely,' she said. 'I've already put my lunch in your boat.'

She pointed to a plastic container in the bow. 'I thought you should know that there's been a development in the Chris case,' she said.

Here it comes, I thought. I was being lulled into a false sense of security.

I imagined being led by handcuffs off the dock, the fishermen wondering aloud in German and Spanish where their number one competitor was going. If they watched the armed response unit sweep in and bundle me into the back of a squad car, perhaps they might concur that the Irish authorities were very strict about maintaining up-to-date rod licences.

I was conscious of Cora staring at me. She had stepped into my boat. She held up some lures.

'Relax,' she said grinning. 'You're off the hook.'

'What?'

'Not funny?' she asked.

'I'd not give up the day job,' I said.

I clambered down into the boat. 'I mean off the hook? Seriously?'

'I think it was better when I said it,' Cora said sitting down on a bench as I untied the mooring lines.

'No,' I said and yanked on the pull cord. 'It was not.'

The engine roared into life, and I steered us out onto the lake.

Others piled into their boats. The water at the docks churned as hundreds of laden boats roared out into the lake before splitting off in different directions, leaving behind white wakes in their sterns.

After a few minutes, I cut the engine and we drifted to a halt. I'd picked a location at a small inlet bordered by reeds. Ideal hunting grounds for pike searching for prey. We had fine views of the homes that dotted the shore.

On one side was a small island that was thought to be man-made— a crannog. Years ago, it would have offered some protection for a family group from wild animals. The threats however evolved into a two-legged menace that emerged from the river itself. Vikings used Ireland's longest river, the Shannon, as a highway. Monasteries on either side of the banks were fair game as monks were put to the sword and precious artefacts like gold crucifixes were stolen and melted down. The dying prayers of monks had long since faded.

Out here on the lake, the fishing boats grew silent as we all drifted. There was little to hear but the sound of water lapping against the side of the boat.

We cast lines out, and let the silence overtake us. Sometimes, other boats in the distance started engines and relocated to better fishing grounds. Mainly there was little to disturb us but the sound of water.

Suddenly Cora's phone rang. She glanced at it but did not take the call. She cut the connection and replaced the phone in her pocket.

'Well? So I'm off the hook?' I said after a while.

Cora nodded and hunched down into her jacket. 'It appears so.'

'Care to elaborate?' I asked.

She idly cast a lure out into the lake, in the way that I had shown her, and reeled it back in.

'There is very little I can say officially,' Cora said, choosing her words carefully. 'However, it's all going to come out anyway. It seems that Chris confessed to driving that car all those years ago. Michael forced a meeting with Chris, and he admitted everything. Chris was persuaded to make good but could not live with the guilt. He decided that life was not worth living and threw himself down the lift shaft.'

'So you only have Michael's word on this?'

Cora shook her head. 'Chris confirmed it.'

'Unless the Gardaí have Ouija boards in their kit, I don't see how that's possible,' I said incredulously.

'A text from the grave, you might say,' Cora replied. 'We unlocked Chris's phone and found an unsent message whereby he said he was sorry for the pain that he had caused Michael and could take it no more. He said he was the driver all those years ago. I'm paraphrasing, of course.'

'So Chris happened to have a lift key on him?'

'They're not that hard to get, anyone in the emergency services has them. Some go missing all the time.'

'You'd have one, wouldn't you?' I asked.

'I didn't need it,' she said. 'I used the hotel one. It's how I got to him.'

'You were first on the scene?'

'I was passing when the call came in.'

Cora herself had taught me to distrust coincidences.

I heard a cruiser in the distance but ignored it. I focused entirely on Cora.

'One question? How did you unlock Chris's phone to discover the message? He kept the PIN secret. The CIA can't unlock those phones?'

'The pathologist tells me that you don't need the PIN if you use the retina scanner.'

'So that will wrap the case up nicely.'

'It appears so. Poor Chris. The guilt must have got the better of him.'

She frowned appropriately.

She reeled in the lure and cast it out again.

So Chris took a dive.

All witnessed by Michael and accompanied by a convenient confession.

Case closed.

'So why did Michael confess to driving then, all those years ago?'

'Blackmail, pure and simple,' Cora said.

I heard the throaty engine of a cruiser slowly approach. I was surprised to see that it was Chris's boat.

In astonishment, I recognised Kyle on the upper deck behind the wheel. He waved briefly.

My mind raced. What was he doing here?

Kyle was supposed to be watching the house.

Cora had a faraway look. She appeared oblivious to the cruiser that throttled back to idle metres away.

'How come you never asked me about that night?' she asked.

She was referring to the accident.

'I didn't need to,' I said. 'Wasn't it all in the papers?'

'Not all of it. You guessed that Chris was there,' she said.

I nodded. 'I figured that the car did not drive itself.'

'It wasn't just a boy's night out, you know.'

I felt the blood drain from my face. 'I'd not thought that far.'

'It didn't cross your mind that I'd be with my fiancé?'

'You were there?'

'We'd left the party, were we going to hang out with a bunch of politicians getting plastered? I don't think so. Chris insisted on driving, it was his pride and joy. Victor was laughing at the baggie he'd scored at the party. Chris was driving fast, showing off. Michael and I told him to slow it down. We came to a checkpoint and Chris panicked. Tore off. He didn't want to lose his licence. He had drink taken, like us all.'

I could see the Mercedes doing a fast U-turn and Chris racing away in the night. Gardaí scrambling to their car before starting a pursuit.

Cora continued; her voice sorrowful. 'We roared at him to stop but we sped on, that car could easily outrun the Ford Fiesta that was after us. We should have gotten clean away but Chris took a turn, too fast. Much too fast.'

I imagined the Mercedes losing traction, a wing clipping a wall, and the car tumbling through a fence into a field. The image of a body out on the road.

'You must understand that we knew then that our careers were over before they started. Christ, they kicked people out of Templemore for having an out-of-date tax disc.'

I thought about three young people sobering up fast.

'Someone had to take the hit,' I said. 'I mean, I'll bet it was clear that Vincent was a passenger. Someone needed to own up to driving. But why not Chris? He was the actual driver.'

Cora's voice betrayed a hint of anger. 'Chris sobbed like a child. He was moaning about what had happened. He bawled and in between his tears, he said we should have made him slow down. He was inconsolable.'

'So even if he admitted it, he'd have brought the lot of you down with him?'

'That's it. He would have caved in at the first opportunity. His confession would mean that Michael and I were washed up. It would mean Laura losing her place in Portiuncula hospital where she was training.'

'What!' I shouted. Fishermen glanced over. 'Laura was there?'

'She and Michael were inseparable. Of course, she was there.'

I listened to the water lapping at the side of the boat as I waited for Cora to continue.

'Laura came up with the idea,' Cora continued. 'I was in bits holding onto Vince. Michael was white with shock. She said that we should draw straws.'

Cora's voice faltered for a moment.

'Michael protested but she insisted. She can be very persuasive when she wants to be. Michael took out a box of matches and broke one in half. He made a fist with three matches poking out. I was crying. I was covered in Vince's blood, but I picked one from his hand anyway. It was intact. Chris was watching. He thought it was a great idea, but he never picked.'

'Go on,' I said, although I doubt Cora heard me.

'That left Laura and Michael. He held up his fist and Laura picked a match. It too was intact. She burst into tears, but Michael was smiling. He told us to take our stuff and hustle out of there. We grabbed our things and slid over a wall. Just as the Garda car arrived.'

'So Michael was out of luck then?' I said.

'Not really.'

'What do you mean?'

'Laura wasn't drinking because she was pregnant. Michael guessed this. Normally, she'd be knocking drink back with the best of us. He would have made a fine detective. As a magician, not so much. I saw his unbroken match on the ground. God forgive me. I saw it. I knew what it meant but I didn't say anything. I wanted the career,' Cora said quietly.

'So Michael had three full matches in his hand?'

'No way would he have seen Laura out of a job. It would never happen. He lied when he said he had the broken one.'

'My God,' I murmured.

'Laura had the idea, but it was Michael that saved us.'

Michael who had suffocated in the night.

'Chris would have brought everyone down with him otherwise. Michael took one for the team. He is just fine, by the way,' she said. 'Kyle was very helpful.' She gestured towards the cruiser.

'He told you?'

'Yep. Don't be mad at him, he did what he felt was best. He came to us and demanded answers. You know how direct Americans can be.'

The cruiser throttled back and slid alongside us.

Michael, in a long coat, stepped out from underneath a canopy to stand at the top of the ladder.

'Go on,' Cora said, indicating the ladder.

'So Laura knows about what we tried to do?' I asked.

Cora sighed.

'She thought it was a good plan. It just needed refinement.'

'What do you mean?'

'Go on, will you,' Cora said in annoyance.

I grasped the ladder and Michael helped pull me up onto the cruiser deck.

Cora expertly tied off my boat to a cleat on the side of the cruiser and Michael reached down and helped her up.

She looked at the open lower deck that contained a built-in table and seats as well as a kitchenette. There was also a helm and a second set of controls should the skipper want the comfort of piloting the boat inside. A small door revealed an entrance to cabins below decks.

'Now this is more like it,' Cora said and sat at the table.

Michael threw her a look.

'I filled him in about that night,' she said, looking him in the eye.

'Sit,' Michael said to me and I slid into a seat.

Kyle took a step down a ladder to the upper deck to check us out.

'Kyle,' I said.

'Martin,' he said. He looked at the others. 'All good here?'

Cora nodded.

Kyle vanished back up to the upper deck. The engine grumbled louder as he turned the cruiser towards the centre of the lake.

'Where are we going?' I asked.

'Taking us for a cruise,' Michael said. 'Somewhere more private.'

I knew that voices seem to carry far over the lake.

Michael opened a fridge and pulled out a few cans of beer. He offered one to Cora and me, and then pulled the tab on one for himself.

'I've a feeling that you've more to tell me,' I said and opened my can.

Cora looked sorrowful.

'Martin,' Cora hesitated. 'There's no easy way of saying it. Laura's gone.'

'What?' I said.

Cora nodded slowly. 'She passed away, peacefully.'

'How?' I said in shock.

Cora pulled out a phone and handed it to me before looking away over the lake.

It was a cheap smartphone that looked like it was just out of the box. Cora opened her can and sipped her beer.

'Play the video,' she said.

I found the sole video file, clicked on it, and stared into the eyes of Laura peering down the barrel of the lens. I recognised our kitchen in the background as she adjusted the selfie.

'Surprise!' she said, summoning a smile. Her expression faded to one of sadness.

'I know what you tried to do, and I get it. I'm sorry. Maybe if I or we'd done something different all those years ago then our story would have turned out differently.'

Her eyes welled up.

'I'm so tired,' she said. 'I don't want to go the way of my parents. I'd not want anyone to see that. You know I am older than my mam was when she passed away?'

My eyes opened wider. I'd seen Laura's trembles and attributed it to drink but when was the last time I actually spotted her take an alcoholic drink?

'The truth is that it would only be a matter of months before I wouldn't even know my own name. Brenda and I visited every expert in the book and despite all the meds, the gaps in my memory are increasing. Did you stop to think that when I got your dose wrong that it wasn't the first time? Did you ever wonder why I would leave a bill with our address on the dashboard? I was in the car park, and for a time, I couldn't remember where I lived. I introduced you to Michael, calling him my husband! Did any of this register?' Laura hesitated, gathering her train of thought.

I saw Michael gazing stiffly into the distance.

'Anyway, it's time to make amends,' Laura said. 'You should come home. I want that. It's your home. Always was. And Liam's. Michael also deserves a break. It's long overdue. I'm sure you all will manage. And it will be paid for.'

Michael took a slug of beer.

'Also, I did find the spider in the car. I guessed how it got there and stowed it in the glovebox until that morning. I felt it would serve you right if it popped out at you. You deserved that,' she grinned.

Laura searched for something else to add.

'I liked that we spoke in the kitchen. That was a good talk.'

Laura smiled. A wide beaming smile.

'By the way, Kyle wondered who you saw out on the lake. I'm guessing Kate. I was always loyal. You need to know that. Plus I hate fucking boats.'

She waved.

The phone panned around the room as Laura passed the phone to Cora – her face briefly appearing in the frame as the phone tumbled. The camera captured Michael standing to the side, as well as Kyle. Brenda sobbed quietly on a high stool. Mrs Keena poured tea. Cora could be heard asking for the location of the stop-record button when the video abruptly ended.

'You made some good plans,' Cora said and reached over and plucked the phone from me. 'The lift was one and Michael went for it. It amused him. He wanted to scare Chris into confessing and doing the right thing, but you know how that turned out. The carbon monoxide was another of your ideas.'

'What do you mean?'

'She decided to leave you in the dark, that it was for the best. She begged Michael to help her.'

Michael looked at me full-on for the first time.

'She was stubborn, that's for sure. Once she made up her mind. That was that,' he said.

He took another slug of beer.

'She lay back on her sofa,' he continued, 'looking through her phone at pictures of Liam. She told me she felt desperately tired. I put on a gas mask, from your workshop, and watched over her.'

Cora waited for a moment.

'When it was done, he promised to let me know,' she said.

I remembered the missed call earlier to her phone.

'Mrs Keena will swear that she saw Laura say goodbye to Michael at her front door. Unfortunately, her cameras are down. Brenda will say that she dropped him to the boatyard.'

They seemed to have thought of everything.

Cora examined her phone and deleted the video. She placed it on the side of the boat. It stood there for a moment as the boat rocked. The boat rose and fell, and the phone toppled over the side, sinking quickly into the water.

'It's what you wanted yes? You even wrote about it.'

I guessed Laura had passed around a copy of the word processing file.

'You shouldn't have suggested that I was fat. It's the stab vest. It adds pounds.'

Everyone's a critic.

'One last thing,' Cora said. 'Laura said to finish your notes. Tell her story. Think of it as a fundraiser. Liam's band needs a new van. Label it, "fiction," of course.'

I stood up and moved to the back of the cruiser. Staring out, we were already far from land.

I suddenly remembered Suzanne's mantra about never making the story fit the evidence. Cora had revealed a lot in the boat but maybe not everything.

Laura no doubt suggested meeting at the hotel. The one building in the town that had a lift shaft several storeys high. Chris had taken the bait, he probably had referred to my lack of promotional prospects, how he could help her out by retiring early. But what would he get in return?

She might have suggested champagne or given some other excuse to make Chris turn back down the corridor. He'd hurried along to find Michael waiting to nudge him through the open doors, opened by a key provided by a serving member of the Gardaí.

Cora, a woman who had never really forgiven the man that killed her fiancé but had allowed another to pay the price.

Chris was doomed, the moment he walked into the hotel; a confession is far less effective if it's retracted. Chris had proved that he could not be trusted.

Cora would happen to be first on the scene. She'd check Chris and quickly peel back his eyelid to unlock his phone. She could then type out a quick confession before leaving the phone back on his body, as firefighters arrived to peer downwards. No one would notice the phone in the melee as it quietly locked itself.

With the confession, Michael would get his life back. Justice would be served for Tim Fagen's son and Cora Halligan's fiancé.

It would be the perfect murder.

However, never underestimate a cornered rat.

Something went wrong.

Of course, something went wrong. Perhaps there was a struggle and Chris found the strength to turn the tables. It was a stupid plan. A desperate man can be stronger than he looks.

The wind blew coldly across the deck, but I ignored it, my mind possessed a clarity that I didn't think possible.

What did Liam say; *maybe anyone can be a murderer.*

There are no coincidences until there are.

There was one thing that Michael, Cora and Laura did not factor in.

Michael moved to stand beside me.

'Liam wasn't supposed to be working that day, but he got called in,' I said in a low voice.

Michael looked at me carefully. He nodded faintly.

'He recognised you?' I asked.

'He looked me up. Googled me. Found me. I've appeared in a few newspapers myself, just not the society pages. He followed me through the hotel. I told you back in the café that he knew me. He watched me open the lift door, and the argument with Chris.'

'There was a struggle,' I said, 'and he wrestled Chris off you. In the chaos, Liam was the one who gave the final push.'

'I told you it was me,' Michael said.

'Of course it was.'

It was something that Michael would admit to without hesitation.

For his son.

'Was Tim part of this?' I asked.

'The minister? Let's just say that he sent each of us a bottle of twenty-year-old Kilbeggan whiskey.'

We watched the wake of the cruiser churning up behind us. In the distance anglers cast lines from their boats.

'Isn't this what you wanted?' Michael said. 'To get away with it. You don't even have to worry about Maggie anymore. Ruairi was behind the one man burglary spree and Cora picked him up. Maggie will play ball if she wants her son kept out of Oberstown.'

I sipped beer.

I'd written that getting away with murder was the hard part. Maybe I was right.

I did know that no one can prove how a gas leak overnight was triggered on a dark winter's night twenty years ago.

A night that I'd summoned in *The Westmeath Independent.*

I flipped open my phone and looked sadly at a picture of Laura on my landing page.

I wrote that I would kill her during the Lough Ree International Fishing Festival.

And I did.

I killed Laura as surely as if I put a bullet in her head.

The End

Acknowledgements

Many people are required to publish a book with only the author making the front cover. This one is no exception.

Many thanks to Drama Studies Alumni Peter McMahon for assisting with the research; to Katie McMahon— the original Riverdance voice for help chasing down Irish lyrics.

I'm grateful to Katherine Mezzacappa of the Irish Writer's Centre for her guidance and to Conor Kostic also of the Irish Writer's Centre for casting a keen eye over the paperwork.

Thanks to the Gardaí who must remain nameless who assisted with the research into Garda operational techniques, any errors are my own.

Much gratitude to Judymay Murphy for her coaching skills and tips to navigate a post-publication world.

My appreciation to the BOC steady crew— Bridie, Nancy, Daniel for their support.

Thanks to Michael McGlynn of Anuna for his advice on Fionnghuala.

A shout out to Valerie Marjoram for checking my Irish.

Thanks to Stephen Walker for casting a jaundiced eye over an early proof to point out some typos and gags that did not land.

Thanks also to proofreaders Steve James; Aquiel Babb and Melani Eksteen who spent so much time reading through the manuscript word by word.

I am thankful to Commissioning Editor Suzanne Mulvey for accepting this work for publication, and all the Pegasus team such as Production Coordinator Vicky Gorry, Production Coordinator Sandra Barber; Chandray Isaacson plus all the editors, graphic designers, publicity crew, etc. I don't know who you all are, but I owe you buns.

Thanks to the Carty clan for the help and support.

Big love and thanks to my parents Nora and Paddy who supported their favourite child to go off and study for an impractical degree.

Hugs to my sisters Jackie and Paula whose support and wit helped refine my gag-making techniques. Both are funnier than I'll ever be.

Much love to my boys Julian and Paul— two irrepressible individuals who overlooked the many times I'd disappear to the home office to work on the manuscript. You appear in the book in name only and any resemblance to the characters involved is purely coincidental.

Finally, much love to Claire who supported me with this novel. Love, hugs and gratitude to you. Thanks for bearing with me. It's always been appreciated even if I was too wrapped up in words to acknowledge your support.

Finally, finally many thanks to you dear reader, to paraphrase Charlotte Bronte, for getting this far.

I hope you enjoyed the journey and that you paid for the book. I invite you to join me on further adventures, even if you did not.

MD.

Athlone 2022